THE BROTHERS BISHOP

Books by Bart Yates

LEAVE MYSELF BEHIND

THE BROTHERS BISHOP

Published by Kensington Publishing Corporation

THE BROTHERS BISHOP

BART YATES

KENSINGTON BOOKS
http://www.kensingtonbooks.com

KENSINGTON BOOKS are published by

Kensington Publishing Corp.
850 Third Avenue
New York, NY 10022

All Kensington titles, imprints and distributed lines are available at special quantity discounts for bulk purchases for sales promotion, premiums, fund-raising, educational or institutional use.

Special book excerpts or customized printings can also be created to fit specific needs. For details, write or phone the office of the Kensington Special Sales Manager: Kensington Publishing Corp., 850 Third Avenue, New York, NY 10022. Attn. Special Sales Department. Phone: 1-800-221-2647.

Kensington and the K logo Reg. U.S. Pat. & TM Off.

Library of Congress Card Catalogue Number: 2004110756
ISBN 0-7582-0911-8

First Printing: July 2005
10 9 8 7 6 5 4 3 2 1

Printed in the United States of America

For Lois J. Yates:
The Mother of all Mothers,
and a damn good friend, too.

ACKNOWLEDGMENTS

The first ten people I want to thank are all Gordon Mennenga. Gordon is a superhero; I once saw him go into a phone booth as himself and emerge a few seconds later as *The Phenomenal and Brilliant Writer/Teacher/Mentor Man.* He deserves a better name than that *(Fictionguy? Storydude?)*—and maybe a costume with a cool cape or something—but the rest is top-notch. Thank you, Gordon, for so many things, not the least of which is letting me get to know your lovely wife, Lynn.

I couldn't ask for a more supportive editor than John Scognamiglio, nor could I wish for a more capable agent than John Talbot.

Gratitude and love to my family, especially my brothers, Jeff and Joel—who, thank God, are not even remotely like the brothers in this book.

Ed Leff was at the wrong place at the wrong time and was foolish enough to answer legal questions for FREE. Sucker! (Thanks, Ed. I owe you a fortune in beer. But please bring Lisa along; she's more fun to talk to . . .)

Sifu Moy Yat Tung (a.k.a. Dr. Robert Squatrito) is a major source of inspiration in my life, and I wouldn't know what to do without each of my kung fu brothers and nephews from the Moy Yat Ving Tsun Kung Fu Academy. The amount of kindness you all heaped on me while I was writing this book was humbling, especially considering how many times I behaved like an idiot during the process. No matter what I tell you to your faces, you guys rock. Special thanks, as ever, to Brad and Liz Schonhorst, John Perona, Peder Bartling, Robert Burns, Mick Benner, Andrew Knapp, Simo (Jennifer Squatrito), Bryan Pierce, Lucas Readinger, and Rob Weingeist.

Paul Robbins gave me a book on archaeology, Jack Manu humored me on the phone, Libby Shannon designed my website, and Rob Shannon is who I want to be when I grow up.

I stole the setting for this story from Mrs. Jeanne Cassidy, but she got even by drinking me under the table—yet again.

And finally, thanks to all of my friends. I wish I could mention each of you, but I'm afraid of leaving someone important out, so please accept this pathetic blanket thanks instead. You never know where friendship will spring up, or how long the driving force behind it might last, but I am grateful beyond words for the people who have shared their lives and their love with me, regardless of how much or how little time we've had together.

That being said, though, I do have a question for two especially benighted souls—Marian Clark and Michael Becker—who have somehow stayed close to me for more than twenty years, in spite of everything that usually gets in the way of deep and abiding relationships like ours:

Are you guys retarded or what?

THE BROTHERS BISHOP

.

CHAPTER 1

When I was five years old I stuck a pencil in a nice man's eye. He was at a desk, typing a letter, and I was sitting on a stool next to him, scribbling a brontosaurus on a sheet of typing paper. I remember looking over at him and wondering why he was so intent on what he was doing, and I remember wishing he'd pay more attention to me. So I held the eraser end of the pencil by the corner of his eye and waited until he turned toward me before making my move. I didn't push too hard and his lashes caught the bulk of the attack, but it still must have hurt like hell.

"Jesus Christ, kid!" he yelled, cradling his eye socket. "What did you do that for?"

I didn't have an answer for him then. I still don't. Sometimes you hurt people for no reason. Just because you can.

So this is how it ends. The day, I mean, with the sun dropping in the dunes at my back, coloring the surface of the water red and gold. I'm standing barefoot in the sand and the cold tide is licking at my ankles like a mutt with a foot fetish. I live half a mile from the beach, so I come here almost every day of the year to clear my head. It's summer now so I don't have the place to myself like I do in the winter, but I can usually find a quiet spot and pretend the ocean belongs exclusively to me.

Tommy's coming home tomorrow, with his new scrotal-buddy and a young married couple in tow. He called last week and asked if he could come see me, but he waited until I said yes before he told me he was bringing an entourage. When I told him I wasn't really in the mood to entertain anybody besides him, he got pissed.

"Don't be a dick, Nathan. You've had the cottage to yourself for three years. Is it going to kill you to have a little company for a couple of weeks?"

I told him that was the whole point, because we haven't seen each other since Dad died, and it would be nice to get together without a bunch of strangers barging in and taking over. He said his friends weren't really strangers, though, because "Philip is practically your brother-in-law" and "Kyle and Camille are my two best friends in the world." He assured me we'd all get along famously.

He's been like this his whole life. He thinks if he loves somebody, everyone else he cares about will automatically love that person too. What an idiot. But of course I caved in. I always do. You can't say no to Tommy.

Tommy's my younger brother and a complete flake. He bounces from one job to another and one relationship to another and one financial crisis to another and all he does is eat, sleep, shit and fuck.

But he gets what he wants from everybody, anyway, because he won the genetics lottery. He got our mother's looks—thick blond hair and startling blue eyes, clear skin, high cheekbones, delicate hands and feet—and he also got every ounce of her charm. I'm a clone of my father—pug nose, high forehead, black hair, brown eyes, sloped shoulders, heavy limbs, and yes, okay, an admittedly unattractive tendency to think of the world as a very screwed up place. If you saw us together on the street you'd never believe we're brothers.

I don't believe we're brothers, either. There is no way in hell somebody as beautiful and lighthearted as Tommy could be carrying around my father's genes. I think Mom took one look at me when I was born and decided she wasn't going to have any more dark, surly children, so she went and had an affair with a surfer or a Swedish porn star or something and got knocked up with Tommy.

I don't really remember our mother. She died when I was five years old and Tommy was only three, so everything we know about her we got from my father. From what he said, though, she sounds exactly like Tommy. Dad said that Mom could make people love her without even trying. He liked to tell the story about the time they were at a restaurant and she couldn't make up her mind about what kind of soda to order. Dad said she must have been over- heard, because within half a minute three glasses appeared on the table—a Coke from the waiter, a Pepsi from the busboy, and a Dr. Pepper from the maître d'.

I guess I should warn you, though, that Dad was a liar. He had at least thirty different versions of that particular story—sometimes he'd say Mom was wearing a black evening gown with long sleeves, and the next time he'd go on about how her tits were spilling out of a skimpy red halter top. He always tailored his stories to fit his au- dience.

But something tells me most of what he said about Mom was true, because my brother can charm the short hairs off a troll, and he sure as hell didn't learn that from anybody he grew up with. I think charm is genetic—a personality fluke equivalent to being able to shape your tongue like a U. Why I didn't get any of Mom's magic and Tommy got it all is just another of life's little inequities I intend to confront God with at the earliest opportunity.

I've been standing in the water long enough for it to have cov- ered my feet with sand and strands of foul-smelling seaweed. It's tempting to just keep standing here until I'm buried up to my neck.

I'm not ready to deal with Tommy yet. Especially not with three complete strangers in tow. This will sound terrible, but my life has been considerably better since Dad died. When we cremated him, it felt like someone took a pillow off my face and I could finally breathe for the first time in my life. Now Tommy is my sole remain- ing relative, and the truth is I hate that someone is still alive in the world who has a familial claim on me. I don't want Tommy to die or anything, I just want him to forget about me and leave me the hell alone.

It's not about love. Of course I love the little shit. But he knows too much about me that no one else on the planet knows, and when he's around I have no choice but to think about everything I hate about myself and my past. He's a gangrenous leg attached to my psyche, and I need to hack him off before he infects my whole fucking soul.

Okay, okay, that's pretty dramatic. But it's exactly how I feel. And if you were me, you'd feel that way too.

A couple of teenage kids run by, both of them dressed in ratty old cutoffs instead of swimsuits. They're probably fifteen or so, and slender and tanned, and one of them slows down and smiles and waves. "Hey, Mr. Bishop."

Great. One of my idiot students. Just what I need today. He's new in town and it takes a second to remember his name. "Hi, Simon. Having fun?"

"Yeah." He picks at some peeling skin on his shoulder. "We've been here all afternoon and now we're getting ready to go out on my dad's new boat before it gets too dark."

I glance at the falling sun. "You better hurry. There's not much daylight left."

He grins. He has straight, white teeth with just the hint of an underbite. "I know. Dad's trying to prove to Mom what a great sailor he is or something. We'll probably all drown just because he won't admit he's not very good at night sailing."

The other boy is waiting for him and Simon gives another little wave. "I guess I should go. See you later."

He runs to catch up, water flipping from his heels onto his back. I watch him go, admiring his speed and lightness.

His ass isn't bad either.

I'm a high school English teacher. I never used to work during the summer, but for the last three years I've been forced to teach remedial grammar courses to kids like Simon who can't tell a pronoun from a potato. And no, I've never done anything improper with one of my students, and I never will. But it doesn't hurt to look.

Is anything more flagrantly sexy than a teenage boy? They're so full of hormones and semen it's a wonder they can walk. Most of them spend every spare minute playing with themselves, but there are a few who haven't yet figured out how to deal with all the sensations in their bodies. You can see it in their eyes—a moist vulnerability, like their corneas are floating in cum and they haven't got a clue what's going on or what to do about it. Simon is like that, I think. He's a true innocent, a kid who would be horrified to know what most of his peers are doing three times a day in bathrooms and bedrooms and behind the bushes. But one of these days his body will override his hang-ups and he'll erupt like Vesuvius, spurting jiz on everyone and everything within a thirty-mile radius.

Mark my words. I know the type well.

A gull flies overhead, calling out. Why do they always sound so lonely? The breeze from the ocean picks up and I raise my arms like wings to let it blow over me and tickle the hair in my armpits. The gull dips and glides and I try to imitate how it moves.

Tommy and I grew up on the beach. Not literally, of course, but we spent almost every day of every summer here when we were little kids, and when we were in high school we were both lifeguards. I can't imagine growing up someplace far away from the ocean and the dunes. What's it like to go home to dinner without salt on your skin and sand between your toes?

I live in southern Connecticut in a little town called Walcott. The name of this beach is Hog's Head Beach, and it's about two hours north of New York City and an hour or so south of Providence. I'm thirty-one years old and except for the six years when I was in college and grad school I've never lived anyplace else and I never will. Sure, the town is backward (like every other small town in America) and the winters are cold and real estate is expensive, but who gives a crap? I own my cottage, and I'm within easy walking distance of a good pub, the public library, and a terrific bakery. A quarter mile from my front door in the other direction is a small cliff with a lighthouse on it (my closest neighbor, Caleb Farrell, lives in the house attached to it), and woods all around, and this beach.

I know almost everybody in town and they know me, and while that sometimes drives me crazy, for the most part it makes me feel safe. Tommy graduated high school and moved away the following summer, but I think he was a fool to not come back after he finished college like I did. He keeps trying to get me to move. He's worried because I never get laid and he says I'm wasting my life and he hasn't been to see me since Dad died because he says that

Walcott is the rectum of the universe and he'd rather glue his nipples to a car bumper than spend another second in "that godforsaken hellhole."

But when I asked him why he was finally coming back for a visit, he said he was homesick.

I knew it would happen, sooner or later. He can pretend all he wants, but he loves this place more than I do.

Walcott is a resort town that no one who isn't rich can afford to live in, unless, like me, you happen to be lucky enough to have inherited a house that's been in the family for over a hundred years. My great-grandfather was a fisherman in the early nineteen hundreds and he built the cottage himself, which apparently made my great-grandmother insane because it took him nearly eleven years to finish it. He'd work on a room for a few days, then he'd leave to go fishing for months at a time, refusing to rush the job or hire somebody else to do it. I feel sorry for my great-grandmother, but I'm glad the old bastard did it that way, because he built the thing with a mind-boggling attention to detail that only comes from sitting around for weeks on end with nothing to do but fish and think about what you want your house to look like.

He built it like a boat. I don't mean that it's shaped like one, but he designed it with the same practicality and space-saving principles you find on small ships—nothing is wasted, nothing is merely decorative. It's two stories high, with the kitchen, guest room, bathroom and living room downstairs, and a gigantic master bedroom upstairs. The woodwork is simple and straightforward, but it's all oak and maple and pine, and when the sun comes through the windows in the morning the walls and the floors shine like church pews. Bookshelves are everywhere; the door to the guest room is actually a bookshelf that swings out on hidden hinges and shuts again with a quiet click. There's a potbellied stove in the corner of the living room, and a modest wine cellar under the kitchen, and in the master bedroom there's a massive old Edwardian desk looking out from an alcove onto the cornfield behind the house. Family legend has it that my great-grandfather stole the desk from some snotty English nobleman who lived in Rhode Island, but like the rest of our family history the story is probably bogus.

My favorite part of the house is the narrow, spiral staircase that connects the two levels. It's the only incompetent piece of carpentry in the house, rickety and uneven and somewhat dangerous to negotiate if you've had more than your share of red wine on a cold winter night. All the upstairs furniture had to be lifted through the windows from the outside because none of it would fit up the staircase. But my great-grandfather built it like that on purpose. He was an exquisite craftsman and could easily have come up with something elegant and functional, but for some inscrutable reason he chose to build an eyesore instead. And what's really funny is that in his will he stipulated that no one was to alter the staircase in the slightest, save for replacing boards if the old ones rotted out.

He never told his son or his wife why he did it that way and no one in the family since has had any clue. Maybe he wanted to restrict access to the upstairs; maybe he thought it was funny to have something ugly and out of place in an otherwise handsome home. Personally, I think he left it that way to piss off his wife. But whatever the reason, whenever I look at it, I wish I'd known the contrary old son of a bitch. The staircase screams attitude, and the only people in the world worth knowing are people with attitude.

There's a note on the front door of the cottage when I get home. It's from the "chairman" of Walcott's Historical Society, Cheri Tipton, politely reminding me that we had an appointment earlier that afternoon, and she was sorry to have missed me, and could I please call her at my earliest convenience to reschedule.

Shit. I forgot all about it. She called last week and asked if she could come over and take a walk with me through the cornfield, because she said she came across some historic papers that seemed to suggest that an old Indian village—predating European settlement by several centuries—may once have stood on my land. I told her I'd never found so much as an arrowhead out there but she insisted on stopping by anyway. I'm not surprised I forgot to be here. I have a bad habit of forgetting to show up for anything I don't want to do.

I crumple up the paper and stand outside the door for a minute, wondering who else is going to invade my house this week. Jesus. Maybe I should just open a Holiday Inn and put up a neon sign advertising multiple vacancies.

I make no apologies for being a hermit. My choice to live alone has been deliberate and entirely voluntary. As a general rule, people piss me off and I'm a much happier man when I'm by myself. I should mine the front yard and buy a couple of dobermans and then maybe I could finally get some privacy.

I take a deep breath. There are two big bushes on either side of the door with cantaloupe-sized white flowers that smell faintly of cat urine. I have no idea what kind of bushes they are, but they've been there my whole life. I could ask Tommy, I suppose, but who cares? I don't need flowers by my door; I need a state-of-the-art security system.

My father was a mean-spirited, petty old man, and a complete waste of human DNA. Aside from that, though, we got along fine.

It's impossible to talk about my dad without getting mad. Tommy says I should get over it and move on, but Tommy has never understood the healthful benefits of loathing someone with your whole heart. He thinks my bitterness is self-destructive and difficult to maintain, but, truly, it's no effort at all. It comes naturally to me, like breathing, or taking a crap.

I'm being flip because I know Tommy's right. My resentment of my father eats at me like cancer. And I should get counseling or a lobotomy or something and maybe eventually learn how to deal with everything he did to us as kids and adults—all the endless cruelties, large and small, he so liberally bestowed on us—except there's one thing I know I can never get past or dismiss so I won't even bother to try.

He loved us.

What a bastard.

Yeah, I know how fucked up that sounds, but there it is. If he'd hated Tommy and me, I think I could maybe forgive him for how he treated us. But he didn't hate us. He loved us, and still he went out of his way to hurt us, time and again, and he never apologized for anything.

His name was Vernon Michael Bishop, and he had a glorious tenor voice. He sang for local weddings and funerals, and people always said it was like listening to an angel. He ran the local paper, the Walcott *Gazette,* for a number of years, and I've been told—ad infinitum—how he generously allowed charities and "good causes" to advertise for free. He was interim mayor for two years when Cloris Adams suddenly died in her office and the town needed a replacement until the next election, and he organized the annual food drive for the Lion's Club every Christmas. He was a big, hearty man who looked you right in the eye and did his best to make you laugh. He was a pillar of the community. So goodness gracious, what's my problem? The man was a saint, right?

Oh, did I neglect to mention that Vernon Michael Bishop liked to beat up little kids? Not all little kids, of course. Just two very special little boys. His sons.

The worst time—though certainly not the first—was when he found Tommy in bed with Jacob Roberts. Jacob had spent the night (he was the last overnight guest we were ever allowed to have, incidentally), so I had given up my bed and slept in the living room on a cot. When Dad got up in the morning and came down to boil water for tea, he decided to poke his head in and see if Tommy and Jacob were awake.

They were nine years old, and they were naked, and apparently Tommy had his fist wrapped around Jacob's puny penis when Dad walked in on them. I was just waking up and came running into the kitchen just in time to see dear old Dad drag Tommy out of the bedroom and begin slamming his head on the counter by the sink. Jacob was scrambling into his clothes in the bedroom and wailing like a cat in heat. I tried to get Dad to stop but I was only eleven, and when I grabbed his arm and begged him to let go of Tommy, he backhanded me hard enough to break my nose and send me flying into the dish cabinet. I still have scars on my neck and shoulders from plunging through the glass.

Tommy told me later that Dad apparently came to his senses

when he looked over and saw me crumpled on the floor in a puddle of blood. He let go of Tommy—who was only marginally better off than me—and calmly told Jacob to stop crying and go home. Dad called an ambulance for us and was soon arrested by the police, but because of his sterling reputation in town and the heinousness of Tommy's actions (discussed, no doubt, in the strictest confidence), the charges were dismissed after a stern warning from the sergeant on duty, who then graciously offered Dad a ride home and probably gave him a cheerful clap on the back as he was getting out of the car.

Dad gave his word that he'd never hit his children again, and, being a man who followed his own peculiar code of honor, he never did. But with physical violence no longer available to him, he was forced to come up with alternative strategies to continue waging war on his children. And that was when he began his long, inspired campaign of verbal and emotional abuse that continued until the day he died.

In retrospect, I wish he'd kept hitting us.

There's a full moon tonight. I like to sit on the porch behind the house at night and look at the stars, but the moon is too bright this evening, blotting out everything else in the sky. The mosquitoes are out in force but I've smeared myself with citronella and vanilla extract so they're mostly leaving me alone. I'll have to check myself later for ticks, though, because nothing discourages those evil little vampires and Connecticut is rife with Lyme disease.

In the moonlight the cornfield looks like something out of a Grade-B horror movie. The rows are in shadow, stretching back a quarter of a mile or so, and the tops of the cornstalks sway back and forth in the breeze, whispering to each other. I think Cheri Tipton is full of shit about my land being the site of an ancient Indian community, but in the stark light of a full moon it's easier to believe her, for some reason. I'm with Hollywood: If there are ghosts in the world, they live in cornfields.

The corn isn't mine, by the way. I rent the field out to a local farmer, Dale Cromwell, who started farming it for my grandfather almost fifty years ago. He pays me enough to cover the land tax, and every spring, like clockwork, he tries to convince me to sell the land to him. I could probably get a lot of money for it, but I don't want to take the chance of him deciding to build a house on the property and blocking my view.

Anyway, I called Cheri again and she's coming back in the morning after my class at the high school. She's bringing what she insists on calling "the evidence" with her, and she thinks it will persuade me to let her dig around out there with a "small team of archaeologists" from my alma mater, the University of Connecticut. I told her I didn't imagine Dale would appreciate her messing up his corn, but she said she thought she could reach some kind of agreement with him if only I'd say yes.

I didn't flat out tell her no, but I'm going to. I'm sure someone in my family in the last hundred years would have known of something like this village she's talking about, and I've never heard a word about it. And even if there is something to her story, she says she doesn't think there will be any "significant ruins," because she says it's just a place this mysterious tribe lived for a few short years and then disappeared from without leaving much behind except vague rumors. So what the hell does she think she's going to find? Chewing gum wrappers?

Whatever, I don't want people traipsing around in my field all summer with pickaxes and shovels and making noise when I'm trying to work. Cheri Tipton can kiss my ass if she doesn't like it.

I get up at sunrise and stumble downstairs to the shower, then I make breakfast and go back upstairs with a cup of tea to sit at the desk and grade papers. While I'm circling misspellings and comma splices, I sip at my tea and stare out the window and play with the loose brass handles on the bottom desk drawer with my toes.

When I was in junior high and high school, mornings used to be when I wrote in my journal. From the time I was thirteen until I left home for college, I got up every day and scribbled down whatever I was thinking. For reasons that are utterly obscure to me now, I used to think I'd eventually want a written record of my teenage years.

I was in junior high at the time and my English teacher was having us read *The Diary of Anne Frank*, which gave me the idea (along with every other overimaginative kid in the class) to start keeping a journal. After all, I did have my very own Nazi living in the same house with me, and our bedroom door was hidden behind a bookshelf, just like Anne's. I bought a fountain pen and one of those cool black leather notebooks with unlined pages, and I used to sprawl out on my bed and write for half an hour or so right after I woke up.

It was all there: daily life with Tommy, first loves, fights with Dad, first sex, jobs, dreams, nightmares, masturbation fantasies, grievances, and an embarrassing amount of self-important, pseudointellectual rambling. There's a place in the downstairs bedroom where Tommy and I (who shared that room our entire childhood) kept things we didn't want Dad to find. It's a cubbyhole in the closet under a loose board, and until I moved out of the house after high school I always kept my journal there. In the five years between when I first started writing and when I moved out, I had seven full notebooks in the cubbyhole.

It's odd but I never once worried about Tommy reading my journals when we were kids. A lot of the stuff in them was about him, of course, but having a common enemy in the same house with us made us considerably closer than most siblings, so I never cared if he read them or not. Besides, he was usually in the room with me while I was writing. I still remember the first paragraph, word for word:

Tommy's fucked-up. He put an empty bottle of ketchup back in the refrigerator and I asked him why and he blushed and wouldn't tell me until I pinned him on the floor and threatened to fart on him. Then he told me he didn't want to throw away the ketchup bottle because the jar of mayonnaise would get lonely.

What a spaz.

Okay, so Anne Frank didn't have to worry about me usurping her rightful place on library bookshelves. But stuff like this made Tommy laugh, and there were hundreds of similar entries. He used to dig my notebooks out at night before bed to read whatever I'd written earlier that day; he said he wanted to "keep an eye on the weird-ass things" going on in my head.

And he was furious when I told him I'd burned all seven of the notebooks. He said those memories were a part of his life, too, and I should have thought to ask him before I did such a thing. I suppose he's right, but I'm not sorry. He wasn't the one who had to sit in the same house with those fucking things day after day, wondering who would find them after I was dead and imagining what they'd think and say about us when they read them. So I got drunk one winter night and carted the notebooks out to the bare ground of the cornfield, poured gasoline over them and struck a match. The burning leather smelled horrible but I didn't budge until all the paper had turned to ash and the covers were only charred, unrecognizable scraps. I was crying while I did it, but the heat from the fire felt good on my face and hands.

Tommy likes to pretend that our childhood was one light-hearted episode after another, but Tommy has yak shit for brains. He never read the journals after he left high school, and he's managed to convince himself that Dad was Andy Griffith and Walcott was Mayberry, and he and I were typical teenage boys. Sometimes I wish I hadn't burned the journals; then I could shove them in his face and make him read the stuff he doesn't want to remember.

But that would mean I'd have to read it, too, and that's the last thing I want to do.

The kids file in one after another, all hormones and pimples and self-conscious posturing. There are twelve of them, freshmen and sophomores, and since there's no air-conditioning in this furnace of a classroom, the girls wear only short skirts and sleeveless blouses (quite a few of them without bras) and most of the boys are decked out in lightweight shorts and tank tops. Simon comes in right before class, still wearing what looks like the same pair of cut-offs he had on yesterday and a T-shirt with big holes in it, one of them gaping open enough to reveal a few inches of his stomach. He smiles at me and sits in an open desk at the front of the room. His blond hair is uncombed and curly and covers half of his ears.

It's nine o'clock in the morning, and for the next hour and fifteen minutes these poor, grammatically challenged dimwits are my prisoners. They don't want to be here and neither do I, but I push back from the desk with fake enthusiasm.

"Okay, did everybody read the chapter about verbs last night?"

In the front row, Vernette Shute rolls her eyes and Peter Russo swats at a fly. Simon shifts lower in his seat and opens his legs wide; his shorts are loose enough to reveal green and black plaid boxers underneath. The rest of the kids stare out the open windows and either scratch themselves or yawn and put their heads on their desks. One boy picks at an inflamed mosquito bite on his left bicep.

I try again. "Who can tell me what a verb is?"

I lead a lethargic discussion for fifteen minutes and then give up and hand out worksheets and a reading assignment to complete by the end of class. I collect their homework assignments from yesterday and sit at my desk to grade them. By nine thirty the heat and the boredom have me fighting to keep my eyes open. I unscrew the lid on my thermos and pour myself a cup of strong, bitter coffee, but what I really need is a hypo full of adrenaline pumped directly into my heart. Sometime around ten they start finishing up their work and stirring, looking at me expectantly, wanting to be dismissed early.

Vernette has fallen asleep with her head on her book, but when I start shuffling papers on my desk she jerks awake and blinks like an iguana on a rock. Peter, a sweet, dumb kid with a sweet, dumb wrestler's body, puts both arms over his head and stretches. His tank top is too big for him and a small brown nipple exposes itself. Simon is watching but looks away quickly when Peter glances over at him.

I clear my throat. "Okay, hand in your worksheets and be prepared tomorrow to talk about the chapter you read today."

They're all out of the room in a virtual stampede before the last word is out of my mouth. That is, everybody except for Simon. He makes no move to get up.

"Anything wrong, Simon?" I ask, getting to my feet.

He glances up at me and blushes for some reason. "No, I'm just tired." He makes up a few questions about the assignment, obviously not interested in my answers, then finally seems to realize I'm waiting to go. He stands up fast, awkwardly scooping up his textbook in front of his groin, but not before I see what he's trying to hide: the poor little bastard has an erection, straining away cheerfully at the fabric of his shorts. His face is strawberry red.

I pretend not to notice and he says good-bye and charges out of the room ahead of me.

What caused that, I wonder? Peter Russo's hairless nipple? A random breeze? Maybe Simon isn't as innocent as I thought.

Jesus. I wouldn't be fifteen again for anything in the world.

Cheri Tipton was a friend of my mother's, a fact she reminds me of every time I see her—which fortunately is only once every six months or so. She's waiting for me on my front steps when I get home from teaching, and she's dressed in Birkenstock sandals and a loose yellow sari type of thing.

Cheri's fat. She's about five foot two, and she weighs over two hundred pounds. The sari hides a lot of her bulk, but her bloated ankles and shins are visible under its hem, and her feet look like they're being choked by her sandal straps. Her short hair is dyed raven black and she's got a mole on her forehead the exact same color. Maybe she dyes the mole, too.

She kisses me on the cheek with wet lips. "Hi, Nathan. I'm a little early."

I tell her not to worry about it and open the door. She waddles in ahead of me without waiting for an invitation, and steps through the kitchen into the living room, looking around with unconcealed curiosity.

"It's exactly like I remember it." For some reason there's a tinge of sadness in her voice.

"You've been in here before? When was that?"

She laughs, and the big silver crucifix earrings she's wearing jiggle against her cheeks. "Years ago. But I used to come here all the time before you were born."

I seriously doubt it. She may have been friends with Mom, but Dad didn't like having company in the house and I'm sure he wouldn't have put up with a frequent guest. I tell her to have a seat and I go upstairs to change clothes. When I come back down she's standing by the sliding doors, staring out at the cornfield.

She hands me a folder. "Take a look at that, would you? I've high-lighted the part that piqued my curiosity."

Inside the folder is a copy of a letter dated March 4, 1708. It's two pages long and signed by someone named Henry Bradstreet. The letter is addressed to his brother, John, in London, England, and is mostly about day-to-day life in rural America, painting a somewhat rosy picture of "the colonies," with the apparent inten-tion of convincing John to relocate across the ocean. I scan through it, skipping over chunks of flowery writing about God's providence and mercy. The highlighted section reads:

"*. . . I heard today of a story that might perhaps interest you, knowing as I do your fondness for tales concerning the Red Man. Minister David Shepard told me in passing of a cache of antique farming implements, of Indian origin, that two of his slaves un-earthed recently as they were clearing a patch of ground behind the main house. Minister Shepard is quite intrigued, because he believes these tools to have belonged to a nomadic tribe of savages no longer extant. . . .*"

When I look up she's staring at me with an expectant look on her face. I return the letter to the folder and hand it back to her. "That's it? That's all you've got?"

She frowns. "The Shepard farm was right here, Nathan. I tracked down the old surveyor's records and figured out where the bound-aries were, and your cornfield overlaps the property almost ex-actly."

"So? What makes you think there's anything else to find out there? Did this Bradstreet leave any other letters behind?"

She has nervous hands. Right now she's worrying at the cuticles of her fingernails with her thumbs. "Not that I can locate. But this actually isn't the first time I've heard reports about the tribe he's speaking of. I've come across several articles in scholarly journals that speculate about a previously undiscovered native people who used to live in this part of Connecticut."

She needs to get out more often. "Look, Cheri. You said yourself there's probably nothing to find." I wave at the cornfield. "Dale Cromwell's been plowing around out there for years and never turned up a thing except rocks and weeds and an occasional dead crow."

She smoothes her dress. Her eyes are brown and bloodshot. "I know. But maybe there's something farther down. Maybe something's been overlooked."

I scratch at a spider bite on my knee. "Why are you so curious about this? I thought the Historical Society was mainly interested in restoring old houses."

She sniffs. "You obviously haven't been to visit our museum in a while. We now have a rather extensive collection of Native American artifacts."

The "museum" she's talking about is a one-room building that used to be a welding shop. The last time I made the mistake of checking it out, there were only three tables in the room, covered with trinkets from the big days of commercial whaling and a few gaudy brochures advertising tours of historic homes. I remember nothing about it really, aside from being distinctly unimpressed.

"I see. But even so . . ."

"Oh, for goodness' sake, Nathan, what's the harm of letting me poke around out there for a bit?" She actually has the balls to sound irritated. "Don't you find this the least bit intriguing?"

I shrug. "Not really." I open the sliding doors for her and step outside onto the back porch. "But I guess it won't hurt if you want to look around."

If she thinks I'm going to let her dig up my cornfield on the strength of a two-hundred-year-old letter and a story about a hole full of rusty old tools she's out of her mind.

She starts to walk toward the cornfield but after a few steps she glances back at me. "Aren't you coming?"

"I don't think so. I've got company arriving in a few hours and I need to get the house ready."

She looks put out but manages a polite smile. "Oh? Anybody I know?"

God, I hate nosy people. I smile back sweetly. "Watch out for the ticks. They're bad this year."

* * *

Tommy said he'd get here "some time after noon," so I decide not to waste the next few hours cleaning the cottage when I could be on the beach getting the last bit of private time I'm going to have for quite a while. I yell out the back door to Cheri telling her I'm taking off and she can call me later if she finds anything. She's bending down by the stone wall on the east side of the cornfield, poking around in the dirt with a stick. She waves at me and yells thanks then goes back to digging up worms for her young or whatever it is she's doing.

When I'm retired like she is, I swear to God you won't find me scratching in the mud with a stick, looking for potsherds and tepee poles and who knows what else. I plan to spend my days on the beach, sleeping on the sand and listening to the waves roll in.

I park the car in the farthest lot from the entrance and cut through the dunes, and when I emerge by the water it only takes a few minutes to get to an isolated spot. I strip off my shirt and sandals and plunge into the ocean immediately, floating on my back and closing my eyes and letting the tide carry me wherever it wants.

I read a poem once that compared waves hitting the shore to the pulse in a human wrist. I can't remember the exact words, but it talked about how the ocean was the world's heart and the beaches were its arteries and veins. I'm not usually too keen on eco-poetry, but that one stuck with me for some reason. I paddle around and hum to myself for a few minutes, putting Tommy and Cheri Tipton out of my mind as much as possible.

"Hey, Mr. Bishop!"

The voice is so close it startles me and I thrash around for a second, searching for who called me, but I can't find anybody. I tread water and spin in a slow circle.

A head explodes out of the ocean not two feet away from me. I lurch away, panicking, before I recognize Simon. He's got a shit-eating grin on his face.

"Simon! Jesus Christ, I could kill you!"

His grin just gets bigger and he pushes his wet hair behind his ears. "Hey, Mr. Bishop," he says again. "Nice day, huh? How are you doing?"

"Fine, fine, couldn't be better. I just peed myself is all." I splash water at him. "Where did you come from?"

He swims a few feet closer to shore so that he can stand. "I was over there in the dunes taking a nap when I saw you and decided to come say hi."

I dog-paddle over to him and put my feet down in the sand, too. He's about six inches shorter than me, because the ocean comes up to his neck while it's only up to my armpits. "So you don't have a job this summer? Or are you getting paid to scare the crap out of people minding their own business at the beach?"

"Dad and Mom won't let me get a job because it's already the middle of the summer and they say I need the time to study. I got way behind last year at my old school and they want me to get caught up before the fall."

A wave pushes into us and moves us a little closer to shore. "And hanging out here counts as studying?"

He shrugs and his shoulders make a brief appearance above the surface of the water. "I'm doing good in my classes so they don't care."

I almost tell him he's obviously not doing so "good" in English but then decide not to be a jerk. "What other classes are you taking?"

"Just remedial math. It only meets on Tuesdays and Thursdays." He turns his head and sneezes, and the sun glints off the moisture spraying out of his mouth, making a brief but delicate snot rainbow. He laughs. "Cool."

Why am I talking to this kid? "Well, I guess I should be going."

He looks disappointed. "How come? You don't teach in the afternoons during the summer, do you?"

"No, but I've got company coming into town. For all I know they may already be here."

He walks with me as I head toward shore, plowing through the water. His ribs unveil themselves an inch at a time, and then his waist and butt, and eventually we're both on dry sand. He digs around in his ear with a pinkie finger. "Yeah? Who's coming?"

"My brother and three of his friends."

Now why did I tell him that? When Cheri Tipton asked me the same thing I made her eat silence.

"Cool," he says again. "Is he older or younger than you?"

"Younger. Two years younger."

He reaches down to brush sand from his shins. The shadow from his body angles off to his left and he suddenly squats to hold his knees. "I've always wanted a younger brother but my folks don't want any more kids."

"Are you an only child, then?"

He nods, squinting at the sun. "Yeah. I had an older sister once but she died when I was a baby." He stares up at me. "I bet you were a pretty good older brother."

I barely know this kid. What makes him say something like that? I pick up my shirt and shake it out. "Yeah, well, I guess I should be going."

He nods. "Okay." He looks forlorn for some reason.

"See you tomorrow in class?"

He nods again.

I head toward the parking lot but when I get to the dunes I turn around. Simon is still hunkered down where he was, watching me.

Cheri left another note on my door. This one says "Hi, Nathan. Thanks for letting me have a look. The site looks promising! I'm going to keep searching through my archives and the Web and see if I can unearth more information. I'll be in touch."

Wonderful. Isn't it precious that she has a hobby?

I've already put clean sheets on the bed in the guest room (after Dad died I sold the twin beds Tommy and I used to have and replaced them with a double), but now I open up the hide-a-bed in the living room and get it ready for whichever couple ends up sleeping out here. Having people visit wouldn't bother me so much if they weren't taking over the whole goddamn house.

I love this room. Books are everywhere, and there's a ponderous old armoire made entirely of oak that takes up most of the north wall. It was already an antique when Grandpa bought it in the nineteen forties, and it's probably worth a fortune by now. But what's inside it is even more valuable: behind the locked doors is a small but impressive collection of first edition books, packed tightly onto three glass shelves. Grandpa didn't have much money, but every time he had a little extra he'd go out and buy a rare book, and quite often he even managed to find a signed copy. God knows how, but he got his hands on first editions of Dickens and Tennyson and Kipling and Emerson and just about everybody else famous who wrote a book in the nineteenth century. If Cheri Tipton and her history-buff friends knew what was in this armoire, their shit would turn green for a month.

On a whim I get the key for the cabinet out of its hiding place (I keep it in a vase that belonged to my mother) and unlock the heavy doors. As I'm swinging them open the distinct aroma of old books— that weird combination of dust and paper and leather peculiar to used book stores and library basements—hits me full force. I love that smell. The best hours of my life have been spent in a quiet corner or under a tree or on the beach with a book in my hands. I've been told on more than one occasion that I should stop reading so much and actually have a life, but do you know what I've figured out? People in books are much more interesting than the people who've told me that.

I pull out a small black copy of essays by Emerson. The cover is slightly water-damaged, but the pages are unmarred except for places in the text where somebody has marked various passages with a pencil. I riffle through it and I'm startled to find that somebody in my family has underlined many of the same sections I've always loved. Whatever our differences, every single member of my family has always felt the same way I do about books in general and the Transcendentalists in specific—even my fucked-up father.

Emerson saved my life in college, by the way. I know that sounds melodramatic, but I'm not joking. I was planning to kill myself one night (attempt number three if I'd gone through with it, but who's counting?) when for some reason I picked up a tattered copy of *The Norton Anthology of American Literature* instead of the bottle of pills next to it on the table by the bed, and I discovered the "Self-Reliance" essay for the first time. It was like I'd been having a nightmare and all of a sudden a sweet old man reached out of a book—and across a century and a half—to shake me awake. Scoff if you will, but I swear I could feel him in the room with me the whole time, sitting beside me and talking softly, like someone keeping watch over a sick friend. I know this makes me sound like a crackpot, but once or twice I even thought I felt a hand on my head.

Are there people still alive in the world who are as wise and kind and modest as everybody says Emerson was? I've never met anyone remotely like him, but I suppose that might simply be a reflection on what I deserve. I mean, look at his social circle: Thoreau, Whitman, Melville, Hawthorne—his journals and letters read like a *Who's Who* from that era. Great people draw other great people to themselves.

And who do I draw to me? Cheri Tipton and Simon Hard-on. Jesus.

I'm standing on one bare foot with my other foot on top of it, and I'm still wearing my swimsuit and reading my favorite dead guy's words when there's a knock on the door in the kitchen. I yell out, "Just a minute," and put the book back in the armoire, but before I can lock it up again I hear the screen door open and footsteps, and then Tommy is standing in the living room doorway staring at me.

He smiles. "Nathan? What are you doing?"

My eyes are suddenly wet and my throat feels tight. "Nothing," I mumble. "Just thinking."

He's dressed in khaki shorts and a white cotton shirt with the two top buttons open, but that's all I have time to notice before he walks over and pulls me close to him, burying his face in my neck. His hands are cool and dry on my back. A lot of people have hangups about touching other people's skin, but that's never been a problem with Tommy.

He pushes me away for a second, holding my shoulders, and says, "You're so dark you look like an Indian," then he hugs me again before finally letting go. He smells like coffee.

I finish locking the armoire. "Where are your friends?"

"They're outside admiring your rhododendrons. Come out and meet them."

"Let me get some clothes on first."

"Don't you dare. I want them to see how beautiful my big brother is."

He's always saying shit like that, but I'd be lying if I said I didn't like it. Compared to him I look like Quasimodo, but he never seems to notice. I can't help but smile at him and he takes me by the hand and pulls me after him into the kitchen.

I may be the older brother, but this is the way it's always been with us. My earliest memories are of him leading me around by the hand as soon as he could walk. I thought I'd finally escaped the leash when he moved to New York, yet every time he comes home I dust off my old collar and let him reattach the chain. I've been told my whole life how lucky I am to be so close to my brother, but I can't tell you how often I've dreamed of being an only child or a member of a family where the siblings can't stand each other.

No matter what anyone tells you, love is not necessarily a good thing.

CHAPTER 2

Tommy is telling a story when I join everybody on the back porch

". . . and he had this thing about snakes. If he saw one while he was mowing he'd freak out and run away. He'd leave the mower on and come get either Nathan or me to finish the lawn while he cowered inside, peeking through the curtains."

He's talking about Dad. Dad pretended to be a bad-ass, but he was the biggest wienie in the world when it came to snakes and rats and spiders.

Tommy puts his bare foot on his boyfriend Philip's leg, and Philip (I don't remember his last name—Ellington? Edgerton?) wraps a hand around it. Tommy smiles at him and resumes his monologue. "So anyway, one morning we all came walking into the kitchen and there's this big fucking garden snake coiled up by the stove. It was at least two feet long, and it's swinging its head around and doing the snake thing with its tongue. Dad ran upstairs, screaming like a bad actress in a slasher movie."

I look around the table. We're sitting in a circle on green plastic lawn chairs, drinking Chardonnay and eating pepper crackers smeared with Brie and hot mustard. Tommy is between Philip and me, and Camille and Kyle—their last name is Colman—are across from us. Philip's a makeup "artist" for some fledgling theater company (which pays next to nothing, so he makes ends meet by working at Blockbuster Video), Camille's a sales rep for Apple Computers, and Kyle's a grunt in an advertising firm. Tommy gave me a brief biographical sketch of each of them when he introduced us, but not much of it besides their jobs stuck in my head—except that the first time Tommy and Kyle met, Tommy tried to get Kyle to go to bed with him.

What a surprise.

Tommy shifts his foot as conspicuously as possible right onto Philip's crotch, and Philip giggles and blushes. I doubt he'd be quite as pleased if I told him how many times I've seen Tommy do the same thing with other guys. The poor bastards—all pretty, all brainless—last about two months.

I'm not impressed with Tommy's latest plaything. Philip hasn't said more than two complete sentences since he got here. (One of those was to complain about his cell phone not working anywhere on my property, and the other was to express his outrage about the absence of a television.) To be fair, it's difficult to make conversation with someone else's tongue in your mouth, but he could at least try.

He is handsome, though. I'll give him that. He's got long brown hair, pulled back in a ponytail, and his skin is flawless, and his smile is genuine and open. He's got one of those faces that doesn't look real, though, because there's absolutely nothing wrong with it. When you look at most people, you can say "so-and-so's nose is his best feature," or "look at those great eyes." But Philip doesn't have a best feature. Even his nostrils are attractive.

Camille is a striking redhead in her mid-twenties, with long legs and perfect, baseball-sized breasts, and Kyle is a skinny, hairy guy with vague green eyes and prominent cheekbones. Camille's wearing the same thing she had on when they got here—a white cotton skirt and a red blouse tied up at the bottom to show off her flat, pale stomach—but Kyle's replaced the pants and a button-down shirt he had on earlier with black soccer shorts and a plain white V-neck T-shirt. A tuft of dark chest hair sticks out at the bottom of the V.

Incidentally, if he's heterosexual, I'm a dachshund.

Ordinarily, I don't even try to figure out what somebody else's sexual thing is, because I've been dead wrong so many times in the past it's embarrassing. But Kyle is a classic closet queer. He's not especially effeminate, but ever since he got here he's been following Tommy and Philip around like a horny puppy, and whenever they touch he gets this hungry expression on his face that's so transparent it's hard to watch. I can't believe Camille married him. She's either the stupidest or the blindest woman in New York. She's obviously in love with him, staring at him every few seconds and falling silent whenever he says something, but he basically ignores her in favor of whatever else is going on.

Tommy takes a swig of his wine and glances around at his audience, making sure he's still got everyone's attention. "The snake isn't really the good part of the story, though, because Nathan and I just got a shovel and tossed the thing out of the house. What was funny is that Nathan wouldn't let me tell Dad we'd gotten rid of it."

All three of them are watching Tommy like he's the most fascinating human being on the planet. Some things never change. Tommy doesn't really have friends. He has groupies.

He reaches over and massages my shoulder while he's talking. "Remember? You went over to the bottom of the staircase and yelled that it had gotten away and we had no idea where it was." He bursts out laughing. "Dad kept calling down to ask if we'd found it yet, and you just sat on the couch saying things like 'Not yet, Dad. Better stay in your room until it turns up.'"

"I'd forgotten all about that." I pour myself another glass of wine. "He stayed upstairs for eleven hours. He wouldn't even come down to use the bathroom."

Tommy's always done a killer imitation of Dad and he does it now. His voice drops about a fifth and he talks really fast and loud. "'You boys better find that damn snake soon, or I'll come down there and wring your scrawny little necks. I mean it. Nathan? Tommy? I'm not messing around.'"

All of a sudden I'm laughing, too. "He ended up peeing out a window, remember? We were cooking dinner in the kitchen when I looked up and saw this stream of water shooting out onto the lawn from the second story. It was sunset and the light caught it just right and I remember thinking, 'Gee, that's kind of pretty.'"

Tommy's taking a drink when I say this and he has to spit it back in his glass because he's laughing so hard. "Oh, God, that's right.

He heard us laughing then and finally figured out we were fucking with him. He came flying down the stairs and we took off before he could get to us. We left the stove on and everything."

Everybody laughs but when Camille asks what happened next Tommy shrugs, smile quickly fading, and changes the subject. She's tactful enough to let it go, but she looks curious. I zone out on the conversation.

I haven't thought about that night in years but now it all comes back: Dad tearing through the kitchen and Tommy and I desperate to get away from him, plunging through the screen door so fast we nearly ripped it off its hinges. He chased us down the path to the lighthouse for at least a hundred yards screaming, "You'd better run, you little sons of bitches!" Tommy wasn't wearing a shirt and neither of us had shoes on. We sprinted all the way to the ocean and stayed there until close to midnight, and even though it was late summer it was a cold night.

I remember sitting next to each other on the beach, pressed together for warmth, laughing about the snake and worrying what Dad was going to do to us. I gave Tommy my shirt because he was quite a bit smaller than I was at the time and he didn't have any body fat to protect him from the wind. I think I was fifteen and he was thirteen. We could have gone to a friend's house, but for some reason we didn't want to. I think the beach was the only place we ever felt safe. Walls and roofs may keep you warm and dry, but they don't give you much room to run if you need it.

Anyway, when we got home Dad had locked the door and refused to let us in. We knocked at the kitchen door for quite a while, and then we went around back to try the sliding doors, and we could see him sitting in his chair in the living room, sipping whiskey and reading. We yelled through the glass and rapped on it for fifteen minutes but he never looked up. We spent the night in a hammock near the cornfield, holding each other and shivering. It was light in the sky by the time I finally fell asleep, and the first thing I saw when I woke up was Dad standing over us with an expression of disgust on his face.

"What a couple of little faggots," he said. "Let go of each other and come inside before the fucking neighbors see you."

Neither of us had the balls to remind him that we didn't have any fucking neighbors.

I don't remember what Dad eventually did to us. Locking us out for the night apparently took the edge off his rage (even though he'd sworn off the physical violence thing years before, I have no doubt he would have killed us if we'd stayed in the house that night) and whatever he came up with to punish us the next day completely escapes me now. His usual method was to make us quit doing something we loved to do—he made Tommy drop out of tennis one year and he made me give up band, for instance. But it must not have been too bad, because I have no memory of it.

And whatever it was, pissing off Dad like that was definitely worth it.

"Nathan?" Tommy's shaking my shoulder again. "Camille just asked you a question."

"Sorry, Camille." I reach for a cracker and smear it with a big glob of Brie. "Whenever Tommy's talking I fall into a coma."

Tommy ignores me and slides his chair closer to Philip.

Camille pushes her hair off her forehead with an elegant finger. She has big blue eyes. "I was just asking if you ever get down to New York."

Tommy snorts. "Nathan barely leaves the yard, let alone the state."

I feel a flash of irritation. "I haven't been there in quite a while. New York is a little overwhelming for me."

"So's downtown Walcott," mutters Tommy.

Jesus, he pisses me off. I keep my eyes on Camille. "I've got quite a few friends there but I'm still working up the courage to go back. The last time I visited I hated every minute of it."

She gives me a pitying smile. "You just need to give it more of a chance. It grows on you." She looks around the table. "I'm always dumbfounded when I meet someone who doesn't care for New York, aren't you? It's as if they're from Mars or something. Why on earth would anyone feel that way?"

I smile back at her. "Because it's hot and dirty and loud, and it smells like urine and stale garlic, and it's full of people who think anyone from a small town is a rube with hay in his teeth who enjoys being spoken to in a condescending fashion."

She recoils and Tommy glares at me. "Stop being so sensitive, Nathan. She was just asking." He turns to Camille. "I should have warned you about Nathan's temper, Camille. I keep hoping he'll mellow out as he gets older but so far there's no sign of that."

She bites her lip. "It's my fault. I didn't mean to sound condescending. I'm sorry, Nathan."

I mutter an apology too, and everybody falls silent for a minute. Tommy returns to his perusal of Philip's earlobe and I stare into my drink.

When I raise my head, Camille's running her fingers through Kyle's hair, but she's doing it mindlessly, as if she's petting a cat. Kyle lets her do it but he doesn't lean in to her touch, either. (He's one of those people whose eyes are never still. They dart from my face to my hands and then around the porch like a bat in an old movie theater.) Camille and he are both watching me now, because Tommy and Philip are whispering to each other and seem to have forgotten us.

Camille leans forward, studying me. "I thought you'd be blond like Tommy." Her voice is pleasant; she seems to have forgiven me for my outburst.

I shake my head. "Tommy's adopted. We found him in the rushes down by the river, singing 'Kum ba yah' and turning water into wine."

Tommy breaks off baby-talking to Philip long enough to look over his shoulder at me. "Nathan's the one who's adopted. He's the bastard love child of Ernest Borgnine and Cher."

I sigh. We could go on like this indefinitely, but I don't want to. It's just our old shtick, and suddenly I'm tired of it. I point at Camille's wedding ring. "So how long have you two been married?"

She holds her hand out to me so I can see it better. It's a delicate gold band with a single small diamond. "One hundred and sixty-three days. But we've been living together for over a year." She gazes at Kyle and her face softens. "I finally talked him into making an honest woman of me."

Kyle grins at her absently and scratches his jaw with his fingernails. He needs a shave. He turns back to me. "How long have you been living in this place?"

Camille frowns.

I sip my wine. "All but ten years of my life. I moved out when I went to college and back in when Dad died."

Tommy grunts. "And now it will take the Connecticut National Guard to get him out of here."

I scowl at him. "Tommy doesn't approve of Walcott. There aren't enough sex clubs and porno shops to keep him amused."

Tommy narrows his eyes but Camille cuts in before he can respond. "It must be strange to still be in the same place you lived as a kid. Doesn't the isolation get to you?"

I shrug. "Sometimes. But it's really not all that isolated. The trees just make it seem like that."

I can see that nobody believes me. They start chatting about the cottage and the weather, and I stand up to go inside and get the vegetables I'm roasting for supper out of the oven.

"What's going on in the cornfield?" Tommy asks.

I look where he's pointing. There's a big patch of freshly dug dirt at the far end of the field, surrounded by broken and uprooted cornstalks. Christ. Dale Cromwell is not going to be happy. "Cheri Tipton was digging around out there today when I went to the beach. She was supposed to leave the corn alone, though."

Camille gets up and walks a few feet toward the field. "What was she looking for?"

"She thinks there might be some relics from an old Indian village out there."

Tommy makes a face. "A what? She's nuts. There's nothing there but crow shit and corn."

"That's what I told her, but she found an old letter that talks about this mysterious tribe who used to live around here."

Camille leans down to pull a deer tick off her ankle. "Really? That's very exciting." She inspects the tick for a second, then calmly pulls it apart with her perfectly manicured purple fingernails, ignoring the chorus of "gross" and "eeugh, yuck," from the rest of us. Kyle's voice is the loudest.

She shakes her head. "What a bunch of sissies."

*   *   *

No one gets why I love Walcott as much as I do. (Except Tommy, of course, who'd never admit, even under torture, that he feels the same way.) To be honest, I'm not even sure myself. My job is just a job, and the people who live here are no different than people everywhere, and there are thousands of small towns up and down the coast that are cheaper or prettier or less infested with tourists, where I could presumably be just as happy. It's not challenging, it's not cultural, and it's certainly not the center of anything that matters.

But Walcott has everything I need or want. I know every square inch of my cottage and my land, and every weed and rock on the path to the beach. I love waking once a week to the "whoosh" of a hot air balloon venting over my roof (sightseers pay Kelly Green fifty dollars per person to take them up for an hour in his balloon, and every Saturday he floats them over my property on his way to the coast), and I love listening to a local pack of coyotes when they come out at night from an abandoned corncrib on the property abutting mine and call to each other across my field, the pups yipping like excited second-graders on a field trip. I love the woods around my house, where I cut down dead trees every October and November and chop them up for firewood, and I love the clean, straight roads that run along the ocean for miles, where (on the rare mornings when I can get my fat ass out of bed to do it) I ride my bike in the quiet before dawn.

But most of all I love the nights. The stillness, the stars, and the slow rise and fall of the moon: these are all I know of God. In this place, in that darkness, nothing of who I am or what I've done matters, and all the demons in my head, cowed in the presence of something sacred, temporarily shut their rabid, carping little mouths, and let me rest. I can't imagine finding that kind of peace anywhere else, even though you'd think I'd be more comfortable far away from here, like Tommy, in an anonymous city where there isn't a bad memory hiding under every rock and behind every tree, waiting to ambush me every time I go for a walk or stop to take a leak.

But what can I say? This is my home. Walcott may be loaded with pitfalls, but after all these years I've finally learned where it's safe to step. And I'm not about to risk moving someplace where I don't know the terrain, or what those who hunt me look like.

Everybody's still in bed when I get up in the morning. Tommy is sleeping on his stomach on the hide-a-bed in the living room with one arm hanging off the mattress, and Philip is curled up on his side next to him. The sheet is down by their feet and they're both naked, the dark tan on their torsos and limbs contrasting starkly with the whiteness of their asses. I try not to stare at the only part of Philip that's awake. They were at it half the night—not being in the least bit quiet about it—and he's apparently ready for more.

I tiptoe past them and when I step into the kitchen I listen for noises from Kyle and Camille in the guest room, but they're not awake yet, either. I take a long time showering and shaving, and by the time I head back upstairs to get dressed, Tommy is sitting up in bed, blinking at the sun.

"Hey," he whispers. "What time is it?" Philip stirs next to him.

"About seven thirty," I whisper back. "I just put on some coffee."

"Seven thirty? Why are you up so early?"

"I teach, remember?"

"I thought you didn't have to be there until nine."

"I don't. I just like to have time to wake up."

He yawns and nods. "Same old Nathan."

"What's that supposed to mean?"

"Nothing. I think it's cool you take your job so seriously."

He doesn't have a clue how little I care about my job. I watch him put his hand on Philip's hip and run his brown fingers over the pale skin. Philip rolls over on his back, still mostly asleep but awake enough to give Tommy better access.

I shake my head. "Same old Tommy."

He grins. "Take your time getting dressed, will you?"

One of Dad's favorite jokes was "Know what AIDS means? Adios Infected Dick Sucker."

Har har har. What a knee-slapper. He had dozens of similar, ven-

omous one-liners; antigay comments flew out his mouth like
pissed-off bees, and most of them were said when he was sure his
sons could hear him.

I'm sure he knew we were gay, and no doubt that's one of the
main reasons he treated us the way he did, but Tommy and I never
spoke of it with him. It's not that we thought he'd disown us or not
love us anymore—that's a given, and we could have handled that
and not cared much at all. But the God's honest truth is we were
afraid he'd kill us if we ever had the balls to actually say the words
out loud. We were absolutely sure he'd cut off our heads—and our
dicks—with Grandpa's old World War II bayonet he kept in his bedroom. He could live with suspicion, but not with truth.

Anyway, the first time I got a blow job, Dad was in the next room,
reading the newspaper. I was fourteen, and it was after school, and
he thought I was reading in Tommy's and my room. I remember
lying on my bed with my legs open, the blond head of another boy
bobbing up and down between my thighs, and I knew if Dad
caught us he'd tear us apart. But as you can probably imagine, by
that time I didn't much care.

It all started innocently enough. The other boy and I were sitting
on the bed together, talking about what had happened at school
that day, and I happened to mention seeing Lee Koslowski's dick in
the showers after gym class. (Koslowski's dick was a local legend. I
swear to God it was at least eight inches long, flaccid.) He noticed
me getting hard talking about it, but when I got embarrassed and
tried to cross my legs to cover it up he wouldn't let me. He put a
hand on each knee and pushed my legs flat, and he stared at the
bulge in my crotch for a while before finally reaching up to touch it.
I remember my mouth going dry and my heart pounding; I remember his fingers opening my belt and unzipping my pants; I remember shifting my hips so he could pull my shorts down past my
knees.

He played with my penis for a while, pulling at it experimentally
and laughing at the expressions on my face, then he said, "I saw a
picture in a magazine of a girl doing this to a guy," and he opened
his mouth, wet his lips and went to work. I remember my hands in
his hair, and how he surfaced for air every once in a while, and how

he whispered, "Better be quiet, Nathan," when I started to whimper right before I came. I remember convulsing on the bed, and the sound of him swallowing several times, and the smell of my semen and sweat in the room. I remember staring up at the ceiling, knowing I should feel guilty about what had just happened, but feeling so fucking good I couldn't quite manage anything remotely resembling guilt.

So I waited until my heart slowed, then I told Tommy to lie on his back for his turn.

Simon comes in late to class with a bad case of bed-hair and red, swollen eyes. Vernette asks him what rock he climbed out from under and he shows her his middle finger before plopping down in his seat. The rest of the class laughs and looks at me expectantly. Why do kids like to see other kids get in trouble?

Vernette gets impatient when I don't say anything. "Did you see that, Mr. Bishop? Simon just flipped me off."

I sigh. "Don't flip off Vernette, Simon."

He stares at his desk, ignoring me.

Vernette glares at the back of his head. "I want an apology." She plays with a dangling earring and starts chewing her gum faster. "I want an apology right now."

The other kids watch avidly, heads swiveling back and forth as if they're trying to keep up with a tennis match. I fight the urge to sigh again. "Apologize to her, Simon, so we can get back to work."

He slowly lifts his head and turns to face her. "I'm sorry you're such a bitch, Vernette."

Vernette slams her book shut. "What is your problem? Why are you being such a faggot?"

"Okay, that's enough," I say in my best no-nonsense teacher's voice. "Simon, why don't you get out of here for today?"

He gets up quickly. "Fine by me."

I call after him before he gets out the door. "Come back after class to get tomorrow's assignment."

He doesn't answer.

Vernette is nearly yelling. "Aren't you going to make him go to the principal? He should be suspended for acting like that."

I tell her to drop it but she isn't through. "That's not right, Mr. Bishop. He called me a bitch in front of the whole class and you, I don't know, you just rewarded him or something by letting him go early."

"Relax, Vernette. I'll cut his tongue out later if that will make you happy, but can we get back to work now?"

She snatches up her purse and her textbook and stalks to the door. "I'm going to talk to Mr. Baker."

Ted Baker is the principal and he and I don't much like each other. No doubt he'll lecture me later on the need to maintain proper discipline in my classroom.

Vernette waits for me to say something else, probably hoping I'll call her back. I shake my head. "Tell him I said hello."

She spins on her heels and flounces down the hall.

The first time I tried to kill myself was November 23, 1988. I got up on a stump and threw a rope over a tree branch in the woods, then I put a noose around my neck and tied my hands behind my back with some phone cord and stepped off the stump.

It hurt like hell. The rope bit into my neck and I tried to scream but I couldn't. I kicked my legs around and was starting to black out when I felt the stump under my toes and pulled myself to where I could stand up again. But I couldn't get untied so I started yelling for somebody to come help me. My legs were going numb and I was beginning to panic when Tommy finally came looking for me. I'd yelled myself hoarse and pissed my pants, and I bawled like a baby calf when I saw him. He bawled, too, after he got me down.

Dad was still at work when we got back to the cottage, thank God, so at least I didn't have to deal with him, but after I took a shower Tommy yelled at me for almost an hour and kept asking me why I'd do something so stupid. I'd never seen him so mad. I couldn't tell him the truth, though, because it would have hurt him too much to hear it. Besides, he wouldn't have understood.

To people like Tommy, suicide is never an option. The idea of killing himself has never crossed his mind. He believes that no matter how shitty today is, tomorrow will be better, and if tomorrow is shitty, too, then next week or next month everything will sort itself out. I can't tell you how many times I've had to listen to him spout obnoxious, cloying bromides like "Just wait: the pendulum will swing from bad to good again," or "You'll see, the wheel will turn full circle," or—the one I hate the most—"You just have to hold on till dawn." In his reality, guilt and pain can be dealt with by simply flipping a switch. And what's especially irritating is that he really, truly has faith that the world works like that for everybody, and all people like me need to do to fix ourselves is to "Turn that frown upside down."

God. I should have hung *him* instead of myself.

The reason he got so pissed at me that day was because he thought I'd made a conscious choice to commit suicide. He probably still thinks that. I'm sure if you asked him he'd tell you that I had a plan about where to tie the rope, and what stump I should stand on, and what time of the afternoon I wanted to try it—as if I had an outline in my head for the whole thing. Something like:

(1) *Get home from school.*
    (a)   *Have snack.*
    (b)   *Brush teeth.*
(2) *Dangle from tree by neck until dead.*
    (a)   *Loll tongue, turn purple.*
    (b)   *Severely inconvenience Tommy.*

But it wasn't like that.

There was no premeditation, no schedule, no design. Blackness just came down in my head, like a curtain at the end of a play. That's all. I don't know how else to describe it. It's as if my mind hung up a sign in the window that said "Out to lunch," and my hands and feet did the rest for me. Instinct took over, and sometimes instinct isn't about survival. Sometimes it's only about stopping the pain, however you have to do it.

I had a bad rope burn around my neck and I had to wear a turtleneck for three days to cover it. Tommy watched me like a hawk for more than a month, and he made me promise not to do anything like that again.

But I had my fingers crossed when I promised, so of course it didn't count.

Simon doesn't come back after class, but Ted Baker is standing in the door when I dismiss the kids. He comes in while I'm erasing the blackboard and perches his fat left ass-cheek on my desk and his fat right foot on my floor. He's wearing bright blue tennis shorts and a polo shirt, and he's got black dress socks on under his sandals.

I can't stand this guy. We've known each other for decades, because we're the same age and we both grew up in Walcott. He was an asshole when we were in school and he's even more of an asshole now. He was the kind of kid who did one stupid thing after another—poured sugar in gas tanks, pulled the fire alarm during basketball games, set fires in trash cans—and he never once got caught. I could have ignored all that, though, because none of it affected me directly, but one time he decided it would be funny to pee on Tommy's clothes in the locker room while Tommy was in the shower. I remember catching him doing it and I remember moving toward him, but I don't remember anything else about the fight until I heard Tommy's voice in my ear whispering, "Please let go of him, Nathan. He can't breathe." Tommy's arms were wrapped around me from behind, and I remember looking down at Baker and seeing that I was kneeling on him and his face was purple and his eyes were frantic and his hands were trying to pry my fingers off his throat. My forearms were scratched and bloody and the right side of my face felt numb. I let go and stood up, and I remember wondering why all the other boys in the locker room backed away from me when I went to my locker to give Tommy my clothes to wear.

Anyway, Baker never did anything to Tommy or me again, but he hates us both, and I know it pisses him off to no end that I work here and he hasn't been able to get rid of me. I was here before he was, and the superintendent, Madeline Huber, won't let him fire me, but he's been a thorn in my side for years, burying me with paperwork and making frequent classroom "visits" to evaluate my teaching. (It's his doing, by the way, that I no longer have a summer vacation to speak of. He somehow managed to convince the school board—over my strident protests—that I should be permanently drafted into the summer school's remedial teaching program.) I have yet to receive a positive evaluation from him, but for some reason Huber doesn't care.

He clears his throat and rubs his hands together. "How's it going, Nathan?"

"It's going fine, Ted. I take it Vernette came to talk to you."

"She did. She said the new kid—what's his name?"

"Simon Hart."

"She said this Hart kid flipped her off and called her a bitch and you didn't do anything about it."

"That's not true. I kicked him out of class. And he only flipped her off because she was rude to him when he walked in the room."

He gestures for me to sit down at one of the kid's desks. "That doesn't justify him giving her the finger."

I stay standing. "No, it doesn't. That's why I kicked him out."

"Why didn't you send him to me? That's why I'm here."

"And what would you have done? Suspended him?"

"Probably. The school has a no-tolerance policy for sexual harassment."

"What are you talking about? He wasn't hitting on her, Ted, he was just flipping her off." I wander over to the window. There's a hot breeze blowing through and I can feel sweat on my back and in my armpits. I turn to face him. "She kind of deserved it. Did she happen to mention that she called Simon a faggot after he called her a bitch?"

He rolls his eyes. "That's hardly the same thing. Kids say 'faggot' more often than they say 'hello.' No one takes it seriously."

Why do I bother? If I admit to him why I take it seriously he'll just try harder than ever to find a reason to fire me. "I'm just saying Vernette was as much to blame as Simon. Look, I'll talk to the kid, okay? I'll make sure he shapes up and apologizes to Vernette, and if he doesn't I'll send him to you and you can castrate him. How's that?"

Ever since he was a kid he's had this weird habit of sucking his acne-scarred cheeks in and blowing them out again. He's doing that now. "There's no need to be defensive. I'm just doing my job."

"Let me handle it, okay?"

He sighs heavily, as if I've asked him for one of his kidneys. "All right, Nathan. But after you've talked to him I want you to write up a report about what happened. I need a paper trail in my files in case this blows up in our faces."

"I don't get why you're making such a big deal out of this. Two kids got pissed at each other, that's all. End of story."

"It's not like when you and I were kids anymore. You can't even believe how fast something like this can turn into an ugly lawsuit."

Whatever. "Okay. I'll write you a report after I talk to Simon."

More cheek-sucking. "Good." I can tell he wants to say more but he finally stands up and saunters toward the hall. I start gathering my things but he turns abruptly in the doorway. "So I heard that Tom's back for a visit."

There are no secrets in Walcott. Tommy could have snuck into town in the middle of a moonless night with his headlights off, dressed in black with charcoal smeared on his face, and somebody still would have seen him. "That's right. Who told you that?"

He shrugs. "I heard it through the grapevine. Somebody saw him pull into town yesterday. Tell him I said hello."

What a hypocrite. "I will. I'll tell him to stop over and see you."

A sickly smile. "That's all right. I'm sure he's got plenty to do without hunting me up."

He says good-bye and scuttles back to the safety of his office.

Camille's sitting at the kitchen table drinking coffee and reading John Irving's *A Widow for One Year* when I get home. She looks up and smiles. "Hi, Nathan. I've been abandoned. The boys all wanted to go for a swim in the ocean before they had breakfast."

How nice of Tommy to leave me with this stranger in my house. "And you didn't?"

She puts the book down and stretches her arms above her head. She's wearing a light blue, sleeveless summer dress; her armpits are shaved. "Not on your life. The water's too cold up here."

"It's not that cold. It feels great once you're in."

She drops her arms and shakes her head. "I grew up in Fort Lauderdale. Swimming in the ocean there was like taking a warm bath. That's what it's supposed to feel like." She gets up and refills her mug from the pot. "How was teaching?"

"Marvelous." I put my briefcase in the corner and tell her about Simon and Vernette and Ted Baker.

She makes a sympathetic face, which may or may not be genuine. "Is it always like that?"

"Is what always like that?"

"Teaching."

I snort. "No. Most of the time it's worse."

She sips at her coffee and plays with the cover of her book. "So why do it?"

I shrug. "It pays the bills." I turn around and hunt for a mug in the dish rack. "I'm a teacher by default. Both of my degrees are in English, and there's nothing else for me to do in Walcott but teach." I pour myself coffee and keep talking with my back to her. "Besides, it's not unbearable, and I can retire when I'm fifty-five."

When I turn to face her again she's studying me. "And how old are you now?"

"Thirty-one."

She frowns. "So you've only got twenty-four more years of doing something on a daily basis that you don't enjoy."

I grimace. "Are you trying to get me to kill myself this morning or what?"

She grins. "Sorry. I just don't understand how you can keep doing a job you don't like, day after day. Especially when you live alone and don't have kids to support. You could go anyplace and do anything you want."

She's starting to piss me off. She's known me for all of twelve hours and already she's trying to fix me.

"Yeah, the world is my oyster." I take a swig of stale coffee and dump the rest in the sink. "But I don't want to live anywhere else, Camille."

She hears the irritation in my voice and bites her lip. "I see."

She stays quiet while I rinse my mug. I take my time doing it, and when I finish and look at her again, she's apparently decided to give up her interrogation, because she changes the subject.

"Is there a basement under the floor in here?" She gestures behind her. "I tripped over the rug this morning coming out of the bathroom, and while I was straightening it I noticed there was a trap door there or something."

She probably rooted around in my underwear drawer, too, while she was at it. I untuck my shirt and kick off my shoes. "It's a wine cellar. Nothing too fancy, but my dad had pretty good taste in red wine. He'd buy a case now and then and toss it down there. I probably still have more than a hundred bottles left."

"Really? I love red wine. Can I look?"

Why are people so fucking nosy? She should get together with Cheri Tipton; the two of them could have all sorts of fun prying into other people's lives.

I shrug. "Sure, if you want to." I kick the rug back and lift the door. It's kind of heavy, but my great-grandfather rigged it with some kind of ingenious weight system that does most of the work once you get it an inch or two off the floor. I prop it in place and grab a flashlight and lead her down the stairs. There's just enough room for both of us down here, but I have to bend my head a little to keep from banging it on the ceiling. The cellar smells like earth and old wood, and it's about twenty degrees cooler than the kitchen. It's basically just a six-by-eight-foot room with a rack of wine on each wall, and each rack is about half full. I've never liked this cellar. It's dank and claustrophobic and there are cobwebs everywhere.

I shine the light on one rack and Camille pulls out and dusts off several bottles to look at the labels. She gasps at one of them. "My God, this is a two-hundred-dollar bottle of wine."

"You're kidding." I move forward and she hands it to me. It's a nineteen seventy-two Chambertin. Dad always went gaga over French wine. I like the stuff but I don't know much about it. "I think I have four or five of these."

She blinks in the beam of the flashlight and checks out another row of bottles. "I'm not exactly an expert, but it looks to me like you have a small fortune down here."

I laugh. "I doubt that."

"No, I'm serious. I haven't seen a single bottle so far that isn't worth at least fifty or sixty dollars, and you said you have more than a hundred bottles. So that's what? A few thousand dollars?"

It's my turn to blink. A few thousand dollars is hardly a fortune, but it's nothing to sneeze at either, since I make less than thirty thousand a year even with my summer teaching. "You've got to be shitting me. Think I should sell it?"

"God, no. Drink it. Enjoy it." She steps to the stairwell and stands in the light from the kitchen, and I can see dust floating around her head. She smiles coyly. "Share it with your friends."

I feel the corners of my mouth turn up against my will. "Now? It's not even noon."

"And your point is?" She pulls cobwebs out of her hair. "It's the only sane way to deal with unwanted houseguests."

I look at the floor and lie. "You're not unwanted."

"Bullshit. Even if Tommy hadn't told us on the way up here that you weren't exactly excited about having us visit, I'd know it. It's all over your face."

Goddamn Tommy and his big mouth. I look up again and she's still smiling at me. She holds out her hand.

Great. She wants to bond. I put the neck of the Chambertin in her outstretched fingers. "What the hell."

She laughs and leads me upstairs.

We're eating fried egg sandwiches and potato chips, and we're well into our second bottle of wine. We've been gossiping about Tommy's former boyfriends for most of the last two hours (Camille thinks, as I do, that Philip is only another anonymous bedmate in a long line of anonymous bedmates) and I've actually been enjoying her company. She just told me that since she and Kyle got married, Tommy's had at least thirteen of these so-called "relationships."

"I'm surprised it's not more. Thirteen in six months is way under par for him."

She fiddles with her wedding ring. "Some of them were actually very sweet men. Let's see . . ." she holds up a hand and begins to count on her fingers, "the first one I met was Vinnie the carpenter, then came Pablo the fireman, then Brad the vacuum salesman, then after Brad was George, the big stupid policeman." She pauses. "Or was his name Greg? Whatever, he had bad teeth and he smelled like lobster bisque. Anyway, you get the picture, I'm sure."

She wets the tip of her index finger and runs it around the rim of her crystal glass, making it hum. "My favorite was this gorgeous Italian guy named Harold. Harold was a charmer. He taught kickboxing at the Y and was always showing up late to everything with bruises and cuts all over him." She grimaces. "I thought he was a good match for Tommy but you know Tommy. He gets bored fast."

I refill her glass. "Maybe he just needs some Ritalin."

She makes a face. "What he needs is a bucket of saltpeter on his cereal every morning for breakfast." She sighs. "I was really angry with Tommy when he dumped Harold, especially because the guy he replaced him with was a revolting pig named Willie who once told me that just talking to women made him sick to his stomach. Willie thought that cologne was something you should bathe in. Sitting in a car with him made me want to gag. I can't believe Tommy brought him to our wedding."

"Tommy was at your wedding?"

She takes a big gulp and nods. "He was Kyle's best man. I wanted him to be my maid of honor instead, but I lost the coin toss." She giggles. "He scandalized the crowd at our reception. He got up on stage with the band and sang a semipornographic version of the theme from *Gilligan's Island*."

"We made that up when we were kids." (*"Just sit right back and you'll hear a tale, a tale of a grateful dick."*) "I can't believe he sang that in public."

"He sure did. Kyle's family is pretty uptight and they were all horrified. Kyle tried to get him to shut up but Tommy just dragged him up on the stage to sing along. Kyle was drunk and got laughing so hard he fell down and knocked over a microphone stand. It almost disemboweled the drummer."

I shake my head. "That's my little brother."

She laughs. "That wasn't even the worst of it. At the end of the night Tommy dropped his pants and took a garter off his thigh and threw it at the priest. My poor mother still hasn't recovered."

I laugh, too, and spill a little wine on my shirt. "It's a wonder no one's shot him yet. He always gets away with murder."

She covers her mouth and burps. "I love that about him." She stands up to get a cloth napkin from the cabinet by the sink and she tosses me one, too, before sitting down again. Her coordination is a little impaired, but she still moves gracefully, like a dancer. "He could care less about what's appropriate, and he's so good-natured no one can stay mad at him for long."

I nibble at a chip. "It'll catch up to him one day, though. He'll lose his looks and no one will think the outrageous shit he pulls is cute anymore."

She stares at me curiously. "Does he make you mad sometimes?"

I hesitate. "No. Not really."

She studies me for a second and looks as if she's going to say something else, but then she takes a lock of her hair and holds it over her upper lip to form a mustache. "Do you think I could pass for a man? My husband might like that. In fact, I'm sure he'd prefer it." She giggles some more. "I think I'm a little tipsy, Nathan."

"Really?" I grin at her. "You seem perfectly sober."

We both start laughing again, then I take a big swallow of my drink and it goes down the wrong tube and I start coughing.

She reaches over to pat my back. "Easy. Don't waste such good wine by pouring it in your lungs."

I laugh some more and wipe my eyes. "Thanks. I'll keep that in mind."

She settles back in her chair and I rest my chin on my fist and sigh. She raises her eyebrows. "What?"

"Nothing." I look at the table. "I was just thinking about the time when Tommy tried to steal some condoms from the drugstore. Lydia Cruise caught him red-handed with two boxes of French ticklers in his pockets."

She chortles. "Now why doesn't that surprise me? So what happened?"

"Absolutely nothing, of course. Tommy gave her a song and dance about how some bullies threatened to beat him up if he didn't do it, and he'd never dream of doing anything illegal otherwise, and he didn't even know what the condoms were for, and *please, please don't tell my dad or he'll kill me.*"

I set my glass down and lace my fingers together behind my head. "Lydia Cruise was the biggest bitch in town. She routinely tossed kids out of the store just for looking at her funny. If it had been me she'd caught, she would have beaten me senseless, then called the cops, and my dad, and fucking Dan Rather and everybody else she could think of. But Tommy just batted his pretty blue eyes at her, and Lydia did everything but roll over and play dead."

I pause to wipe my lips on my sleeve. "I couldn't believe it when Tommy told me about it later. He said that before she let him go she even patted his head and gave him a free Snickers bar. Jesus." Bitterness seeps into my voice. "Even Lydia couldn't resist him. Precious little Tommy is everybody's golden boy."

She winces at my tone. "I thought you said he didn't make you mad."

I sniff. "Yeah, well, I guess I was lying."

The screen door bangs open and Tommy, Kyle and Philip finally come trooping in, talking about something or other. They stop to stare at us.

Tommy looks at his watch and raises his eyebrows in mock surprise. "Wow. Not even one o'clock yet. I guess the sun passes over the yardarm earlier here than it does in New York."

I grew up on the beach and I'm used to seeing beautiful young people (and quite possibly the wine has lowered my standards or something), but Tommy and Philip look like matching bronze gods, all long limbs and toned muscle and smooth chests—I know Tommy shaves his and I'd bet Philip does, too—and even though Kyle is too skinny and too hairy, he's strong and healthy, with a nice firm ass and a perky set of nipples. His eyes flit over me momentarily, but he's mostly watching Tommy, of course, and doesn't even notice at first that Camille has put out her hand for him to take. He finally sees it and lets her pull him over, but when she tilts her head back for a kiss he pretends not to notice and releases her fingers so he can rejoin Tommy and Philip by the sink.

Camille looks hurt at first and then pissed, but she tries to mask it. She takes another sip of wine. "So how was the beach?" she asks no one in particular. Her voice is too bright.

"Awesome." Philip throws his arms around Tommy and nuzzles his neck. "Tommy and I made a sand castle."

Tommy gives him a perfunctory hug, then lets go and gets a

wineglass out of the dish rack. "It was a good one, too, but for some reason all the towers ended up looking like gigantic penises."

I pour for him. "Imagine that." I turn to Kyle. "And what were you doing while these two juveniles played in the sand?"

Camille snorts and pops another potato chip in her mouth. She's glaring at Kyle. "Yes, I can't imagine you not wanting to participate while something phallic was happening."

There's sudden acid in her voice. The transformation is jarring. When it was just the two of us here she was relaxed and cheerful. Now suddenly she's breathing hard and trying not to cry.

Silence. Kyle gets a glass out of the rack, too. "What's that supposed to mean?"

"Nothing, dear." She slugs down the rest of her wine and holds her glass out for more. "Nothing at all."

Tommy plops down in the chair next to me and picks up my sandwich for a bite. He smells like salt and sweat. "So what's up, big brother? It's not like you to hit the booze so early."

I take my sandwich back before he can eat the whole damn thing. "Camille made me."

She smiles but there's no humor in her eyes. She shifts in her chair. "That's right. I didn't want to drink alone and since my husband left me to go prancing about at the ocean, I twisted Nathan's arm and forced him to join me."

Kyle fills his glass, glaring at her. "I hate it when you get like this, Camille. What's your problem?"

"I don't have a problem." She stands up. "It would just be nice to get a fucking kiss from my fucking husband every once in a while without having to beg for one."

Five minutes ago she was goofy but completely in control. Now her face is bright red and she's weaving a little. Philip's staring at the floor and even Tommy is looking embarrassed. He reaches for the sandwich again. "Hey, Camille. Chill out, okay? Let's have a good time."

She doesn't even look at him. "Hey, Tommy. Fuck you, okay?"

There's a knock at the screen door and everybody but Camille turns to find out who it is. She's standing in my way with her eyes fixed on Kyle, so I have to lean around her to see.

It's Simon. Wonderful. Just wonderful.

I push my chair back and step around Camille. "Simon? What are you doing here?"

And who was the idiot who told you where I live?

I open the screen door.

"Hey, Mr. Bishop." He smiles sheepishly. He obviously heard Camille's last comment. "Can I talk to you for a minute?"

Tommy comes up next to me. "Who's this?" He sticks out his hand and puts on his most charming smile. "I'm Tom. Nathan's brother."

Simon takes his fingers. "I'm Simon."

"Hi, Simon. You must be new. I know everybody in Walcott and I haven't seen you before."

Philip comes up behind Tommy and sticks his tongue in Tommy's ear. Simon's eyes get big and he drops Tommy's hand like it's burning him. Tommy just grins and drapes an arm over Philip's shoulders.

Goddammit. Now every kid in school is going to know I've got a house full of fags.

"I just moved here a few weeks ago," Simon mumbles, trying not to look at anybody.

Tommy motions for him to come in. "Want a glass of wine?"

I put my hand on Simon's shoulder and move him back so I can step outside. "Simon is one of my students, Tommy." I shut the screen door behind me. "Let's talk out here."

We move away from the front steps. Tommy is watching from the doorway and when Simon can't see him he shapes his mouth in an O and bobs his head up and down, miming a blow job. I flip him off behind my back and lead Simon around the corner of the house, out of sight.

It's another brutally hot day. I'm still wearing the shirt and shorts I had on at the school, but my shirt is unbuttoned and I'm barefoot. Simon is dressed in his habitual cutoffs and T-shirt; there are sweat stains on his chest and under his arms.

I lead him into the shade of a red maple. "Don't mind my brother and his friend. They're both retarded. So what's up?"

He looks up at me then drops his eyes. "I wanted to say I'm sorry about how I acted in class today."

"Yeah, I needed to talk to you about that. What's going on?"

He shrugs and still won't look at me. His chin is quivering. "Nothing, really. I'm just having a bad day, that's all."

Why is it you have to browbeat people into talking about what they obviously want to talk about? "That's not good enough, Simon. You were being a jerk today, and besides that, you got me into trouble. What's up?"

"You got in trouble?" He glances at me, surprised, from under his hair. "Who with?"

"Mr. Baker. He came to see me after class because Vernette complained about you. I got a lecture because I didn't send you to him."

"Shit." His chin quivers some more. "I'm sorry. I didn't mean . . . ." A tear runs down his cheek.

A kid blubbering on my lawn is all I need. "Don't worry about it." I touch his shoulder awkwardly. "It's not a big deal."

He sniffs and wipes his nose on his sleeve. "My dad's being a dick." He blurts the words out. "He found a joint in my room this morning and he flipped out and started pushing me around and shit. Mom tried to stop him but he just yelled at her to get out of the room and let him deal with it."

He pauses and I have to prod to get him talking again. "What happened then?"

He lifts up his shirt and shows me an ugly, fist-sized bruise on his side. The skin around it is angry and red.

"Jesus." On impulse I reach out to touch it but I stop myself before my fingers connect. "Does it hurt to breathe?" My hand falls to my side.

"Not really. I'm just kind of sore." He drops his shirt and he looks up at me wordlessly, his eyes full.

I feel myself getting pissed. Why are fathers such fucked-up human beings? "You should get it checked out anyway and make sure you're okay. You might have a cracked rib or something."

"I'm okay. I cracked a rib once and it doesn't feel like this."

"Is this the first time he's hit you?"

He nods. "He's slapped me once or twice but never very hard. I don't think he meant to . . ."

"It doesn't matter if he meant to or not. No one has the right to hit a kid."

Tommy pokes his head around the side of the house. "You guys doing all right out here? Need anything?" He comes closer, smiling at Simon.

For Christ's sake. His boyfriend's in the house and he's out here lusting after a fifteen-year-old. "We're fine. We're just having a private conversation."

"Okay, but you might want to come inside soon. Camille's getting a little out of hand."

What does he expect me to do about it? I wave him away. He makes a pouty face and turns around.

Simon's eyes follow him as he disappears around the corner. "You guys look a lot alike."

I snort. "Now I know you need to see a doctor. Your eyesight is definitely messed up."

He looks at me curiously. "No it's not. His hair's a different color and you're a little taller but you're obviously brothers."

Whatever. "Look, Simon. We need to call somebody and tell them what your dad did to you."

He looks horrified. "No! Please don't tell anybody, Mr. Bishop. I don't want to get him in trouble."

"I have to tell, Simon. As a teacher I'm required by law to report stuff like this. If it ever comes out that I didn't say anything I could get in deep shit."

"I'd never tell anybody that you knew." He grabs my arm. His fingers are damp. "Please? I only told you because I wanted to explain why I was such an asshole this morning. I didn't want you thinking I was like that all the time."

Why does he care what I think about him? I pull away from him gently. "I know you're not like that. That's why I was worried about you." A mosquito lands on my elbow and I flick it off. "Did your mom see your dad hit you?"

"Yeah. She's really pissed at him. They were still screaming at each other when I left the house this morning."

"Have you been home since? Is it safe for you there?"

He nods. "It's fine. Dad's usually a lot cooler. But it's his job. He's an assistant DA and he gets really weirded out about drugs and shit."

I think I knew the new DA's last name was Hart but I hadn't made the connection between him and Simon yet. "It still doesn't give him the right to hit you."

"Yeah, I know, but I guess he can't help it. He kept yelling stuff like 'I could get fired if people knew I had this in my house.'" His eyes well up again. "Please don't tell anybody, Mr. Bishop. Okay? I'm sure he's calmed down by now."

He looks pathetic. I chew on my lip. "Simon . . . I can't . . ."

He's crying soundlessly, one tear after another leaking from his eyes and running down his face. Goddammit.

I sigh. What am I going to write in my report to Baker about this conversation? "Okay, okay. I won't say anything."

"Promise?"

For some reason I get a lump in my throat. I don't know why. Maybe the wine is making me sentimental or maybe it's just because this poor dumb kid is still stupid enough to believe in adult promises. "I promise. But if he does anything like this again I want you to come to me right away."

"Okay."

I am such a sap but I can't help myself. "Promise?"

He smiles through his tears. It's a sweet smile, relaxed and trusting. "I promise."

We don't say anything for a minute and in the silence I can hear crickets and birds and the sound of the wind blowing through the tall grass. He looks around for the first time since we came out here. "You sure have a lot of privacy. You can't even see any other houses."

I start to say something but just as I open my mouth Camille starts screaming inside. I can't make out the words but she sounds like she's gone postal. Simon and I gawk at each other but before he can ask any questions I tell him I'll see him in class tomorrow.

He nods and starts walking toward the driveway. "Thanks a lot, Mr. Bishop."

I almost tell him to call me Nathan but decide at the last second not to. It's dangerous as a teacher to let kids get too close. I watch him disappear into the woods before I head back inside.

Camille is standing with her face in the bookshelves on the closed door of the guest room (where Kyle has apparently barricaded himself), and she's yelling nonstop. Her voice sounds ragged and the only clear words are "fucking little chickenshit" but she shows no sign of stopping anytime soon. It's hard to believe this is the same woman I was having lunch with just a short while ago. Tommy and Philip are nowhere in sight. I let the screen door slam behind me, hoping she'll quiet down if she knows I'm in the room with her, but she doesn't even bother to turn her head. There's a broken plate on the kitchen counter and books all over the floor.

She grabs a dictionary and steps back to hurl it against the door.

Where the fuck is Tommy? All of a sudden I'm mad as hell. "Camille!"

It's scary how much I sound like my dad when I'm angry.

She jumps and swivels clumsily to face me. Her hair is going every direction and her cheeks are streaked with tears. She points at the guest room door. "That son of a bitch called me a bitch. And he said I was drunk. I am not drunk."

I step forward and take the book away from her. "You need to calm down right now, Camille, or you need to get out of my house."

Her face falls and she crumples to the floor as if I've kicked her in the stomach. She starts to wail. "I'm sorry, I'm sorry, I'm sorry. I'm so sorry, Nathan."

I squat down next to her and try to quiet her. She's sobbing uncontrollably, and when I put my hand on her back she lurches forward and wraps her arms around me and cries on my shirt.

Tommy reappears in the doorway to the living room and Philip is behind him. I look over Camille's head and Tommy mouths, "Good job."

"Eat shit," I mouth back.

He looks confused and whispers, "What's your problem?"

He brings a lunatic into my house and leaves me to deal with her and he wonders why I'm pissed.

The four of us don't move for quite a while. Kyle finally pokes his head out of the guest room and gapes at us; we must look like a tableau in a wax museum.

Camille lifts her head off my chest. Sweat is beaded on her forehead and under her eyes, and her nostrils are wet and runny. "I don't feel so good." She tries to get her legs under her but before she can her eyes get huge and panicky.

"Uh-oh," she says, and leans forward to vomit on my lap.

CHAPTER 3

It's nearly midnight and I'm sitting on the back porch alone. Kyle and Camille have gone to bed (Camille's been in the guest room all day), and Philip and Tommy are sprawled out on the hide-a-bed in the living room, talking baby talk to each other again and no doubt getting ready to fuck their brains out once I call it a night and go upstairs. It's not like Tommy to show this much restraint; on a normal night he'd already be riding Philip like a cowboy on a mustang and if I happened to walk through the room he'd just smile between thrusts and ask how I was doing. But he's been uncharacteristically considerate since Camille puked in my lap this afternoon—except, of course, for the ten minutes after it happened when he couldn't stop laughing.

Camille passed out right after she was sick, and I went immediately to the bathroom, stripped, and took a scalding hot shower. When I came back to the kitchen everything was cleaned up, Camille was out of sight, and Kyle, Tommy, and Philip were playing a quiet game of euchre. By then Tommy had gotten himself under control, and he and Kyle each apologized to me about three hundred times. I ignored them, grabbed another bottle of wine, and went upstairs to drink it by myself. Now I've got a splitting headache and I'm nursing a cup of chamomile tea, and I'm trying to figure out the best way to throw my brother and his traveling troupe of clowns out of my house.

I hate scenes like the one this afternoon. One of the main reasons I live alone is because I can't stand the histrionic horseshit that inevitably occurs whenever two or more people share the same space for any length of time. Granted, Camille's little temper tantrum was an extreme example, but even when the people involved aren't drunk (or mentally deranged), there's always a conflict of some kind, whether or not it leads—like this afternoon's fiasco—to missiles and obscenities hurtling through the air. The best of friends and/or lovers may handle togetherness more gracefully, but they're not exempt either, and the older I get the less patience I have for any of it.

Yeah, I know what the shrinks say: "Conflict and conflict resolution are the mainstays of human intimacy." That fatuous little axiom may be true, but it presupposes that human intimacy is a desirable thing. I have never been nearly as happy with somebody else in the room as I am when I'm by myself. It seems to me that loneliness is a small price to pay for peace and quiet.

I used to think that one day I'd find someone or something that would beat back the perennial emptiness in life that's impossible to ignore when you live by yourself. I had childish, intricate fantasies about some modern-day Prince Charming (who in my imagination always looked like a shaggy hybrid of Han Solo and Luke Skywalker) showing up on my doorstep or in the cereal aisle at the grocery store, and *Presto!* my life would be fixed and I'd never be lonely again. Or I'd dream about having a career that consumed me, a "calling" from on high—a colossal artistic talent, like painting or writing or playing an instrument—that would take all of my energy and passion and leave no room and no need for anything else. I drank a lot of booze and I smoked a lot of pot and I fucked a few pretty strangers, and I even tried praying a bit—anything I could think of to try to avoid reality.

But I've grown up since then. I know now that nothing will ever come along to fill the gap inside of me for more than a short while. Every time I've believed otherwise and gotten used to having something there, sooner or later it's always disappeared, taking another chunk of me with it when it goes. It's happened so often I feel like a cow carcass in the desert after the vultures have stopped by for a snack. Loneliness is just a permanent fact of life. And if you buy into the illusion that you can somehow escape it, you're in for a world of hurt.

Want to know the biggest lie ever written? *'Tis better to have loved and lost than never to have loved at all.*

What an unmitigated pile of shit.

"Nathan?"

I look over my shoulder. Tommy's standing behind the screen door; the light from the living room surrounds his body and head like an aureole. I turn back to face the night. "What?"

He slides open the screen and steps outside. "What are you doing?"

"Watching the stars." As kids we spent a lot of time out here at night. One of the only cool things Dad ever taught us was the names of the constellations. I point at a cluster directly to the south, right above the cornfield. "Why do you think Sagittarius is called 'The Archer?' It looks much more like a teapot than a guy with a bow."

He closes the screen and plops down in the chair next to me. "I don't know. Maybe the guy who named it got off by fantasizing about butch men." He laughs. "Think about it. Besides Sagittarius, there's, let's see," he points high, "well, there's Hercules, of course, and Ophiuchus, and back there . . ." he waves a hand behind us vaguely, not bothering to look, "is Orion, and Castor and Pollux, and Auriga, and . . . Jesus, it's like looking in the window at a queer bathhouse."

Leave it to him to turn the night sky into a homoerotic mural. I don't say anything. Being gay is his entire identity. Every cylinder is a penis, every hole is an anus. It gets old. I like sex as well as the next guy, but Tommy's turned it into a religion. No, that's not quite right. He's too irreverent for that. It's more like a mixture of religion and slapstick.

I don't know why he does what he does with so many men. He claims he craves a "connection" with other human beings, and that sex is the best medium he's found for "bringing down the barriers between people." But as usual, I think he's full of shit. Every time one of his boyfriends tries to have a relationship with him that goes deeper than a few orgasms, Tommy runs like hell. I asked him once if he kept a running tally of how many times he spooged with each guy; I accused him of counting to fifty and then moving on to his next victim. He got pissed, of course, but he didn't deny it, either.

Whatever, that's Tommy. I could spend a lot of time analyzing why he feels the need to be a poster child for promiscuity, but I guess the more pertinent question for me is why I'm not more like him. We have the same blood running through our veins; we grew up in the same house with the same parents. Yeah, in college I did some dumb-ass things with my dick, but like I said, I outgrew that when I realized that casual sex didn't do much for me except mess with my head.

Tommy says I have no right to judge him because I've never had a lasting relationship, either, and at least he's getting laid. He's probably right. Maybe I am no better than him; maybe his serial-killer approach to relationships is as legitimate a way to live as my self-imposed celibacy routine. The bottom line is that we're both seriously fucked-up, because the only way he can feel good about himself is by making one pointless conquest after another, while the only chance I have of dealing with myself at all is by avoiding all forms of intimacy with anyone or anything. So pick your dysfunction: I'm as bad as he is.

But I'll be damned if I'll tell him that. Especially when he's so convinced that his neopagan, in-your-face brand of homosexuality is the only permissible way there is to be a gay man.

He puts his feet up on his chair and rests his head on his knees. "Are you still pissed at me?"

I scratch at the stubble on my chin. "Of course not. Don't be silly. Your friend trashed my kitchen and blew chunks all over my shorts while you hid in the living room and left me alone with her. Why on earth should I be pissed about that?" My voice gets a little louder. "Oh, and you hit on my student, and let Philip hump your leg in front of him, too. What makes you think I'd still be mad?"

He shushes me. "You're exaggerating. The kitchen's fine, and all Philip did was stick his tongue in my ear. And I wasn't hitting on Simon. I was just checking him out. Besides, what do you care what some kid thinks?"

"Because it's not just him, you asshole. He'll tell all his friends, and they'll tell their friends, and before you know it . . . Maybe you've forgotten, but Walcott isn't exactly Manhattan. A lot of people here still get really uptight about gays—especially in the school system—and I'd just as soon not hang a banner advertising my sexuality."

"Same old Nathan."

"What are you talking about?"

He sighs. "Aren't you getting a little sick of the closet? Jesus."

"I'm not in the closet, you self-righteous prick. Just because I don't run around screaming my orientation to total strangers . . ."

"I don't run around screaming. I just do what I feel like doing, when I feel like doing it."

I wish I owned a gun. "That's because you have the luxury of living in a place that . . ." I stop. My head hurts and I'm tired of this. "Forget it."

He sits quietly for a minute, watching me, then he reaches over and lifts my hand out of my lap. "I didn't mean to make you mad."

I take a deep breath and relax my shoulders. "I know."

He kisses my knuckles. "It's so good to see you again, Nathan. I'm sorry I'm such a pain in the ass."

I don't say anything but I squeeze his fingers before letting go.

I can never stay mad at him for more than a few seconds. He pushes every button in me but just when I'm getting ready to tear his throat out, sweetness oozes out of him like sap from a maple tree.

There's a warm breeze rustling through the corn, and an owl is hooting in the woods close by. I yawn and take another sip of tea.

Tommy points at the black hole in the cornfield where Cheri Tipton went digging for buried treasure. "I can't believe Cheri dug up Dale's field. Has he seen it yet?"

"I doubt it. I'm sure I'll hear about it as soon as he does."

"So Cheri's still nuts." He pauses. "Is she still fat, too?"

I can see his grin in the light from the living room. I smile back, recognizing where this is going. Tasteless fat jokes were a staple of our childhood, mainly because Dad always wrestled with his weight, and anything we could make fun of him about behind his back was fair game.

I nod, playing along. "Fat as a rhino."

"Really?"

"Fatter. I heard that somebody mistook her for a whole city. One time when she went swimming they even tried to build a harbor around her navel."

"Wow." He scratches his bare chest. "You know, I've been thinking. Maybe I should gain some weight."

No matter how it starts, I always end up as Tommy's straight man. "Why's that?"

"Because then I wouldn't need pockets anymore. I could just keep my keys and wallet and stuff in the folds of skin under my tits."

I laugh. "Gross. Shame on you. It makes baby Jesus cry when you talk like that."

"Yeah, well, baby Jesus never had to sit next to a fat guy in an airplane and listen to him oink down a box of Ritz Crackers and half a jar of peanut butter."

The light in the house goes off; Philip has apparently gotten tired of waiting for Tommy. Tommy glances over his shoulder but doesn't make any move to get up.

He lowers his voice and leans toward me. "So what do you think of him?"

I look down in my mug and whisper back. "Philip? He's nice."

"That's it? Just nice?"

"What do you want me to say? He's cute, and he seems sweet."

"But?"

"But nothing. As long as you're happy with him, I'm happy too."

He shakes his head. "I hate it when you talk like that. Stop spouting shit and tell me what you really think."

Here we go again. "Why do you care if I like him? He's your boyfriend, not mine."

"I care because you're my brother. I want you to like the person I love."

I cough on the last mouthful of tea. "Love? That's a laugh."

He flares. "What do you know about how I feel?"

"Oh, let's see. Maybe it's because I've lost count of how many men you've loved in exactly the same way. You'll use Philip just like you've used everybody else in your life, and then you'll kick his pretty little ass out of bed for the next guy who catches your eye a week or a month from now."

There's a quick intake of breath behind us. We both turn in time to see Philip standing next to the screen door. His ponytail is draped over his left shoulder like an epaulet and he's wearing white boxer shorts. "I'm sorry," he stammers, "I was just . . ." His lower lip suddenly scrunches up and he disappears from sight.

Tommy jumps to his feet. "Nice going, Nathan. Thanks a lot."

"How was I supposed to know he was listening? Besides, you did everything but torture me to get me to say what I thought."

"Whatever. Maybe if you ever got a boyfriend of your own you could stop being such a dick." He charges inside.

Great. A perfect ending to a perfect day. I hawk up a loogie and spit it on the lawn.

I suppose I should feel bad, but Tommy will have Philip eating out of his hand (or more likely, his crotch) in twenty minutes. He'll convince him this time is different and that I don't know what the hell I'm talking about. They'll make plans for the future and the house they'll buy together and the trip to Scotland or Ethiopia they'll take on their anniversary. And Philip will be ancient history by no later than Labor Day.

I have got to get these people out of my house.

Until Dad died Tommy and I had never gone more than six months without seeing each other, not even when he was in school in Boston and I was at the University of Connecticut in Storrs. We made it a point to get together as often as possible, and if we didn't feel like staying with Dad in Walcott (where we weren't particularly welcome, anyway), we'd meet in Providence and sleep at a youth hostel, and get drunk with snooty rich kids from Brown University. And after college we saw each other even more often, because by then he'd gotten a job in New York and I was back in Walcott in my own house, and he loved to drive up every few weeks (usually with his latest disposable boyfriend) and spend a couple of days on the beach.

But when Dad died, all that stopped.

In ways I'll never understand, Dad was the single most important element in Tommy's and my relationship. He wasn't the reason we loved each other, but he was the reason we needed each other.

Dad was a fun house mirror. Whenever we looked at him, we saw nothing but the most grotesque aspects of ourselves. I used to think that once we moved out we'd be free of him, but I was wrong, because every time we thought of him we'd still see ourselves through his eyes, even from hundreds of miles away. And the only way we could live with that distorted reflection was by looking at each other instead of him.

But when he died, it seemed the mirror was broken—bad luck for Dad, good luck for Tommy and me. After the funeral Tommy helped me move back into the cottage before he returned to the city, and we said we'd see each other in a few days. But a week went by, then another, and even though we called now and then, neither of us suggested getting together. Thanksgiving came and Tommy had something come up; Christmas rolled around and I decided to spend it with friends in Maine. We bragged on the phone about how well we were doing, and we joked about how "we should have gotten this divorce a long time ago." A year passed, and then another, and then another, and we kept making plans that one of us would cancel, using whatever excuse came to hand: sickness, or work, or bad weather.

But we both knew the truth. It's too painful to be together now, because Dad's mirror isn't really broken. It's just split in two, and both halves still show all the wrong things.

Somebody's beating on the front door. I roll over and look at the alarm clock. It's five thirty-four in the morning. I blink stupidly at the red digital numbers, trying to figure out who would be rude enough to wake me up this early. More banging. I swear and sit up, but when I try to swing my legs over the side of the bed my right foot gets tangled in the sheets and it takes me a few seconds to kick it loose.

The knocking is getting progressively louder. I trip down the crappy spiral staircase and into the living room. Philip and Tommy are both awake but they just stare at me and don't say anything as I lurch past them in my underwear on the way to the kitchen.

I charge across the floor and rip open the door, catching Dale Cromwell in mid-pound. He checks his fist and glares at me. "What idiot did that to my corn, Nathan?"

Dale is in his late sixties, but he's strong as a Budweiser Clydesdale and just about as big. He's wearing old jeans, muddy boots, and a T-shirt, and he leans a huge, hairy forearm on my door frame while he waits for an answer.

"Jesus, Dale. Do you know what time it is?"

He glowers down at me. "Sorry it's early but this can't wait. I need to know who's been ripping up my field."

"Cheri Tipton. She thinks there's an old Indian village buried under your corn."

"What?" His face is always ruddy but now it turns a frightening shade of purple. He's standing close enough that I can smell the coffee on his breath when he starts to yell. "She thinks what?"

"She thinks there's some kind of Indian . . ."

"That woman is out of her fucking mind." He takes off his baseball cap and runs a hand through his stiff white hair. "Christ, Nathan, why did you let her do it? Your dad would never have let her."

"I didn't let her do anything, Dale. I told her she could walk around out there but I never gave her permission to touch the corn. I told her you rented the land from me and . . ."

"And the crazy old cunt went ahead and tore up my field anyway. What did she use, a pitchfork?" He keeps talking before I can answer. "There's no rhyme or reason to what she did. There's just a pile of ruined corn and a bunch of chicken scratches around it." He steps away from the door and turns away. "Sorry for bothering you," he calls over his shoulder.

I stare after him as he climbs on his tractor in the driveway and heads away from the house. It doesn't take a genius to guess where he's going; I'd bet my left nut that Cheri Tipton will be getting a rather unpleasant wake-up call in about five minutes.

The door to the guest room opens behind me and Camille sticks her head out. She's wearing a lacy, black chemise and her hair is scattered and knotted. We stare at each other for a minute and she murmurs good morning but when I start to answer her, she talks over me. "Nathan, I am so sorry about yesterday. I can't even believe I behaved like that." She folds her arms over her breasts and actually blushes. "I love red wine but it apparently hates me."

I shrug and close the front door behind me. "Don't worry about it."

She pulls at her hair and looks like she's going to start crying again. It's too early for this. I've already had a farmer with bad breath screaming in my face this morning, and I'm not about to babysit Camille while she rends her garments and begs for forgiveness. I head for the living room. "I'm going back to bed for a couple of hours."

I get about four steps away before she starts to sniffle.

Shit. I make myself stop and turn around. "Everything's fine, Camille. Really."

She nods and wipes her eyes, but before she can say anything else I hurry out of the room. Philip is on his back with a pillow over his face and Tommy has the sheet pulled over his head with nothing showing but his nose.

"Thanks for getting up and answering the door," I mutter. Neither of them stirs.

Simon's waiting for me, sitting on the floor in the hallway by my classroom. None of the other kids are there yet; I came in early today to write the show-and-tell report Baker assigned me after yesterday's incident.

He smiles up at me. "You look tired."

I dig my keys out of my pocket and unlock the door. "What are you doing here so early? Couldn't wait to discuss gerunds?"

He gets to his feet and follows me into the classroom. "No, I just wanted to get out of the house."

I put my books down and face him. "Any problems since yester-day?"

He shakes his head. "It just feels weird. Dad and I aren't talking much and neither are him and my mom." He sits at his usual desk. "Besides, I forgot to get yesterday's assignment from you and thought maybe I could look it over before class."

He smells a little sour, as if he didn't take a shower this morning or he forgot to put on deodorant, but he's young and pretty enough to get away with that. Hygiene is for people like me; I've reached an age where I can no longer afford to smell like myself. Simon, on the other hand, could rub dog shit in his hair and he'd still have no trouble finding somebody to sleep with him.

I tell him I have to write the report for Baker and he asks if he can stay in here and read his homework assignment while I'm working on that. I shrug and tell him what pages to read and he opens his text and starts before I even sit down at my desk.

I pull out a sheet of paper and gnaw on the end of my pen. This report is a farce, especially since I promised not to say anything about the only thing that might possibly excuse Simon's behavior yesterday in Baker's eyes. I scribble a few vague lines about Simon's "personal family problems" and I lie about how harshly I repri-manded him for his attitude. I look up once, thinking, and catch Simon watching me. His eyes are disconcertingly blue, like Tommy's.

I raise my eyebrows. "Trouble with the assignment? Something you don't understand?"

He mumbles no and starts reading again, embarrassed. I study him for a minute, enjoying how the sun from the windows lights up the right side of his face and body. He's sitting upright and one foot is completely out of his sandal except for his toes, curling and un-curling around the ankle strap.

Would you believe me if I told you I'm not sexually attracted to this boy? A lot of my old college friends wouldn't. When they ask me about my job, they smirk and make cracks about "after-school tutoring sessions." But it's the truth, or at least mostly. Simon's too young, too naive, too much a kid for my taste.

But I love watching him. It's got nothing to do with wanting to shtumpf him, or father him, and no, he doesn't remind me of who I used to be, or make me weep for lost innocence, or any other half-assed Freudian bullshit like that. It's just simple aesthetic pleasure. Period. I love the sight of his bare heel swaying back and forth above his sandal, and the thin shin above it, and his knobby, scabby knee resting against the underside of the desk. He's a boy, and he's beautiful. That's all there is to it.

He looks up and sees me watching him and it's my turn to be embarrassed, but for some reason I'm not. We even smile at each other a little bit.

I clear my throat. "You'll need to apologize to Vernette today, Simon. I told Baker you would."

He frowns briefly but then nods. "Okay."

"Really? You can do that without being a smart-ass and pissing her off again?"

"Yeah. I don't like it, but if it's what you want me to do, I'll do it."

He says this matter-of-factly, without a hint of self-pity or teenage angst. I tell him thanks and he grunts something unintelligible. There's a comfortable silence and he starts reading again. I go back to writing the report but every now and then he looks up at me or I look at him, and I think both of us are glad for the company.

I had a cat once named Patroclus. Patroclus was a big gray eunuch of a cat with gigantic paws, a belly that scraped the floor when he walked, and breath that always smelled faintly of rotting fish. All he did was eat and sleep and shit and lick himself, but I loved him dearly, because he was the sweetest soul I've ever met in my life. He never used his claws on me, never hissed at anything but the vacuum cleaner, never was anything but slow and gentle and patient. We lived together during the time when I was through with college but before I moved back into the cottage.

He slept on my bed at night, but during the day, in warm weather, he slept in the sun on the front porch of my house. He was a deep sleeper, too; strangers could walk up and rub his stomach and he'd never wake up, or if he did he'd just stretch and purr and fall back asleep. I think he thought of himself as a sunbathing, feline god, and the world was a wonderful place made exclusively to serve him, full of nothing but kind creatures with soft hands.

Anyway, one summer morning when I was in the kitchen washing the dishes I looked out the window just in time to see an unleashed, one hundred and twenty pound rottweiler charge across the lawn and sink its teeth into my cat's throat. The dog flung him around like a rubber squeak toy, spattering blood, and Patroclus was dead before he even knew what had hold of him.

I grabbed the nearest weapon I could find, a cast-iron skillet, and flew through the door, screaming. The rottweiler dropped Patroclus in time for one lunge at me but I swung the skillet like a baseball bat and damn near tore its head off. It staggered off the porch and I chased after it and didn't stop swinging until the ugly fucker was nothing but a red, matted pile of fur on my lawn.

If I'd had time to think I never would have done that, because the dog was just doing what dogs do to sleeping cats, and it wasn't his fault that his dumb-ass owners didn't have him tied up. But he killed something I loved, and he made the mistake of doing it where I could see him.

I cried for a week, and I never got another cat. I will not take the chance of getting attached to something else that's too trusting and kind to take care of itself. If you're sweet all the time, you're eventually going to get your throat ripped out. Anyone who tells you different is a fool. Patroclus was the sweet one. Not me.

Camille is sitting at the kitchen table, drinking coffee and reading her book, just like yesterday. She puts the book down when I walk in and gives me a tentative smile. "Hi. Déjà vu, huh?" She has her bare feet up on the chair next to her. Her toenails are painted red.

I ask her where everybody is and she tells me they're all at the beach again. I try to hide the look on my face but she sees it and grimaces. "I know. I tried to tell Tommy that after yesterday you probably wouldn't be thrilled to come home to just me, but you know Tommy."

"Don't be silly. It's fine."

Goddamn Tommy. I'm going to kick his ass for this. And what's up with Camille's husband, leaving her alone like this again? He's either dumb as a stuffed toy or he's got a serious death wish.

I ask her if they said when they'd be back.

She shakes her head. "I just made a fresh pot of coffee. Want some?"

"No thanks. If I have any more caffeine today my heart will explode."

She stands up and walks over to the coffee machine to refill her mug. With her back to me she asks, "How about a glass of wine, then?"

"No fucking way." It comes out harsher than I intended.

She looks over her shoulder and tries to grin. There are circles under her eyes. "I'm just making a bad joke, Nathan. If I even see another bottle of red wine I'll start throwing up again."

She looks so pathetic I have to smile. "Just do me a favor and aim for Tommy and Kyle the next time."

She manages a shaky laugh. "That's a deal."

I kick off my sandals and start to head upstairs to change my clothes. She stops me before I get out of the room. "You had a phone call about half an hour ago from Cheri Tipton. She sounded excited. I guess that loud farmer who woke us all up this morning paid her a visit, too."

"Good. Maybe next time she won't be so eager to rip up somebody else's property whenever she feels like it."

"Actually, she said something about how she got everything worked out with him and now all she needs is your permission to continue digging."

"What?" I don't believe this. "Cromwell told her it was okay?"

"That's what she said. She wants you to call her back."

I don't give a rat's ass what she wants. She's not digging up my field.

While I'm upstairs changing I hear the screen door slide open and closed, then I see Camille walk across the back lawn and into the corn. She makes a beeline for the ripped-up patch of ground at the end farthest from the house, and when she gets there she squats in the middle of it and picks around in the soil with her fingers.

What is it with her and Cheri Tipton? What is so fascinating about a cornfield that they can't keep their hands out of it?

I finish changing clothes and head downstairs. Camille's still sitting in the dirt, but now her hands are motionless and she's just staring at the ground. I go to the kitchen and get an apple from the fridge, and when I come back to the living room a few minutes later she hasn't moved a muscle. Something about the way she's sitting makes her look brittle and lonely, and after I watch her for a while I can't stand it anymore and I go out to join her.

The sun is hot on my head and on the back of my neck, and there's not much of a breeze today. I take my time getting over to her, but Camille is still pretending to be a scarecrow or something and she doesn't see me until I toss the apple core into the corn when I'm a few feet away from her. She hears it land and looks up, startled. Her face is red and there are tears on her cheeks.

Does this woman ever stop crying? I turn to go back inside. "Sorry. I didn't mean to disturb you."

She stops me. "Please don't leave. I'm just feeling sorry for myself, that's all. I'll be all right in a minute."

I know she wants me to ask her what's wrong, but I'm really not in the mood to play counselor and wheedle it out of her, so I kick at the dirt with my sandal for a second then hunker down beside her wordlessly.

She picks up a clod of dirt and crumbles it. The earth is parched; it's been a dry, hot summer. She squints at the sun and winces. "I was just sitting here trying to figure out why I married a gay man."

I blink. I guess she's not as stupid as I thought she was.

I don't know what to say so I put a bland expression on my face and play dumb. "Are you sure he's gay?"

She snorts. "As gay as a tulip festival." She looks over at me and makes a face. "Oh, please. Don't act like you didn't know, Nathan. It's so bloody obvious."

"When did you figure it out?"

She twists her hair and gets her fingers caught in a tangle. "I guess I've always kind of known. But sex has always been okay with us and he swears up and down that he's not attracted to men, so I've lied to myself for a long time. Pretty funny, huh?"

She picks up a small rock and heaves it at the stone wall lining the field. It clicks against one of the flat stones on top and skitters off into the woods. "But ever since Kyle met Tommy, he's been less and less interested in me. Every time I touch him now he acts like I've got the plague." She glances at the sky then back at the ground. "I am such an idiot. My mother even had it figured out before the wedding and kept telling me I was making a mistake. I told her she was wrong and to mind her own business." She laughs and actually sounds genuinely amused. "What a retard."

"So what are you going to do?"

"I don't know. He still insists he's straight, and that he's not attracted to Tommy, and that I'm imagining everything." She scowls. "He even went down on me last night to prove it."

What am I supposed to say to that? I grunt sympathetically, wishing I could change the subject. She seems to realize I'm uncomfortable and she falls silent.

I look around. In spite of the drought the corn is nearly five feet tall and almost ready to pick, with tufts of white silk sticking out at the top of each ear. I can't believe Cheri convinced Dale to let her uproot his corn. She probably told him she'd wait until after he harvests it, but knowing Dale I'm sure she also must have had to offer him quite a bit of money for him to agree. Her Historical Society must do better financially than I thought.

I don't care what she offered him. I don't want a bunch of Indiana Jones wannabes strutting around my property, unearthing bottle caps and rusted beer cans and trying to pass them off as ancient Indian artifacts.

She's watching me. "Do you think it's possible Cheri Tipton's right?"

I stare hard at her, surprised. "What are you, a mind reader?"

"You were looking at the corn and frowning. It wasn't hard to guess what you were thinking." She pauses, then prods again when I don't say anything. "So what do you think? Could she be right about the Indian village and all that?"

I make a face. "I seriously doubt it. And even if she is I don't care. It's not like we're squatting on King Tut's tomb or something."

She nods. "Still, you never know. It could be kind of fun to let her do it. Maybe she'd find something interesting."

"It's not just that. If I let her do it, I'll have a bunch of strangers rooting around in my backyard for God knows how long. I like my privacy."

She studies me. "You and Tommy are about as different as you can be, aren't you?"

"You're just figuring that out?" A single blade of grass is by my foot and I pluck it from the soil and wind it around my finger. "If it were up to Tommy he'd tear down the cottage and put up a stage in its place, with seats all around it and a crowd of adoring fans to watch his every move."

"And you?" Her voice is serious; she's analyzing me.

How nice. It seems I've got a new therapist.

I let the blade of grass fall from my hands. "I just want to be left alone."

She gets a hurt look on her face. "I'll go inside if . . ."

Oh, for Christ's sake. "I didn't mean right now, Camille. I just mean in general."

We sit in silence. The sun is baking down on us and my shirt is sticking to my back. I make a move to get up. "I've got to get into the shade."

She nods but doesn't stand up when I do. Her skin is already starting to burn; she's wearing a sleeveless blouse and her arms and shoulders are looking red and blotchy.

Whatever. If she wants to sit here and stew in the hot sun that's her business. I head toward the house, but after a few steps my feet stop of their own accord, like a couple of balky mules. Goddammit.

I turn around and go back. "Are you coming?"

She looks up and of course she's crying again. I offer her my hand and help her to stand. She follows me back to the house like a lost kid.

Since when did I become a babysitter?

*   *   *

I was only two years old when Tommy was born, so I don't have any memories of Mom's being pregnant, nor of the day she and Dad brought him home from the hospital. I don't know if I was jealous of the attention he must have gotten from my parents, or if I doted on him, or if I even noticed him at all. I've never heard any stories from those first few years of our lives, because Mom died before I was old enough to ask her about them, and whenever I approached Dad about stuff like that he'd tell me he didn't remember, or he'd say helpful things like "Stop pestering me." You'd think something as momentous as a younger brother popping into my life out of nowhere would have made a lasting impression, but apparently I just took it in stride and didn't pay any more attention to him (at least initially) than to the flowers on the dining room table or the telephone on the desk.

Regardless, my earliest memory is still of Tommy. It's only a fragment, but I seem to remember sitting next to him in front of the wood stove in the living room, watching him smash a fistful of Silly Putty on the Sunday comics page from the newspaper. I couldn't have been more than four, but in my mind I can see his small, pudgy hands lifting up the putty to reveal a flattened, gray and black copy of a panel featuring Charlie Brown and Snoopy. I remember his face, intent and serious and proud, and I remember him offering me the sticky blob as a gift, and I remember our hands touching when I took it from him. His fingers were sweaty and warm.

You'd think something more important would be the first thing I'd recall, but for some reason my brain has chosen to hang on to that image above all others. I don't know why. I'm not surprised it picked something to do with Tommy, but I'm puzzled why it glommed on to something so trivial. Maybe that's just the way consciousness works: one minute you're oblivious and the next you're not, and whatever happens to be going on when that switch gets flipped in your head is the thing that sticks with you, no matter how insignificant it might be.

But it's probably simpler than that. Tommy's given me dozens of things through the years—everything from a papier-mâché dragon with a red plastic fork for a tongue, to a homemade necklace with a brass pendant shaped like a dildo. (He even gave me the most revered object of my childhood: a Princess Leia action-figure doll that I carried around in my rear pocket for almost three years, until Leia's head finally popped off after I wiped out on my bike one tragic afternoon and landed on my ass in our driveway.) But the Silly Putty was different. Not because it was any better or worse than his other presents, but because it came first, and as such it was my introduction to Tommy's take-no-prisoners brand of generosity.

With Tommy, gift-giving is an art form. Whatever he bestows on you is more likely than not going to be something absurd and cheap and tacky, but the way he offers it always makes you feel as if you were receiving an oblation. I don't know how he does it. It's a bizarre kind of magic; he somehow makes you believe that the use-less thing in his outstretched hands is actually a chunk of his heart that he's torn out, just for you. He holds it up for your inspection, and it glows between his fingers like a candle in a cave. And as if that weren't enough, he makes it absolutely clear that he doesn't want anything in return, not even your gratitude, so all you can do is stand there with a stupefied look on your face and humbly accept what he's vouchsafing you.

It's one of the more effective ways he has of binding people to him. Oh, I'm sure he doesn't do it on purpose—it wouldn't work if it were intentional—but no one can resist such unconscious, ruth-less benevolence. After receiving that kind of keepsake, you no longer really belong to yourself; you belong to him.

So I guess there's no mystery about why my first memory is what it is.

It's not every day you give up your soul for a glob of Silly Putty.

A thin green line of pistachio ice cream dribbles down Philip's chin and falls on the front of his shirt.

"Dammit." He sponges at it with his napkin. "I should have got-ten it in a cup like you did. This stupid cone is melting faster than I can eat it."

I scoop another spoonful of hot fudge into my mouth and don't say anything.

I got stuck with Philip this afternoon. Kyle and Camille and Tommy all wanted a nap after lunch and when I told Philip I was going for a walk he asked if he could tag along. Since then all he's done is whine about how hot it is, and blather on and on about his favorite movie (*Lara Croft: Tomb Raider*). I told him I hadn't seen it and now he's made it his mission in life to describe each scene in excruciating detail.

The air above the brick street in front of Pearson's Dairy Queen is shimmering in the heat. We're both wearing sandals and T-shirts and shorts, and he's got a ridiculous wide-brimmed straw hat on his head that makes him look like Huckleberry Finn. (He was smart to bring it, though, because right about now I could fry an egg on top of my hair.)

Another big glob of pistachio falls off his cone and lands with a splat between his feet. He glares down at the mess and shakes his head. "Fuck." He tosses the rest of the ice cream into a trash can on the street. "I give up."

I hold my cup out to him. "Want some of mine?"

"What flavor did you get?"

"Coffee."

He hesitates for a second then takes it from me. "Thanks." He dips the spoon in for a delicate bite before handing it back. He looks up and down the street and sighs. "You must get bored to tears in this town. What on earth do you do for excitement around here?"

I shrug. "Sometimes I let them put gummy bears on my ice cream instead of hot fudge." I'm getting a sugar headache so I dump the Styrofoam cup in the garbage.

He laughs. "That's something my Tommy would say."

I grimace. "Yeah, your Tommy is a laugh a minute." I start walking toward the post office. "I need to pick up my mail."

He falls into step beside me. His toes are long and thin and hang off the edge of his sandals. "Don't you have it delivered?"

I shake my head. "My family's never had a box at the house. We've always walked to town to get our mail."

He glances at me from under his hat. His ponytail is damp with sweat. "Why?" He asks this as if I've just said the stupidest thing he's ever heard.

I frown. "I don't know. I like the exercise, I suppose."

He snorts. "If you really want to know what exercise is you should move to New York. We have to walk *everywhere* there."

My voice takes on an edge. "No thanks. When I go for a walk I like to breathe air that actually has oxygen in it."

He darts a look at my face and flushes. "I just pulled a Camille, didn't I? I'm sorry."

I wave a hand. "Forget it. The heat's making me cranky."

We climb the steps to the post office lobby in silence and open the door. Cold air rushes out and both of us sigh in relief. He trails me to the wall of metal mailboxes and watches me work the combination lock on mine. "Was this the same box you guys had when you were kids?" He touches the knob on the little door when I open it. "Did Tommy used to come here like this to get the mail?"

Oh, for God's sake. Poor lovesick bastard. His voice is hushed, as if he's watching me push the rock away from the entrance to Christ's tomb. I grin at him. "You've got it bad, don't you?"

"Got what bad?"

I raise my eyebrows and he blushes a little. "Oh. Yeah, I guess I do. I've never felt like this before about anybody in my life. Tommy's like . . ." He breaks off when Mary Purpleton, the cross-eyed town librarian, wanders into the lobby. She says hello to me and stops to chat for a minute. (As usual, I don't know which of her pupils to look into.) Philip barely acknowledges her when I introduce him, and as soon as she walks off he starts talking again. "Tommy's like a godsend to me. I couldn't believe it the first time I saw him. He was so . . . you know, so perfect. I couldn't believe he liked me."

I shut the box and we go back outside. The asphalt on the street in front of the post office is soft and sticky underfoot. "Where did you guys meet?"

"At the Union Square Café."

I stare at him blankly.

"You've got to be shitting me." He blinks when he realizes I don't have a clue what he's talking about. "It's a famous restaurant, Nathan. I can't believe you haven't heard of it. Everyone knows about it."

I shrug and he pauses, wide-eyed. I roll my eyes and keep walking.

He clears his throat after a few steps. "Anyway, I was there one night after work when Tommy came in for dinner with some skanky piece of farm-boy trash from Iowa or Indiana. But Tommy and I were checking each other out the whole time they were eating, and when the pig-slopper finally got up to use the bathroom, Tommy came over and got my phone number. Just like that. I about *died.*"

He shakes his head, his face full of wonder. "It was like fate, you know? Ordinarily, I can't even afford to eat there, but I just happened to be there with my friends Mikey and Chris that night— they're absolutely fucking loaded, because Mikey's some kind of computer genius, and Chris models underwear for Calvin Klein, and they took me out to celebrate Mikey's birthday, and at first I thought it was just blind luck that Mikey's birthday happened to fall on the only day Tommy was there, too, because he said that was his first time, too, but the more I think about it, the more it seems like it was *supposed* to happen that way. I mean, come on, what are the odds of us meeting like that in a place neither of us had ever been in before?"

He looks at me for confirmation of this miracle, but when I become absorbed with a tea stain on my shirt instead of responding, he prattles on, more than happy to fill the silence:

"Anyway, my friends were so freaked when they saw Tommy coming over, because they'd noticed him, too, of course, and kept whispering stuff like, 'Oh, my God, I think he likes you, don't look now, he's watching you again,' and other dumb stuff like that. Those guys are so funny. Well, after that had gone on for what seemed like hours, they about *died* when he finally got up to talk to me. It was so funny, it was like being in a movie. I felt like Doris Day."

He hugs himself and sighs, "Mmmm," through his nose in a contented descending glissando. "So anyway, to make a long story short, a few weeks later Tommy and I were living together. Can you imagine? It was so romantic."

I'm beginning to understand why some people enjoy beating up gays.

I cough. "A few weeks? What took so long?"

The sarcasm is lost on him. "Tommy had a hard time settling down at first. He kept insisting on dating that corn-fed little Gomer, too, until I told him I wouldn't share him with anybody anymore." His face darkens. "We had a couple of bad fights at first because I'm kind of the jealous type, but we're all done with that stuff now."

I don't say a word. His relationship with Tommy has the probable shelf life of a jug of milk, but it's none of my business.

Simon shows up at the door again late afternoon. Camille and Kyle are at the grocery store, Philip's taking a nap in the living room, and Tommy and I are in the kitchen, getting ready to head to the beach for a short swim before dinner.

I'm at the table and Tommy's sitting on the counter, wearing a god-awful Hawaiian luau shirt and drinking a beer, and before I can get up he reaches over and pushes the screen door open. "Hey, Simon! Come on in."

Simon says hi and sidles past him, then stands in the middle of the room, eyes darting nervously from me to Tommy, then back again. He's dressed in a white T-shirt with the sleeves cut off that says "Westport Wrestling" in big black letters, and a dark blue swimsuit that's about three sizes too big for his legs.

I need to say something that will let him know he can't just keep showing up at my house, but he looks so awkward I can't quite do it. "Hi, Simon. What's up?"

"Nothing, really." He doesn't know what to do with his hands; he clasps and unclasps them in front of him, then lets them hang at his sides for a second before finally parking them in his swimsuit pockets. "I was just on my way to the ocean and I thought I'd stop by and see what you were doing."

Tommy answers before I can. "We were just getting ready to go for a swim, too. Want to come?"

Damn him.

Simon smiles, surprised and pleased. "Sure." He glances at me and his smile fades when he sees my face. "I mean, if that's okay with you guys."

I push back from the table and look pointedly at Tommy. "It

would be fine, but we're not going to be there very long. We need to get back for dinner. Maybe some other ti . . ."

"He can join us for dinner, too, then." Tommy hops off the counter and takes another swig of his beer. "Camille's cooking lasagna and there'll be plenty."

Jesus Christ. Why doesn't he just invite him to move in with us?

I give him the evil eye. "I'm sure Simon already has plans, Tommy."

Simon shakes his head. "Not really. I'll just call home and tell them I'm eating over here. They won't care."

His eyes are even bluer than Tommy's, and there's something defeated in them, as if I've already turned him down and now there's nothing left for him to do but go join a nunnery or something.

I am such a pushover. I make myself sound excited. "Okay, then. Great! Give your folks a call and we'll get going."

His face lights up like a star going nova. I point him to the phone in the living room and he bounds across the floor. He'll probably wake up Philip.

I glare at Tommy and whisper, "I could kill you."

He makes a face. "Oh, chill out. He's a sweet kid. What's your problem?"

"My problem is I know you."

"What's that supposed to mean?"

I move close to him just to be sure Simon won't hear us. "It means leave him alone. He's only fifteen."

"Would you relax? I'm just being polite. Besides, I've already got a boyfriend."

"Since when has that mattered?"

"Fuck you." He turns and dumps the rest of his beer in the sink. "For your information, I haven't cheated on Philip in months."

"Congratulations. There's a first time for everything."

"God, you're an asshole. Look, Nathan, I'm not stupid. I'm not going to get involved with a kid. What do you take me for?"

"Oh, let's see. The horniest bastard on the eastern seaboard?"

Our faces are close together and he turns his head to belch. "So I like sex. Who doesn't? Oh, sorry, I forgot you had your hormones removed."

"Just because I don't sleep with everything on two or four legs. . . . This is stupid. Just control yourself. Please? Just this once. That's all I'm saying."

His face is bright red. I haven't seen him this pissed in a long time. I must have hit a nerve.

He listens to make sure Simon is still talking on the phone, then he leans forward so his nose is only an inch from mine. He smells like beer and expensive shampoo. "You are such a shit. I am not some goddamn pedophile. You know me better than that."

I stare into his eyes for a few seconds, then I drop my gaze because I can see I've hurt his feelings. "I know you're not," I mumble. I look up again. "But, Jesus, Tommy, what do you expect me to say? I grew up with you. When we were kids your fly was open more often than the twenty-four-hour laundromat. If your dick had been a gun you could have outdrawn Doc Holliday."

His eyes get big and all of a sudden we both burst out laughing. He reaches over and pulls me close. I can feel his ear against my cheek.

"Mr. Bishop?" Simon comes back into the kitchen.

I give Tommy another squeeze then break away. "What do you need, Simon?"

He looks at the floor, embarrassed. "My dad wants to talk to you. Is that okay?"

I can hardly wait. "Sure."

He looks worried, as if he's thinking I might say something to his dad about the bruise on his ribs. I pat him on the shoulder to reassure him, then I walk into the living room to get the phone. Philip is sprawled out on the futon bed, facedown with his head between two pillows, snoring. I pick up the phone. "Hello?"

"Is this Mr. Bishop?" Simon's dad has a high-pitched, clipped voice and he sounds irritated. He's probably angry that Simon's not there to slap around.

"Yes, this is Nathan." I have to struggle to keep my voice pleasant. "How can I help you, Mr. Hart?"

A pause. "I just wanted to be sure Simon wasn't being a nuisance. He says you invited him to supper tonight."

"That's right. Is that a problem?"

"He says you're the English teacher at his high school?"

"That's correct."

Another pause. "So how long have you been teaching there?"

What does this guy want? My curriculum vitae? "Several years."

He probably thinks he's being a good parent by asking these questions, but I'll be damned if I'll play along with his father-of-the-year charade.

He waits a while longer as if expecting me to say something else, but I stay silent. He clears his throat. "Well, I guess that will be fine, then." He still sounds suspicious. "Just send him on home whenever you get tired of him."

"Will do." I hesitate. "Simon's a terrific kid, by the way. I'm enjoying having him in class."

I want him to know that I'm keeping an eye on Simon. Maybe he'll think twice before hitting him again if he knows I'm watching.

His voice is suddenly warmer. "Thanks for saying that. His mother and I are very lucky." He seems genuinely pleased.

There's another awkward silence, then he says good night and hangs up.

I stare at the phone for a minute, thinking.

Hart wasn't faking the pride in his voice after I complimented Simon. I think I even heard love there, too. But now I'm twice as mad at him as I was before.

Love and pride don't count for shit if they're interspersed with random punches.

I walk back into the kitchen. Simon is sitting at the table, waiting for Tommy to come out of the bathroom. He hops up when he sees me. "Is everything okay?"

Tommy steps into the room in time to hear me say everything's fine.

The tension on Simon's face dissolves and Tommy claps me on the back. "Then let's go swimming. Need a towel, Simon?"

It's almost five o'clock but the sun is still beating down on us as we walk to the beach. Simon's on my right and Tommy's on my left, but they both have way too much restless energy and keep pulling ahead, trying to get me to hurry up, like two big dogs on leashes.

I try to make conversation. "So, Simon. How are things going? Have you made any friends yet?"

He slows down for a second and waits for me to catch up. "No, not really. Just you guys."

This boy is way too honest for his own good. I guess I'm kind of flattered but it makes me uncomfortable. "How about that kid I saw you with a few days ago at the beach?"

He shakes his head. "That was my cousin. He was in town visiting but now he's gone back to Massachusetts."

"Is that where you're from, too?"

He nods. "Yeah. I grew up there."

"Let me guess. Westport?"

His jaw drops. "How'd you know?"

I point at his wrestling shirt.

He looks down and grins. "I forgot I had this on. It's not even mine. It's my dad's."

Tommy looks over his shoulder. "I swear to God, Nathan, is there a way you could possibly walk any slower?"

"What's your hurry? The ocean's not going anywhere."

"Neither are we, apparently." He turns to Simon. "Isn't Westport where Horseneck Beach is?"

Simon bats at a black fly buzzing his head. "Yeah. I used to go there all the time."

Tommy stops and waits for us. "I was there a few years ago with some friends. The place was swarming with queers. I felt like I'd died and gone to homo heaven." He throws his head back and laughs. "There was this one guy I met with the most magnificent ass you've ever seen. I think his name was Steve, or Sean, or something like that, I guess it doesn't matter. Anyway, I took him back into the dunes and . . ."

I break in. "Shut up, Tommy. I don't think that's something we need to hear about right now."

Simon blushes and doesn't say anything. Tommy smiles innocently and falls into step with us.

Sometimes I hate my brother.

I suppose it's good that he doesn't hide his orientation, but when he meets people who are disconcerted by it, he loves rubbing their noses in it. He says he's only "being himself" when he does that kind of shit, but he's really just a spoiled little brat having fun at someone else's expense. I've seen him do it a million times and it gets old. Anyway, now that he knows Simon is easy to mess with, I guarantee he'll make at least a dozen more sexual references in the next fifteen minutes.

We come up to the lighthouse and then the beach. A lot of people have already left for the day and we find a stretch of beach right away that's mostly deserted.

Tommy tosses down his towel. "Is this okay with you guys?"

I put my towel beside his and Simon lays his on my other side, so I'm in the middle. Tommy pulls his luau shirt off without bothering to unbutton it and kicks his sandals onto his towel. "Last one in has the smallest penis."

He charges toward the water and when he's only a few steps in he dives and disappears.

"Watch," I tell Simon. "This will blow your mind."

Tommy is a natural athlete, and he swims like a dolphin. He can also hold his breath for an ungodly amount of time, and he loves to show off, especially to people who've never seen him swim.

The seconds tick by and he still hasn't surfaced, and Simon starts to look concerned. After at least a minute goes by he glances at me, then back at the water. "Is he all right?"

"Just wait."

I've seen Tommy do this again and again but I still get a kick out of it, because even though part of me knows he's just fine, he stays down so long even I start to worry. He always times it perfectly, as if he can sense when his audience is starting to panic.

Simon gets to his feet after what feels like an eternity and shades his eyes with his hand. "Maybe we should get a lifeguard."

I tell him it will be fine, but after another fifteen seconds I slowly get to my feet too. Another ten seconds pass. It's been too long. He's never stayed down this long before. My heart speeds up and I begin to move toward the water. Maybe the stupid son of a bitch really did get snagged on something out there this time and I'm going to have to find him before he drowns.

"Goddammit, Tommy," I mutter, and I start to run. I can hear Simon following close behind.

Right as we reach the ocean Tommy pops out of the water like a cork from a bottle of champagne. He's at least a hundred feet out. Simon and I both give a yell of relief and grind to a halt.

I cup my hands by my mouth so my voice will carry. "You asshole!" I scream. "I could kill you for that."

I can't see Tommy's face and I don't know if he can hear me, but he gives a showy wave, then plunges back in.

"Jesus," Simon says. He laughs. "That was awesome. He scared the shit out of me."

I shake my head. "Yeah. Me too. One of these days his lungs will explode and I'm going to laugh my ass off."

We wander back to our towels and take off our shirts and sandals. The bruise on his side is about three inches under his left nipple. It's faded from black-and-blue to a sickly yellow, but it still looks painful.

He sees me looking at it and touches it with his fingertips. When he pokes it the skin turns white for a second. "It's okay. It looks worse than it feels."

"Good, because it looks like it hurts."

He shrugs. "Dad said he was sorry about a thousand times."

"That's big of him."

Tommy yells from behind us and we both turn to face him. He's near the shore again, standing about waist-deep in the water. "Are you guys coming in or what?"

We start walking toward the ocean. Simon's feet leave even, narrow tracks in the wet sand. He stops to turn over a hermit crab that's on its back. The next shallow wave washes over it and we watch it burrow out of sight.

He looks up at me. "Can I ask you a personal question, Mr. Bishop?"

"Sure. I guess so."

"Are you, you know, like your brother?"

Shit. I thought he was going to ask me something about, I don't know, my favorite television show or what flavor Pop-Tart trips my trigger. I stall for time. "How do you mean?"

He stands up and brushes the sand from his fingers, and even though he looks sheepish he doesn't avoid my eyes. "I mean gay. Are you gay, too?"

"Simon, I'm not sure that's an appropriate question. You're my student, remember?"

He drops his gaze. "Sorry. I was just curious."

All of a sudden I'm ashamed of myself. Tommy's right. I need to grow some balls. I clear my throat. "It's okay. Yes, I'm gay. Is that a problem?"

He looks up again and shakes his head emphatically. "Not at all. It doesn't matter one way or the other. I just wanted to know."

"Are you sure you're okay with it?" I don't know why I care, but I do. "When Tommy and his boyfriend were fooling around at the cottage yesterday you seemed a little taken aback."

"Not really. I'm just not used to seeing guys do that kind of stuff with each other, that's all."

Tommy bellows something at us and we wander farther into the surf, but we stop again when the water reaches knee level. Tommy looks exasperated and shouts, "Oh, for God's sake," then takes off again, apparently tired of waiting for us.

Two gulls fly overhead calling to each other, and an overweight jogger runs by behind us, huffing and puffing. The water is cold on my legs but it feels good; I'm still sweating from the sun and the hot breeze.

Simon turns toward me. "Can I ask you something else?"

I nod and wait. What's it going to be this time? Boxers or briefs? My social security number?

He hesitates. "When did, I mean, how old were you when you knew you were gay?"

Ah. I think I finally see where this is going and why he wants to play twenty questions.

I move forward another couple of steps but stop before the water reaches my crotch. I'm not quite ready for the shock yet. "I don't really remember. Probably younger than you." I look back at him. "Why do you ask?"

He takes a deep breath and lets it out slowly; I watch his stomach expand and shrink. He's standing so the sun falls on the left side of his body, exposing his ribs and highlighting his bruise like a tumor on an X-ray. I see a few random hairs on the middle of his chest, and he's also got peach fuzz on his chin. He looks thin and vulnerable, and it kind of hurts to look at him.

He opens his mouth and closes it, then tries again. "I don't know. Sometimes I think that maybe . . . I don't know. No real reason."

Tommy bursts from the waves a few feet away and charges me. He throws his arms around me and tackles me; I gasp as the icy water hits the rest of my body. I struggle to my feet and push him off. "Not now, Tommy. We're talking."

He ignores me and attacks Simon. Simon flinches when Tommy grabs him, but he starts to laugh as they struggle. Tommy loses his footing and begins to fall, and he grabs Simon's arm at the last second and yanks him down with him. They both go under and come up spluttering.

I shake my head. "Boys will be boys."

Tommy gets to his feet and pulls Simon up next to him. "Come on, Simon. I'll give you a dollar if you'll help me drown my big brother."

Simon grins. "Okay."

They move toward me and I back away. "I'm not in the mood for this, you guys."

"Tough shit," Tommy says.

They both hit at the same time, and the next few minutes are a blur of arms and legs and ocean water. At one point I pick up Simon and toss him on top of Tommy; soon after that Simon is holding my hands above my head and Tommy has both of my feet and they're counting to three and heaving me into a wave. I finally get Tommy in a full nelson and even though Simon climbs on my back I manage to drag them both to the shore and we all collapse in a heap, laughing and swearing.

I roll off Tommy and disentangle myself from Simon, then sprawl out flat on my back. "Assholes," I pant. "I think I'm having a heart attack."

Tommy sits up. "Good. If you die, can I have the cottage?"

"You already own half of it. Don't be greedy."

"I know. But if I owned the whole thing I could turn it into a gay bed-and-breakfast and make Dad's corpse do backflips in the grave for the rest of eternity."

Simon is lying on his back, too, but now he rises up on his elbows. Sand is caked on the sides of his legs and arms and shoulders. He's between Tommy and me and he swings his head back and forth, watching us. "Your dad's dead? When did that happen?"

I grunt. "Not nearly soon enough."

Tommy tosses a broken scallop shell at me. "Don't be like that, Nathan."

"Me? What about you? You're the one still looking for new ways to piss him off."

"Yeah, but I'm mostly joking. You're not." His eyes travel casually over Simon's body. Simon notices and blushes a little, but Tommy just goes on checking him out, unembarrassed at being caught. He reaches out his hand when he sees the bruise. "Jesus. How'd that happen?"

Simon recoils at first but then he relaxes and lets Tommy touch his ribs. "My dad and I were playing catch and the baseball caught me there."

He's not a very good liar. I can tell Tommy doesn't believe him, but all he says is, "That must have hurt."

Simon shrugs and doesn't answer, probably because he's too busy watching my brother's fingers explore his bruise. Tommy's taking his sweet time, tracing the yellow and green outline. Simon doesn't look like he's breathing.

Christ. I relax my guard for two seconds and Tommy moves in for the kill.

I sit up and make my voice brisk. "We should probably get back soon. Camille might need help with dinner."

Tommy nods and gets to his feet. "I'm going back in the ocean for a minute to get the sand off me." He reaches a hand down to Simon. "Coming?"

Simon glances at me nervously, but after a second he takes Tommy's fingers and lets himself be pulled up. Tommy lets go of him as soon as he's standing, but as I watch them walk into the water together it's as if Simon is still tethered to him. They stay close to each other, and Simon is smiling a lot and not taking his eyes off of him.

Tommy and I are going to have a long talk this evening.

Camille's lasagna is spicy enough that it makes the back of my neck sweat and my nose run, but it's so good I can't stop eating it.

We're all sitting around the kitchen table, because even though it's cooler outside there's too much food and too many people to fit around the table on the back porch. Camille and Kyle are sitting on one side of the table, Tommy and Philip on the other, and Simon and I are at the ends.

I have to hand it to Camille; she's putting on a good show. She's cheerful and relaxed, and looks for all the world as if nothing is bothering her. She laughs at every joke she hears, and she pats Kyle's arm affectionately now and then, and she pretends not to notice that her husband's attention is completely focused on the other side of the table. She is also, thankfully, drinking iced tea with Simon, even though the rest of us are guzzling red wine.

I compliment her on the meal and she smiles graciously. "Thank you, Nathan. It's my mother's recipe. I'm glad you like it."

Everybody else chimes in with, "Yeah, this is great," and "Thanks, Camille," and "I didn't know lasagna could taste like this," then there's a lull in the conversation while we all shovel food in our faces.

Philip is on my left and he turns to me. He's got a big glob of ricotta cheese and a patch of red sauce on his chin. "Oh, Nathan, I forgot to tell you that Cheri Tipton called twice while you guys were at the beach. She said it was important."

I frown. "Thanks. I'll be sure to call her back sometime next year."

Simon looks curious and Tommy explains. "She's this fat old cow from the Historical Society who thinks our cornfield is the site of some ancient civilization. Nathan and I think she's full of shit."

Tommy keeps turning his head away from Philip to talk to Simon, and Philip is starting to pout. I can't say I blame him, really; ever since we got back from the beach Tommy has basically ignored him in favor of showing Simon around the cottage and the yard.

Simon, for his part, has chattered nonstop about school and Walcott and Camille's food, but most of his comments have been aimed directly at Tommy, even though now and then he'll look over at me as if for reassurance.

It's too hot in here. I've got a window fan blowing cooler air in from outside but it's not helping much. Camille's dressed in a flimsy red halter top and white cotton shorts, and the rest of us are wearing swimsuits or Bermuda shorts, and our shoulders and chests are shiny from sweat. The air is stuffy and claustrophobic.

I take a big swig of wine and ask Kyle to pass the Parmesan cheese. He looks away from Tommy long enough to hand me the bowl, and when our fingers accidentally connect he gives me a shy smile.

"There you go," he says. "Fresh-grated is the only way to go."

All of a sudden I'm irritated beyond all reason. I'm hot and tired and I should have taken a shower when we got back from the beach. The salt from the ocean is mixing with my sweat, and my skin feels like wet sandpaper, and it's making me crabby. The last thing I want to do right at the moment is engage in small talk with a closet queer about the many merits of fresh-grated cheese.

It's an effort to keep my voice friendly. "Thanks."

Tommy, of course, is having a great time. Nothing makes him happier than to find a new member for his fan club. He's pouring so much charm on Simon it's a wonder the poor kid hasn't drowned yet. Right now Tommy's talking about his job:

"I work for a publishing company in Manhattan. It's really cool because all I have to do is read novels all day, and pass along the ones I like to my boss. I still can't believe I'm actually getting paid to read great new books." He takes another bite of lasagna. "The only thing better would be to work at home. I figure I can eventually talk my boss into having the manuscripts delivered to my apartment so I can lie in bed all day in my underwear, with my head on a pillow and a plate of grapes on my nightstand."

Everybody laughs except for me. I drink more wine.

What he's not bothering to say is that he's only a temp, filling in for a lady on maternity leave, and as soon as she comes back he'll be out on his ass, yet again, with no savings and no clue what to do with his life.

Out of the corner of my eye I can see Kyle watching me. When my glass is empty he grabs the wine bottle in the middle of the table and refills it. He waits for a break in Tommy's monologue, then raises his own glass and proposes a toast.

Everybody lifts a glass.

Kyle grins self-consciously. The hair on his chest and stomach is damp and with his free hand he wipes some of the sweat off and rubs it on his shorts. He clears his throat. "To Nathan. For putting up with all of us and being so generous with his home and his wine."

We all clink glasses and drink. The conversation resumes.

What the hell was that about?

Tommy keeps talking about his "career." Camille is smiling so much it looks like her cheeks are going to shatter. Philip is glowering at Simon, but Simon doesn't notice because he's too busy being hypnotized by Tommy. Kyle's foot touches mine under the table. He says excuse me but after half a minute passes he does it again, and this time his foot, warm and damp, just stays on mine. I look over at him and he makes eye contact with me.

What the hell is wrong with this guy? His wife is sitting on his other side and he's actually playing footsie with me.

I sit up straight and try to pull away from him, but his toes stay glued to mine. He's pretending to listen to Tommy, but he's got this weird smile on his face and he's blushing. In spite of myself I start to get hard.

I'm disgusted with myself but I can't help it. He's cute, and it's been a long time since anyone's come on to me.

I let his foot rest there for a minute, but when his toes move up to my ankle, I finally yank my legs away, shifting in my chair so that I'm facing Philip and as far from Kyle as I can get. I accidentally jostle the table and everybody stops talking and stares at me.

I mumble something about a charley horse and rub at my thigh like I'm trying to loosen a muscle. They make sympathetic noises and resume their conversation.

Kyle looks at me reproachfully and I glare back at him until he turns away. No one else notices. For the rest of the meal he ignores me.

Good. I refuse to be part of his sick little dream world. I don't care how good it feels to be wanted again.

CHAPTER 4

Tommy wakes me at dawn by pouncing on me in bed. One second I'm sound asleep, and the next he's jumping up and down on my mattress, making me jiggle around like an earthquake victim.

"Rise and shine, big brother!" he yells.

"What the hell . . ." I try to grab him to make him stop but he leaps out of reach and puts a foot on each side of my knees.

"Wakey, wakey, wakey!" He bounces on the mattress with each word, then pauses for a second and looks down at me. He's wearing a pair of green boxers with a picture of Homer Simpson stretched across his fly.

"Tommy, I'm trying to sleep. What the fuck are you doing?"

He smiles, and then screams "Incoming!" right before falling flat on top of me. I say something like "Oosh," as all one hundred seventy pounds of him lands on my chest and collapses my lungs.

"Goddammit, Tommy." I try to shove him off but I can't budge him. "You're acting like a five-year-old."

His breath is warm on my face and smells like garlic. He grins. "Good morning to you, too, sunshine." He puts a hand on my forehead and makes a "tsk, tsk" sound. "You're burning up."

"I feel fine."

"No, you don't. You feel awful. Stick out your tongue."

I comply and he grunts. "Gross. I was right. It's all purple."

I push at him again. "We drank red wine last night, dumbshit. Yours is purple, too."

He rolls off me. "Nonsense. You've got the plague or something. I'm going to call the school and tell them you're too sick to teach today." He stands up and pads over to the phone. "Who do I call? Ted Baker? I haven't talked to Teddy-poo in ages."

"I'm not sick, Tommy. What's gotten into you?"

He scowls at me. "Work with me here, Nathan. I was talking to the gang last night after you went to bed, and we all decided that today would be a perfect day for a road trip up to Newport, but . . ."

I pull the sheet over my face. "I don't want to go to Newport."

". . . but if we wait until you get home from school, we won't have enough time to do everything we want to do, so we need to leave in about an hour or so. Which means you can't go to work today."

"So go without me."

He walks back to the bed and yanks the sheet away. "Not an option. You're coming."

The sun is poking through the blinds and the room is hot. My skin feels wet and sticky. "I don't have any sick days left," I lie. "And I'm not going to use one of my personal days for something I don't want to do."

"You get personal days? Perfect." He goes back to the phone. "If you use one of those instead, then you won't get in trouble with Baker if someone sees you playing hooky when you're not really sick."

I sit up. "Put the phone down, Tommy. I'm not supposed to use personal days for stuff like this, and besides, there's no way in hell Ted will let me take off on such short notice."

He makes a face. "Okay, so you'll just have to be sick again, then. You poor thing. You're on death's door. What's Ted's number?"

I shake my head. "Tommy . . ."

He frowns. "Will you stop being such a turd? You don't want to teach today, anyway. What's the big deal? We'll have fun."

"Why do I doubt that?" I snort at the pouty look on his face. "Give me a break, Tommy. You're not going to guilt-trip me into this."

He steps close and puts his hands on my shoulders. "Please, Nathan?" He rests his head on mine. "Come on, don't make me beg. I'll drive, so you can sit in the back and drink Bloody Marys all the way there. How does that sound? I'll even let you bitch about my driving, and you know how much you enjoy doing that."

There are small beads of sweat in the hollow of his chest. I breathe into his neck and sigh. "You're not going to give up, are you?"

He pulls back and a smile breaks over his face. "Nope."

I grimace and yawn. "Ted's number is in the phone book. Tell him I've got a bad fever."

"Awesome!" He lets go of me and trots back to the phone. He's going to wear a hole in the floor between the desk and the bed. "This is going to be such a good day. We'll sneak you out of town in the trunk or something." He paws through the phone book. "Now all we have to do is figure out how to get Simon out of class, too."

I'm on my feet in a second. "Don't you dare."

He looks up at me and laughs. "Jeez. I'm just joking. Chill out."

Tommy and Philip are in the front of Tommy's car, and Kyle and Camille and I are squeezed into the back. (Tommy's driving a Toyota Camry these days, though God only knows how he affords it. I make more money than he does and all I've got is a twelve-year-old Chevette.) Kyle's holding a gallon thermos full of Bloody Marys in his lap, and every time somebody's blue plastic cup is empty, he gives them a refill. Camille is still sipping at her first one, but the rest of us are working on cup number three. The air conditioner is going full blast but the car still feels stuffy.

Tommy blows past a semi on the road and I lean forward. "Slow down, Tommy. You're going to get us all killed."

He glares at me in the rearview mirror. "Would you relax? I'm only going five miles over the speed limit."

I turn to Camille. "Tommy's miles are like dog years. Five means thirty-five."

She smiles. "I've noticed." She reaches up and taps him on the shoulder. "Nathan's right, Tommy. You've been drinking and you can't afford to get pulled over."

"Oh, Jesus," he mutters. "You, too? Fine." He eases up on the accelerator.

I lean back against the seat and click my drink against Camille's. "Congratulations. What's your secret? He wouldn't have done that for me even if I'd put a gun to his temple."

She laughs. "He's afraid of me. Aren't you, Tommy?"

"Damn right." He drains his glass and hands it back to Kyle for more. "Anybody with hair as red as yours is a walking time bomb."

Kyle grins. "You've got that right." He puts his hand on Camille's head for a second and ruffles her hair. "Kaboom."

She drops her ear on his shoulder and watches him pour Tommy's drink. She's wearing a white blouse and white shorts, and she smells like Noxzema. Kyle finishes pouring and then puts his arm around her neck, and she snuggles into him and closes her eyes with a contented smile.

Kyle's pretending as if nothing happened between us last night, but he's avoiding my eyes, and aside from a curt greeting at breakfast, he hasn't spoken to me today. He's been playing the "doting husband" all morning, and Camille is eating it up. She's so used to being ignored by him that she'll probably try to eke out every ounce of affection she can get, even though she's smart enough to know it's all a lie. I guess I can't really blame her. When you're starving for love, you'll take whatever scraps get tossed your way.

Philip is half-turned in his seat so that he can see Tommy and us at the same time. "I wish I had a camera. You guys look so cozy back there." He reaches up to tickle Tommy's ear. He's got a piece of soft leather tied around his wrist with what look like shoelaces.

"What's that on your wrist?" I ask. "I kind of like it."

He stares at me. "You're joking, right?"

Tommy bursts out laughing. "Nope. Nathan's an innocent. He's never seen a cock-ring before."

Philip shakes his head. "Wow. What kind of a homo are you?"

Tommy laughs harder and I start to get irritated. "Why are you wearing a cock-ring on your wrist?"

Philip politely explains that a cock-ring on your left wrist means you're a "top," but if you have one on the right, like he does, then you're a "bottom."

Camille opens her eyes. "You're such a cliché, Philip. Why do you need to advertise what you do in bed?"

Philip frowns. "I'm not advertising. I'm just, I don't know, saying what I enjoy."

She makes a face. "That's very tasteful. I'm sure everybody you meet is dying to know what sexual position you like." She sniffs. "Personally, I prefer doggy style. Do they make a bracelet for that, too?"

"Don't be a prude." He turns his back on her. "Everybody's wearing these, Camille."

She takes another sip of her drink. "Yes, I'm sure you're right. I think President Bush had one on the other day when he met with the Russian ambassador." She giggles. "In fact, I think he was wearing four of them, and they were all on his right arm."

I grin at her. "Maybe that wasn't his arm."

Everybody but Philip laughs. He looks out the window and stays silent.

"I think you hurt his feelings," Kyle whispers.

"Then he's too fragile for his own good," she whispers back, but after a second she leans forward and touches Philip's hair. "I'm sorry, Philip. I'm just teasing you. Your cock-ring is lovely. I wish I had one just like it." She looks over her shoulder at me and rolls her eyes, and I have to bite my lip to keep from laughing again.

He doesn't answer and for a few miles we ride in silence. I stare at the oak and maple trees lining the interstate for a while, then I watch the sun make fake puddles of water on the road that disappear as soon as we get close to them.

Tommy turns on the stereo and slides in a disc, and Van Morrison's "Into the Mystic" fills the car. (Tommy only listens to the stuff we grew up with. As kids we were always listening to Springsteen, or The Who, or Creedence Clearwater—or when we were feeling more mellow, James Taylor and Elton John. Now when I'm by myself I usually prefer classical or jazz, but I forget how much I love this stuff, too.) When the second verse rolls around, he starts singing. He's got a good voice—not like Dad's, but still good. I like hearing him sing, and when he gets to a place where I know the words, I join in. His eyes meet mine in the mirror again and we both start to sing louder.

Philip turns in his seat and raises his voice to talk above us. "I hate this song, you guys. Can't we listen to something good?"

Tommy ignores him and cranks up the stereo for the chorus. *"I wanna rock your gypsy soul,"* he bellows, *"... just like way back in the days of old ..."*

I bellow along with him. *"... and together we will float, into the mystic."*

Philip winces and sinks down in his seat.

Camille is watching me with an amused expression and says something I can't hear. I lean closer to her and she puts her lips next to my ear. "Your whole face changes when you sing. It's fun to watch."

I pull back and frown. "How do you mean?"

She touches my face and smiles. "Stop that this instant." Her fingers are cool on my cheek. "Less frowning, more singing, okay? Trust me on this."

Her voice is kind, and before I can help it I smile back at her. She drops her hand and I face the front again in time to rejoin Tommy for the last few lines of the song. Kyle tries to sing, too, but it comes out in a monotone and Camille shushes him.

I hate to admit this, but I think I like her.

Newport, Rhode Island, is the site of the most ostentatious display of wealth in the entire country. There's an enormous cliff that runs for miles along the ocean, and on top of that cliff sit dozens of vast mansions, each more ridiculously hulking and opulent than the next, lined up one after another like swimmers beside a pool. (Somebody should shoot off a gun into the air someday and see if he can get one of them to jump in. The splash alone would probably trigger a tsunami, and months later stuffy old butlers and grand pianos and Oriental rugs and Tiffany lamps would still be washing up on the shore.)

We're taking the "Cliff Walk"—which means we're hiking along a paved path that cuts through the front yards of the mansions, near the edge of the cliff. Kyle and Camille are in front, Philip is next to Tommy, and I'm bringing up the rear. A lot of people are on the path today: Japanese tourists, and Portuguese families from Fall River, and old married couples dressed in clean white sweaters in spite of the heat, and single young joggers in running shorts, leashed to panting golden retrievers. Tommy and I have been here many times, but Kyle and Camille and Philip have never seen it, so Tommy's strutting along listening to the others "ooh" and "aah," and chuckling to himself like a demented tour guide.

But I don't mind. I'm kind of glad I came today. It's cooler up here than at ocean level, and there's a pleasant breeze coming off the water, and I've got an agreeable buzz going from all the Bloody Marys. Walking feels good, and I like looking at the flowers and weeds lining the edge of the drop-off, and I enjoy hearing the waves slap the cliff face far below. Some of them are hitting hard enough that I can feel the impact through the soles of my feet.

Philip and Tommy are walking so close their shoulders and forearms are touching. Philip stops to gape at one of the palaces and Tommy pauses with him.

"My God," Philip breathes. "You could fit twenty good-sized houses inside of that."

Tommy grins and takes his hand. "Just think of all the beds we could fuck in."

Philip blushes and Tommy laughs and leans over to kiss him. He slides his free hand under the waistband at the back of Philip's shorts and Philip melts against him.

There are footsteps behind me and then a loud, angry voice. "Fucking homos."

I whip around to find two young men standing there, both in their early twenties. The one in front is dressed like a spoiled frat boy in a designer black muscle shirt and polyester basketball shorts, and he's glaring at Tommy and Philip. His shoulders and biceps are overdeveloped and his thighs are twice the size of mine, but his shaved head is too small for his body, and the beard he's trying to grow is spotty and laughable. His friend, a tall blond guy in a blue polo shirt, is standing behind him, looking uncomfortable.

Tommy wraps both arms around Philip and glares back at the guy who spoke. "Yeah, that's right, we're homos. What gave it away?"

The blond guy nudges the beefy bald one and says, "Come on, Sal, let's go."

Sal keeps his eyes on Tommy. "Why can't you fags keep that shit in the bedroom? There are little kids out here, for God's sake. You should be ashamed of yourselves."

I start moving toward him and he shifts his attention to me. I stop a foot away from him and when he meets my eyes he backs up a little. This close he looks more nervous than mad. He's also younger than I thought, maybe only eighteen or nineteen, and he's got pimples on his chin.

"Nathan," Tommy says behind me. "Don't."

I ignore him. "Say 'fag' again, *Sal*, and I'll show you how to cliff-dive."

The blond guy steps up. "We're leaving right now." His voice trembles.

"The fuck we are," Sal says.

A vein starts throbbing in my temple. "Better listen to him, Sal. He's smarter than you are."

Sal puffs out his chest and moves toward me. "I'm not afraid of you, you pussy son of a bitch."

"That's because steroids have made your brain even smaller than your penis."

He starts to throw a fist but his friend steps between us. "Stop it, Sal!"

Sal shoves him aside. "Get out of the way, Ben!"

I bring my fists up but Tommy suddenly grabs me from behind. "That's enough, Nathan. What are you, thirteen?" He yells over my shoulder at Ben, who's still fighting to restrain his asshole friend. "Get him out of here, would you?"

Ben takes hold of Sal's arm and drags him past us. Sal swears at him but lets himself be pulled away. Ben calls back over his shoulder. "I'm sorry about this. He's an idiot."

"So's my brother," Tommy answers. Sal spits at me in passing but the other kid doesn't let go until they catch up to Kyle and Camille, who are looking back at us with frightened expressions.

I break free from Tommy and turn to face him. He's got his patented I'm-so-disgusted-with-you look on his face and my temper explodes. "Don't you dare start with me, Tommy! That was all your fault, and you know it." I grab a sunflower from the side of the path, yank it out of the ground and chuck it off the cliff.

He rolls his eyes. "Attaboy, Nathan. There's a dandelion over there that looks like it wants a piece of you, too." He rejoins Philip and nuzzles his neck, but he keeps talking to me. "Relax, would you? That's exactly what that little prick needed to see. Maybe the next time he sees a gay couple he won't be such a toolbox."

I stalk past them. "Yeah, good thinking. Why didn't you show him how Philip's cock-ring works while you were at it? That might have really loosened him up."

He lets go of Philip and catches up to me. "What's your problem? I'm not the one who almost got in a fistfight on top of a cliff."

"I don't have a problem. I just don't think groping Philip's ass in public is appropriate. Look what happened."

He clears his throat and spits into the weeds. "I obviously didn't see them coming. But even if I did, who cares? Breeders do that kind of shit all the time, and no one thinks twice about it."

"Well, maybe they should. I don't like watching anybody . . ."

"Oh, here we go again," he huffs. "Another holier-than-thou lecture from Nathan Bishop about why all sexuality should be outlawed unless it's done behind locked doors with the shades pulled and the lights off. Don't you ever get tired of listening to yourself?"

"Fuck you, Tommy." A grasshopper lands on my sandal and I flick my foot to get rid of it. "If you had a normal brain instead of the criminally retarded one floating around in the head of your dick, maybe you'd figure out that some things are private."

"Like affection? Like love?" He smirks. "You're right, we wouldn't want people to see things like that. Civilization as we know it might collapse."

"You're so full of shit, Tommy." I have to struggle to keep from yelling. "You had your hand stuffed down Philip's pants. People like that dildo Sal go haywire when they see shit like that. What if there had been more than two of them, or if his friend had been a jerk, too? You could have been beaten up, or worse. You never think about consequences, and someday it's going to get you hurt."

We catch up to Kyle and Camille. Camille pushes her hair off her face. "What was all that about?"

Tommy pulls up next to them and tries to smile. "It was no big deal. Just another run-in with a redneck from central casting."

I make a face. "A completely unnecessary run-in."

He picks at a red spot in his hairline. "Since when did my thirty-one-year-old brother turn into a ninety-year-old Baptist minister?" Philip rejoins us but Tommy keeps his eyes fixed on me. "You were being so much fun in the car on the way here, Nathan. I actually thought you weren't going to be your usual pissy, uptight self today."

I step close to him. "And I actually thought you wouldn't feel the need to be an exhibitionist today. Why don't you just drop your shorts and whack off for the next homophobic pedestrian we pass? Or if you don't feel like doing that, then maybe you could give Philip head in front of a Girl Scout troop. Wouldn't that be fun?"

"Okay, boys," Camille steps between us. "Time out. We're here to have a good time, remember?"

A young, pregnant mother pushing a stroller comes by and we fall silent while she passes. Kyle and Philip wander off a little bit and pretend to be interested in something on the path between them. Philip seems embarrassed.

Tommy glowers at me over Camille's head. "It's hard to have a good time when you're in the company of a Puritan. I'm surprised Nathan hasn't tried to burn me at the stake."

I glower back at him. "Anybody got a match?"

Camille covers both of our mouths with her hands. "That's enough." I push her hand away but before I can say anything else she cuts me off. "I mean it, Nathan. You too, Tommy."

Tommy stalks away, disgusted, and I glare after him. "God, he pisses me off."

Camille pats my bicep. "Well, if it's any consolation, I think you piss him off, too."

"Good," I mumble. "As long as we're even, that's all that counts." The Bloody Marys are wearing off, and the sun feels hotter, and I'm starting to get a headache. I look down at her and sigh. "I'm sorry, Camille. That was pretty tacky."

She shrugs and smiles. "There's no need to apologize, believe me. You saw me behave much worse than that. And besides, I understand. I've got a little sister."

"My condolences." I kick at a rock on the path. "But I doubt very much she's as annoying as Tommy."

Her smile broadens. "Wanna bet? Last Christmas Mom sent us to bed without supper because we were fighting so much."

I laugh a little and look ahead to where Kyle and Philip and Tommy are standing. Tommy has his back to us, but Kyle and Philip are shading their eyes and looking in our direction. "I suppose we'd better catch up. Think anyone would notice if I accidentally pushed Tommy off the edge?"

She starts walking. "You two are funny. I know you squabble a lot, but it's obvious how much you love each other. In New York, all he talks about is Nathan this and Nathan that." She squints up at me. "He adores you, you know. You're very lucky to have a brother like that."

I fall into step with her. "Yeah, right, I'm the luckiest guy in the universe." I heave a sigh. "But in my next life I'd prefer a puppy, okay?"

We're close enough to the others that Tommy hears me and turns to face us. I prepare myself for Round Two, but the anger is gone from his eyes, and he even grins a little as he puts his arms around me.

"Woof," he whispers in my ear.

And of course, my stupid arms come up of their own accord and wrap around his waist.

We get back to the cottage right before sunset and find Simon sitting on the front porch, waiting for us. Philip mumbles something I don't catch but Tommy frowns over his shoulder at him and tells him to relax. Camille's the first out of the car.

"Hey, Simon," she calls. "How long have you been sitting there?"

He stands up and walks toward us. "I don't know. Not too long." He grins at me. "How are you feeling, Mr. Bishop? Mr. Baker taught class this morning and he said you were pretty sick."

I flush. "I woke up with a fever but it went away before lunch. I don't know what my problem was."

Tommy comes up next to me and laughs. "You're a terrible liar, Nathan." I scowl at him but he ignores me. "I made Nathan play hooky today so that he could come with us to Newport. Don't tell anybody, okay?"

Simon laughs. "Okay. That's cool." He follows me toward the cottage. "Mr. Baker really sucks as a teacher. All he did for the whole class time today was read the textbook out loud to us."

Tommy snorts. "I'm surprised he knows how to read. The guy's as dumb as a Chia Pet."

I step onto the porch and open the kitchen door. I never lock the cottage; there's really no point. The kitchen is boiling hot from being shut up all day, and everybody trailing in after me groans.

We're all tired and hung over, but aside from Tommy's and my argument this morning, the rest of the day went without incident. We wandered around Newport and ate a late lunch, and then sat at an outdoor bar by the pier and chatted and drank for a few hours. The ride home was mostly quiet because we were all talked out. Kyle sat up front with Tommy, and Philip passed out with his head on the window in back. Camille fell asleep on my shoulder.

Kyle peels off his shirt and kicks off his shoes. He's got a purple birthmark on his right shoulder blade. "I've got dibs on the shower."

He goes into the bathroom and shuts the door before I can tell him I need to pee. I make a face and wander over to the table. Camille steps around me on her way to the refrigerator and starts pulling things out to make supper. She says she's going to whip up a goulash. I tell her I'll cook but she insists she wants to. Tommy reaches around her for a beer.

I plop down on a chair. "I'll take one of those, too."

He tosses me a bottle. Philip heads for the living room, unbuttoning his shirt. He walks by Simon and Simon says hello, but Philip doesn't answer. Simon stares after him with a confused expression.

I hear the shower turn on and I grimace at the bathroom door. My bladder's about ready to burst, so I excuse myself and head back outside.

"Where are you going?" Tommy calls after me.

"Outside for a minute. I have to piss."

He nods. "Yeah, I need to do that, too. I'll come with you."

Simon's looking lost, and as I walk out the door I hear Camille ask him to help her chop up some vegetables. Tommy steps out after me and the screen door bangs shut behind him.

I go over to the weeds next to the cars and stand with my back to the cottage. Tommy comes up beside me and unzips his fly, too, and then we stand together and sip at our beers while we piss. The weeds are riddled with goldenrod, and yellow and red wildflowers, and the sun turns our urine bright orange, like Tang.

He burps. "So what do you think of Kyle and Camille?"

"I like Camille."

He glances at me. "But not Kyle?"

I shrug. "He's all right." I shake off and zip back up while Tommy's still going. He can urinate longer than any human being on the face of the planet.

He nods. "Kyle grows on you. He's really sweet once you get to know him."

I lean against my car without answering, and I wait for him to finish his business. It takes forever. His stream finally slows to a trickle and I talk to the back of his head. "Jesus, Tommy, that's ridiculous. Your bladder must be the size of Lake Erie."

He grins over his shoulder as he zips up. "Remember when we used to time how long we could pee? I always won."

I grin back. "Ah, the good old days. Kids these days don't know what they're missing. Who needs a Game Boy when you've got a dick and a stopwatch?"

He hops up and plants his butt on the hood of my car. His feet are bare, but he's still wearing the white T-shirt and khaki shorts he's had on all day. "Dad even got into the contest once, remember?"

I stare at him, startled. "He did not."

"Honest to God."

I shake my head. "No way. The Great Vernon Bishop would never have allowed himself to participate in something so frivolous. Especially with us."

He drums his fingers lightly on the hood. "I'm serious, Nathan. He heard us arguing one time about who could go longer. You were mad because you'd downed two quarts of Gatorade in less than five minutes to try and beat me, and you accused me of cheating because you still lost."

"I would have won, but you counted too fast."

"I did not. I timed it on my watch. You were the one who always counted too fast." He scratches his nose. "You got fifty-seven seconds, I got one hundred and three."

"I had a lot more than that. I distinctly remember . . ."

He talks over me. "Anyway, Dad heard us arguing, and the next time he came out of the bathroom and walked by us in the kitchen, he turned at the living room door with this deadpan expression on his face and said, 'Forty-three seconds.' We both laughed at him, remember?"

I shake my head again and swallow another mouthful of beer. "You must have dreamed it."

He looks puzzled. "No, I didn't. He even smiled a little when he said it, then he went upstairs without saying anything else." He studies me. "I can't believe you don't remember that. We talked about it afterwards because we both thought it was really weird. You said you thought an alien with a sense of humor had possessed him or something."

I look away. The moon is already coming up in the east even though the sun is still above the trees in the west. I don't know why, but this conversation is really unsettling me. I fall silent, thinking, and I sip at my beer and listen to the sounds coming through the kitchen door: Camille talking to Simon, pots and pans banging around, water running.

Tommy puts his hand on my shoulder. "What's wrong?"

"I don't know." I look up at him again. The hair at his temples is damp with sweat. "I have no recollection of Dad doing that. None whatsoever. Which means that either you're full of shit, or my memory is playing tricks on me."

He tugs at the collar of my shirt. "It's not a big deal, Nathan. You've just got selective amnesia when it comes to Dad."

"What do you mean?"

He rubs his jaw. "You don't let yourself remember anything good about him, that's all. You've got it set in your brain that he was nothing but a son of a bitch, twenty-four-seven, and anything that doesn't fit with that assessment gets tossed out, for some reason."

I stand up straight. "That's absurd."

He holds up a hand. "Please, Nathan, I don't want to fight anymore today, okay? I'm just saying you like your world black-and-white, that's all. It's not wrong, it's just . . ."

"Just what?" I demand.

He grins. "It's just not right."

I start to splutter and he hops off the hood and keeps talking. "Nope. I'm not going to let you get mad again today. You can yell at me more tomorrow, I promise, but for now let's go inside and have supper and a nice evening, okay?"

He turns and walks toward the cottage. I stare at the ground for a few minutes, stewing, then follow him in.

What really pisses me off is I think he may be on to something.

When I walk back in the kitchen, Camille is in the shower and Kyle has taken over as chef. Philip is sitting at the kitchen table across from Simon—the two of them are shelling green beans into a big bowl—and Tommy is lifting the door to the wine cellar.

The kitchen is still really hot, and Kyle is standing in front of the stove with a towel wrapped around his waist, stirring the goulash in a big pot. The skin on his back is tan, but it's lightly pocked with small scars. He must have had acne when he was a kid.

He looks up when I walk in and gives me a tight smile. "Hey, Nathan."

It seems he's forgiven me for not playing footsie with him last night. "Hey." I watch Tommy disappear into the cellar and I walk over to the hole and tell him to bring up some Chianti. I hear the shower shut off in the bathroom; Camille is a lot faster than Kyle.

"Hey, Mr. Bishop." Simon pushes the bowl toward me. "Want to help?"

"Sure." I sit in the chair at the end of the table and grab a handful of unshelled beans. "Do your folks know you're here?"

He nods. "Yeah. Mom says I should start paying you rent."

"Good idea," Philip mutters, but then he puts on a phony smile. "I'm just teasing, Simon."

Philip has an odd habit of lightly rubbing the middle of his chest, as if he's tickling himself. He catches me watching him and he drops his hand, flushing, but after a few seconds he forgets and his fingers drift back up to his sternum.

Tommy reappears with two bottles and drops the cellar door back in place, but then he abruptly stands still. Philip starts to ask him what's the matter, but he shushes him. "Listen."

Camille is humming to herself in the bathroom. I don't recognize the song, and her voice isn't particularly appealing, but Tommy doesn't move or let any of us speak until the bathroom door swings open a minute later and she steps out, still humming. She sees us all staring at her and falls silent. Her hair is wet and clinging to her neck, and she's wrapped in a towel that matches Kyle's, except hers is tucked at the armpits to cover her breasts.

Her eyebrows go up. "What?"

Tommy smiles and sets the wine bottles on the table. "Nothing. It's just weird to hear a woman sing in this house. I like it."

She smiles back, embarrassed. "Thank you. I take requests, by the way. I'm particularly good at Aretha Franklin songs." She glances over at Kyle. "Mmm. Who's that adorable man in a towel? Can we have him for dinner instead of what he's cooking?" She pads over to him and takes the spoon from him to taste the goulash. "It needs more paprika, and more salt."

He turns to get the salt and while his back is to her she suddenly grabs his towel and gives it a hard yank. "Abracadabra!" she yells.

He tries to grab the towel but misses, and in an instant he's standing bare-ass naked in front of the spice rack. His pubic hair is a dark patch of fur and his dick is long and thin.

"Camille!" he yells. "That's not funny!" He uses one hand to cover his crotch and another to try to regain the towel. She dances away from him, laughing, and the rest of us start laughing, too. Kyle's chest, neck, and face all turn bright red as he runs after her, his white butt jiggling with each step.

She almost makes it to the guest room door when he catches her. "Goddammit!" he screams, "Give it back right now!"

The rest of us stop laughing when we hear the anger in his voice, but Camille, even though she looks shocked, seems to want to pretend that this is still all in fun. They tussle for a minute, grunting, and she fights to hold his towel away from him, but while her arms are over her head, his hands dart forward and latch on her towel instead.

"Okay, you bitch," he snaps. "Let's see how you like it."

She flinches at the fury in his voice, and a second later she's as naked as he is. She has a small mole between her breasts, and her ribs stick out a little over her stomach. Her face is stunned and hurt.

There's a moment of silence while we all gawk at them.

"Wow," Tommy blurts. "You really are a redhead."

She doesn't bother to cover herself. She stands there gaping at Kyle for another instant, then she disappears into the guest room. Kyle stares at the floor for a minute, breathing hard, then follows her in without looking at us.

The door slams shut behind him, and a few moments later Camille's sobs begin to bleed through the bookshelves.

CHAPTER 5

I watched my mother die. It's the only vivid memory I have of her. We were all eating breakfast at Stevenson's Coffee Shop in downtown Walcott on a Saturday morning, and Tommy and I were fighting over the maple syrup. Dad was reading the newspaper and ignoring us, and Mom was eating eggs and sausage and trying to get us to behave. She was threatening not to let us watch cartoons when we got home, then she took another bite of sausage and started to say something else but all of a sudden her face turned red and she put her hand to her throat. Dad looked over the top of his newspaper and asked if she was all right. She shook her head. Tommy made another grab for the maple syrup and I held it out of his reach. Mom pushed back from the table with this wild look on her face and Dad dropped the newspaper and asked if she was choking. She nodded frantically; by then her cheeks and forehead were almost purple.

Dad lurched to his feet, knocking over his chair, and rushed around the table to her. He made her stand up and he put his arms around her and I remember wondering why he was hugging her like that. The other people in the restaurant were all looking at them with these scared expressions on their faces. He squeezed her hard and I could see it hurt her, and I remember saying something like, "Don't hug her so hard, Daddy." He squeezed again, and again, and the fourth time I heard a snapping sound from her rib cage. Dad was saying over and over, "Come on, Vicki, come on, come on," and her eyes were huge and she flailed her arms around and he almost dropped her. Tommy started to howl and I handed him the maple syrup to get him to shut up but he just kept bellowing, as if he were providing music for Dad and Mom's strange little dance. It seemed to go on forever.

Then Mom went limp in Dad's arms. Her head lolled back against his shoulder and the toes of her shoes dragged along the floor, and a wet spot suddenly appeared on her skirt. Dad just stood there holding her with his mouth open and his eyes shut.

I don't remember much else about it. I know an ambulance came, and when they put Mom in it Dad crawled in after her and left Tommy and me with some lady in the coffee shop. I remember she bought us each a candy bar.

Tommy and I both had nightmares for years. Even when we were in high school Tommy would still wake up screaming now and then, his body drenched with sweat, and I'd hold him while he sobbed and gibbered. Dad must have heard him, but he never came to check on us. I'm sure he thought he had better things to do with his time than "coddle" us.

Before Mom died my memories of my father are good ones. I don't like to admit that for some reason—maybe because it makes a better story to say he was a colossal failure as a parent from day one, like a character in a Grimm's fairy tale, the wicked stepmother who is never anything but wicked. But the truth is, until I was five I adored him. I remember him holding me on his lap and reading to me, I remember him giving me piggyback rides all the way to the beach, I remember him swinging me around by my heels in the yard.

But when Mom died, he went from being a patient, loving man to a brooding, sarcastic, hateful old despot in what seemed the space of a few minutes. I don't remember much about the transition. One moment he was kind and the next he wasn't. Tommy tells me I should be compassionate because Dad loved Mom so much and losing her tore him apart, but that's a load of horseshit. Lots of people lose someone they love and don't become cruel sons of bitches overnight. He used his grief as an excuse to be an asshole to his children. End of story.

He blamed us for her death. He never said it in words, but I know he did. In his mind, it was Tommy's and my argument that morning at Stevenson's that led directly to him losing his wife, and as stupid as it sounds, I think everything he did to us from that point on was a way of punishing us. Tommy thinks I'm wrong, of course. He thinks Dad blamed himself for not being able to save Mom, and all of his anger at us was just misdirected self-hatred. I think Tommy spends way too much time reading self-help books, but whatever, it doesn't matter, even if he's right. Misdirected self-hatred is still hatred.

Simon's waiting for me in the hall by my classroom again.

He gets off the floor when I walk up and gives me a huge smile. "Hey, Mr. Bishop."

"Hi, Simon." The door is swollen from the humidity and I need both hands to get it open, so I hand him my book bag. "I wasn't sure I'd see you today. You had a pretty late night last night, didn't you?"

He left the cottage well after midnight. He would have stayed even later, but I threw him out when I realized he wasn't going to leave unless I told him to. Kyle and Camille—who eventually reappeared after their nude brawl and tried to act, without success, as if everything was back to normal—went to bed at eleven, and the rest of us sat up talking until I couldn't keep my eyes open. Tommy was holding court, perched in the middle of the couch with Philip on one side and Simon on the other, and I was across the room, feeling like a chaperone.

"Not really. I'm usually awake until at least two or three in the morning anyway."

"What is with this thing?" I grunt. "It was fine yesterday."

The door (a heavy oak monster with a frosted windowpane in its top half) isn't budging, no matter how much I wrestle with it. In frustration, I give the bottom of it a solid kick, and it flies open so suddenly I lose my grip on the knob. It swings in and crashes into the wall, then bounces back and starts swinging toward us again. I put my foot out to catch it, and the windowpane pops from its frame and falls directly in front of us. There's an explosion of glass; I grab Simon instinctively and pull him back into the hall.

We stare at the mess for a minute, then silently look at each other.

Simon laughs. "Oops."

I step forward, and flick on the light in the classroom. Glass shards are everywhere, scattered under the desks and out into the hall. "Shit." I wave Simon back when he tries to come in. "You're wearing sandals. I don't want you to get cut."

"Nathan? What's going on here?"

It's Ted Baker. Fabulous. Just what I needed. He pushes past Simon, wearing a Nike T-shirt the size of a circus tent. He looks pissed off.

I force a smile. "Good morning to you, too, Ted. I had a little accident with the door."

"I can see that. What happened?"

"It was stuck and when I kicked it to get it open, it . . ."

"You kicked it?" He shakes his head and makes a face. "What did you expect it to do after you did that? Did you think it would just slowly open for you?"

I feel my face turn red. "No, Ted, actually I was hoping it would fly through the window and decapitate a couple of cheerleaders in the parking lot." I take a deep breath. "I didn't kick it hard. It just got away from me, that's all."

"Well, you've made quite a mess. We can't have kids coming in here until it's cleaned up." He rounds on Simon. "What are you doing here so early, by the way? Students aren't supposed to be in the building until five minutes before class starts."

Simon has been watching us quietly and looks taken aback at Baker's sudden aggressive tone. "I was just . . ."

"I asked him to come in early," I lie. "I'm helping him with an assignment."

"Well, that will have to wait." He turns back to me. "You need to go find the janitor first and borrow a broom to clean this up."

My temper flares. "If you weren't standing here wasting my time and ordering me around I'd already be doing that, Ted."

He pauses, pursing his lips. "It's not appropriate for you to speak to me like that in front of a student."

"And it's not appropriate for you to talk to me like I'm in kindergarten, either." I should stop there, but I can't control myself. "May I go get the broom now, or would you like to spank me first?"

He turns prune-colored and rubs furiously at his ear. Simon is staring at us with wide eyes. Baker is clenching his fists, but when he talks his voice comes out tightly controlled. "Come see me after your class is over, Mr. Bishop."

He pivots on his heel and stomps down the hall. When he's out of sight Simon visibly relaxes. "You guys don't like each other much, do you?"

"Not much."

He looks worried. "He's not going to fire you, is he?"

I shrug. "He'll probably try." I let my head fall to one side then the other, trying to loosen the muscles in my neck. "I'm sorry, Simon. We shouldn't have been arguing in front of you."

"It's not your fault." His voice drops to a whisper. "He's really an asshole."

"No comment." I kick at some glass. "How about helping me find a janitor?"

When I was a senior in high school I fell in love for the first time. I'd had dozens of crushes by then (none of which amounted to anything but adolescent fantasies, based on a furtive glance from some boy at the beach or a casual slap on the butt from a friend in gym class), but until I met Andy Strauss I'd somehow managed to avoid any serious emotional involvement with another guy.

Part of that, I suppose, is because Tommy and I fooled around with each other on a fairly regular basis for nearly four years, which kept me from drowning in my own cum and gave me a way to diffuse desire.

I suppose I should talk about that for a minute. My sexual relationship with my brother is something I know I'm supposed to be ashamed of, but I'm not. Not really. Tommy and I have always been ridiculously close; we slept in the same bedroom (and quite often the same bed) our entire childhood, and took baths together even as teenagers, and once we figured out that it felt good to touch each other one thing just led to another. It's not like we fucked on a nightly basis or anything, but we were both gay, and horny as hell, and we ended up doing just about everything to each other that two people can do in bed.

And you can believe me or not, but it was just innocent fun. I'd wake up in the middle of the night with a hard-on, and while other kids in other houses would deal with the same situation by jerking themselves off, I had the luxury of a willing partner, and more times than not Tommy would be awake and in the exact same boat as me. He'd roll over on his back and tell me to get in bed with him, and we'd go down on each other, or sometimes we'd just lie next to each other and whack each other off. After the first year or so, we did it less and less, but even after Andy and I started messing around, Tommy would occasionally wake me up by sticking his hand down my shorts, or I'd come home from school and find him in the shower, so I'd get in with him and one of us would end up pressed against the tiles while the other one went to work from behind.

I mean, what the hell, it wasn't like either of us was going to get pregnant and give birth to a retarded kid or anything. I know it sounds fucked-up, but we both enjoyed it and it didn't hurt anybody else, and it died a natural death as we got older.

It's kind of odd, but aside from an occasional lewd joke, we've never talked about that aspect of our relationship, not even as adults. I don't feel guilty or squeamish about it, and I'm sure Tommy doesn't, either. But for some reason we shy away from the subject, probably because talking to each other about it would be as absurd as talking to your own hand after masturbating, and thanking it for a wonderful time.

Anyway, I was going to tell you about Andy.

Andy moved to town our senior year from somewhere in Florida, and quickly became Walcott High School's golden boy. He played basketball and football, and was a straight-A student, and he was polite and charming, and good-looking in the same anonymous way as every blond teen idol on every television show you've ever seen. (Tommy once described him as "the kind of person who never gets food stuck in his teeth," and that about says it all.) We met in an American Lit class and started hanging out almost immediately, and the first night I spent at his house we were all over each other almost as soon as the lights went off.

I remember staring up at his bedroom ceiling while he blew me; his folks were downstairs watching David Letterman and the television was loud enough that I could hear the studio audience laughing and clapping every few seconds. A particularly loud burst of applause erupted from the television at the exact moment I ejaculated, and Andy and I both thought that was hilarious. He looked up at me after he finished and said, "Okay, now let's try for a standing ovation."

And the next day in school we both acted as if nothing was different. We waved to each other in the hall and grinned, and we sat next to each other in Lit class and wrote notes back and forth about stupid shit (I remember one of his comments verbatim: "Maybe if Emily Dickinson had owned a dildo she wouldn't have been so fucking serious all the time"), and we made plans to go get a pizza after he finished football practice. We got the pizza to go and took his car out to the country, and while we looked for a secluded spot to park, he pretended my dick was a gearshift and kept saying things like, "Vroom vroom." After we ate we fucked like monkeys in the backseat, and talked for hours about God and prejudice and cars and movies and books and family. I remember resting my head on his chest and hearing his heart with one ear and his voice with the other.

For the next two months we made love in bathrooms and closets, and on the beach and in the cornfield, and once even behind City Hall. When we weren't together I walked around in a trance with an idiotic grin on my face and a bulge in my crotch, and for the first time in my life people actually started complimenting me on my "sunny personality." (Tommy was the only one who knew why my attitude had taken a major turn for the better; he kept telling me to announce to the next person who mentioned it that I owed it all "to regular homosexual intercourse with a nonfamily member.") Andy and I started making plans for where we would go to college, and I began to believe that life didn't necessarily suck all the time.

And then Andy met Dad.

I'd purposely never brought Andy to the cottage when Dad was going to be home, because by that time the only way Dad and I could tolerate each other was by never being in the same space for longer than a minute or two. I also avoided being seen with Andy anywhere that Dad was likely to be, for the explicit reason that part of me knew that Dad would likely figure out far more than I wanted him to, and he'd somehow find a way to ruin everything. Oh, he would never admit to himself or anyone else the possibility that one of his sons was fucking another boy, of course, but he'd still try to destroy any close friendship I had, just to make sure.

Anyway, Andy and I made the mistake of going downtown one day after school to get a milk shake at Stevenson's, and on our way we ran into Dad on the street. I had no choice but to introduce the two of them. Dad shook his hand and looked at him suspiciously (in Dad's view anybody who wanted to spend time with me was obviously a seriously flawed human being), then his eyes went from me to Andy, and back again.

That's all it took. I don't know how he knew, but he did. It was all over his face.

He dropped Andy's hand and sneered. "Where are you girls going? On your way to buy dresses for the prom?"

I knew what kind of things he was capable of saying and doing, but his sudden hostility even took me by surprise. Andy was completely flustered; I tried to guide him around Dad and get him out of there, but Dad stepped back and blocked our way again.

"I asked you a question, Nathan. Where are you going?"

"Venice," I muttered. "I hear they've got good spaghetti there."

He dropped his hand on my shoulder and squeezed hard. "Don't get smart with me, son."

I yanked away from him. "What's your problem? We're just hanging out."

"Well, isn't that cute? I think you've probably done enough hanging out for today, though. Why don't you say good-bye to your sweetheart here and go on home."

I rubbed my shoulder where his fingers had dug in. "Why don't you go fuck yourself?"

He raised his hand and stepped toward me.

I glared up at him and wouldn't let myself flinch. "Go ahead, Dad. Hit me in public. That will help you sell a lot of newspapers, won't it."

Andy edged away from us.

Dad slowly lowered his hand. Somebody drove by in an old Chevy Nova and honked, and he put a big smile on his face and waved at them until they were out of sight.

He was calm when he looked at me again. "Go home now, or don't come home at all." He turned to Andy. "I don't want to see you with my son again."

Andy looked at me, then at Dad, then he turned away and ran down the street. He never looked back once, not even when I called after him. My sight blurred as I watched him disappear around the corner, his blue shirt reflecting for an instant in the glass of the drugstore window. I tried to say his name again, but my throat closed around the sound.

I wheeled about to confront Dad, and found him waiting for me with a satisfied, almost friendly smile on his handsome face. Something sharp and murderous rose in my chest, and as he studied my expression his smile vanished.

"That was for your own good," he said calmly. "You'll thank me when you're older."

I couldn't speak. Rage and grief were suffocating me, and I could feel hot tears on my cheeks.

He pressed his lips together and sighed. "Don't make a scene, Nathan. I didn't raise you to be a crybaby."

I somehow found my voice. "I'll kill you for this. I swear to God I will."

He rolled his eyes. "You're behaving like a child."

I choked on my words. "What gives you the right to do something like that, Dad? Andy was my friend."

He snorted. "I could tell."

"What's that supposed to mean?"

He waved a hand, dismissing the question. "You're better off without him. He obviously doesn't care much about you, or he'd still be here."

My head snapped back on my neck. "Fuck you, asshole!"

Ordinarily that kind of comment would have put me in the hospital, but all he did was flush a little and loom over me, threatening. "Go home, Nathan. You're an embarrassment."

I wiped my nose on my sleeve and stared straight in his eyes. I spoke as clearly as I could, savoring each syllable. "Fuck you, you fat sack of shit."

He blinked. "I wouldn't say that again if I were you."

I took a deep breath and began to repeat myself. "Fuck . . . you . . . you . . . fat . . ."

He clapped a hand over my mouth. "That's about enough." He squeezed so hard I felt something in my jaw pop. "Are you finished?"

I bit his hand and tasted blood, and he swore and shoved me away from him. I stumbled on the sidewalk and fell down just as Sam Templeton, the owner of the town's only accounting office, stepped out of his office across the street with one of his daughters. He started to wave at Dad but stopped still when he saw me sprawled on the ground.

"Is everything okay?" he called out.

Dad forced a grin and raised his voice to answer. "Hi, Sam. Everything's fine. Nathan just tripped over his own feet again. He's growing so fast these days he doesn't know how long his legs are."

He bent down toward me, still speaking loudly enough for Sam to hear what he said. "Are you all right, son? I wish you'd be more careful." He grabbed my right bicep and pulled me up to stand beside him.

Sam laughed and led his girl over to their car. Dad waited until their doors were closed before he released me and stepped back. "We're done talking about this. Now go home."

We glared at each other for a long minute as he waited for me to obey him. I didn't budge.

A vein in his right temple twitched under his skin like a worm. Sam Templeton backed his car into the street and drove by us and Dad broke off the staring contest to nod pleasantly at him, but I kept my eyes fixed on my father. When he looked back at me I was waiting for him.

"You're a son of a bitch, Dad." My voice was quiet, but the hatred in it was palpable. "And I hope you burn in hell."

He actually recoiled a little, and he paused before answering. He filled his lungs and let the air out slowly, and he began to nod his head several times as if I'd just made a polite comment about the weather. We were standing close and I could feel his breath on my face. It smelled like Listerine.

"I wouldn't worry about that." His lips parted in the semblance of a smile as he looked down at me. "Haven't you noticed, son? We're already there."

Something in his tone made me catch my breath. He held my eyes for a moment longer, then he turned and walked away from me, following in Andy's footsteps.

Baker's secretary, Cleo Norton, is sitting at her desk in the outer office when I walk in. She's a big, good-natured woman in her early twenties with huge dimples and two extra chins. The air conditioner is going full blast, and the room is at least thirty degrees cooler than the rest of the school.

She looks up at me. "Hi, Nathan." Her smile is a little forced, and she nods at Baker's closed door. "He's waiting for you."

Cleo's a friend. We don't hang out together or anything, but we get along fine and she's about the only person in the school I like.

"I'm sure he is. How are you?"

"Fat. Depressed. The usual." She leans toward me and whispers. "You've really done it this time."

I grin. "You always say that."

"Yeah, but today I mean it."

I sigh and walk over to Baker's door. He calls out "Come in," when I knock.

It's even colder in here, and it smells like dry, nervous sweat. Baker is sitting behind his desk, staring at a computer screen.

He looks up. "Close the door and have a seat, please."

I sit down facing him. The bookshelves behind him are full of football trophies from our high school days; there's even one from when we were in junior high. Christ. Is there anything more pathetic than a man in his thirties who still holds on to shit like that?

He pushes back from the desk and rests his pudgy hands on top of his beer belly. "I'm putting an official reprimand in your file for your behavior this morning, Nathan, and I'm going to speak to the superintendent about the possibility of dismissing you."

"Again? What makes you think she'll be more inclined to fire me this time than she has been before?"

"This time is different. You were openly disrespectful to me in front of a student. I won't tolerate that."

This pompous twat pisses me off like no one else I can think of, but I make myself stay calm. "I'll be sure to tell her how respectful you were to me, too, Ted. I particularly liked how you ordered me to go get a broom."

He raises his voice. "I didn't order you. I asked politely." He leans forward and his chair creaks. "Besides, you're forgetting why all this happened in the first place. You destroyed school property this morning."

"Oh, Jesus. I'll pay for the goddamn door. Stop acting like I set off a firebomb in the lunchroom."

He pauses for a long time and worries at his lower lip with his tongue. His tongue is more white than red. "Can I ask you a personal question, Nathan?"

His tone is almost conversational and I'm suddenly leery. "What?"

"Why do you hate me so much? I know we weren't friends in high school, but that was a long time ago and we're both grown-ups now. Why not let bygones be bygones?"

What a fucking hypocrite. "I'm not the one who's been trying to get you fired for years, Ted."

He pushes back again. "I'll admit I was initially reluctant to have you on staff because of our previous relationship, but the reason I don't want you working here now is because I can tell you don't like teaching, and I don't think kids should have teachers who don't want to be here. And that's the God's honest truth."

He's looking me straight in the eye, and I can tell he believes what he's saying. On one level it's utter bullshit, because no matter what he says I know he's lying to himself about his motives for doing this, but unfortunately, his assessment of my desire to teach is pretty accurate, and it silences me for a minute.

He's right, of course. I'd be a liar if I said otherwise. I do my job and I teach what I'm supposed to, but sometimes I feel guilty because there's part of me that believes teaching should be more than that.

But I'm not going to admit that to this asshole.

I clear my throat. "If that's the case, there are probably fifteen teachers in this school who want to be here less than I do. Why not go after them too?"

He drops his gaze and moves a pile of paper on his desk. "Who says I don't?" He waves a hand. "You can go. I expect you'll hear from Madeline later on today about how she wants to discipline you."

I get up slowly. "Well, Ted, it's been a pleasure, as always."

He ignores me.

Cleo looks up as I close Baker's door behind me. "How did it go?" she whispers.

"About like you'd expect," I whisper back. "How can you stand working for him?"

She shrugs. "He's a lot nicer to me than he is to you." She gives me a shrewd look. "I can't say as I blame him, either. You're hardly at your best where he's concerned."

I grimace. "So I've been told."

The only time I ever saw Tommy get violent was with some kid who made the mistake of making fun of how Mom died. We used to eat breakfast in the school cafeteria (mostly because the sooner we could get out of the house and away from Dad for the day, the better), and one morning when Tommy was in junior high, this punk named Ethan Abernathy decided it would be funny to pretend to choke to death on a waffle.

Tommy and I were sitting together as usual, but when Ethan did his comedy routine I was up getting my tray refilled—which was fortunate for Ethan, because as badly as Tommy took it, I would have been ten times worse. Anyway, apparently Tommy had been teasing Ethan for chewing with his mouth open, so Ethan got everyone's attention at the table we were sharing by saying, "Guess who I am," and from what I gathered later, began to perform an elaborate mime of Mom's death, first taking a bite of waffle, then holding his hands to his throat and gagging. To the credit of the other kids at the table, almost no one laughed.

When Tommy realized what Ethan was doing, he picked up his oatmeal bowl (one of those heavy porcelain things schools used to use before plastic took over the world) and bounced it off Ethan's head. Ethan hit the floor like a wet swimsuit, and he ended up with a mild concussion and ten stitches in his scalp. Tommy was suspended from school for three days, even though the principal at the time, Marjorie Hicks, told him in private she didn't blame him a bit for losing his temper. He cried so hard in her office that she came and got me, and gave me permission to leave school and take him home.

The reason I bring all this up is because it was the one time in our entire childhood I can remember Dad being gentle with either of us. The principal had apparently called him earlier, because when he came home in the evening he put his hand on Tommy's head and left it there for a few seconds, and his face looked soft and almost kind. He opened his mouth to speak, and I was sure he was finally going to say something like, "I love you, son," or "I'm sorry I've been such a crappy human being." What he said was, "Don't you dare apologize to that little son of a bitch. Not ever."

Heartwarming, isn't it? Words to live by.

Simon is tossing a Frisbee with Tommy and Philip and Kyle when I get back to the cottage. They're out in the yard on the east side of the house, and Camille is sprawled under a tree with a mug of coffee, watching them.

It's not even eleven in the morning and it's already unbearably hot. Kyle's wearing bright yellow gym shorts and a yellow tank top (he looks like a canary), and Philip and Simon are apparently having a contest for who owns the tackiest pair of cutoffs. Tommy is wearing a black Speedo swimsuit and nothing else.

Christ. If his genitals were squeezed any tighter against the fabric I could count his pubic hairs.

When I slam the car door Simon gives me a big wave and comes running over. His hair is wet from sweating, and there's a small red pimple in the middle of his chest.

"Hi, Mr. Bishop. What happened? Did you get fired?"

Tommy comes over, too, before I can answer. Kyle tosses the Frisbee at him and he makes a showy one-handed catch, then flicks it toward Philip and turns to me. "What's going on? Simon said you got in trouble with Turd Baker."

I narrow my eyes at Simon. "What are you, the town crier?"

His face clouds up. "I'm sorry."

Tommy scowls and drops an arm over Simon's shoulders. "Don't be a jerk, Nathan. He was just worried about you, that's all." He gives Simon a squeeze and Simon leans into him a little.

"Sorry, Simon," I mutter. "I didn't mean to snap at you. I'm just in a bad mood."

"It's okay." He suddenly seems to realize that he's being held by Tommy and he steps away a little and looks embarrassed. "So what happened with Baker?"

I shrug. "Nothing out of the ordinary. Hugs and kisses, that sort of thing."

"Heads up!" Kyle yells.

We all turn in time to see the Frisbee rocketing toward Simon's head. Simon makes a grab for it but before he gets his fingers on it Tommy tackles him for no apparent reason and it sails harmlessly by, into the woods. I look down at the tangle of bare limbs on the ground.

"Oof." Simon's head appears from under Tommy's shoulder. He's laughing.

Tommy smiles down at him. "I hope you noticed I just saved your life."

I wipe sweat from my forehead. "Either that or you broke every bone in his body."

Tommy grunts. "Don't bother me with details. I'm a hero." He starts to push himself up and Simon shifts under him, but for a second their eyes lock and both of them stop moving. There's a charged silence.

Philip comes running over. "This isn't football, Tommy. Get off the poor kid before you crush him."

A car suddenly noses out of the woods and swings in behind mine. It's Cheri Tipton. Her right side mirror has been knocked loose and is dangling like a distended eyeball.

This day just keeps getting better and better.

Tommy climbs to his feet and offers a hand to Simon as Cheri pulls to a stop and gets out of the car. Philip tries to step between Tommy and Simon after Simon is standing, but Tommy gives him an irritated look and stays in the middle.

"Is that little Tommy?" Cheri calls out. She trundles over and grabs hold of Tommy, kissing him on the cheek, then she steps back and looks him up and down, making a valiant effort not to gape at his Speedos. Her upper lip is beaded with sweat. "My goodness, I haven't seen you in at least ten years."

"Hi, Cheri." Tommy smiles sweetly. "You look gorgeous."

She blushes like a pubescent schoolgirl and fingers the silver crucifix necklace wedged between her huge breasts.

Tommy is so full of shit. He knows what effect he has on middle-aged women (not to mention gay men) and he plays it to the hilt. Cheri is wearing a white dress and looks about as gorgeous as a marshmallow.

Kyle wanders up to see what's going on and Tommy introduces everybody. "This is my friend Kyle, and this is Simon, and this is my boyfriend, Philip."

Even though I know Tommy deliberately introduced Philip that way to get a reaction, Cheri doesn't bat an eye, which surprises me. She just shakes everyone's hand politely, then notices Camille sitting under the tree. Kyle calls for Camille to come over but she frowns at him and looks away.

Kyle tries to smile, but he's embarrassed. "And that's my unsociable wife, Camille."

Cheri brushes it off tactfully. "I don't blame her. It's too hot to be in the sun. What on earth are you all doing out here? You should be hiding inside, in the air-conditioning."

Tommy laughs and wraps an arm around Philip's waist. "You obviously haven't met my brother, have you? Nathan won't pry open his wallet to buy a decent toaster, let alone an air conditioner or a television."

I ignore him. "So, Cheri. What brings you back so soon?"

Her smile fades. "Don't be difficult, Nathan. I've been trying to get hold of you for two days. Dale gave me the go-ahead on the cornfield and all I need is your permission now to bring in my team and have a look around back there."

Team? What team? The Boston Red Sox?

I shake my head. "I don't think so, Cheri. What would be the point?"

She speaks slowly and with exaggerated patience, as if she's talking to a foreigner with mild brain damage. "I thought I'd already explained that to you. You may be sitting on a major archaeological find."

Kyle looks bored and drifts off to find the Frisbee. Tommy casually drapes his free arm over Simon's shoulder again and Philip frowns. Simon looks a little uncomfortable, but he doesn't pull away, and after a few seconds he even tilts his head back and rests it on Tommy's bicep.

Goddammit Tommy.

I force myself to focus on Cheri. "I thought you said you didn't expect to find much."

"I know, but the more I think about it, the more I'm convinced something's here that's worth finding."

"Why? What's changed? You haven't come across any more evidence, have you?"

"No, but I've got this really strong feeling that this is something we should do."

I grunt in frustration. "Look, Cheri, I'm not going to let an army of morons with pickaxes and shovels invade my privacy just because you've got a 'really strong feeling.' I need a better reason than that."

She opens her purse and pulls out a check and some papers. "I've been authorized by the Historical Society to offer you two thousand dollars, and of course we'll also pay for any damage to your land when we're done." She holds the check out to me but I pretend not to notice. "And it's hardly an army. It will be a professor from the university, and a couple of her grad students, and me. That's all." She waves the check in front of my eyes. "Take it or leave it."

I look at Tommy and he shrugs. "It's up to you. I think it's a waste of time, too, but it's not a bad deal." He's still got his arms around Philip and Simon, and both are watching him as he talks. The three of them look like a cheesy advertisement for a weekend getaway to Fire Island.

Kyle comes out of the woods with the Frisbee. He leans down and checks his legs and feet for ticks, then he looks up and sees me watching him and he smiles and starts walking toward me.

I turn back to Cheri. "I'm not saying yes yet, but if I did, how long would it take?"

The sudden eagerness in her face is almost indecent. "I'm not sure. Maybe only a few weeks, since the site is quite small. We'd get started right away."

I stare at the check in her hand and finally reach out to take it. If Ted Baker has his way, I'll need all the money I can get.

Kyle appears at my side and hands me the Frisbee. "So are you coming to the beach with us today or what?"

Dad was the smartest idiot I've ever met. I don't know what his IQ was, but it had to have been off the charts. He knew a staggering amount about just about everything, from astronomy and geography to math and music. He never went to college, but he could quote extensively from authors like Emerson and Jung and Nietzsche, and he spent every spare minute with a book in his hand. He could prattle on for hours (usually while he was tinkering with a car engine or listening to a Mahler symphony) about Shakespeare's sonnets, or Rilke's Duino Elegies, or Messier's catalogue of nonstellar objects, and his brain was stuffed with religious esoterica, like what pope did what to whom. His intellect wasn't limited to academics, either; I never once saw him lose an argument with anybody.

If he had been a stupid man, I could maybe have understood the way he was. But he had the brain of a genius, and no one that smart has a right to behave like a malignant retard. The wisdom and kindness in the books he read were in the end nothing but pretty words to him, and had no influence on how he lived his life.

I've often wondered what sort of man he would have been if Mom hadn't died so young. If Tommy is right about her death being the catalyst for everything he became, maybe if she'd lived I could still hear the word "father" without flinching. And maybe if we'd had even one decent parent, Tommy and I wouldn't have needed to bond to each other in the way we did. Sexual experimentation between siblings is supposedly a common enough occurrence, but in a "normal" home, where tenderness is easier to come by, it usually doesn't last for four years or get nearly as hot and heavy as it did for Tommy and me.

I was lying earlier when I told you I don't feel any guilt about what Tommy and I did together. Of course I feel guilty, sometimes—especially because I'm the older brother. Granted, Tommy was always an enthusiastic participant, but I probably should have stopped things before they got out of hand. But it was always so hard to say no to him. Every time I tried to put the brakes on by telling him I didn't think we should do what we were doing, he just kept touching me until I was so horny I couldn't think straight and I'd give in and do what he wanted.

But I'm not blaming Tommy. I'd be lying if I said I ever put up much of a fight. I liked the sex as much as he did, and there were days that it was all I could do to not tear his clothes off in front of other people. We'd pass each other at school and his eyes would flicker at me, and I couldn't wait for the bell to ring at the end of the day, because I knew what was going to happen as soon as we got home.

It was wrong, but we couldn't help it. We were kids, and we loved each other, and I refuse to beat myself up about it anymore, like I used to. What would be the point? It's over and done with.

"Nathan?" It's Tommy, calling from the front door of the cottage. I'm staring after Cheri, who just left to go call her "team." She was so excited I thought she was going to pee all over her Birkenstocks.

I walk towards him. "What?"

"Madeline Huber's on the phone."

"Shit." I chew on my lip. Ted Baker must have already contacted the superintendent. "I'll take it upstairs. Keep everyone quiet, okay?"

I run upstairs to my desk and pick up the phone. "I've got it, Tommy." I wait until he hangs up the downstairs line before I start talking. "Madeline?"

"Hi, Nathan. We need to talk." I hear her take a drag on a cigarette. "What happened this morning between you and Ted?"

"What did he tell you?" I demand. "I'm sure he exaggerated."

She sighs. "Probably. What's your side of the story?"

I've known Madeline forever. She and Dad were friends once, a long time ago, and even though I don't know what happened between them, I know their friendship ended badly not long after Mom died.

I twist the phone cord around my finger. "It really wasn't a big deal. I accidentally broke the door to my classroom and Ted threw a hissy fit and started ordering me around. I got a little angry and we both lost our tempers. That's about it."

"He says you asked him to spank you."

I wince. "That's a lie."

"Really?"

"Well, sort of. I didn't ask him to spank me, I just asked him if he was *going* to spank me."

There's a long silence.

I sit at my desk. "Madeline? Are you still there?"

She finally clears her throat. "Yes, I'm still here, unfortunately." Another pause. "And you chose to have this conversation in front of a student? This new boy," I can hear her shuffling papers, "this . . . what's his name?"

"Simon Hart."

"Right. Ted tells me he's been a problem in your class." She coughs. Madeline smokes more than anyone I know. "He's not happy about how you handled that situation, either, by the way."

"Simon's not a problem." I can only imagine what she'd say if I told her that the boy she's asking about is downstairs right now with Tommy and Philip, probably listening to what I'm saying. "And I could care less if Ted is happy or not. I handled it fine. But yes,

Simon was there this morning. I'm sorry. I do feel bad about that. But Ted was being an idiot."

"It seems he wasn't the only one." She sounds irritated. "I swear, Nathan, what nonsense was going through your head? When are you going to grow up? I am sick to death of this childish pissing contest between you two."

I can feel myself blushing. "He started it," I mumble.

"Oh, for God's sake. Do you hear yourself?" She laughs, which gets her coughing again.

After a minute I laugh a little, too, in spite of myself. "Okay, okay. I'll admit I was part of the problem. But I couldn't help it. He's such an ass."

She gets herself under control. "I can't keep overriding Ted for you, Nathan. He's unreasonable when it comes to you, but he's a good principal, and this time he's right. You did go too far."

I lurch to my feet. "I can't believe this. You're firing me?"

"Calm down, please. No, I'm not firing you. But I'm allowing him to put a reprimand in your file, and if something like this happens again, your job will be in serious jeopardy." She takes a breath and I can hear a phone ringing in the background. "I like you, Nathan, and your students like you, but you can't run around shooting off your mouth at Ted just because he annoys you."

"What about . . ."

"I've already warned Ted to behave more professionally toward you, as well."

"Will his job be in serious jeopardy, too, if he doesn't?"

I hear the flick of a cigarette lighter as she sucks in air. "Just worry about yourself. I'll take care of Ted."

"Fine. I'll be a model employee from here on. Scout's honor."

She snorts. "You are so much like your father it frightens me. I've got to go." She hangs up.

I sit down again and glare at the phone until Tommy yells upstairs and tells me everyone is waiting for me.

When I was eight years old Tommy and I broke a vase while playing catch in the house, and we tried to tell Dad a bird had somehow gotten inside and knocked it over.

He nodded. "I see. A bird."

He got a hammer out of the kitchen closet and walked into our bedroom and proceeded to smash every breakable object in sight: a piggy bank, and a glass jar with Tommy's seashell collection in it, and the clock radio Tommy had given me for my birthday that year. We were screaming at him to stop and that we were sorry but he kept right on going, taking out a lamp, and a Lego castle on the floor, and a model airplane or two on the desk. He was absolutely calm while he did it, and he had a slight smile on his face.

He handed me the hammer on the way out of the room and said, "Fucking birds. I guess we need to find a way to keep them out of the house, don't we?"

We're at the beach. Even Camille came, but she followed along behind the rest of us on the way here, dragging her feet and pretending to be interested in the wildflowers along the path. At first Kyle walked with her and tried to get her to match speed with the rest of us, but after a while he got pissed and left her by herself. Now she's sitting on a corner of the blanket, playing with a strand of her hair and digging her toes into the sand. Simon and Kyle are tossing the Frisbee back and forth in the ocean, I'm sitting beside Camille, and Tommy and Philip are sprawled on their stomachs next to us, napping in the sun. The air is hazy and smells like suntan lotion and seaweed.

Camille finally stops staring at the sky and turns to face me. "I don't think I can stay here much longer."

She's got a lot of freckles on her shoulders and arms but she poured about a gallon of sunscreen on before we left the cottage. I touch her forearm to see if she's getting too much color. "Are you burning?"

"No, I mean here in Walcott. I need to go home."

I lie back, prop myself up on my elbows and stretch my legs out in front of me. "Do you guys have to get back to work or something?"

She shakes her head. "No. We've still got more than a week off." She fiddles with the fringe on the blanket. "Didn't Tommy tell you?

We all coordinated our schedules to take two weeks off together and come up here. We've been planning it for months."

I glare over at Tommy. Both he and Philip are sound asleep. "You might not have noticed, but Tommy's not very good at keeping people in the loop. I suppose I should be grateful he remembered to call a few days beforehand and warn me you were all showing up."

Her eyes travel over Philip and me, then linger on Tommy. "Jesus. Look at that body. He could work as a model for Michelangelo."

I grunt. "I wouldn't go that far." I turn my head to look at him, too. Every muscle in his back and legs is clearly defined by the sweat glistening on his skin. He's outrageously beautiful, but for some reason I don't want to say that to Camille. "Besides, I doubt Michelangelo would approve of Speedos."

She glances down at me. "You don't need to be jealous, Nathan. You're pretty easy to look at, yourself."

I flush and change the subject. "Why do you have to get back to New York?"

She flicks a hand toward Kyle. "I've got to get away from my husband before he actually jumps in bed with Tommy and Philip." Her eyes bore into mine. "Or you, for that matter."

I stare at the hair around my navel. "What are you talking about?"

"Oh, please, Nathan. His eyes follow you wherever you go. Whenever Kyle's around you must feel like you're in a room with the *Mona Lisa.*"

"That's silly." I sit up and wrap my arms around my legs. "If he's interested in anybody besides you, it's Tommy."

An old man with mottled pink and white skin and a turgid paunch stumbles around our blanket and leers at Camille on his way to the ocean. She makes a face as if he offered her a plate of pigeon entrails and he instantly hangs his head and looks away.

I rest my left ear on my knees and study her. Her hair is long and thick and she's wearing it up right now, off her neck. She's thin and strong, and her bikini—red, to match her hair—reveals a flat stomach and an exquisite set of pelvic bones. Her forehead is lined, though, and she looks unhappy.

I lift my head. "You're a knockout, Camille. Do you know that?"

Her eyes dart to my face to see if I'm teasing. "I used to." She glances down at her body and laughs self-consciously, then her eyes fill with tears and she looks away.

A battered old seagull with filthy feathers and sallow eyes passes within two feet of our blanket, holding a piece of hot dog in its beak, and a few seconds later half a dozen sandpipers skitter by after it, thin legs churning comically fast under their plump bodies. I watch them move down the beach and wait for Camille to get herself under control again.

She swallows a few times and turns back to me. "Sorry." She tries to smile. "It's been such a long time since anyone who said that meant it. I'd forgotten what it felt like."

I clear my throat. "Have you told Kyle you want to leave?"

She reaches over and bats at a black fly hovering by my head. "No. I haven't wanted to see the look of glee in his eyes when he realizes I'll be out of the picture and he can stop pretending to be straight."

I don't know what to say. I should probably argue with her to make her feel better, but I don't have the heart for it. She's right.

"So what are you going to do?"

She sighs. "You mean about going back to New York, or about my farce of a marriage?"

"I mean about Kyle."

She shrugs. "I don't know." She picks up a scallop shell from the sand and holds it to the sun. "I know I should get out, but I keep telling myself that maybe I'm wrong and he just needs time to figure things out." She tosses the shell away. "Isn't it scary how easy it is to do exactly the wrong thing?"

I look away and pick at a scab on my elbow. "Tell me about it."

She covers my elbow with her hand. "Stop. You'll just make it worse."

I pull away from her and show her the fresh drops of blood on my skin. "Too late for that."

She studies my face for a minute. "It always is, isn't it?"

I don't answer and after a while she starts talking again. "Kyle was the one who pushed to get married so fast, and I was stupid enough to think it was because he was in love with me." She pauses and digs a paper towel out of her beach bag to wipe her nose. "He was sweet, and cute, and shy at first, and he treated me really well. Really, really well, you know? He bought me things all the time, and he never yelled or got mad, and he never looked at other women or talked about them." She sniffles. "That should have been my first clue."

She watches Kyle leap in the air to snag the Frisbee. He makes a good catch but a wave hits him when he lands and knocks it loose from his fingers again.

She chews on her lip as he runs after it. "My last two boyfriends were cosmic losers. The first one used to hit me when he was angry, and the other one cheated on me, and Kyle seemed so normal and kind in comparison, and I fell in love in about four seconds." She traces a fingernail around a mole near her left breast. "He couldn't wait for me to meet his parents, and I actually thought that was a good sign." She snorts. "I should have just sent him to the costume shop to buy a phony beard. It would have worked just as well. Christ."

She balls up the paper towel and stuffs it back in the bag. "Why don't you goddamn gay guys get your act together and stop fucking around with stupid, gullible women like me?"

I can't help but smile. "We've got nothing better to do with our time, I guess."

She glowers at me. "I'm serious, Nathan. Bring it up at the next meeting or something, will you?" Her eyes fill again. "This hurts like hell."

She drops her face on her legs and takes a deep breath. I put my hand on the base of her neck and she leans into it and rocks back and forth as I rub her shoulders.

Tommy rolls over and sits up, blinking stupidly. It takes him a few seconds to focus. "Hey. What's up?" He yawns and looks around. "Where's Simon?"

I look out at the ocean. Kyle is walking toward us with the Frisbee, but Simon's nowhere in sight.

"Where did Simon go?" I call out.

Philip stirs and rolls over on his back. He reaches up and runs a finger along Tommy's ribs, but Tommy's watching the ocean and doesn't respond.

Kyle looks back over his shoulder for a second then faces us again and shrugs. "I don't know." He gets to the blanket and drops to his knees between Camille and me. "I told him I was going to get out of the water and he said he wanted to swim for another few minutes. I don't know where he went."

I scan the waves. A few people are playing close to shore, but none of them are Simon. Tommy slowly climbs to his feet, but just as he starts to look worried, a familiar blond head surfaces about fifty feet out.

Tommy grins and sits back down. I toss a clump of sand at him. "Nice going, shithead. He's trying to do your trick, and he'll probably end up drowning."

Philip stretches his arms above his head. "Good," he mutters.

Tommy frowns at him. "Why is that good?"

Philip closes his eyes. "I'm just joking."

Kyle asks Camille how she's doing, but as she's lifting her head to answer him he turns to me and puts a hand on my ankle. "Want to play Frisbee with me, Nathan?"

I glance at Camille. She looks back at me with a wan smile. "Go ahead. He won't leave you alone until you play with him."

Simon's made his way back and I watch him emerge from the water. He stands up and with both hands pushes his hair back behind his ears, then he reaches down to scratch his right knee. Tommy's watching him, too, and the intent expression on his face bothers me. All he needs is a tail and a mane and he'd look like a lion preparing to spring from the bushes on an unsuspecting gazelle.

When Madeline compared me to my father I wanted to climb through the phone and extinguish her cigarette in her left nostril. She knows full well what I think of my dad, and I can't believe she said that. She's not usually that unkind; she must be more irritated with me than I realized.

And she's right, of course.

I am all too much my father's son. I have his hands, I have his temper. I am fully capable of being just as petty and vindictive as he was, and I can no more control my tongue than he could. I sometimes feel like the repository of every foul impulse he ever gave in to and every despicable act he ever committed—a spiritual chamber pot, so to speak, where he dumped all of his worst smelling shit.

Yeah, I know. I overstate my case.

Dad did that, too.

Tommy is, in every way, a better person than I am. He's not deeper and he's not smarter, but he's infinitely better. Sure, his dick rules his life and he can't commit to anyone or anything and he's insensitive and buffoonish and completely unconcerned, initially, with how his actions might affect somebody else—but whenever he hurts someone, it's always unintentional, and he's always horrified by what he's done. Even when he tried to replace Ethan Abernathy's skull with a bowl of oatmeal, he was just acting on instinct. He's not capable of premeditation, or malice.

But I am.

After Andy abandoned me in the street with Dad that day he began to avoid me. He told me we needed to stop messing around because it was too dangerous and it wasn't worth risking what my father would do to us if we got caught. He stopped taking my phone calls and he stopped sitting next to me in classes. When we passed each other in the halls he wouldn't even meet my eyes. I tried for weeks to find a way to be alone with him, but he always made sure he was surrounded by at least three or four other people, usually some of his jock friends. He'd see me coming and he'd frown and turn his back, and after a while I'd see those same friends smirking whenever I walked by. I don't know what he told them, but I imagined the worst. I was sure he was saying things like, *"Bishop is a fucking faggot. He made a pass at me and when I told him no he started stalking me."*

I've never been so miserable. I moped around the house and the school for days and wouldn't talk to anyone—not even Tommy. My grades took a nosedive and I started blowing off classes, and I'd come home in the middle of the day and steal shots of Dad's Irish whiskey and lay on my bed and whack off to recent memories of sex with Andy.

And then Andy started hanging out with Joe Allerton.

I'd always liked Joe. He was a gangling, sweet-tempered kid with moist brown eyes and thick black hair, and he had huge hands and feet, and jug ears, and a low voice that cracked at least once in every conversation. He grew up in Walcott and was in the same class with Ted Baker and me all the way through school, and he played wide receiver on the football team. What he lacked in brains he made up for in civility and decency, and even though he was a mediocre athlete, he worked hard at it and was a favorite of the crowd at games. (I remember one game in particular during the fall of our sophomore year when he got lucky and ran the ball in for a touchdown, and everyone in the bleachers, including me, started chanting, "Go, Joe! Go, Joe!" He spiked the ball and pranced around in the end zone like a chimpanzee on acid.) He owned a black Labrador who went everywhere with him, and he worked at the local grocery store, and he told me once that when he got out of school he wanted to join the air force and become a fighter pilot.

But unfortunately for Joe, he made the mistake of getting involved with my ex-boyfriend. A few weeks after Andy and I stopped fucking, I began to notice the two of them looking at each other in the same way Andy and I used to look at each other. At first I thought I was being paranoid, but after a couple of days I became convinced and decided to try to find a way to spy on them when they were by themselves, just to be sure. One day after school I got on my bike and rode out to the same secluded spot in the woods where Andy and I liked to go to be alone, and I hid my bike in the brush and climbed up an embankment directly above where Andy used to park his car out of sight of the road.

It was mid-November and the trees had lost a lot of their leaves, but there were still enough to offer privacy from anyone driving by, and I settled in to wait until football practice was over. If Andy and Joe were messing around it was likely they'd come here then, because I knew Joe had a big family and his house would be off-limits, and Andy preferred fucking in a car to taking a chance in his own house, and late afternoon after football practice was always his favorite time of day to have sex. All the blocking and tackling and post-practice locker room stuff made him horny, and he liked to get his rocks off before going home for supper.

I sat there for over an hour and a half that first afternoon, sniffling in the cold air, and they never showed up, and the same thing happened the next day. But the third time (I still remember the date: Thursday, November 17, 1991, at exactly five twenty-two p.m.) Andy and Joe pulled up in Andy's monstrous old Cadillac and turned off the engine under my nest.

I was about a dozen feet above them, but I could see most of the backseat from my vantage point, and even though it was a cold day and the windows soon got steamed up, I saw Andy pull Joe's dick out of his pants (it was surprisingly thick for such a skinny kid) and start to suck on it, and a few minutes later I also got to see Joe's face, wincing a little, flattened against the glass on the passenger side of the car as Andy mounted him from behind.

It went on for quite a while. The car rocked back and forth, and I could hear both of them groaning and finally Andy cried out and Joe's face fell away from the window. A few minutes later they crawled back into the front seat and drove away. I climbed down from the embankment and got on my bike and went home.

And that night, in bed, I stared up at the ceiling for a few hours and didn't fall asleep until I'd come up with a plan to expose their relationship to their families.

I should tell you that from the beginning Tommy was against me doing anything to them. He felt sorry for me because of how Andy had abandoned me after our little run-in with Dad, but he'd always liked Andy and said I should forgive him and move on. He had a soft spot for people who were intimidated by Dad.

Oh, yeah. His soft spot also had something to do with the time he and I had an impromptu circle jerk with Andy in the woods beyond the cornfield.

Tommy knew that Andy and I were fucking, of course; I always told him everything. Andy, on the other hand, knew nothing about what Tommy and I had been doing together for years, and I had no intention of telling him. (I could just imagine that conversation:

"You know that thing I do with my tongue you like so much? Well, my little brother taught me that. Pretty cool, huh?") I'd kept them apart intentionally because it was just too weird to think about the three of us being in the same room together, and I was also afraid if Andy got to know Tommy he'd like him better than he liked me. I know that's pretty pathetic—but if Tommy was your little brother you'd be insecure, too.

I managed to compartmentalize my life for a few weeks, but one Saturday morning in early October—Dad always worked on Saturdays—Andy came by the house unannounced just as Tommy and I were finishing breakfast. He came in and sat at the table while we washed the dishes. I felt awkward at first because Tommy was making innuendos and being his usual dipshit self (at one point he stuffed the dish towel down the front of his pants and claimed to be an alien from Planet Blue-Balls), but after a while I relaxed when I saw that even though Andy was enjoying Tommy he was still mostly paying attention to me. We got laughing and suddenly it seemed like the most natural thing in the world for us all to be together.

It was a perfect fall day, crisp and clear and sunny, and the three of us decided to go for a walk, but as soon as we got a little ways into the woods and squatted down to catch our breath, I looked at Andy and without warning my heart changed to a gallop and I put my hand on his thigh. Just like that. I didn't really know what I was doing, but I couldn't help it. He started to freak and he pushed at my hand but I kept it there and I told him Tommy was cool and it was okay. His eyes darted from Tommy to me and back again. Tommy nodded enthusiastically and, being Tommy, sprang to his feet, unbuckled his belt, and pushed his jeans and boxers down to his ankles.

On cue, his dick immediately popped up and bobbed around in the cold air like a bloodhound sniffing out a rabbit. Andy sat there ogling it, his eyes the size of dinner plates and his mouth partly open. I swallowed hard, once, squeezed Andy's knee, and reached up and wrapped my free hand around Tommy's dick—he gasped a little and said, "Your fingers are cold!"—and then I got to my feet and pulled Andy up to stand beside me. We ended up in a rough tri-angle. There was a flurry of fingers and zippers, then, just like magic, I had a dick in each hand. Tommy took turns squeezing Andy's balls first, then mine, and Andy stroked me off with one hand and with the other helped me work on Tommy.

It only took about thirty seconds because we were all so horny. Tommy shot first, then Andy, then me. The leaves on the ground between us looked like an insane baker had run amok with an icing gun. Tommy leaned over and rested his head on mine, and after a second Andy did the same thing on the other side, and we all stood there, watching our breaths commingle and steam in the cold air. Tommy started to giggle, and a few seconds later we were all out of control, laughing hysterically. I gave each of their shrinking penises a final affectionate pull and stepped back.

We never did that again. It was fun, and it's one of my favorite sex memories. But something about it was too weird, even for Tommy and me. What we had between us was private, and in retrospect it felt wrong to bring somebody else, even a willing boyfriend, into our relationship. Andy asked me later if Tommy and I had ever done that sort of thing before and I lied and told him no. Andy may have been the first person I fell in love with, but Tommy was my brother, and even at that age there was never a question which mattered more.

Just a side note: Tommy and I never kissed each other on the mouth. After what I've told you that must seem pretty strange, but what can I say? Blow jobs and anal sex were par for the course, but a kiss on the lips would have been too weird, even for us.

Anyway, I was telling you about what I did to Andy and Joe after I caught them screwing around in Andy's car. My plan was simple: get an incriminating picture of them together, make copies of it and send it to their parents.

Taking the picture was easy. I borrowed Dad's fancy-ass Minolta camera with a zoom lens (without asking him, of course) and climbed back up the embankment the next afternoon to wait for the Dynamic Duo. They showed up right on schedule, and within minutes of their arrival, I snapped a terrific shot of Joe kissing the head of Andy's dick.

The angle couldn't have been better. They were in the enormous backseat of the Cadillac again, and Andy was sitting with his head resting on the deck under the rear window, his pants around his knees and his eyes looking straight up at the sky. (I still can't believe he didn't see me; if he had turned his head an inch he would have been looking right at me.) Joe was kneeling on the floor between Andy's legs, and I took the picture just as he raised his chin and puckered up his lips. The car was facing west, but it was an overcast day, so even though there was plenty of light, there was no glare off the rear window. Their faces were crystal clear through the zoom lens, and neither the Strausses nor the Allertons would have any trouble recognizing their sons. Joe's lips were wet and his eyes were half-closed; Andy's mouth was open and he was smiling. Even Andy's dick was cooperatively photogenic—it stood up tall and proud against Joe's mouth, like a purple-headed microphone he was thinking about singing into. I got some other interesting poses, but that was by far the best.

Developing the film was more problematic. The only place in Walcott that developed pictures was the local drugstore, and it was owned by Burt Thorne—a cantankerous old Baptist who would never have allowed pictures like that to be printed—so I ended up hopping a bus to New Haven. It took a while but I finally found a one-hour photo shop with a bored, pimple-faced attendant, who just leered and said, "Sure," when I asked for three copies of the blow job picture. I went across the street to a Dunkin' Donuts and had a cup of coffee and a chocolate cruller while he printed them up.

The rest was easy. I took the bus back to Walcott, bought a Scotch tape dispenser and some typing paper, and sat in Tommy's and my bedroom that night for an hour or so, taping the pictures to pieces of paper and trying to figure out the perfect caption to write under them. I finally settled on "Congratulations, Joe and Andy, on your fine karaoke act," then I addressed an envelope to Mr. and Mrs. Allerton, and another to Mr. and Mrs. Strauss, and I stuck a copy of the picture in each. Tommy sat with me, telling me nonstop that I shouldn't do this. I told him to shut up and mind his own business, and I mailed the letters first thing in the morning.

So far, so good, right? I'd pulled off the perfect plan and made

Joe and Andy's lives miserable for the foreseeable future. Their parents would shit bricks and neither of them would get a moment's peace for the rest of their senior year. And best of all, Andy would eventually figure out it was me who had done this to him.

It was the finest "fuck you" I'd ever given anyone, and even though part of me knew I shouldn't gloat, I didn't care. I felt vindicated. Whatever stories he'd told to his friends about me were now completely obliterated. I'd shown the light on his lies (or so I told myself), and given him exactly what he deserved for being such a chickenshit as to let my father scare him away from me. I couldn't wait to see Andy's face after his parents found out the truth about him and Joe.

I still remember how I strutted around the house that evening. Tommy was strangely subdued and was barely speaking to me, but not even that dimmed my overall mood. I chattered at the back of his head while he sat at his desk in our room and ignored me.

"Do you think they've already gotten the pictures? I stuck them in the mail this morning in time for them to get delivered." I paced around the bed while I jabbered. "No one fucks with me and gets away with it. Andy and Joe are so screwed it's not even funny." I chortled. "They'll be lucky if they don't get crucified, don't you think?"

He turned and stared at me. He was trying to repair a mangled shortwave radio somebody had tossed in the trash downtown and he was holding a soldering gun and some wire. His eyes were red and he looked like he was trying not to cry.

"What's the matter with you?" I demanded.

He made an odd, helpless gesture with the wire, then turned away again. "Nothing," he whispered.

I stared at his head for a few seconds, then returned to the satisfying business of patting myself on the back. It was as if I'd written a perfect play, I crowed. I was a modern-day Shakespeare, manipulating characters and events and controlling every aspect of a complex plot, leading up to a final, crushing denouement. I was a puppet master; I was a genius. Shit, God Himself couldn't have done a better job feeding those two assholes their just deserts . . .

Blah, blah, blah.

Jesus, I was so stupid. I can sometimes almost forgive myself for my cruelty and my pride, but I can never forgive myself for such epic stupidity.

I didn't see Andy again for almost seven years. When I went to school the next morning he wasn't in any of his classes, and neither was Joe. I found out later that Andy's parents had withdrawn him from Walcott High School without any explanation, and sent him to live with his grandmother in Tucson. (His mother still lives in Walcott, so now and then when he comes to visit her, I'll see him walking uptown. I tried to talk to him once and he flipped me off and turned away.)

Joe, though, returned to school two days later, sporting a cast on his left arm. He told people he'd broken it by falling down the stairs at home, but every few weeks after that he'd show up with a new bruise on his face or somewhere else on his body and eventually the school counselor figured out that his dad was beating the shit out of him and sent a social worker to the Allertons' house to put an end to it. The result was Joe being taken away from his family and put into foster care in another town. Until he left Walcott, every time I passed him in the hall he refused to look at me.

So my brilliant plan came down to this: I wrecked two families and got an innocent kid beaten up—all because I couldn't stand being dumped. It's the single worst thing I've ever done in my life.

Besides Andy and Joe, Tommy is the only one who knows what I did. I tried to pretend that I was okay with everything, but the night after we'd heard Joe had been sent away, too, I lay on my bed and stared at the ceiling, not moving or saying a word until Tommy curled up next to me and put his arms around me. I turned away from him and told him to please leave me alone. He ignored me and after a while I started shaking so hard the mattress rattled in its metal frame. I opened my mouth to scream but nothing came out.

I still have my copy of that picture somewhere. I don't know why I keep it. All I know is that whenever I come across it, it hurts to see it. A few years ago Tommy found out I still had it and he got mad at me and told me I was rubbing my nose in old guilt for no reason. He called me Hester Prynne and said he was going to have the picture made into a T-shirt so I could wear it on my chest like a scarlet letter.

But I'm not trying to punish myself or anything, not really. I just don't want to forget what I'm capable of. I owe Andy and Joe at least that much, don't you think?

And I don't have a clue why Tommy still loves me.

CHAPTER 6

Dale Cromwell and Cheri Tipton are standing next to the cornfield with Caleb Farrell when we get back from the beach. Caleb is my nearest neighbor—he lives in the old Cape Cod cottage attached to the lighthouse—and the closest thing my dad had to a friend. Caleb and Dale are leaning on one of the wheels of Dale's John Deere tractor and Cheri is pacing back and forth in front of them, waving her arms around and pointing at the field. They break off their conversation and stare at us as we come up.

Caleb takes one look at Tommy and his face wrinkles in distaste. "Put some clothes on, boy. This ain't the south of France."

Tommy's still wearing his Speedos and a pair of sandals, and he's got a blue towel draped around his neck. He narrows his eyes and scowls. "What the hell are you doing here? I was hoping you'd be dead by now."

There's a stunned silence from Tommy's friends, but Dale and Cheri are grinning. Caleb glares at Tommy and pushes away from the tractor. "You should be horsewhipped for saying such a terrible thing to an old man."

Tommy nods. "Probably." He tilts his head and studies Farrell's face. "Christ, Caleb, you've got more ear hair than Bigfoot. Don't you ever look in the mirror?"

Caleb stomps over and places himself squarely in front of us. The top of his head only comes up to Tommy's chin, and he probably weighs less than Simon. He's fighting to look pissed but all of a sudden he bursts out laughing and pulls Tommy into a fierce bear hug. "You little asshole." There are tears in his eyes as he rests his chin on Tommy's shoulder. "It's about time you came home."

Tommy hugs him back hard and his voice comes out muffled. "I know. I'm sorry."

Kyle and Camille and Philip are staring at them curiously, and Simon looks up at me, trying to figure out what's going on. I shrug and we all watch them for a moment in silence until Dale shakes his head and rolls his eyes at me. "Very touching. Do you mind if I puke on your lawn?"

Tommy laughs and he and Caleb finally step apart. Tommy wipes his eyes on his towel.

"Hi, everybody," Cheri burbles. "I was just showing Dale and Caleb where we're going to start the dig. Dale's going to mow down the corn this afternoon, and then tomorrow morning Dr. Hampstead and her students will be coming in." She turns to me. "Don't worry about a thing, Nathan. You'll hardly notice they're here. They're bringing their own Porta Potty and everything."

"Wonderful." I glower at Dale. "How in God's name did she talk you into this?"

He grimaces. "The same way she talked you into it."

Tommy's busy introducing everybody to everybody. When he gets to Philip he calls him "my partner," and an uncomfortable expression flits across Dale's face. Caleb raises an eyebrow, but he shakes Philip's hand and says, "Pleased to meet you, son." Philip blushes and steps closer to Tommy.

Caleb Farrell was the only person my dad actually went out of his way to see on a regular basis. They played chess at Caleb's house every Sunday for nearly thirty years, and Dad usually came home in a good mood, reeking of Guinness Extra Stout and Caleb's pipe smoke. I have no idea what they talked about during those games, or if they talked at all, for that matter, and I also don't know who was the better chess player, since neither of them would ever admit having lost a game to the other one. But I know Dad wouldn't have kept going back if he wasn't being challenged. It's a funny thing, but as much as he liked to dominate people in every other arena of his life, he hated playing chess with anybody who couldn't put up a good fight. (I made the mistake of beating him once and he was after me for days for a rematch. After that I made sure to bite the dust several times in a row so he'd lose interest and stop hounding me.)

I've never understood Caleb. He's not like Dad at all, and it never made sense to me that they were friends. They shared a love of books and music, I guess, and they were both widowed young, but that's where the similarity ends. Caleb comes across as gruff and irritable, but that's just for show. He's the kind of guy who sits out on the rocks behind his house every morning at dawn, drinking coffee from a thermos and humming and singing to himself and waving at passing joggers on the beach. Dad would never have been caught dead doing something like that.

I'll never forget the time I was down at the recycling center with Caleb, helping him get rid of all his empty wine bottles. There was a young mother there with a little boy, and the kid was trying to help her throw a bunch of plastic milk jugs into one of those gigantic green bins, but the opening was too high for him and he kept missing. The mother was spending her whole time picking up what he was dropping, but she didn't seem to mind, not even when he chucked one at her left temple and nearly toppled her. Caleb watched the whole thing and laughed himself hoarse, and I remember thinking how refreshing it was to be with an older man who genuinely liked other people. Dad pretended to be a "hail-fellow-well-met" kind of guy, but it was just an act. Underneath that surface show of good will (which he trotted out reflexively for everybody but my brother and me) was a bone-deep contempt for most of the human race.

Anyway, Caleb's always been good to Tommy and me. He taught us how to fish, and how to sail a boat, and how to cook a lobster. He never had children of his own, so we spent a lot of time in his house when we were kids and he was fond of both of us—especially Tommy—but he told us early on that he didn't want to hear about any problems we were having with Dad. And even though Dad didn't care if we spent time with Caleb or not, he made sure we were never around when they were together. The message was clear: their friendship had nothing to do with us.

I haven't seen him for a while and I stick out my hand for him to shake. "Hi, Caleb. What brings you here?"

He points a stubby thumb at Tommy. "I heard this little bastard was back home and I thought I'd come over and see if he was still as ugly as he used to be." He reaches up and flicks my head with his middle finger. "Thanks a lot, by the way, for not letting me know he was coming."

"Sorry. I just found out myself a few days ago. You know Tommy."

"Unfortunately." He leans in close. The others are talking to each other and aren't paying any attention to us. "Who's that Philip character? I was hoping Tommy'd gotten over that phase by now and settled down with a nice girl."

Some things never change. Tommy came out to Caleb right after Dad's funeral, but Caleb just shook his head and changed the subject. To his credit, he never made a big deal out of it or treated Tommy any differently, but he also never took it seriously—which is why I've never bothered to tell him that I'm gay, too, when he pesters me about needing to date this or that available woman he's just met.

I sigh. "I don't think it's a phase, Caleb."

He grunts. "He'll get tired of it eventually, mark my words." His eyes fix on Simon and he steps away from me. "Aren't you Harold Hart's boy?"

Simon nods. "You know my dad?"

"I surely do. I met him at a luncheon at the Lion's Club the other day."

"Really? What was he doing there?" Simon sounds genuinely interested and steps closer to talk to Caleb. Caleb says something about the fine job Simon's dad is doing as DA, and then starts to gush a little about how much he enjoyed meeting him and what a nice guy he is. Simon smiles, pleased, and I have to bite my tongue to keep from revealing to Caleb how Simon got that "nice" big bruise on his ribs.

Dale interrupts to say good-bye to Caleb, then hoists himself up onto his tractor. We all back away as he turns it on and swings into the cornfield, dragging one of those scary-looking plow things behind him. It immediately sinks its teeth into the soil and starts ripping up the corn. The green stalks fall like a line of soldiers in a bad war movie.

I shake my head, wishing all over again that I'd said no to Cheri. I can't believe Dale didn't insist she'd have to wait at least until the corn was ripe and he'd harvested it. Aside from anything else, this is a criminal waste of good food. And for what? A few trinkets and a clay bowl, if she's lucky?

For no reason at all I suddenly get tears in my eyes. Tommy notices, of course, and starts to move toward me, but I shake my head and turn away before anyone else sees that I'm upset. I don't know what my problem is. It's not even my corn. The next thing you know I'll be weeping over soybeans and asparagus.

Cheri's almost jumping up and down, she's so excited. I don't want to watch this anymore, so I tell Caleb and Simon good-bye and say I'm going inside to take a nap.

Tommy and I had a huge marble collection when we were kids. We had everything: agates and shooters, steelies, migs, taws, cat's-eyes and boulders, and we had close to four thousand of them. We kept them in a wastebasket that was made to resemble a red fire hydrant, with a pointed yellow lid and a matching valve and spout that protruded from each side like jaundiced breasts. We occasionally dumped all the marbles out in our bedroom and they'd pour from the can in a loud wash of color, covering every square inch of available floor space between his bed and mine.

I don't know why we had so many of the things. We won a lot from other kids at school, but I think we also bought a bunch every time we got money from our grandmother (Dad's mom, who was the only grandparent still alive when I was born, died when I was nine), and I seem to remember Caleb once giving us several hundred at Christmas. Anyway, regardless of where they all came from, for some reason we were nuts about them.

We used to sit facing each other with our backs against our beds and our legs straddling our treasure, and Tommy would scoot forward until the bottoms of his feet touched mine, creating a diamond-shaped corral between us. We'd sink our hands into the mound and let the marbles run through our fingers, then we'd cull the herd by removing those with chips or gouges, setting them to the side for use the next day on the playground, because we didn't want to risk anything better in grudge matches with our classmates. After that we'd clear a space in the middle for the "crown jewels" of our stash: ten unique marbles that were permanently exempted from any and all games and contests, because the thought of losing any of them was unacceptable to Tommy and me. All of these ten were considered royalty, of course—from the black and tan shooter with a lime green splotch I found in the gutter behind the school, to the red and purple cat's-eye that looked like it was winking at you whenever you picked it up—but even in this rarefied company there was a distinct hierarchy: a small yellow and black agate that looked like a bumblebee was our all-time favorite, followed closely by a walnut-sized turquoise boulder, flecked with gold and silver.

It's stupid, but there is nothing more precious to me than the memory of sitting with my brother this way, squirreled away in our bedroom with all of our marbles in front of us. I remember his bare feet pressed against mine, and the sound of our voices overlapping as we plotted about how to get our hands on even more loot, and the kaleidoscope of colors that shifted and sparkled like the surface of the ocean whenever I ran my hand through the pile.

Every time we did this—and there were dozens of such times—I loved every minute of it. I don't know why. It wasn't always perfect; sometimes we'd argue about dumb stuff like who'd won the rusted steelie from Billy Oakley, sometimes Dad would destroy the moment by barging in and telling us to go outside because he was sick of us always "holing up" in our room (although I think his real reason for interrupting was because he hated knowing that we were having fun). Sometimes it was nothing but an hour or two of sheer idiocy; Tommy would fill his cheeks with marbles until he looked like a squirrel and I'd stick a couple up my nose and we'd pretend to have a serious conversation until one of us couldn't keep a straight face any longer and Tommy would end up spraying shrapnel from his mouth while I rolled around on the floor, convulsed with laughter.

But I guess it doesn't matter why I loved it. I just did. Playing with Tommy like this seemed like such a good thing to do. It felt so normal.

I don't mean normal for us. I mean *normal.* Like something other kids would do.

It's late afternoon when I wake up, and I feel disoriented and woozy. My bedroom is stuffy and hot and my skin is slimy and the sheet I've been sleeping on is soaked with sweat. There's a fan in the window pointed directly at me but it's just blowing hot air in from outside and it doesn't help at all. I sit up and put my feet on the floor. I can hear Tommy laughing softly downstairs, and then I hear Simon say something and both of them laugh together. I listen for other voices but they seem to be alone.

Goddammit. Why is Simon still here? And where is Philip? I stand up and pull on a pair of cotton shorts and start to move toward the staircase, but apparently I've gotten up too fast because the room spins and I almost black out for a second. While I'm waiting for my balance to come back there's another burst of muffled laughter from downstairs, which cuts off almost instantly.

There's something about the silence that makes my skin crawl. I take a deep breath and edge closer to the staircase before stopping again to listen. Nothing. If Tommy and Simon are talking, the noise from the fan is completely obscuring their voices. I lie down on the floor so that my head is hanging over the top step of the spiral staircase. There are no boards between the stairs, so I have a clear view of the futon couch they're sitting on.

Tommy has replaced his Speedo swimsuit with a skimpy pair of red tennis shorts, and Simon is still wearing nothing but cutoffs. Tommy's hand is on Simon's right knee, and the two of them are kissing. Their eyes are open, watching each other, and when Tommy lifts his head to come up for air, a thin string of saliva hangs for an instant between their lips like a spiderweb, then falls on Simon's chest. Tommy smiles and wipes it off with a finger, then he whispers something I can't hear, and moves his hand farther up Simon's thigh. Simon opens his legs for him and Tommy's hand disappears quickly under the faded denim of the cutoffs. Simon's mouth falls open and he drops his head to watch Tommy's progress.

I shove myself off the floor and stand still in the middle of the room, breathing hard.

I am going to beat the absolute living crap out of Tommy. It's all I can do to not charge down there and yank him off the couch right in front of Simon. What the fuck do they think they're doing? And what am I supposed to do about it?

I wait a few seconds, thinking, then I step quietly back toward the bed before stomping over to the staircase again. I cough a few times before heading down. By the time I get to the bottom they're sitting on opposite ends of the couch. They both have their legs crossed in exactly the same way, trying, no doubt, to hide matching erections. If it weren't so pathetic I'd laugh.

"Hey, big brother," Tommy says casually. "How was your nap?"

Simon forces a smile, trying hard to look innocent. "Hi, Mr. Bishop."

I fake a yawn. "Where is everybody?"

Tommy massages a bicep. "Philip wanted to cook dinner for us tonight so they all went to the wharf to buy some fish."

"I can't believe Philip went without you. You guys are usually attached at the hip."

"I told him I wanted to take a nap, too."

I can't quite manage to keep the edge out of my voice. "With Simon still here?"

Simon flushes and talks really fast. "I was going to go home and get a shirt and a dry pair of shorts before dinner but Tommy invited me in for a Pepsi and we got talking."

"I see."

There's an uncomfortable silence and Tommy gets suddenly preoccupied with a toenail. "Philip's a great cook. He's going to grill some tuna steaks for us."

"Sounds good." I make myself smile at Simon. "Why don't you run on home and get changed, kid, and while you're doing that Tommy can help me with something here."

Simon springs to his feet as if I've just poked him with a cattle prod. "Okay." He looks at Tommy, then at me, then back at Tommy. Tommy gives him a reassuring smile and tells him to hurry back. Simons says okay again, then heads for the kitchen.

I wait for nearly a minute after the screen door slams behind him to make sure he's out of earshot. Tommy sneaks glances at me every few seconds but doesn't say anything.

I lean down beside him and put my hands on my knees so that he has to look at me straight on. "Are you out of your mind?" I'm talking quietly, determined not to lose my temper. "He's a fifteen-year-old boy, Tommy. Does the word 'jailbait' mean anything to you?"

"What are you talking about?"

"Don't give me that. If I hadn't come downstairs when I did you'd have had him bent over the coffee table."

He jumps to his feet, his face full of indignation. "I can't believe you're accusing me of . . ."

"I saw you, Tommy. I saw you kissing him and feeling him up."

He sits down again and drops his head. "I thought you would have had enough of spying on people," he mutters. "Remember what happened the last time you did that?"

I can't believe he has the balls to bring that up. All of a sudden I'm yelling directly in his face. "This is my home, you asshole, and I'll do anything I fucking want in it! And don't you dare try and make me feel guilty for catching you doing something you *know*, you absolutely fucking *know*, you shouldn't be doing." I grab him by the shoulders and start shaking him. "Don't you realize you could get sent to prison for this stupid shit?"

He yanks away from me. "Calm down, Nathan. All I did was kiss him."

"And what's next? Jesus, Tommy, I've known quahogs that are smarter than you. Stop thinking with your dick for once in your sorry life. If you're not worried for you, then what about me? Simon is my student. Did it ever occur to you I could get fired for this?"

He rolls his eyes. "You obviously don't need me for that."

"You fucking *asshole!*" I lurch forward but he catches my wrist and my fist barely grazes his chin. I try to pull away but he won't let go. He drags me down on the couch with him and wraps his arms around me, immobilizing me for a second. I'm stronger than he is but not by much, and he's got a good grip.

"Calm down right now, Nathan," he whispers in my ear. "You're right, okay? I won't let anything else happen with Simon. I promise."

My laugh comes out harsh and loud. "Oh, you promise. I feel so relieved now. Do you cross your heart and hope to die? Let's do a pinkie swear, okay? That will make things all better."

He keeps talking quietly to me. Most of it is just nonsense words. I struggle halfheartedly for a minute but he's holding on tight and I finally give up and go limp. My face is pressed to his side and I can hear his heart, pounding fast. We're both sweating so much that when I lift my head my cheek sticks briefly to his skin.

I glare at him. I'm suddenly too tired to move. "You are the stupidest son of a bitch I've ever met."

He loosens his arms but doesn't let go. "I know. Stupidity runs in our family."

"You can say that again. I should have moved years ago and not left a forwarding address." I sigh. "Jesus, Tommy. What were you thinking?"

He shrugs. "I don't know. It just happened. We were talking about this and that and he kept checking me out and . . ."

"And you had no choice but to leap across the couch and jump his bones? Christ. You're almost thirty years old and you're still as horny as a goat." I shift to get more comfortable.

He studies me for a minute, then gives me a sly grin I remember all too well from our childhood and bends his head down to nibble at a patch of hair in the middle of my chest. "Baaa."

I smile in spite of myself. "Pervert."

"You're one to talk." He pulls back, still eyeing my chest, then he lowers his head again and touches my left nipple with the tip of his tongue.

My penis pops to attention in my shorts and I can feel him getting hard, too, under my back. I turn my head so I can bite him on the shoulder.

He yelps. "Ow! Quit it."

I rest my forehead against his neck, then I lightly head-butt his chin and pull away. We stare at each other for a while. His face registers one emotion after another—sadness, surprise, hilarity, tenderness—flipping by like different channels on a television set. I wonder if my own face is doing the same thing.

I finally clear my throat. "We should probably . . ."

He nods. "Yeah."

I sit up, and this time he lets me go.

When I get up in the morning, Cheri is running around in the ruin of the cornfield with three strangers. I hear them before I see them, their voices flattened and their words distorted into gibberish by the fan in my bedroom window. One is a woman about Cheri's age, but she's thin and tall, with wild gray hair and wire-rimmed glasses. The other two—a homely, skinny male, and a dumpy, unhappy-looking female—are considerably younger, and presumably here to assist the older woman.

Dr. Hampstead and her "team," I presume. From the University of Connecticut. I watch them for a minute from my window, then I get dressed and go downstairs. Tommy and Philip are still in bed, but they're about as far apart on the mattress as they can get, sleeping with their backs to each other.

They had a fight last night after Simon left and Kyle and Camille had gone to bed. I was already upstairs, but I could hear them whispering angrily to each other. At one point Philip raised his voice and said, "You are so full of shit, Tommy. I've seen the way you look at him." There were more whispers, then I heard Tommy say, "Why are you being such a jealous little bitch? I'm just being friendly with the poor kid." I couldn't hear the rest of it, but one or the other of them—probably Tommy—eventually got fed up with the argument and went outside, opening the screen door and sliding it shut again with enough force to rattle the headboard of my bed.

Tommy was an embarrassment during dinner. In spite of what he'd promised me just two hours earlier, he kept putting his hand on Simon's wrist while he talked to him, and once he reached up with his index finger and delicately brushed a piece of food from the corner of Simon's mouth. I tried to catch his eye but he ignored me, and Philip, on his other side, grew more and more sullen as the evening progressed.

Camille, meanwhile, watched in silence while Kyle babbled at me, and one time she even raised her eyebrows behind his back and mouthed "See?" when he hopped up to get more food for me before I'd even finished the first plateful.

I tried to keep my distance from him for the rest of the night, but while I was washing dishes he insisted on drying them, and every time he took a plate or a glass from me he managed to find a way to touch my hand or my arm. Camille was putting the clean dishes away, but when we were halfway done she murmured something about it looking like we had things well in control and she left us alone in the kitchen. Kyle watched her go but made no move to follow her, and when we finished cleaning up he asked if I wanted to go for a walk. He tried to act like it didn't matter one way or the other, but when I said no he looked like I'd just torn the head off his favorite teddy bear, and part of me wanted to take it back and say yes.

I couldn't help it. I know it's stupid and he's fucked-up and I feel like I've stumbled into the middle of an Oscar Wilde soap opera—but he's got soft green eyes, and long, delicate fingers, and last night he smelled salty and clean, like the ocean.

It makes me want to vomit saying something like that, but it's the truth.

And yes, okay, dammit, I haven't been laid in almost five years.

It's an extreme understatement to say that I haven't had much luck with boyfriends. Part of that, I suppose, is because there's not much to choose from in a town like Walcott, but even when I was away at college it was still pretty much the same story. Besides Andy, I've only been involved with a few other guys, and none of them lasted more than a week or two. And all of these so-called relationships ended badly; it seems I'm not very good at breaking up with people without also pissing them off royally.

The last one was the worst, though. His name was Richard Woolf and he was a landscape architect from Boston. Walcott's city council hired him to come and redesign the town park, and he moved here for a couple of months while he worked on it. I met him on the beach one weekend and he began stalking me until I was stupid enough to agree to have supper with him. (I should have known better, but what can I say? He was almost as pretty as Tommy, and he caught me on a bad day, when I was feeling especially lonely and didn't have the strength to trot out my standard rejection speech.) I drank too much and we ended up in bed that night, and the next morning he phoned three times in as many minutes to say things like "The memory of your kisses is driving me wild," and "I can't stop thinking about you."

God. How preposterous can you get? The dumb-ass didn't even *know* me.

Anyway, I immediately started to avoid him, but he didn't take the hint, so I eventually had to break off all contact with him to get him to leave me alone. He got desperate then and showed up on my doorstep one night, crying and screaming when I wouldn't let him in. It got so out of hand I had to shove him off the porch and threaten to call the cops before he'd go away.

Jesus. Why am I even thinking about sex again? The last thing I need is more shit like that in my life.

Philip stirs and opens his eyes. He blinks at me for a minute then raises up on an elbow. "What's up?"

"Morning. I didn't mean to wake you. I was just getting ready to go outside."

He nods and glances over at Tommy, who from all appearances is still sound asleep. Philip makes a face and turns back to me. "Can I talk to you later?' he whispers. "In private?"

You would not believe how many of Tommy's fuck-buddies have asked me that. They always want reassurance that he still loves them, or advice on how to keep from losing him. Poor bastards.

"Sure. Anytime."

I open the screen door and head out to the cornfield. Cheri sees me coming and waves. "Hi, Nathan," she calls out. "Come meet our archaeologists."

Jane Hampstead looks me in the eye and gives my hand a firm squeeze, and she thanks me for the opportunity to give her grad students—"Bill" and "Sally"—some "on-site experience." She has a

bit of a mustache, and her voice dips from high to low in the middle
of words, like Big Bird's on *Sesame Street.* Bill is a walking advertisement for malnutrition, with pallid skin, sunken eyes, and painfully
thin arms and legs, and Sally is anxious and chubby and monosyl-
labic. Even if Hampstead hadn't told me they were grad students I'd
have known it anyway; they're much too intense and self-involved
to be anything else. I shake their hands and wish them good luck.

Jane studies me with an amused look on her face. "Cheri tells
me you're skeptical about this project."

"That's an understatement. I think all you're going to find is a lot
of dirt and rocks and a couple of worms."

Cheri looks irritated but Jane just nods. "Ninety-nine percent of
the time that's all there is. We're really not expecting much here, either, but I accepted Cheri's invitation because I thought it would be
a good introduction to scavenge archaeology for Bill and Sally. And
you never know what you might unearth."

She scratches a sagging breast unconsciously. "Four years ago I
did a similar dig in Minnesota. A farmer uncovered some mysterious bones on his land and thought he'd found some kind of ancient burial ground." She snorts. "It turned out to be a private
cemetery for a family that lived there thirty years before he bought
the property."

She looks up at me. "But while we were investigating the site we
accidentally exhumed a three-thousand-year-old statuette of a
woman suckling a child that's remarkably similar to many Egyptian
artifacts from the same time period. We're still trying to figure out
how it got there."

She shakes her head and sighs. "It was the damndest thing I've
ever seen. Half of my colleagues are still insisting it's a hoax I
cooked up to make a name for myself." She gives me another little
smile. "I've participated in eleven other digs since then and haven't
found anything remotely as interesting, and I don't expect to find
anything noteworthy this time, either."

"So why do it?"

She shrugs. "Because it's fun, of course. And educational for my
students."

She excuses herself politely and wanders off. Bill and Sally trail after her like children in the wake of a pied piper.

Cheri waits until she's out of earshot then leans close and whispers, "Fun, my foot. She got almost half a million dollars from the Tate Museum for that statuette, but she spent that a long time ago and has been down on her luck since. That's why we were able to get her so cheaply."

I wince. "You're inspiring a lot of confidence here, Cheri."

She pats my arm. "Oh, don't worry. She's very good at what she does. And don't believe that stuff about her not expecting to find anything this time. She wouldn't be here if she didn't think there was a good chance to find something of value. Archaeologists are practical people."

"So what happens if you do find something valuable? Who gets the money?"

She sniffs. "By all rights the Historical Society should have complete ownership of any artifacts that surface, since we're the ones who are financing the dig in the first place. But we couldn't get Dr. Hampstead to sign on to the project without promising her a substantial share of anything we might choose to sell." She glances at me. "Not to worry, Nathan. If we find something significant, you'll get a small share as well, as owner of the property. Our lawyer is drawing up the contracts this week for everybody to sign. It's all aboveboard."

She goes to join the others and I watch them all as they walk to the far end of the field. At that distance the sun is already hot enough to refract the air around them and turn their bodies into vague silhouettes. Not far from them is an old oak tree, and from here its leaves look black. As they get close to it, the branches suddenly erupt, and it takes me a minute to figure out that what I thought were leaves were really enormous crows, now swirling around in the sky, crying out to each other in loud, raucous voices before settling once again on the tree.

Where did they come from? I've never seen that many crows in my whole life. I squint at the four humans by the tree again, but the sun is too bright and I can't tell them apart. They look like cartoon stick figures, and the crows over their heads sound like the laugh track in a bad sitcom.

I can't believe I agreed to this.

I ask Simon if I can speak to him after class. He says sure and waits patiently while I answer another kid's questions and argue with Vernette about the grade she got on a recent assignment.

Simon told me he apologized to Vernette like I asked him to, and he must have, because I'm sure she would have complained if he hadn't. They seem to have reached some kind of understanding, but there's still obvious hostility between them: when Vernette stumps past Simon's desk on her way out of the room they pointedly ignore each other.

I walk over and close the door behind her. It closes easily now; the janitor apparently filed down the wood so it wouldn't stick anymore. The glass pane has already been replaced in the frame, but the school opted for clear glass this time instead of the more expensive, old-fashioned frosted stuff. Baker will no doubt deduct the cost from my next paycheck, and I won't be surprised at all if he charges me for the labor as well as the supplies—even though it never would have happened if the stupid door hadn't been sticking in the first place. He's probably sitting in his office right now adding up the numbers and rubbing his fat, greasy hands together.

God, I hate that son of a bitch.

I turn back and sit in the desk next to Simon. He's trying to look cheerful and relaxed, but his fingers are fidgeting with his notebook.

"What's up?" he asks.

"Not much. I just thought we should talk for a minute." I lean forward and put my elbows on my knees. "This is kind of awkward, Simon, and I don't want you to misunderstand what I'm saying, but I think it's probably better if you don't spend so much time at my cottage for the next few days."

The expression on his face is awful. If I'd slapped him he couldn't look more surprised and hurt.

But I was awake most of the night thinking about this and I've made up my mind. I rush on. "You're a great kid and this has nothing to do with you, and after my company leaves you're more than welcome to come over now and then to visit. But . . ."

I can't go on. He's crying.

"Why?" he asks. "What did I do?"

I have to be careful here. I can't tell him I saw Tommy and him fooling around on the couch, because if that ever gets out and there's legal trouble I won't be able to claim I didn't know what was going on. I know how cowardly that sounds, but I'll be damned if I'm going to take a fall because my stupid brother can't keep his dick in his pants. So I have no choice but to lie.

I clear my throat. "You didn't do anything. Everybody really likes you. But I was talking to all of them this morning and they said they needed some private time now to do some couples kind of stuff. That's what they came up here for, after all."

He drops his head. I put my hand on his shoulder. "Please don't take this personally, Simon. They want time apart from me, too."

I'm making myself sick, so I stop talking. The truth is Philip hates him, and most of my lovely house guests weren't even awake this morning when I left, and the only "couples stuff" any of them seem to want to do is argue with or ignore each other.

He raises his head after a minute. His eyes are red. "I don't understand. The last thing Tommy said last night was that he'd see me tomorrow after you and I got out of class."

He looks and sounds completely baffled as to why, after several days of welcoming him into my home, I'm now telling him to take a hike. I'm suddenly remembering when he called Tommy and me his only friends in Walcott, and I feel like shit for lying to him.

But he's not as innocent as he wants me to think. I also need to remember that he knew enough yesterday to try to act like nothing was going on between Tommy and him when I interrupted their make-out session on the couch. I'm sure his hurt is genuine, but I'm equally sure it's got more to do with frustrated sexual desire than with feeling left out.

I squeeze his shoulder. "I know he did. But to be honest, Philip is a little jealous of how well you and Tommy are getting along, and they need some time to work on their relationship."

He blinks at me nervously. I can almost read his mind; he's wondering if I know what's really going on between Tommy and him. I play dumb. "I know that sounds silly, but Philip's kind of insecure." I give his shoulder another squeeze and let go. "Tommy doesn't exactly have the best track record when it comes to treating his boyfriends well."

There. I've done everything I needed to do. I've let him know I like him and he's welcome to hang out with me after my guests leave, and I've given him a legitimate reason for staying away, and—just in case he was having any fantasies about some kind of future with my brother—I've even warned him a little bit about Tommy's propensity for infidelity. Now maybe he'll make himself scarce until I've got my house back to myself, and all of this messy stuff will just go away.

Simon licks his lips. "Mr. Bishop, did Tommy tell you that we kissed yesterday while you were taking a nap?"

Fuck. Now what?

I put my hands together. My palms are sweating. "He didn't have to tell me. I figured it out."

He flushes. "I thought so. You were acting pretty strange when you came downstairs and saw us sitting on the couch."

"Simon, I . . ." I chew on my lip for a minute. "I don't know what to say. But what happened between you and Tommy shouldn't have happened. He's almost twice your age. It's not right. He shouldn't have done that."

He shakes his head, and when he talks I can barely hear him. "It wasn't like that. Please don't be mad at Tommy. I wanted him to kiss me." He picks at the wire binding on his notebook. "I asked him to."

I sigh. "Even if that's true, he still shouldn't have done it. You're only fifteen." I tilt my head so he's looking me right in the eye. His irises are so blue they almost look fake. "Did you really ask him to?"

He nods.

"Are you sure?"

The words come out in a torrent. "Well, no, I didn't say it out loud but it's what I was thinking. I was watching his face while we were talking and when he leaned toward me I moved closer to him, too, and shit, I don't know, it just happened." He looks back down at his notebook. "I haven't been able to think about anything else since then. All last night during dinner I was hoping he'd find a way that we could do it again."

Goddamn my brother. I knew I should never have allowed Simon to come within a hundred feet of him.

I reach over and put my hand on the side of his face. "That's exactly why you shouldn't be around him anymore. He can't control himself and you're way too young to get involved with somebody like him." Tears start rolling down his face again and I pat his cheek. "I'm sorry, Simon."

He nods again and suddenly lurches out of his seat. The next thing I know he's on his knees and he's got his arms wrapped around me and he's crying into my shirt. His hair smells like apples. I pat him on the back a few times and wait for him to get himself in control.

From the corner of my eye I sense movement and look up. Ted Baker is standing in the hall, looking through the clean new window of my door. His lips are pursed together and he's got a wide-eyed, panicky look on his face. He reaches for the knob.

I shake my head at him and even though he glares, he surprises me after a second by nodding, then stepping out of sight. I give Simon a final squeeze and gently pull away from him.

The second Simon walks out, Baker charges in and slams the door behind him. The glass trembles in the frame and even though he flinches he pretends not to notice.

He leans against the wall and crosses his beefy arms over his chest. "Just what do you think you're doing? Have you lost your mind?"

"You should be more careful, Ted." I walk over to my desk and start collecting my things. "If the principal catches you slamming the door like that he'll put a note in your folder saying you've been naughty."

"Don't you dare take that tone with me. Not after what I just saw."

I know where this is going but I'm not going to give him the satisfaction of seeing me squirm. "What are you talking about?"

"You know full well what I'm talking about. You were just touching a kid in a very intimate way, and if that isn't bad enough, you did it when the two of you were all alone in a classroom. I didn't think it was possible for any teacher to be that stupid. Not even you."

"Give me a break, Ted. Simon's got some problems at home right now and he practically threw himself on me. What was I supposed to do? Shove him down on the floor and call him a mama's boy?" I stuff papers in my briefcase and snap it shut. "All I did was give him a hug."

He pushes himself off the wall. "Oh, is that all? Just a hug? How sweet." He starts to pace. "Teachers get fired for things like that and schools get sued, Nathan. What if that kid turns out to be some kind of psycho who decides to accuse you of molesting him?"

"Simon's not like that. He's just . . ."

"Or what if he's a queer? What if he's got a crush on you and he goes home and tells his folks that Mr. Bishop just gave him the nicest, sweetest hug ever and would they mind if he started wearing makeup and titty-tassels now?"

My mind flashes back to when I almost strangled this dumb-shit for peeing on my brother's clothes. I should have ignored Tommy that day and finished the job. I'm tempted to try again but now the weight of his jowls would probably snap my fingers before I could get a good grip.

I pick up my briefcase and head toward the door. "You're being ridiculous."

He steps in my way, putting his hand up like a traffic cop. "I'm just telling you this for your own good. That kid is bad news, Nathan."

I brush past him. "Thanks for your concern, Ted. I'll be sure to knee him in the groin the next time he has a meltdown in my room."

As I'm opening the door he calls after me. "I'm afraid I'm going to have to speak to Madeline about this."

I look over my shoulder. He's got his hands in his pockets and a grim expression on his face. I shrug. "Go ahead. Do you really think she'll have a problem with a teacher for trying to comfort a kid?"

All of a sudden I'm all too aware of why Simon needed comfort in the first place. Jesus. What if either Ted or Madeline talks to Simon and finds out what happened between him and Tommy? Or what if they talk to Simon's parents and find out how much time he's been spending at the cottage? Will they suspect something inappropriate is going on between him and me? A bead of cold sweat runs from my armpit to my waist.

He nods. "I'm afraid so. This isn't an episode of *Little House on the Prairie,* Nathan. You just can't touch kids like that anymore, and if I don't say something and it comes back to bite us in the ass we could both get fired. I'm sorry. It's a damn shame things are like that nowadays, but that's the way it is. I don't want to report you, but I've got to protect myself and the school."

The most troubling thing about all of this is the look on his face. I'd expect him to be gloating, but he actually seems a little sad.

I roll my eyes and walk out the door, pretending I've never heard anything half as stupid in my entire life. But all the way to the car my heart is racing in my chest, and my stomach has a knot in it the size of a football.

By the time I pull into the clearing by the cottage, Dr. Hampstead and her slaves have already staked out the southeast corner of the cornfield. I get out of the car and walk around the house to see what they're up to.

It's still just as hot as it's been for the last week, but as I get close to the field a big black cloud blocks out the sun for a few seconds and the temperature drops nearly ten degrees. I sigh with relief at the sudden change, but the cloud passes by and the sun immediately resumes its slow roasting of the earth. I peel my shirt off and wrap it around my head like a turban. Ever since I left the school, nervous sweat has been pouring out of me and my armpits smell sour and acrid. I can't wait to get to the ocean and wash the stench away.

Bill and Sally are doing something with twine between several of the stakes, and Dr. Hampstead is standing a few feet away, scribbling in a notebook. Cheri Tipton is nowhere to be seen, even though her car is still in the driveway. Sometime in the last couple of hours a long metal table has materialized next to the field, and there's a Porta Potty discreetly tucked away at the edge of the woods farthest from the cottage.

Hampstead looks up and waves as I get close, but then sticks her face immediately back in her notebook without saying anything. She's wearing a white baseball cap with a "Smithsonian Museum" logo printed over the bill, a long-sleeved white cotton blouse, and dark green corduroy pants. As an added fashion bonus, she's also sporting a pair of high-top, black Reeboks on her feet, and the fly of her pants is partly open, revealing a disturbing glimpse of faded pink panties.

Bill and Sally are playing with their string and their sticks too intently to even notice me. Bill is a scarecrow of a man, all elbows and knees and shoulder blades, and his head is mostly teeth. His ass and chest are nonexistent, and his legs and arms look like skewers sticking out of the meager shish kebab of his torso. But what he lacks in body fat Sally more than makes up for. Her gut is straining at the fabric of her yellow T-shirt, and as she bends over, the crack of her ample butt smiles vertically at me over the top of her belt. I'd expected to see shovels and pickaxes and a bunch of mole holes in the ground, but so far there are no tools at all, and it looks as if they haven't done any digging.

"Dr. Hampstead?" Sally calls out, "Is this how you wanted it?"

Hampstead glances up and scowls. "No, Sally, it's not. The stakes still need to go deeper. How many times do I have to tell you that?"

She returns her attention to her notebook, and Bill shrugs at Sally and suddenly mimes whacking off behind Hampstead's back. Sally lowers her bleached-blond head and titters, making her breasts jiggle. Hampstead shoots a glare over her shoulder, but Bill is now standing perfectly still, absorbed in his work. She narrows her eyes at Sally and turns away again. Bill sees me watching them and gives me an innocent smile.

Cheri steps out of the Porta Potty. "Hi, Nathan," she calls out. Instead of walking across the field to get to me, she picks her way along the edge. Apparently the field is now off-limits to nonarchaeologists.

I wait until she's standing next to me before I say anything. "Hi,

Cheri. When do they start burrowing? Shouldn't they be squirreling away a few acorns by now to get ready for next winter?"

"You have the strangest sense of humor." She shields her eyes from the sun. "They won't start to dig for several days. They have to survey the land and lay out a grid first. They're coming up with a plan of attack."

"Why don't they just bring in a backhoe and get it over with?"

"Don't be stupid," she snaps. "You know full well it's not done that way."

I blink, surprised at her burst of temper. "Too much caffeine today or what?"

She sighs. "Sorry. Every once in a while I hear your father's voice when you're talking and it sets me off. He always went out of his way to goad me."

I grimace. "Thanks a lot, Cheri. You know how much I love being compared to my dad."

She smiles a little and pats my arm. "It's only once in a while. Most of the time you sound like your mom."

There she goes again. I want to pin her down and ask where she gets off pretending to have been bosom buddies with my mom when I'm reasonably sure they were never more than passing acquaintances, but it's too hot and I don't have the energy for it.

She waits for me to say something but when I'm quiet she gets uncomfortable and keeps talking. "Jane says a cornfield is usually the worst possible place for a dig because of all the surface disturbance, but what we're looking for is at least six or seven hundred years old and she's hoping that all the farming since hasn't gone deep enough to ruin whatever might be there. It's even possible the indigenous peoples who lived here before the Puritans weren't necessarily . . ."

I exaggerate a yawn and she falls silent.

Another cloud skims over the sun and I glance up at the sky, hoping for evidence of approaching rain, but the clouds are few and far between. I look at the field again in time to catch Bill scratching his crotch with one hand and picking his nose with the other.

I step close to Cheri and nod my head towards Bill. "If he finds something old in his nostril, will it belong to the Historical Society, too?"

She tries to scowl at me but after a second her hand comes up and covers her mouth and she giggles. "Stop it, Nathan."

I grin. "Maybe you should pay for permission to excavate his butt, too, while you're at it. He may have the mother lode hidden up there."

Her other hand flies up to her mouth, too, and her whole body shakes with laughter. Hampstead and Bill and Sally all stop what they're doing and stare at us.

Hampstead frowns. "Excuse me, but we're trying to work here. Perhaps you could have your conversation elsewhere?" She's irritated, but her voice is still doing its muppet thing, and it's hard to take her seriously.

I nod. "Of course. I'm so sorry." I turn to go but stop for one last whisper to Cheri. "Jeez. I didn't know Big Bird could be such a bitch."

Cheri turns bright pink and swats at me. "Go away, Nathan. Right now."

She heads for Dr. Hampstead, calling out an apology but still trying not to laugh.

When I slide open the screen on the back door of the cottage and step inside, the first thing I see is Philip, propped up on the futon, reading a book. Instead of his usual ponytail, his hair is loose and hanging over his shoulders. He's wearing a white T-shirt with a doctored picture of Mount Rushmore on it, displaying the likenesses of our four greatest presidents: Marilyn Monroe, Judy Garland, Barbra Streisand, and Bette Midler.

Cute. If this guy weren't gay, he'd have to throw out his entire wardrobe.

He looks up when I slide the screen door shut. "Hi, Nathan. I didn't know you were home."

"I just got here."

He leans forward and looks past me at the screen door. "Is that little shit with you?"

"Simon? He's not coming over today."

He smiles. "That's too bad." He leans back again, tickling his chest. "Did you see Cheri's makeup? What in God's name was she thinking? She must have applied it with a dust mop and a spatula."

"Uh-huh. Where is everybody?"

"Kyle and Camille went for a walk on the beach, and Tommy's having coffee with some old friend of his who called while I was in the shower. He said he'd be back in just a little while."

"What old friend was that?"

And why the hell didn't this bozo go along, too, so I could have some time alone?

He sets the book on the table next to him. "Karen something-or-other. He said they were in the same class all the way through school."

I knew every kid in Tommy's class and there was no one named Karen. I tell Philip that and he looks confused. "I must have heard him wrong. But I could have sworn he said Karen."

I shrug. "It doesn't matter. I'm just curious, because Tommy pretty much hated everyone in his class. He once told me he'd rather pour boiling oil in his navel than go to a high school re-union."

He nods, but I can tell he's not really listening. I excuse myself and start to head upstairs to change into my swimsuit.

He stops me before I get to the steps. "Can we talk for a minute?"

"Sure." I walk over and he moves his feet to make room for me on the futon. I sit down next to him. "What's up?"

He bites his lip and plays with a strand of his hair. "What you said to Tommy the other night . . . you know, that stuff about him using one guy after another and then dumping them and moving on. Was that for real?"

"I'm sorry. I never would have said that if I'd known you could hear us."

"That's okay. I just need to know if . . . I mean, he's not really like that, is he?"

I study him, wondering how honest I should be. I'm struck again by how physically beautiful he is. His face is still and perfectly sym-metrical, like the face of a statue. His eyes are big and soft and brown, and his body is a walking wet dream, and there's a vulnerability in his expression, especially now, that's almost irresistible. Tommy's a sucker for guys like Philip, but for some reason I'm mostly immune to their sex appeal. What turns me off about these interchangeable pretty boys is that even when they're not coming on to you, they know all too well how they look, and they know how to use their looks to get what they want.

And right now what Philip wants is for me to lie to him. He wants me to tell him Tommy has been a bad boy in the past, but now he's completely ready to settle down, and I've never seen him so in love with anybody before, and the two of them will live happily ever after. He's thinking if he bats his eyes just so and puts the right amount of trust and sweetness on his face, I won't be able to do anything but tell him exactly what he wants to hear.

I shouldn't admit this, but part of me always enjoys unsettling these spoiled little mannequins of Tommy's, even though I know their feelings for him are genuine enough and it's kind of cruel to dash their hopes so abruptly.

I sigh. "I'm sorry, Philip. I know you don't want to hear this, but Tommy is the skankiest whore in the world. He makes Madonna look like Mary Poppins."

His face falls, but he shakes his head stubbornly. "Maybe he used to be like that, but he told me that I'm the first person he's ever really loved, and he wants to spend the rest of his life with me. He said that last week."

There are tears in his eyes and he looks miserable, but I'm not about to sit through a second crying jag this morning. I pat him on the shin and stand up. "You're probably right. Maybe he's changed."

I'm halfway up the stairs when he clears his throat. "You don't suppose he's with Simon right now, do you?"

I get another knot in my stomach. "No. I had a little talk with Simon this morning and I don't think we'll be seeing him anymore."

He locks eyes with me for a second, then he tries to smile. "Good. I hope you're right."

He thanks me, then he picks the book up again and I go on upstairs. I change into my swimsuit and my sandals, but as I'm getting ready to head back down, his last question starts to grate on me. I walk over to the phone and stand beside it for a minute, then I pick it up and punch in star-six-nine, and the computer voice comes on and tells me the number of my last incoming call. I don't recognize it. I stare at the phone for a long time, then I dial the number. After the fourth ring a machine answers and tells me I've reached the Hart residence, and if I want to leave a message for Harold or Bonita or Simon, I should do so after the beep.

I hang up.

Goddammit, Simon.

He must have run home and called while I was still talking to Ted Baker. Right after I told him to stay the hell away.

I stare at the floor, wondering where they are. My brother knows every hidden nook and cranny in Walcott where you can go when you need a nice, quiet place to fuck.

I can't believe this is happening. I run a hand through my hair and look out the window at the field. Twine is everywhere, stretched taut like a giant spiderweb, waiting patiently for hapless prey to stumble into it.

Tommy, you stupid, stupid son of a bitch.

The second time I tried to kill myself, I decided drowning was the way to go. I'd read somewhere that after you got past the initial panic of running out of air and finally managed to fill your lungs with water, the end would be painless and quick, and even peaceful, owing to some chemical reaction in your oxygen-starved brain. Besides, I'd never been afraid of the ocean, and it seemed kind of comforting to know that the last thing I'd feel would be saltwater on my skin.

What an idiot.

I snuck out of the cottage an hour before dawn one morning when Tommy was still asleep. I got dressed in the darkness and he turned over once and muttered when I opened our bedroom door, but he didn't wake up, and Dad, of course, was still upstairs, snoring loud enough for me to hear him in the kitchen. It was late spring and I was sixteen. I was wearing sneakers and sweatpants and a Windbreaker, and I had a canvas backpack to fill with rocks once I got to the beach. I ran most of the way there because I knew the water was going to be cold and I wanted my body to be warm when I first went in.

It was still dark at the beach, but the sun was close enough to making an appearance that I could see just fine, even though everything had a grayish-red tint. The backpack was a big one, and by the time I crammed it with stones it probably weighed close to seventy pounds. I tied it tightly to my waist with rope, took a last deep breath, and started running toward the water as fast as I could.

I got as far as knee-level in the surf when I heard sudden footsteps echoing mine. I shot a startled glance over my shoulder just in time to see Tommy plunging through the water a few feet behind. I yelled in surprise and tried to run faster but he closed the gap in seconds and tackled me. We both went under, and the backpack squeezed all the air out of my lungs at once.

I came up swearing and spluttering. "God damn you, Tommy! What the fuck are you doing here? Leave me alone!" My teeth were chattering.

He hauled off and punched me in the jaw hard enough to knock me down again, then he grabbed hold of the backpack and yanked me to my feet and started screaming in my face. "You stupid fucking cocksucker! Who the hell do you think you are?" He punched me again but grabbed me before I could fall. "You goddamn stupid fucking asshole!"

Then he burst into tears and fell on his knees in front of me. He wrapped his arms around my waist and buried his face in my stomach. The water came up to his ribs. I stood there dazed, with a throbbing jaw and blood running from my nose. Both of us were shaking from the cold.

He looked up at me. There was snot on his upper lip and his eyes were red and full. His skin was pale blue. "I'll kill you myself the next time you pull something like this, Nathan. I swear to God. Don't you fucking dare try to leave me."

I started to cry, too. "I can't do this anymore, Tommy."

"Can't do what?"

I wiped my nose on my shoulder and left a smear of blood on my jacket. "I can't handle . . ." I tried to keep talking but couldn't.

He waited for me to go on but when I didn't say anything else he squeezed my waist hard. "Can't handle what?"

My tongue refused to move. I looked over his head at the beach.

He shook me in frustration. "Nathan? What can't you handle?"

I fought without success to untie the knot in the rope holding the backpack on me. "Us," I whispered, staring down into his face.

He pulled back a little. "What are you talking about?"

I made my voice work. "You know. Don't pretend you don't."

He bit his lip and looked away. "Don't be a moron. Everything's fine. We're fine, I mean."

"No, we're not, and you know it." I pushed at his arms. "Why can't you just let me go?"

He swallowed a few times and gazed around me at the ocean. A fresh batch of tears welled up in his eyes, but after a few seconds he looked up at me again and forced a smile. He reached up and put his hand on my cheek. "If you'd really wanted that, you wouldn't have made so much goddamn noise leaving the house. Next time just hire a brass band to play a fanfare for you."

I flushed and knocked his hand away. "I don't know what you're talking about."

He snorted. "Bullshit. Do you think I don't notice when you're getting ready to do something stupid? Do you think I haven't been watching you for the last two weeks, waiting for you to try something again? Christ. You're the most transparent person I've ever met. You wanted me to stop you. It would serve you right if I'd let you come here by yourself."

"I wish to God you had. Next time I'll . . ."

His head snapped up and I fell silent when I saw his expression. He got slowly to his feet and when he started talking again his voice was grim. "There's not going to be a next time, Nathan. I'm sick of this shit, and I know how to make it stop."

I forced a laugh. "What are you going to do? Stay awake twenty-four hours a day? Chain me to the radiator?"

He shook his head. "Nope. I don't have to do that. I'm done fucking around and worrying about you." He got a weird half-smile on his face. "So this is how we're going to play it from now on. If you die, I die."

I glared at him. "What's that supposed to mean?"

He reached out and began fumbling with the rope at my waist. "I mean it, Nathan. If you pull this shit again and I'm not here to stop you, then as soon as I hear you're dead, I'll kill myself, too."

My breath caught in my throat and I shoved his fingers away. "That's the stupidest thing I've ever heard. You'll do no such thing."

He grabbed my arm and hauled me toward dry land. "Try me, asshole."

I'm still standing by the phone in my bedroom when Kyle and Camille get back from the beach. I can hear them talking to Philip for a minute, then Camille calls my name from the bottom of the stairs. I don't answer.

The stairwell creaks and her head appears. "Nathan? What are you doing?"

I clear my throat and shrug. "Nothing. Just getting ready to go to the beach."

"You look upset. Is everything all right?"

"Perfect. Couldn't be better." I take a deep breath and blow it out. "Do you need something?"

She frowns and comes the rest of the way up the stairs. "Kyle and Philip and I are going to head uptown to the grocery store. Want to come?"

I shake my head. "I don't think so."

She looks disappointed. "Can we borrow your car, then? I was going to use Tommy's, but he's apparently out visiting an old school buddy."

I dig my keys from the pocket of the shorts I was wearing earlier and toss them to her. "Can you drive a stick?"

She nods and pushes her hair behind her ears. "We'll be back in about an hour, if that's okay. I want to stop at that clothing store I saw the other day." She gives me a sad smile and drops her voice to a whisper. "I want to buy something sexy on the off-chance Kyle might notice I'm alive. Pretty pathetic, huh?"

"You're not pathetic."

She waves a hand. "Actually, I was thinking what might do the trick is if I bought a lot of men's clothes, shaved my head, and stuffed a roll of socks down the front of my pants. What do you think?" Her lips tremble. "Don't you want to come along and give me a few pointers on how to look butch? Philip and Kyle won't be any help at all."

She stands in the same place for what seems like an eternity, and it suddenly occurs to me she's waiting for me to say something else.

I force a smile. "No, thanks. I'll stay here. Have fun."

Her face falls but she tries to smile back. "Are you sure I can't talk you into it? I'll let you be mean to Kyle and Philip."

"That's really tempting, but I don't think so. I'm sorry. I'm not up to it today."

She hesitates and her expression changes. "Are you sure you're okay? You're not acting like yourself."

"I'm fine. I'm just tired, that's all. I think I may take a nap before I go to the beach."

She keeps standing there. What the hell does she want from me?

I sit on the end of my bed. "Really, Camille. I'm fine."

"Sure you are." She wanders over and squats in front of me, looking up into my face. "What's going on? You're behaving as if I'm not the only person in the world with a problem, and if you don't stop it right now, I may have to alter my entire view of how the universe works."

I laugh a little and lean down so my eyes are a few inches from hers. She looks fragile and strung out. "Better start altering, sweetheart. I'm the High Priest of self-involvement. You're a mere acolyte."

She reaches up and touches my chin. She's wearing perfume that smells like apricots. "What's wrong, Nathan? Tell me."

I try to keep my voice steady. "I can't, Camille."

"Please? It would make me feel better to know that someone else's life is as fucked-up as mine."

I stare at my lap. "No problem there."

She tugs on my ear. "So tell me."

I shake my head. "If I say it out loud, I'm afraid it will come true." I lean into her touch. "Okay?"

Her finger travels up my cheek and into my hair. I expect her to argue more, but she finally nods and drops her hand. "Fair enough. But if you change your mind . . ."

I nod back. She waits a while longer, then stands up again and tells me she'll be home soon.

She goes downstairs and I lie on the bed and put a pillow over my face. I hear her tell Philip and Kyle that I'm not going with them. Kyle says something I can't hear and Camille whispers back and then there's a quick, heated exchange, most of which I miss, but Kyle has apparently decided not to go, either.

Wonderful.

The front door slams a few seconds later. I hear my car start up and pull away. Jane Hampstead calls out something to Bill in the cornfield, and then there's silence. I take the pillow off my face and stare at the ceiling.

What the hell am I going to do about Tommy and Simon? If they're doing what I think they're doing, I've got to find a way to stop it before anyone else finds out. I've got to get Tommy back to New York and then somehow convince Simon to never say a word to anybody. Surely he'll understand that nothing good can come of this.

Who am I kidding? The damage is done. If they've already had sex, Simon will latch on to Tommy like a barnacle on a rock. We'll be lucky if he doesn't take out an ad in the Walcott *Gazette* announcing their impending marriage.

My thoughts are flying around in my skull like fireflies in a jar, but all of a sudden I'm unbearably tired and can't stay awake. I roll over and close my eyes.

I'm just starting to doze off when I hear footsteps on the stairs. Kyle. He's trying to be quiet, but the staircase gives him away. I hear him reach the top, then he stops. I keep my eyes closed, hoping he'll turn around and leave me alone if I don't acknowledge him.

He starts moving again toward the bed. Christ. What the hell is he doing?

I jump a little when he touches my shoulder, and I roll onto my back and pretend to be waking up. "Kyle? What's going on?"

"Were you asleep?" He sits down next to me. He's wearing a pair of putrid lime green shorts and a black T-shirt. His eyes travel over my body for a second before settling on my face. "Camille said you were upset about something. I thought I'd see if you wanted to talk."

"I'm not upset. I'm just tired. I didn't sleep very well last night."

"How come? Is something bothering you?"

Yeah, something's bothering me, you moron. My job's in jeopardy, my brother's banging one of my underage students, a bunch of strangers are ripping up my backyard, and a loser with really bad taste in clothes is perched on my mattress drooling over me when he should be with his goddamn wife at the grocery store.

I put my arm over my eyes. "Not really. I've just got a lot on my mind."

"Uh-huh."

I wait for him to get up and go away, but he keeps sitting there. He shifts his weight on the mattress a little and I hear him swallow, then a second later he drops a sweaty hand on my stomach.

I take my arm off my face and look up at him but he won't meet my eyes. He's watching his fingers move along my ribs. "You're in really good shape." His voice comes out strained. "It must be all the swimming you do."

My breathing is getting faster and my heart is speeding up. "Kyle." I need to stop this before it goes any farther. I raise up on my elbows. "What do you think you're doing?"

He doesn't answer. His hand drops to my navel and tugs lightly at the short hairs there. My hard-on is obvious, pushing upward and turning the loose rayon fabric of my swimsuit into a miniature pup tent. He stares at it, mesmerized, then he swallows again, loudly, and snakes his fingers under the waistband.

I grab his wrist just as he takes hold of my cock. "Quit it, Kyle."

He doesn't let go. "Why? We both want to."

He's right, of course, but the last thing I need right now is more complications. I take a ragged breath. "Oh, well, let's see. Remember the woman who was here a few minutes ago? Red hair, about yea-high? I think she might have a little problem with this."

He grimaces. "Things haven't been so good with us lately. She keeps asking if I'm gay."

"I wonder where she got that idea." I'm still holding his wrist, but he's working away, undeterred. I gasp when he squeezes the tip of my penis, and he smiles.

I do want this. What he's doing feels great, and I'm horny beyond belief, and I would love to lose myself for a few minutes in the oblivion of another man's body. Even this clown. Tommy would do it in a heartbeat, and to hell with the consequences.

Shit. I pry his fingers off and slide away from him.

He reaches for me when I get to my feet. "What's the matter?"

I step back. "I'm going to the beach."

"Come on, Nathan, please? I really want to . . ." His voice rasps a little. "I'll do anything you want."

I'll say one thing for him: he's direct. I shake my head. "Correct me if I'm wrong, but weren't you claiming to be straight just a few days ago?"

He looks at the floor. "I thought I was." When he looks up again the expression on his face is pathetic.

I straighten my swimsuit. "Look, Kyle, I'm flattered and everything, and under different circumstances I'd like nothing better than to mess around with you. But I'm not about to go to bed with you while Camille is a guest in my home and you guys are still theoretically together. Call me old-fashioned, but that's just too tacky for words."

He looks like a starving urchin outside a restaurant window. "But I really like you," he says.

"I don't think you know what you like. And I don't want to be your guinea pig while you try to figure it out."

He drops his head again.

I grab a towel. "I'll be back in a while."

He calls out when I start down the stairs. "Don't tell Camille, Nathan, okay? Please?" He sounds frantic.

I look over my shoulder. He's hugging himself and there are tears on his cheeks.

I nod. "Absolutely not a problem."

I was with Dad when he died. You're probably expecting me to say we reached an understanding before he passed away—something along the lines of him gazing at me lovingly, speechless, while I held his hand and Pachelbel's Canon in D played in the background.

Well, no such luck. Dad was true to his code: he was an asshole to the bitter end. Granted, he had liver cancer and was in a lot of pain, but as I sat in his hospital room for the better part of three days, watching him fight with the tubes sticking out of his nose, he never said a word to me except for things like "Get me some water," or "Tell the nurse I want more morphine."

He ignored Tommy, too, but when Caleb Farrell came to visit, Dad would rouse himself and try to smile, and he'd tell me to get out so they could speak in private. I asked Caleb later what they talked about, and he just shook his head and said Dad wouldn't want him to answer that.

Which, of course, begs the question: what exactly was the nature of their relationship? Why did Dad not want Tommy or me to hear what they discussed? I'm not suggesting they were lovers or anything like that; the idea of those two grizzled old homophobes getting it on is ludicrous. Nor do I think Dad had any deep dark secrets to hide, or any deathbed confessions. For all I know they may have talked about the weather, or football, or chess. It doesn't matter, I suppose, but the secrecy bugs the crap out of me.

Was Dad kind to Caleb? Was he funny, or thoughtful, or wise? Did they laugh together, or bitch about women, or argue about the existence of God, or compare notes on the best single malt Scotch? I'll never know. But Caleb wept at Dad's memorial service. Tommy and I didn't. The decent side of my father—and he must have had redeeming qualities, because people like Caleb don't cry for you if you're a complete piece of shit—was a side he never bothered to show Tommy and me.

Except, of course, by accident. Like when he sang at Claudia Burke's funeral, the year before he himself died.

Ed Burke, who used to work for Dad at the paper, asked Dad to sing something when his wife passed away. I remember watching Dad totter up to stand beside the piano at the church, and I remember he surprised everyone by singing Brahms's Lullaby. I don't know why he chose a cradle song for a funeral, but he just opened his mouth and the thick German words spilled off his tongue like melted butter. Maybe he was inspired by the memory of losing Mom and he had a fleeting moment of empathy for someone else's pain, or maybe he just loved the music so much that his hateful old soul stepped out of the way for once and let him be a normal human being—but whatever, he was magnificent that day. His voice filled the church, resonating like an old bell, and it was so pure and rich I almost couldn't bear to listen to it. He was sixty-eight, and overweight and sick, but it didn't matter at all. I remember thinking that no one who could sing like that could be all bad. I still believe that, I guess, in spite of all the evidence to the contrary.

But when I drove him home after the service, I made the mistake of complimenting him on his performance and telling him there wasn't a dry eye in the place while he sang.

He made a dismissive gesture with his hand. "I wonder how many of those saps bawling their eyes out knew that Claudia was screwing Walter Anderson for the last seven years, right under Ed's nose? I shouldn't have sung for her funeral. It makes me feel unclean."

My dad, the compassionate. Why is it that people who need the most forgiveness are always the least forgiving?

Anyway, he died in his sleep. I heard his last breath, and I saw his heart monitor go flat. Dad's doctor had filled out a do-not-resuscitate order, so that was it. I signed a few forms, picked up his personal things, and went to find Tommy, who was down the street at Manchester's Pub, eating an early supper.

I sat down beside him at the bar. "Dad just died."

He looked at me for a second, put down his fork and drained the rest of his beer. His hands were perfectly steady. He signaled the bartender to bring two more.

"What are we drinking?" I asked.

"Guinness, of course."

"Dad's favorite. How appropriate."

We drank the Guinness, then we had several shots of Irish whiskey, then a few pints of Bass Ale, then a double-shot each of Jim Beam, then we decided that Bloody Marys were a wonderful idea. We laughed a lot, and Tommy talked about what was going on in his life, and he even pretended to be interested in what I was up to. He flirted relentlessly with the irritable, overtly heterosexual bartender, and we ate a couple platefuls of fried cheesesticks.

We didn't speak about Dad all evening, but when we were so drunk we could barely sit without swaying on our stools, I finally picked up my glass and proposed a toast.

"To Dad," I said. "The coldest, fattest, shittiest father . . ." My voice broke.

Tommy clinked my glass with his own. "Hear, hear."

Walking home that night Tommy fell to his knees on the side of the road and vomited. While he was wiping his mouth he let out a single, wrenching sob.

I put my hand on his back to comfort him, but he got to his feet immediately and gave me a crooked smile.

"I'm just drunk," he said. "Really. I'm fine."

To my knowledge those are the only moments of grief for my father either of us ever allowed ourselves to show. Sometimes I feel this weight in my chest that I know belongs to him, but it's buried so deep I'll never be able to root it out.

When I get back from the beach late in the afternoon, Jane Hampstead and Cheri and the others are packing up to leave for the day. I ask Cheri if they've found anything yet and she shakes her head in exasperation.

"Of course not. We're still in the preliminary stage. These things take time."

"Uh-huh." I'm hungry and tired and worn out from too much sun. I'm also seriously dehydrated, and even though I'm dark enough by now that I don't burn anymore, my skin feels hot and leathery, and I'm speckled with sand and salt.

Bill and Sally have apparently had a rough day. They're both wearing wide-brimmed hats and shirts and shorts, but their arms and legs are an angry red, and their clothes are coated with dirt. Bill's shirt is soaked with sweat and plastered to his ribs, and Sally's left knee is scraped and raw. They look exhausted and pissed off, like they'd gladly mow down a roomful of kindergartners for a bath and a glass of Kool-Aid. Hampstead and Cheri, on the other hand, are comparatively clean and dry, and probably spent most of the day in the shade, watching Bill and Sally do all the work. The field is neatly divided into sections now, cordoned into small, separate squares with bright orange twine and dozens of stakes.

Hampstead comes over to me. "Cheri tells me your family has lived on this land for several generations." Her blouse is wrinkled and coffee-stained, but at least (praise God) the fly of her pants is now fully zipped up.

I nod. "Four, to be exact."

"I see." She reaches down and brushes dirt from the knees of her corduroys. "To your knowledge, did any of them ever mention anything that might suggest someone had lived here before?"

"Not a word." I scowl at Cheri. "You didn't tell her?"

Cheri flushes. "What we're looking for was here a long time before your family . . ."

"True," Hampstead interrupts, "but you'd think that someone would have turned up something along the way before now."

Bill sidles closer. He has a huge Adam's apple, and his voice is timid. "Dr. Hampstead, I was looking at the surveyor's records of this property last night like you asked me to, and even though I'm sure Ms. Tipton knows what she's doing, I wasn't able to confirm her findings."

Cheri bridles. "I can assure you I've double- and triple-checked those records, and there's no need for you to concern yourself with that aspect of this project."

He flinches and withdraws. Hampstead looks at him, then back at Cheri. "Perhaps I should also take a look at the records, just to be sure?"

Cheri shakes her head vigorously. "My father was a surveyor, Jane, and he taught me everything he knew. And absolutely no one is more familiar with this part of Walcott than me. Or any other part, for that matter. You can see the records, of course, but it's a waste of your time."

Hampstead studies her for a minute. There are age spots on her hands and wrists, and crow's-feet next to her eyes. "I'm sure you're right, but I think I'd like to check your work, just to be sure."

Cheri's face darkens, making the mole on her forehead stand out. "That's insulting."

Hampstead shrugs. "I'm sorry, Cheri, it's nothing personal, but we can't afford to have any disagreement over where we should be digging. I was initially willing to trust your coordinates for the site, but now that Bill has expressed some doubt, I'd like to make sure we're on the right track." She turns toward Bill. "Why didn't you say something this morning, before we did all this work?"

He blinks. "I didn't think it was my place to dispute Ms. Tipton."

Cheri's voice has acid in it. "You're right about that, Bill. It isn't your place."

Bill crosses his scrawny arms in front of his chest.

Cheri wheels back to Hampstead. "And I hate to say this, Jane, but it's not your place, either."

Hampstead's eyes go wide and her cheeks redden. "I beg your pardon?"

Cheri blanches a little but she holds her ground. "*I* am in charge here, and you were hired to investigate *this* site, not to question my coordinates and argue with me over where we should dig."

Hampstead draws herself up to her full height and raises her voice. "I was *hired* to lead this team in excavating a viable site, not to risk wasting my time on a possible blunder."

Cheri puts her chubby fists on her hips like a sumo wrestler preparing to enter the ring. "There hasn't been any blunder, and I can't tell you how much I resent your attitude."

Hampstead's gray eyes turn to ice. "And I can't tell you how much I resent being scolded by a defensive dilettante."

Cheri gasps and stomps on the ground. "How dare you!" Her body is shaking so much her triceps start jiggling. "The only reason you're here is because I brought you here! I might not have a fancy degree in archaeology, but about *this* site and *this* town, I certainly know more than you can ever hope to."

Hampstead smirks. "Yes, that's quite true. I must have been absent from all of the classes at Yale when the vast archaeological significance of Walcott, Connecticut, was discussed. But nonetheless, I *do* know how to read a surveyor's map, Cheri, perhaps even better than you."

Bill and Sally are watching this exchange with rapt expressions, as if they can't believe someone would dare to take Hampstead on face-to-face. Sally catches my eye and fights back a smile. You could roll a quarter through the gap between her two front teeth.

Cheri is so worked up she can't talk, and Hampstead uses the opportunity to hammer her point home. "Any *professional* archaeologist would never balk at having her research confirmed by a colleague, no matter how familiar she was with a particular site. Surely you can understand that?"

Cheri doesn't answer, and there are tears of rage in her eyes. They glare at each other for a while, and in the silence a large black dragonfly hovers between them, then shoots across the cornfield like a plane on a strafing run.

Hampstead finally takes a deep breath and moderates her tone with an effort. "Let's discuss this calmly, shall we? I apologize for losing my temper. What I said was uncalled for, and I didn't mean it. I'm sure your coordinates are correct, but wouldn't you rather we be absolutely certain before proceeding any further?"

Cheri purses her lips, not at all mollified. She's breathing very fast, and her face is scrunched up and splotchy, like an overripe apple. "I am already absolutely certain about my coordinates, Jane." Her voice could freeze gas. "This is the site, and this is where I expect you to dig. If you have a problem with that, then I'm sure I can find someone else to do the job."

Hampstead locks eyes with her and doesn't say a word for nearly a minute. When she speaks again she sounds as if she's choking. "Fine. As you say, you're in charge. But I'm going to call the other board members from the Historical Society tonight and tell them you're not allowing me to do my job as I believe it needs to be done." She steps close to Cheri and her voice drops to a threatening growl. "And if there has been an error, I will not be held accountable for it."

Cheri blinks and Hampstead turns away. Bill and Sally avoid looking at both of them, but I see Sally glance at Bill and raise her eyebrows. Cheri turns to me and lifts her hands in a "See what I put up with?" gesture. I keep my face blank and her hands fall slowly to her sides.

I say good night and head for the cottage, but before I get to the back door Hampstead calls my name.

She gestures toward the front of the house. "Somebody parked behind my car a while ago. Could you please get them to move so I can leave?" Her tone is polite, but all the muscles and veins in her thin neck are bulging out and her left eye has developed a slight tic.

I nod and walk around the cottage to see whose car is in the way. It's mine. Camille had the whole yard to choose from but decided to park squarely behind Hampstead's SUV. Tommy's car is here, too, but he was smart enough to leave it off to the side so that the other vehicles could get out.

I walk in the front door and kick my sandals off, then head directly for the refrigerator to get a pitcher of water. No one's in the kitchen but I can hear voices scattered throughout the house.

"Hello?" I call out. "Camille?"

There's silence for a minute, then the bed in the guest room creaks and a second later the door of books swings open and Camille pokes her head out. "Hi, Nathan."

I start to get a glass, then on impulse drink directly from the pitcher. I take several deep swallows and wipe my mouth. "Do you have the keys to my car? The dirt people are done playing for the day and they need to go home."

She nods listlessly. "Sorry. I'll do it." She picks up her purse off the floor and roots around in it.

"Thanks." I take another long pull on the pitcher. "Watch out for Hampstead. She and Cheri almost came to blows just now, and she's so pissed off she'll tear your tonsils out with her fangs if you even look at her funny." I lean my shoulder against the refrigerator. "Where is everybody?"

She shrugs. "I don't know. I've been reading for the last couple of hours. I haven't seen Kyle since I got back, but I thought I heard Tommy and Philip a while ago."

She finds the keys and goes outside. The screen door bangs shut behind her.

I pick up a jug of spring water and refill the pitcher. We've got an artesian well out here but I don't trust the water in it because of all the chemicals Dale dumped on his corn when we were kids. He switched to organic farming a few years back, but I think I'll wait another decade or two before I start drinking from the well again. I had somebody from the city run a test on it and they claim it's at least as safe as the municipal tap water, but I don't find that particularly reassuring, since Walcott's tap water is thick enough to chew.

I wander over to the window above the sink and watch Hampstead and Cheri pull away from the house in separate vehicles, pointedly ignoring each other. Bill and Sally are in the back of Hampstead's SUV, and Sally sees me and waves good-bye. I wave back and head for the living room, hoping to avoid Camille on her way back into the house. It's stupid, but I'm afraid she'll take a closer look at me and somehow figure out what happened between Kyle and me this morning.

I need a shower really bad, but I should find Tommy first. The living room is empty but I can hear him talking to someone upstairs in my bedroom.

I walk over to the stairs and call up. "Tommy?"

It takes him a second to answer and when he does his voice sounds strange. "Yeah."

"What are you doing?"

He doesn't answer and I start to go up, but before I can see into the room he appears at the top of the staircase. He's fully dressed for once, with sandals and knee-length shorts and a tight red shirt. "Philip and I are talking."

He looks conspicuously sober and sad and I've seen that exact expression on his face before, many times. It's his patented I-just-dumped-my-boyfriend-and-see-how-I'm-suffering-because-of-it look. In the silence I can now hear Philip snuffling from the vicinity of my bed.

I lower my voice. "Jesus, Tommy, do you have to do this in my bedroom?"

"It's the only private place in the house."

I shake my head. "Okay, but when you're done I need to talk to you, too."

He nods, as if he was expecting me to say that. "We're almost through."

Philip sobs loudly. "We are not almost through!" he yells. "You fucking prick!"

Tommy turns away from me. "Philip, buddy, I understand that you're angry, but . . ."

"Fuck you, Tommy!" Philip stomps across the floor and comes nose to nose with Tommy at the top of the stairs. He's shirtless and the belt on his pants is undone—either a last-ditch effort on his part to seduce Tommy or a feeble attempt by Tommy to console him—and his face is red and puffy. "What kind of an asshole are you? You've spent the day fucking a zit-faced infant and now you want to break up with me? Just last night you told me you loved me!"

Tommy reaches for him. "I do love you," he whispers.

"You fucking liar!" Philip screams, then lunges forward and shoves Tommy with all his strength.

Tommy loses his balance and grabs for Philip to catch himself, but Philip is still charging right at him and the two of them rocket off the top step and plow into me. I manage to keep on my feet for about one second, then all three of us topple to the bottom of the staircase. I bang my head on the wall on the way down and my tailbone on the floor when we hit, and Tommy lands with both elbows in my stomach, aided by the full weight of Philip on top of him.

We all lie still for a few moments, stunned. Then Philip squirms off the pile and starts to hit Tommy with his fists. I try to get out from under them, but Tommy's got me pinned and can't move himself because he's too busy trying to ward off Philip.

Most of Philip's punches are ineffectual, but he finally lands a good one to the side of Tommy's head.

"Goddammit, Philip!" Tommy bellows. He grabs Philip's wrist and gives him a violent yank. Philip tears away from him and falls on his butt when Tommy lets go. He sits there for an instant with a surprised, comical expression on his face, but after a second he recovers and leaps to his feet and grabs a glazed porcelain lamp from the coffee table.

"Don't!" Tommy yells, and flings up an arm to protect his face and head just as Philip hurls the lamp at him.

The lamp's electrical cord is plugged into the wall and it snags the lamp out of the air midflight and brings it crashing down about a foot away from Tommy and me. Pieces of it jet across the room but by some miracle none of them hit us. Tommy uses the moment of shocked silence to jump up and tackle Philip, then he crawls on top of him and traps his arms before he can recover. Philip starts to cry.

I stand up. My wind is knocked out of me and my legs are shaking. Camille is in the doorway between the kitchen and the living room. Her eyes are huge.

Tommy tries to hush Philip but Philip doesn't want to be hushed. "Get away from me," he howls.

The more Tommy tries to console him, the worse he gets. I finally put my hand on Tommy's shoulder and tell him to get out of here for a while. Tommy starts to argue for a second, but then he grimaces and lets Philip go. He has a wary expression on his face, as if he's expecting to be attacked again, but Philip just curls into a ball like a pill bug and sobs. Tommy stands over him for a while, then gives up and goes out the back door.

I sigh and lie down on the floor next to Philip. When I put my arms around him he turns over immediately and clamps me in a bear hug. His skin is hot against mine and I can't tell if the moisture on my neck is his sweat or his tears. I hold him while he cries himself out.

Camille goes over to Philip's suitcase and pulls out a fresh shirt for him. She smoothes it out and drapes it over the end of the futon mattress, then disappears back into the kitchen to get a broom.

After Philip finishes bawling and gets dressed he immediately insists on leaving. While I'm on the phone trying to find out train departure times for him he gets impatient and walks out the front door with his suitcase, and he's halfway down our lane when I catch up. He gets in the car without a word and slumps in his seat and stares out the window. He looks like a little boy.

Just as we're getting ready to pull on to the main road, we see

Tommy, wandering along the shoulder with a stick in his hands. He sees us and starts walking toward the car, and Philip loses it.

"If that bastard tries to talk to me I'm going to fucking kill him!" He sticks his head out the window and begins yelling. "Fuck you, you sick fucking asshole! Don't be surprised if the police get a phone call about what you're doing with Simon."

Tommy stops dead in his tracks.

Philip's laugh comes out high and sharp. "That's right, you stupid fucking whore, did you think you could do this to me and get away with it?"

I put my hand on his arm. "Shut up, Philip, you're only making it worse."

He whips his head around. "*I'm* making it worse? He's fucking a child, Nathan. Maybe you've forgotten, but that's a felony, the last time I checked." He turns back to the window to yell again. "Didn't Simon say his Dad was a DA, Tommy? Maybe I'll just give him a call and see what he thinks about his precious little boy getting sodomized by some fucking NAMBLA reject."

Another car rolls by with its windows open. It's the older sister of a woman Tommy and I went to school with. She sees me and waves. Philip leans farther out the window to get her attention. "You better keep your kids away from that guy in the road, lady, or he'll . . ."

I jab him pretty hard above the kidneys to shut him up. He jumps and bangs his head on the car roof. The woman looks shocked, but I hold up my hands in a carefree "everything is fine, we're just screwing around" gesture, and give her a goofy grin. She smiles indulgently, then waves again and drives out of sight.

Tommy's eyes meet mine for an instant, and I see panic in them. I pull out onto the road before Philip can say anything else.

I glance over at him after a few blocks. He's rubbing his back and glaring at me.

"Sorry," I mutter. "But you were making a fool of yourself."

He shakes his head, disgusted. "I know he's your brother, Nathan, but I can't believe you're protecting him. Simon is your *student,* for God's sake. You should put an end to this."

"I'm not protecting Tommy," I lie. "I know for a fact that nothing is happening between them."

He guffaws. "Right. Is that why Tommy smelled like the floor of a porno theater when he came home this afternoon? Is that why he won't tell me anything about the person he went to see?"

I don't answer him. I should probably try to diffuse his anger some more, but there are limits to my hypocrisy, and anything I say probably won't do any good anyway.

We drive in silence until we get to the train station. I stop the car by the platform stairs and wait for him to get out, but he doesn't move.

I clear my throat. "Well, it looks like we're here."

No reaction.

I put the car in neutral. "Look, Philip. I'm really sorry things worked out this way."

He wipes his nose on his sleeve. "It's not your fault. You tried to warn me."

I make one more feeble try. "Will it help if I tell you that Tommy really does care for you?"

He looks up at me. His eyes are full of tears and his nose is red and runny. He manages a pathetic little smile. "Sure he does. And Brad Pitt wants to have my baby."

For the first time, I feel as if I could like him. I smile back. "It could happen. You never know."

He sighs, then leans over and gives me a quick hug. "You can relax, Nathan. I won't say anything to anybody. I just wanted to make Tommy worry."

Relief floods through me. "Thanks. I'll make sure things don't go any farther."

He shrugs. "I really don't give a shit about Simon. Tommy can skull-fuck him with an electric mixer for all I care." He makes a face when I raise my eyebrows. "Yeah, I know. I'm full of shit. I was just pretending moral outrage a minute ago because it made me feel better. But the truth is I think that manipulative, pimple-popping little queer knows exactly what he's doing. Simon acts all naive and sweet but . . ." He trails off. "Whatever. Fuck it."

He gets out of the car and hauls his suitcase from the backseat. "So long. It was nice meeting you."

I watch him trudge up the stairs, his head down and his feet dragging. Right before he goes through the glass doors he glances back at me and nods. I nod back and he disappears into the station. I stare at the reflection of the sun in the doors for a while, surprised by how much pity I feel for him.

Poor bastard. Philip's not my favorite person in the world, but I guess the only thing he really did wrong was to love Tommy, and how can I fault him for that? Just because everybody else knew from the beginning that things would turn out this way doesn't mean Philip had any choice in the matter. He's hardly the first person to get run over by Tommy Bishop's Joystick Juggernaut; the streets of New York are littered with my brother's rejects, splattered all over the concrete like so many dead ants.

All of a sudden I'm pissed as hell. Why is it *me* sitting here trying to deal with Philip? Why am *I* stuck at the train station doing damage control while Tommy, yet again, escapes all responsiblity for his actions? Right now he's skipping down the lane at home, whistling happy songs and diddling himself through a hole in the pocket of his pants, completely oblivious to what he's just put Philip and me through.

And why shouldn't he be? He always gets exactly what he wants, and he expects me to trail along after him like an obedient stable boy, cleaning up his messes.

Goddamn him.

Now that I think about it, something like this happens every time he comes home. He flies into town, tossing around dozens of penis-shaped grenades (like when he hit on the Mormon undertaker's newly married son at Dad's funeral, right in front of the poor kid's wife), and after the damn things go off he prances back to New York in his magic fairy shoes and leaves me to deal with the carnage.

But I'm sick of it. I won't do this again. The next time he screws up, I won't be there to pick up the pieces. I am sick of being used, and I'm sick of his ridicule about how I choose to live, and most of all I'm sick of his self-righteous attitude. He should be forced to wear a T-shirt that says *"Hi, I'm Tommy, and I'm going to fuck you over if you're stupid enough to fall in love with me."* At least then people would be forewarned about what they were in for before they got hooked on him.

I'm finally starting to get my own life here in Walcott, but Tommy doesn't even notice that. He waltzes in after three years, swinging his dick around like a wrecking ball, and he assumes I won't mind him making a shambles of everything. Just who the hell does he think he is? I am not his fucking butler, or his nursemaid, and my home is not an orphanage for the lovelorn.

My rage builds and I begin to slam my palms into the steering wheel again and again, not caring that there are two teenaged girls gawking at me as they come down the stairs. I don't know either of them—Walcott gets a lot of tourists during the summer because of the beach—but they both have long blond hair (cut identically, of course), and they look about as bright as a pair of twin gerbils. They glance at each other and start to laugh nervously.

I yell out the window at them. "Why don't you mind your own fucking business?"

They stop walking and one of them raises her hands up by her shoulders and makes a face. "What's your problem, mister?" Her voice is high-pitched and grating.

I glare at her and hit the steering wheel one more time, bruising my left thumb, then I pop the car into gear and floor the accelerator, burning rubber on the pavement directly in front of them. I blast by some old man I don't recognize stuffing a bag in his trunk and he shakes a finger at my face and yells at me to slow down.

Goddamn tourists. I flip him off and fly across the parking lot, ignoring the stop sign and peeling out onto the road. Three blocks later I almost hit a dog in a crosswalk, and I swerve over to the curb and slam on the brakes, cursing. The engine stalls out and a second later I turn the key off and let my hands fall in my lap. I close my eyes and rest my chin on my chest, not bothering to look up when someone behind me honks his horn several times before going around me.

I don't want to move, ever again.

Maybe I'll just sit here until my flesh rots. Maybe I'll just roll up the windows and roast like a chicken for a few days, so that when Tommy finally comes to find me he'll have to scrape my rancid carcass off the seat into a garbage bag before he can bury me in the backyard. Maybe I'll even be more liquid than solid by then, and he'll have to use a Shop-Vac to suck me out of the upholstery. I hope he chokes on his own puke while he's doing it.

It would serve the little son of a bitch right.

The sun is hammering down on the left side of my body. I ignore it as long as I can, but when I can't bear the heat anymore, I lift my head and glance in the mirror at my face. My cheeks and forehead are red and damp, and my eyes are bloodshot and swollen.

I look exactly like my dad did after one of his temper tantrums.

Fuck. Goddamn *fucking* hell.

I sit still for several minutes, listening to other cars pass me on the street. I'm slick with sweat, and my legs and back are sticking to the seat. I lean forward and rest the bridge of my nose against the steering wheel, and I wrap my arms loosely around my waist and listen to my heartbeat gradually get slower. It seems to take forever.

Another horn blares at me and when I wave my arm out the window for whoever it is to pass by, a car creeps around my bumper and stops next to me, brakes squeaking. I look over to see who it is.

Fabulous. It's the old man I flipped off in the parking lot.

He's alone in his car, and his passenger window is open. His face is angry and his wrinkled bald head has blue veins on it. He leans across his seat as if he's going to say something.

I try to forestall him by talking first. "I'm really sorry about that back there." I make my voice as polite as I can. "I'm just having a bad day. I apologize."

He raises his right hand in the air and slowly gives me the finger. His voice is tremulous and harsh. "Fuck you, buddy."

My whole body stiffens and I stick my head out the window to confront him. "Relax, okay? I said I was sorry."

"*You* fucking relax. No one treats me like that." His bony middle finger is still sticking straight up, daring me to do something.

I lock eyes with him and my head starts pounding again. I don't believe this. The old bastard wants me to come after him. He's got to be eighty years old, and he wants to fight. Crazy old fucker.

Something in me boils over.

Fine. If he wants to fight, I'll fight. I've put up with more than enough shit for one day.

My voice is thick with fury. "I hope you've got good dentures, asshole, because in about two seconds you're going to be eating that finger." I reach for my door handle. "Make sure to chew before you swallow."

He gets a scared look on his face, but he doesn't budge.

We'll see about that.

I'm actually putting a foot on the ground when shame hits me in the chest like a mace.

I've witnessed this kind of scene before, way too many times. And I know all too well where I learned to act like this.

Christ. My father would be very proud of me.

I force myself to close my door again, even though everything in me still wants to reach over and jerk the scabby old prick out of his car and use his fat fleshy skull for a basketball. I face front and look out my windshield, trying to ignore him.

He snorts. "That's what I thought." There's triumph in his voice.

I stare back into his eyes and he finally drops his hand.

"Feel better now?" I ask.

"Fuck you," he says once more, but there's less heat in it this time. I look away again and a few seconds later he drives off.

There's a familiar state motto printed across the bottom of the license plate on his car; it says "Live Free Or Die." Of course. New Hampshire. I should have known. Those people are all lunatics.

I close my eyes again and breathe a few times before I restart the car and head for home.

Okay, so I'm a dick.

But it's not completely my fault. I'll take most of the responsibility for how I just acted, but no small portion of the blame belongs to Tommy and Dad. One's living and one's not, but when I put them together in my head they make me crazy.

And someday they're going to be the death of me.

CHAPTER 7

Shit.

Kyle is sitting on the front steps of the cottage when I pull into the driveway. Would you believe I'd almost forgotten our little encounter earlier today? The mess with Philip and Tommy and Simon (not to mention the run-in with the old man on the street) pushed it right out of my mind. I really don't want to talk to him right now but I guess there's no avoiding it.

He watches me as I get out of the car and walk toward him. He's drinking a Heineken and he offers the bottle to me when I reach the porch steps.

I take a swig and hand it back. "Thanks."

"Sure." He shifts to make room for me. "I hear Philip is gone."

"Yeah. I just dropped him off at the train station." I sit beside him. The blossoms on the rhododendrons are starting to wilt and fall apart. I reach down and pick up one of the white petals from the ground. It feels like old silk.

He flicks an ant off his bare leg. "Camille said I missed quite a scene."

"Yeah. All we needed is a couple more props and a laugh track and we could have made our own Three Stooges movie." I shred the petal into tiny pieces and let them fall one by one. "Where's Tommy?"

"Out back, I think. He found your dad's old hammock somewhere and said he was going to put it up in the shade."

He's trying really hard to be cool and detached, but he's having a rough go of it. He can't meet my eyes for more than a second at a time, and his fingers are picking nervously at the label on the beer bottle. I guess I can't blame him.

Neither of us can think of anything to say. I wait a minute longer to make it seem like I'm not in a rush to get away from him, then I put my hands on my knees and start to get up. "I should probably go find my brother."

"Okay," he says, but before I'm halfway up he grabs my hand and pulls me down again. He leans close to whisper, and I can barely hear him even though his mouth is right by my ear. "Listen, Nathan, I'm really sorry about what happened this afternoon. I was out of line."

"Forget it. It's fine."

"No, it's not. I was an asshole. I should have asked you first before I . . . well, you know. I've never done anything like that before. I don't know what I was thinking."

His face is so red it's almost purple. I kind of want to relish his embarrassment for a few more seconds, but he looks so pitiful I can't make myself do it.

"Forget it," I repeat. "Like I said, I'm flattered."

I squeeze his fingers and he squeezes back, then all of a sudden he kisses my cheek. His lips are wet and his breath is warm and smells like beer, but his gentleness takes me by surprise, and before I can help myself, I turn my head and kiss him on the lips. Twice. He closes his eyes during the second one.

It's been years since I've kissed another human being. I'd almost forgotten what it feels like. The softness of it. Something inside me I'd thought was gone a long time ago stirs and kicks, like a sleeper rolling over in bed. I pull delicately at Kyle's lower lip with my teeth and he lifts his chin a little and air rushes from his nose. When I let him go he doesn't move or open his eyes, and I nearly kiss him again before I catch myself and recoil in horror.

Goddammit. I can't believe I just did that. How many kinds of an idiot can I be?

I drop his hand as if it's a cockroach and stand up so fast I almost black out. "I need to go find Tommy."

Confusion and something else—anxiety? happiness?—are having a war for control of his face. I open the screen door and go inside before he can say anything else.

Tommy's strung the hammock up in the backyard, between the two maple trees we used for the same purpose when we were kids, and he's stretched out in it with one hand behind his head and the other holding a book upright on his stomach. Even though it's hot he's still wearing the red shirt he had on earlier, and I can see big wet patches under his arms. His feet are bare and he's got them tangled up in the loose rope mesh of the hammock.

He doesn't look up until I'm standing right beside him. "Hey," he says.

"Hey."

He lays the book flat on his stomach; it's the Emerson essay collection from the locked cabinet in the living room.

I lift it off him carefully. "You're going to get it all sweaty, Tommy. It's a first edition." I set it on the grass in the shade.

"Sorry." He scootches over a little. "Somebody's underlined a bunch of stuff in it. Was that you?"

"No. I just saw that the other day, too." The hammock rocks wildly as I crawl in beside him, and the sides fold up like a taco and toss us against each other. "Oof. We're a little bigger than we were the last time we did this."

"You can say that again. Move your elbow, would you?" He shifts to get comfortable. "Camille said you took Philip to the train station."

"Yeah. Thanks a lot, by the way. I can't remember the last time I had so much fun."

He puts his head on my shoulder. "Sorry."

We don't say anything for a while. I study the cornfield and the sky, and I listen to a woodpecker bang his head against a tree someplace in the woods behind us, and I feel my brother breathe against my side. We're out of the sun here, and the heat of the day is finally backing off a little. It's a nice moment.

Maybe if I keep quiet everything will be fine. Maybe if I just close my eyes and fall asleep, when I wake up Simon will be a distant memory and Kyle and Camille will have disappeared and I won't have this almost irresistible urge to beat Tommy's brains out with a sharp, heavy rock. Maybe Ted Baker will stop being an asshole, and Cheri Tipton will crawl back in her hole, and Jane Hampstead will take Bill and Sally to Egypt and they'll all get entombed in a pyramid with a homicidal mummy.

And maybe Jerry Falwell and Trent Lott will hold hands and French kiss on a big pink float in the next Gay Rights Parade.

Tommy's breathing slows. He's falling asleep. I nudge his head with my shoulder. "Hey. Wake up. We need to talk."

"What about?"

"Simon."

Silence. "What about him?"

"Are you guys fucking?"

He lifts his head from my shoulder. "What? Of course not."

"Don't lie to me, Tommy. I know he called here this afternoon and you went to meet him."

He rolls over so his back is to me. "So what? We were just talking."

I can see his spine through his shirt. "What about? Condom versus no condom? Ways to keep from shooting your load until your father figure is ready to shoot, too?"

"I said we were just talking."

I'm starting to get pissed again. I'm sick of being lied to. "Philip said it was more than that."

"Philip is a jealous little bitch who's grasping at straws because I dumped him, and he can't believe I only did it because I'm tired of him."

I grab his shoulder and pull him over so he has to look at me. "Wasn't it just a couple of nights ago you were telling me how much you loved him? Strange that you've had a change of heart after spending an afternoon 'talking' with Simon."

"Simon's got nothing to do with it." He's getting angry, too. His voice is strained and I can see the veins in his neck. "I finally woke up to what a dildo Philip is. End of story."

"I can't believe you're lying about this. Especially after you promised me you wouldn't let anything else happen."

"I am *not* lying!" He sits up abruptly and the hammock almost dumps us both on the ground. "Why won't you believe me?"

He's looking straight at me, with his eyes wide open and his chin trembling, the very picture of outraged innocence.

I study him for a minute. Is it possible he's telling the truth?

I sigh. No way. I know my brother. It's not in him to be able to resist someone as blatantly ready and willing as Simon.

Tommy's first boyfriend was a kid named Owen Olson. The two of them were in eighth grade together, and for nearly three weeks after they started fooling around, Owen was all Tommy talked about. I was force-fed a steady diet of endless, saccharine monologues about how they were going to be together forever, and how Tommy couldn't imagine loving anybody more than he loved Owen, and how tragic it was that the two of them couldn't live together now that they'd finally "found" one another.

Fast forward to a week later, when Owen "found" Tommy in the dunes at the beach, on his knees in front of an older boy named Terry. Owen flipped out and Tommy transferred his allegiance on the spot to Terry, mainly because Owen had pimples and glasses, and Terry had big biceps and a hairy belly.

So much for true love.

Anyway, four days after that Terry got bumped for Edward, and Edward got bumped for Rick, and so on and so on. You get the picture.

Granted, Tommy was a kid back then, and people do grow up. But some things never change. No matter what else happens in the universe—the fall of communism, the destruction of the ozone, the death of punk rock, whatever—you can at least put your faith in one thing:

If a man is pretty, available, and breathing, Tommy will stick his dick in him.

I sit up, too, slowly, and when I'm upright our faces are close together. "You are so full of shit. You can say anything you want, but we both know exactly what's going on." I jab a finger at his chest. "And you better get the fuck out of Walcott before it goes any further. You're playing with fire, Tommy. If you get caught . . ."

He slaps my hand away. "I'm not going to get caught because I'm not doing anything wrong!" There are tears in his eyes. One of his feet is still caught in the hammock and he tries to yank it free and just gets it more entangled. He swears and starts to cry.

All of a sudden—and in complete defiance of logic—I'm not sure what to believe. Despite everything I know about how he operates, I've seldom seen him this upset. If he's lying, he's giving an Oscar-worthy performance. How am I supposed to know what's true?

I watch him struggle with the rope and then he gives up and puts his face in his hands and sobs. "I don't need this shit from you right now, Nathan."

His shoulders are shaking, and he's hunched over as if his appendix just burst. I can't take it anymore. "Okay, okay, please stop crying. I believe you, okay?" I reach down and work his foot free. There are small rope burns on his ankle. I finger them lightly and he pulls away.

"Don't touch me." His face is wet and he sounds choked. "You are such an asshole."

I throw up my hands. "What did you expect me to think? I asked both you and Simon to stay away from each other and the first chance you get you run off for a secret rendezvous."

"All I promised was that I wouldn't mess around with him anymore. I didn't promise not to see him." He dabs at his eyes with his shirtsleeve. "You should have trusted me, Nathan. You had no right to ask him to stay away."

"The hell I didn't." A big crow bursts from the branches of one of the maples supporting the hammock and soars into the sky, startling us. It caws a few times and flies over the cornfield, no doubt seeking a quieter place to nap. "You guys were all over each other on the couch yesterday and I know he wants as much of that as he can get. You might have been able to control yourself today, but how long do you think you can manage to keep your hands off him?"

He shrugs and looks away. "That's my problem."

"Maybe so, but it's not just about you, Tommy. Ted Baker saw me hugging Simon this morning in my classroom—that was thanks to you, by the way—and he ran off to tattle to Madeline because he thinks it was inappropriate. The last thing . . ."

"Why is that my fault? You were the one who . . ."

I ignore him. "The last thing I need right now is for you to mess things up even more by hanging out with Simon in public. God knows what people will think if they see the two of you together."

"What people are we talking about? And what's the big deal, even if you do get fired? You'll find something else. Quit acting like it's life or death."

"What else am I going to do in this town? And that's not even the point. Just how easy do you think it would be to keep living here if I got let go for having a suspicious relationship with a high school boy? I love Walcott. I plan on spending the rest of my life here."

He rolls his eyes. "That's my brave big brother. Shoot for the stars."

Blood rushes to my head and something in me snaps. "Fuck you!" I give him a shove and he falls backward off the hammock, but on his way he grabs the side of it and spills me out, too. He hits the ground first with a satisfying thump and I land right on top of him.

Both of us have the air knocked out of us and we don't move for a second. I entertain the idea of taking his skull and mashing it into the soil, but I'm suddenly too damn tired to sustain a good mad-on, and my anger begins to dribble away. A cool breeze is blowing over us, and the tangy smell of his sweat is mixing pleasantly with the espresso-like odor of the earth. I breathe in and out a few times and the muscles in my neck and shoulders slowly relax.

He finally stirs. "Jesus, Nathan." He lifts his head off the grass then lets it fall again. "When are you going to learn to control your temper?" He pushes at me. "Get off."

He sounds so put out that I start to giggle in spite of myself.

"It's not funny," he snaps. "I'm getting really tired of people knocking me down, today."

"I know." I laugh harder. "But that's the most fun I've had since you got here."

He tries to move me again, then gives up and starts to laugh, too. I nuzzle his neck briefly, then roll off him so that we're both flat on our backs.

I clear my throat when we've both quieted. "Kyle stuck his hand down the front of my swimsuit today."

"What?" He sits up and gapes at me. There's a grass stain on his left shoulder and a few scrapes on his forearm.

"Yeah. I made him stop at the time, but when I just saw him out front I accidentally kissed him on the lips." I laugh again. "Oops."

He raises an eyebrow. "So the whole time you were up on your pulpit lecturing me about Simon, you'd just finished making out with a married man?"

I rub my temples. "Something like that."

He grins. "Good for you. I was beginning to think you'd gotten too old to be interested in sex anymore."

"All I did was kiss him. I didn't even use my tongue."

"You're a saint. I'm sure Camille will appreciate the distinction."

"Oh, God," I groan. "You don't think he'll tell her, do you?"

"Kyle? No way. He's too much of a chickenshit. I'm amazed he actually made a pass at you."

"It wasn't just a pass. He nearly pulled my dick off."

He throws back his head and chortles. "Really? Wow. I always knew he was gay but I thought he'd never have the balls to admit it to himself, let alone someone else."

"Well, he did a pretty good hatchet job on that old closet door of his today. He damn near tore the hinges off on his way out."

"You haven't lost your charm after all, Nathan." He tickles my armpit. "You slut. I bet you could turn John Ashcroft into a demure little bottom-boy."

"Gross. I'd rather hump a tree."

"Me too." He pauses for effect. "Speaking of which, have you seen that adorable little sapling by the mailbox?"

That sets us off again. We joke back and forth for a while until I finally start to sober up. One of Tommy's gifts is how easily he can distract people and keep them away from any topic he doesn't want to talk about. But I'm not going to let him do it this time.

I turn my head and gaze up at him. "Can we be serious for a minute?"

His smile fades. "Sure, I guess."

I sit up and put my hands on his shoulders. "You need to be careful." He starts to protest but I shake him gently and stop him. "I mean it, okay?"

For better or worse, this is my job. I look out for my brother, because he can't look out for himself. I'll do whatever it takes to keep him safe, no matter how much he pisses me off.

He makes a face and doesn't say anything, but when he finally figures out I'm not going to let go of him until he gives me an answer, he nods once, reluctantly. "I will if you will."

"Deal."

I've been lying to you a little about my father. I told you I have no good memories of him after Mom died, but that's not entirely true.

There's one.

When I was a freshman in college and Tommy was a junior in high school, I came home in February for winter break. I'd managed to avoid coming home for Thanksgiving or Christmas, so this was the first time I'd seen Dad in almost six months. (I'd seen Tommy frequently, of course; he hopped the bus every few weeks to get away from Dad and would show up outside my dorm room with a sleeping bag and a toothbrush, and nothing in his pockets but a handful of change and a return ticket.) I'd had no intention of spending the break in Walcott, but my plans to visit my roommate's family fell through, and since the dorm was closed and no one else was available to impose on, I had no choice but to head back to the cottage.

It was a frigid, bitter day when I pulled into town. I'd called Tommy the night before to let him know when I'd be arriving, but he was working that afternoon (he had a part time job at a gas station) and couldn't pick me up, so he told me Dad would be there instead. I got off the bus and waited for half an hour, but Dad didn't show up, so I zipped up my coat and trudged home through the snow, carrying my suitcase first in one hand, then the other. I'd misplaced my gloves somewhere and I was trying to warm my fingers in my pockets.

Walcott in February is stark and brutal. The sky is usually overcast, and the wind coming off the ocean freezes the moisture in your eyes and makes your face hurt. Several people I knew stopped in their cars to ask if I wanted a lift, but I told them no. It was after five o'clock and I knew Dad was probably already at home, and I was in no hurry to see him, in spite of the cold.

It only took me twenty minutes, but by the time I got to our property I was shivering violently and my feet were numb. The sun was already down, and the lane through the woods was dark and still. I paused once or twice to listen to the trees groaning under the ice on their limbs, and I jumped when a small fox skittered across the snow in front of me and plunged into the brush at the side of the road.

When I reached the clearing, there were several lights on in the cottage. An autumn storm had ripped a lot of shingles from the roof, but otherwise it looked the same as always, sturdy and silent and glowing like a beacon, and I stopped again to stare at it.

Dad was washing dishes and peering, presumably, at his reflection in the kitchen window. I was in the shadows under the trees and invisible to him, but I could see him clearly; the bare lightbulb over the sink lit him up like an actor on the stage. He'd aged quite a bit in only half a year. His cheeks were sagging and his hair was thinner, and his skin was loose and gray. I watched him for a few seconds, studying his face and trying to determine his mood, then I realized I was stalling and made myself step into the circle of light directly in front of the house. He saw me and froze, then flipped on the switch for the outside light above the porch.

And that's when it happened. The minor miracle. Tommy didn't believe me when I told him, but I swear to God this is true: tears sprang to Dad's eyes, and then, completely against my will, into mine, too. It was almost as if we were a normal father and son, and we were glad to see each other. His lips turned slightly upward at the corners in what was meant to be a smile, but ended up looking like a spasm of pain. I felt my own mouth do something similar, then I shifted my suitcase and shrugged a little, and he nodded as if agreeing to something I'd said.

And that was it. The moment passed, and by the time I got in the door, it was as if it never happened. I think I said hello, and he told me to take my shoes off so I wouldn't track snow into the house. I asked him why he hadn't come to pick me up and he told me he'd been too busy that afternoon to notice the clock, and then we stopped talking and pointedly ignored each other for the rest of the vacation.

Those tears were an airborne virus, a twenty-four-second flu kind of thing that came out of nowhere and vanished into the February night. I don't know why the connection between us was so fleeting, or why it never came back. Maybe—and let's beat this simile to death, shall we?—it was like a case of chicken pox or something, and once we'd had it and survived, we were immune to future outbreaks, with nothing to remind us of how sick we'd been, except for a few small scars on our chests, very near the heart.

Or, much more likely, he was drunk and I was tired. It's an easier explanation, true or not, so let's leave it at that.

Camille knows something's up.

With Philip gone and Simon at least temporarily out of the picture, there's only the four of us for dinner. Tommy and I are sitting at the ends, and Kyle and Camille are facing each other on the sides. Nobody is talking, but Kyle is picking at his food and sneaking glances at me, and Tommy, although blessedly silent, is watching Kyle from the corner of his eye and smirking like a two-year-old. Camille is studying each of us in turn with a small frown on her face.

I smother my cheeseburger with ketchup and red onions and try to make conversation. "Cheri said they haven't found anything in the cornfield yet."

"What a surprise," Tommy says. "I was sure they would have turned up the missing link by now."

I grunt. "Or at least a dog turd or two."

Kyle laughs uproariously, as if I'm the funniest human being he's ever had the honor of sharing a meal with. Tommy rolls his eyes and hides a grin behind his hand. I glare at him.

Camille waits until Kyle stops laughing, then turns to me. "Did Philip say what he was going to do once he got back to New York?"

I shake my head. "No. I don't think he knows. He was pretty upset."

"You don't think he'll do anything stupid, do you?"

Why is she asking me? I barely know Philip.

I raise my eyebrows. "Like what?"

She shrugs. "I don't know. I'm just worried he might try to hurt himself. He seems kind of unstable."

Tommy looks bored, as if we're talking about a stranger.

Kyle speaks up. "He'll be fine, Camille. Philip is tougher than he looks."

"Since when did you become an expert on Philip?" Camille snaps. "We only met him a couple of months ago, and you didn't see him this afternoon after Tommy . . ." She stops abruptly and darts her eyes at Tommy. "Sorry."

Tommy takes a deep pull on his beer, upending it like a baby bottle, then sets it down again. "It's fine. And Kyle's right about Philip. He was upset, but he'll get over it."

We're having a late supper. The sun went down a while ago, and the only light in the room besides a small lamp on the table by the door is a lit candle in the middle of the table. The radio next to the lamp is on, softly, playing classical music from the NPR station in New Haven—Rachmaninoff, maybe.

Camille pries some wax off the base of the candlestick and feeds it back into the flame. "You probably could have handled that situation a little better, Tommy."

He looks pissed but doesn't say anything. If it had been me criticizing him he'd have bounced the mustard bottle off my head.

There's a knock at the door. Tommy looks up and smiles, and I turn around with a sinking sensation in my stomach.

It's Simon.

Tommy's on his feet before I can say anything. He doesn't even look at me on the way to the door. "Simon! I was just thinking about you. Don't just stand there. Come on in."

I stand up slowly. Simon comes in the room, takes one look at me and drops his eyes to the floor. He moves closer to Tommy, and

Tommy whispers something in his ear and gives him a quick peck on the cheek. Simon raises his head again, and the look on his face confirms everything I've been afraid of.

I'm a fool.

"What can I do for you, Simon?" My voice is cold.

I can barely hear his answer. "Tommy said I should . . ."

Tommy takes his hand and guides him over to the table. "I told him to come over tonight, Nathan."

I'm so angry I can't even speak. I stand there, livid, and watch Tommy fetch another chair. He sets it between him and Camille, then he gestures for Simon to sit, making fluttery motions with his hands like a hostess in a restaurant. Simon slides onto the chair with an embarrassed grin, but his eyes never leave Tommy's. Tommy ruffles his hair and sits down beside him.

Kyle and Camille are both watching me, and Tommy finally looks up, but only after handing Simon a plate and a napkin. "What's your problem? Are you going to stand there all night or what?"

My throat feels tight and my fingernails are digging into my palms. "What do you think you're doing?"

Simon jumps a little in his chair. Tommy drops an arm over his shoulders and glowers at me. "I'm getting our guest something to eat. What does it look like?"

"Oh, offhand, I'd say about the stupidest thing you've ever done. Does that sound about right?"

He rolls his eyes. I glance at Kyle and Camille. "I'm sorry to do this in front of you guys, but Tommy and Simon aren't leaving me much choice. Simon, you need to go home. I told you this morning you shouldn't . . ."

Tommy shoves back from the table. "This is my home too, Nathan, and I'll have whoever I want . . ."

"That's exactly the problem, Tommy. You always have whoever you want."

He's on his feet in an instant, yelling. "Since when do you get to decide who my friends are?"

"Ever since you lost your mind and started screwing a fifteen-year-old!"

Simon's looking back and forth between Tommy and me with a

panicked expression on his face. Kyle's mouth is open and Camille's eyes are wide and frightened.

Tommy slams both of his fists down on the table and everything on it jumps. Camille rescues a full glass of water, but Kyle's beer falls over before he can get to it. He grabs it before much spills. The candle sways, flickering wildly and casting strange shadows on Camille's blouse.

Tommy is fighting for control. He takes a deep breath and lowers his voice. "I can't believe you just said that. I already told you . . ."

"I know what you told me, Tommy. And I don't believe you anymore. Look at the two of you. Any idiot can see what's going on."

Simon stands up next to him. "It's not like that, Mr. Bishop. Really. We're just good friends."

My laugh comes out as a high-pitched bark. "Oh, please, Simon, call me Nathan. After all, it looks like we're going to be brothers-in-law. We can go as a family to visit Tommy when he's in the federal penitentiary."

His lips are trembling and he's trying not to cry. He's wearing a tank top and his exposed collarbones are thin and delicate, like a handle on a coffee mug.

Camille reaches up and puts her fingers on my wrist. "Nathan, you're behaving badly. Why don't you sit down and we can discuss this calmly, and maybe . . ."

I yank my arm away from her. "I'm behaving badly? Should we have some red wine while we discuss it?"

She flinches and drops her hand. Tommy puts his arms around Simon. "It's all right," he whispers to him. He looks back at me with contempt. "Hi, Dad," he says quietly. "Welcome home. I thought you were dead."

The words hang in the air like black balloons. I look at each of their faces in turn: Tommy's, furious; Simon's, pale and hurt; Camille's, insulted; Kyle's, confused.

The anger drains out of me and I sit down. "Go home, Simon. Please. We'll talk in the morning at the school."

Tommy starts to argue again, but Simon stops him. "It's okay. I guess I should probably go."

Tommy studies him, then nods and turns him loose. "I'll walk you home." He steps to the door, stopping briefly to put on san-dals—mine, of course, because he likes them better than his own. Simon says good night under his breath and follows him outside.

Camille is staring at her plate and Kyle is playing with the fringe on the tablecloth. The music on the radio seeps back into the room, low brass at first, then cellos and violas and a nasal-voiced clarinet.

I sigh and take a big gulp of beer. "I'm sorry, Camille. I shouldn't have said that."

"It doesn't matter." She refolds the napkin on her lap. "Surely Tommy isn't having sex with Simon?"

I reach out and feed a glob of dry wax from the base of the can-dle into the flame. "I don't know. A minute ago I was so sure . . ." I meet her eyes. "What do you think?"

Kyle clears his throat. "He's smarter than that."

Camille's eyes flit over her husband and back to me. "I don't know."

There's one other memory of my mother that bears mentioning. It's more vague than the one of watching her die, but still potent, nonetheless.

I was probably four years old or so, I don't remember exactly, but I was old enough to walk to the end of the lane with Dad to buy some potatoes. (Dale Cromwell and his wife used to own a fruit and vegetable stand there every summer, selling fresh produce from their farm at ridiculously cheap prices.) Tommy was too small to walk that far and had to stay with Mom—which pissed him off—but I was thrilled because I seldom got Dad to myself anymore.

I don't remember the walk at all, except for the end of it. I couldn't wait to gloat to Tommy about everything he'd missed, so once the clearing came in sight, I ran ahead of Dad down the final steps of the lane and burst from the woods like a flushed pheasant. Tommy was sitting on the front porch steps, still pouting, and Mom was wa-tering some flowers with a hose.

The instant I saw her my feet stopped moving.

It was early evening, past the worst heat of the day, but the sun wasn't quite down yet, and the water coming from the spray nozzle of the hose was catching the light and turning the air into waves of color. It looked like Mom was waving a magic wand. Her hair was under a red bandana, and she was singing the alphabet song to Tommy, trying to cheer him up. I think she was barefoot.

I couldn't have told you then why I stopped running, and I'm not sure I can even now. All I know is that it had something to do with love.

Quit rolling your eyes, please.

Love doesn't "grow." It doesn't wait for you to discover it, it doesn't fall like a gentle rain from the sky, it doesn't tiptoe into your heart like a happy little bunny, and it doesn't have a fucking thing to do with familiarity. Love is neither patient nor kind.

Love attacks. It sneaks up like a pride of lions or a pack of hyenas and eats your heart out while you watch. Love is the bully on the playground who takes your lunch money and gives you a black eye in return, the arsonist who burns your house down with you in it, the witch who lures you into her home with candy and boils you alive for dinner. Love is raw, and violent, and instantaneous. You don't fall in love; you get trampled by it.

I was only four years old, and I had never known what love really was until that day I saw my mother singing to my brother. Before then it was only a word, just an abstract concept I confused with simple affection. But that was the day it became a reality, something palpable and awful and heart-stopping.

If it doesn't drop you to your knees and make you shake like a wet dog, it's not love.

Anyway, it was only for a moment, then everything went back to normal. (That's another thing about love. It's always hit-and-run.) Dad came up behind me with his bag of potatoes and asked me if anything was wrong, and I told him no and skipped over to Tommy to brag about the turtle we'd seen in the lane on the way home. Mom flicked the hose at me as I passed her and got me wet.

I can't remember her face that day. I don't remember the color of her blouse, or if she was wearing pants or shorts. I don't remember if her voice was high or low, or how tall she was compared to me, or why she was watering the flowers out front instead of the ones in back.

But I remember I loved her.
I still do.

It just occurred to me that all of my best memories involve Tommy. And all of my worst ones, too. Every time something significant happens in my life, Tommy is part of it. Without him, there's no me to speak of.

After the dishes are cleared I tell Kyle and Camille I'm going for a walk. Kyle offers to come with me but I tell him I need to be alone. Tommy's not back yet with my sandals, so I grab a pair of sneakers from the closet, then a flashlight off the kitchen counter on my way out the door.

It's almost cool outside. The humidity has dropped and the sky is cloudless, and the stars are so bright I don't need to turn the flashlight on to see where I'm going. I kick at the grass for a minute, then I wander out back.

The cornfield looks like a graveyard. The twine is almost invisible, but the stakes are all too clear, standing in neat rows across the field, jutting up in the air like tombstones. A coyote howls in the distance, and a sudden breeze blows by from the north and tugs at the back of my shirt. Gooseflesh crawls up my spine.

When Tommy and I were kids, we used to play out here after Dale harvested the corn. We would attack the empty stalks with long sticks we pretended were samurai swords, swinging them around and screaming "Sushi!" (The only Japanese word we knew.) And sometimes after Dale had plowed the corn under at the end of the summer, we'd have campfires on the bare ground, and sit around talking until the flames died and the coals burned out. But now Cheri's turned our familiar field into a low-budget movie set, and I can't stand to look at it.

I turn around and head for the lane. The living room lights are on in the cottage, and as I'm passing by I can see Camille in Dad's old rocking chair, reading. She's by herself, and there's a light on behind the closed curtains of the guest room, so I assume Kyle is in there, avoiding her. I hope to God he doesn't decide to tell her about our little escapade.

The memory of his hand in my shorts pops into my mind and I get an erection. I can't believe I made him stop. His marriage is already down the tubes, and if he doesn't cheat on Camille with me, he will with somebody else, soon enough. I should have given him what he wanted. I should have unzipped his fly and dived in like a falcon after a snake.

I take a deep breath and force myself to think about Tommy and Simon.

I'm at a loss. The way Simon was looking at Tommy tonight—not to mention the obvious physical ease between them—had me utterly convinced for a few minutes that Tommy was lying to me about their relationship. But Simon's shocked reaction to my accusations unsettled me, and now I haven't got a clue what the truth is. If I'm right, then I have to find a way to stop it. If I'm wrong . . .

My feet grind to a halt behind the parked cars in front of the cottage. God. Who am I kidding?

If Tommy was lying about something like this, I would know, wouldn't I?

Of course I would.

Without a question, without a doubt. No one knows him better than me, and the more I think about it, the more I realize he had to be telling the truth, both this afternoon and tonight. He's never been able to hide feeling guilty, and there was no guilt in him. Not a speck. I'm suddenly sure of it.

So what the hell is the matter with me? What came over me? Am I jealous of their friendship? Did I let Philip's certainty cloud my judgment?

Not that it matters. The cardinal point is I was being a complete asshole, and the look on Tommy's face before he left was devastating. He's never looked at me like that before, not even when I was getting ready to mail obscene pictures of Andy and Joe to their parents. I'll be lucky if he ever speaks to me again. I called him a liar and a pedophile, and I did it in front of his two closest friends and an innocent boy who adores him. I am such a piece of crap.

And he was absolutely right in what he said: Dad is alive and well. Tommy's told me before that I should get therapy and deal with all this father-hate crap, but I don't need a therapist.

I need an exorcist.

I've got to find Tommy and try to fix this between us.

I start walking again, faster. Maybe I can find him on his way back from Simon's. I'm not sure where Simon lives, but if I know Tommy, he'll be too pissed to come home right away and he'll swing by Manchester's for a beer. I'll try there first.

It's darker in the woods, but I still don't have to use the flashlight. The lane is dirt and gravel, with a strip of knee-high grass running down the middle of it. It's full of potholes that are treacherous for cars and unwary hikers, but I know every inch of this lane and these woods. Tommy and I spent as much time fooling around out here when we were kids as we did at the beach.

The only sound for a moment is my feet on the earth, but then a bird or a bat flaps by my head and I stop abruptly, startled. A dog barks in the distance, and a truck rumbles by on the old highway, half a mile from here. The night is so still I can hear the truck's wheels whining on the pavement. The sound fades away and is replaced by a human voice murmuring.

There's no one else out here. I strain my ears and wait, sure I imagined it, but just as I take another step I hear it again. It's coming from back in the trees, to my left. I look around, getting my bearings, and something clicks in my brain.

About thirty feet from me, further in the woods, is the foundation of an old abandoned farmhouse that my great-grandfather tore down when he bought this land and built the cottage. I think he actually used some of the wood from it, but everything else was hauled off except for a flat slab of concrete and one jagged, waist-high wall. Tommy and I used it as a kind of poor man's fort when we were little, but in high school it served mainly as a place to hide our pot pipes and our booze. There was a driveway leading out to it at one time, but all that's left of that is a narrow deer path. No one else besides Tommy and me—and possibly Caleb Farrell—even knows it's there, and I haven't even thought about it in years.

I hear the voice again, but when it falls silent this time another voice answers. My stomach clenches.

I find the deer path and follow it, taking my time and stepping quietly, like a hunter. The trail is covered with undergrowth and broken branches, and this far in the woods it's harder to see what I'm doing, but there's still enough light to avoid the worst of it. I pick my way along, one step at a time, letting my eyes adjust gradually.

The voices are intermittent, and male. I can't make out individual words yet, but I know who's talking: Tommy and Simon. Tommy's voice is low and relaxed, and Simon's is higher and a little breathy.

As I get closer to the foundation, I can see better again. Young trees have started reclaiming the earth around it, but there's still a patch of clear sky overhead, and in the starlight I can easily make out the uneven contour of the wall, and a large, moving mound next to it. I creep closer, and the mound becomes two people, one on top of the other. There's a dark patch under them, probably some kind of blanket or tarp (Where did they get that, I wonder? Tommy's car?), and a small pile of something by their feet. I take another couple of steps and drop to a crouch beside a bush at the edge of the clearing. I'm less than a dozen feet from them, but I'm in no danger of being discovered, because all their attention is focused on what they're doing.

The pile by their feet is their clothes; from this vantage point I can see Tommy's naked back, and the paler flesh of his bare butt bobbing up and down in the night air. Simon's ankles are riding on Tommy's shoulders, like matching parrots on a pirate, and one of his hands is in Tommy's hair. I can't make out his other hand, because it's hidden between their groins, but the forearm attached to it is pumping up and down with clocklike regularity.

I can hear them better now, too, but neither is saying much. Simon is panting and moaning a little, and Tommy drops his head to kiss him, then pulls away again. "How you doing?" he asks.

"Great," Simon gasps. "I'm doing great."

"Me too." Tommy voice is getting as ragged as Simon's. "I'm getting close."

"Me too." Simon's legs stiffen. "Oh God. Oh my God."

Tommy shushes him. "Wait just a little longer, okay? Wait for me."

They kiss again. It lasts a long time, and all I can hear for a while is the usual forest noises: rustling leaves, an owl, random animal movement at ground level.

My legs are cramping. I can't seem to move, and I don't know what to do. Rage is inside me like a living thing, beating at my temples and making it hard to breathe. I should stop this or I should leave, but I'm paralyzed.

I want to hurt them. It frightens me how much I want to hurt them. I want to leap out of the darkness with my flashlight and impale them in its beam, then I want to smash their frightened faces together until bones break and blood flows. My whole body is trembling with the need to hurt them.

But I can't. I need to know something first.

Simon throws his head back and groans. "I have to cum."

"Just a little longer," Tommy grunts.

Simon arches his back and cries out and Tommy puts a hand over his mouth to stifle him. A few frantic thrusts later he lets out a short "ah," and then a muffled, "Oh, Jesus!"

They gradually stop moving, decelerating to a halt like a windup toy, and I hold still, too, not daring to breathe in the abrupt silence. Simon's legs drop from Tommy's shoulders to the ground. I feel something crawling on my shin and even though it makes me shudder I leave whatever it is alone.

A minute passes, and Tommy raises his head again. I can barely hear him. "That was amazing," he whispers. "Even better than this afternoon."

Thank you, Tommy. That's all I needed to know.

I aim the flashlight at them and snap it on. "I hope you guys sprayed yourselves with some Deep Woods Off before coming out here. You're begging for Lyme disease."

They fly apart in a flurry of arms and legs. Simon lurches against the wall and wraps himself into a ball and Tommy leaps to his feet and throws up a hand in front of his eyes to try to see me. His skin is dripping with sweat and his dick is still half-hard.

I stand up and step closer to them. A vein is pulsing in my head and there's a flood of acid in my stomach, but I keep my voice offensively pleasant. "Fancy meeting you out here, Tommy. I thought you were walking Simon home." I flick the light in Simon's direction. He winces at the light and tries to block it with his arm. "Oh, look, there's Simon now. What a coincidence. Say, why are you guys naked?"

"Stop it, Nathan." Tommy leans over and grabs his shorts from the pile of clothes at his feet. "Turn that damn light off."

"Oh, I'm sorry. How rude of me." I leave it on. "I'm sorry to interrupt you guys, but I just wanted to apologize for what I said at dinner. How can I ever make it up to you?"

Tommy's having trouble putting his shorts on because his hands are shaking. "I can't believe you were spying on me," he mutters. "That's pretty low. My brother, the eternal voyeur." He finally gets the boxers past his feet and yanks them up to cover his groin.

My control starts to slip. "Don't you fucking dare try to make this about me, you lying son of a bitch."

He recoils at the animosity in my voice, then he steps toward me, pleading. "I didn't want to lie to you, Nathan, but I knew you wouldn't understand. You didn't leave me any choice."

My fingers dig into the flashlight. "Yeah, I can see your point. You're right. From here on, I'll try really hard not to be such a close-minded prick about child abuse." I hold up my hand to stop him from getting closer to me. "Don't say another word, Tommy, or you'll leave me no choice, either, except to beat the living shit out of you."

He flinches and I stab the light at Simon again. "Get dressed, Simon. Now."

He scrambles across the foundation to his clothes, covering his crotch with one hand.

I shift the light back to Tommy. "This ends tonight. Either you do it, or I will."

He's putting on his shirt but he freezes mid-motion. "What's that supposed to mean?"

"It means you leave first thing for New York in the morning, or I call Simon's dad and let him know what I just saw."

Simon lurches toward me with just his shirt on, modesty forgotten. "Please don't do that, Mr. Bishop. He'll kill me."

"I don't want to, Simon, but nothing else I've said has gotten through to you two idiots. You're not leaving me any options."

He falls on his knees in front of me and starts to sob. "I promise we'll stop. I promise. Please don't tell my dad."

Tommy is fully dressed now. He comes over carrying the rest of Simon's clothes. "Don't worry, Simon. Nathan won't tell anyone. I'll leave tomorrow morning, and everything will be fine." He kneels down next to him and hands him his underwear. "Finish getting dressed, okay? I'll walk you home."

"Over my dead body." I snatch Simon's cutoffs and sandals out of Tommy's hands. "You go back to the cottage. I'll walk Simon home."

Tommy gets to his feet, glaring. "Stop ordering me around, Nathan."

"Fine. Don't go to the cottage. Go to Afghanistan or Bumfuck, Egypt, for all I care. Or better yet, go to hell. Just get away from Simon."

Simon is still sniveling but he gets to his feet and pulls on the rest of his clothes. Tommy puts his arms around him but Simon is watching me the whole time and doesn't hug him back. Tommy pulls away with a hurt look.

I take Simon's arm and shine the light on the deer path. "Let's go."

Tommy calls my name after we take a few steps. I turn around to face him, shining the flashlight at his torso. For the first time I notice how the foundation behind him has changed since we were kids; the wall is crumbling apart and several tree roots have broken through the pavement and pocked it with holes.

He runs a hand through his hair. "Remember what Dad did to Andy and you?"

Something in my chest starts to ache. "Andy and I were the same age, Tommy. It's not the same thing, and you know it."

His eyes are glistening. "Maybe not, but it sure feels like it."

Simon takes a step back toward him, but I keep a firm grip on his arm and he doesn't try to break away. I shrug. "Tough shit, Tommy. I don't care how it feels."

He blinks, then drops his head and backs blindly toward the foundation, where he stoops to pick up the blanket. I turn Simon around again and lead him back to the lane.

After I ask him where he lives and he tells me, we don't talk at all on the way to his house. He stares at his feet and occasionally wipes his nose on his sleeve. A few cars pass us and I want to kick myself for not driving him home; no doubt someone will recognize me and start rumors about what I was doing out at this hour with one of my students.

His parents bought the old Carroll place on Market Street, which is less than a quarter mile from the school and about two miles from the cottage. His driveway is U-shaped and lined with pine trees. I stop at the head of it. The walk should have calmed me down, but I'm still seething. I put my hand on his shoulder and give him a shove up the driveway. "Go inside, Simon. I'll wait here and make sure you do."

He meets my eyes for the first time since we left Tommy. "I don't blame you for being mad at us."

I sigh. "I'm not mad at you, Simon."

"You're not?"

"No. I'm not even close to mad. I'm fucking furious." The whispered words come boiling out of me. "It's taking every ounce of willpower I've got to not beat your brains out with a rock. I tried to warn you but you were too goddamn stupid to listen. And not only that, but you lied to me. You stood there in my fucking kitchen and looked me right in the face and lied to me."

Tears spring to his eyes again. "I'm sorry, I really am. But I couldn't help it. We fell in love and it was like something took over my brain and . . ."

"And the next thing you knew Tommy's dick was in your ass. Give it a rest, Simon. I don't want to hear it. It's not love, it's just sex. Go find another teenager and spread your legs for him, or go out for football and have an orgy with the whole team. I don't care. Just stay the fuck away from my brother. He is not going to prison because of you, you stupid little shit, do you get that?"

His face is a mess. The whole time I've been spitting venom at him he's been crying without a sound, and snot is running freely from his nose. He tries to talk and fails, then finally manages to blurt out, "I would never tell anybody about Tommy. Never."

Even through my anger I'm all too aware that part of me is enjoying hurting him, and it's making me sick. But I have to finish this in a way that will prevent further damage to any of us, and I don't know what else to do.

I drop the flashlight and grab his arms. "You better not, Simon." I turn my head and glance at his house, and I make my voice as cold as I can. "I know where you live, now, and if you ever say anything about Tommy to anybody, I'll come find you." I shove my nose in his face and squeeze his biceps as hard as I can. "How's that for a promise?"

He recoils and cries out in pain, and I immediately want to take it back. He's the *victim,* for God's sake, and I'm threatening him like a Mafia thug in a bad movie. But, Jesus, what else can I do? His puppy love for Tommy will lapse eventually, and then what? What if he decides he wants to blackmail Tommy or me to buy his silence? I'm not about to sit around for the next ten years, waiting to see if he has a change of heart. If he fears me, then maybe this will go away and we can all get on with our lives.

He's crying so hard that tears are literally spurting out of his eyes. I can't bear to look at him. I let go of him. "Go to bed, Simon." I sound hoarse. "We'll talk some more later and . . ."

I trail off, unable to finish. I stare at the ground, listening to him cry and hating myself. If I had a knife I'd slit my throat.

The next thing I know, his head is on my chest and his arms are around my waist. "It's okay, everything's okay," he murmurs. "I know you didn't mean it."

I let my face fall into his hair for an instant. He smells like my brother. I push his arms off and pick up the flashlight. The glass over the bulb is cracked.

"Go inside, Simon." I turn away. "Do us all a favor and forget about Tommy."

*   *   *

When I get back to the cottage, Kyle is still in the guest room with the door closed, and Camille hasn't moved from the rocker in the living room. She's got her legs curled under her like a little girl.

She puts down her book when I walk in. "Did you have a nice walk?"

I hear the words but they don't make sense to me. "Is Tommy here?"

She frowns. "No, he's not. How far away does Simon live?"

"I don't know." I mutter something about being tired, and I head for the staircase.

"Is anything the matter?" Worry creeps into her voice. "Did something else happen?"

I stop with my foot on the bottom step. I want to tell her what's going on, but my tongue isn't working. I shake my head.

She gets up and stands with her arms crossed in front of her chest. "What is it, Nathan? You're frightening me."

I swallow. "I'm sorry. It's nothing, really."

She steps closer but I turn away quickly and say good night. Her eyes follow me up the stairs.

In my bedroom I get undressed, dutifully checking my body and clothes for ticks. I find one on the inside of my shirt, nestled in the seam at the collar. I pluck it out and put it on the desk. By the time I find a cigarette lighter in one of the drawers, it's crawled a couple of inches toward me, still after my blood.

"You bastards don't give up, do you?" I flick the lighter on and incinerate it, burning a black spot on the desk's surface in the process. The tick shrinks back, then pops. I let the flame stay on until the lighter gets too hot to hold, singeing my thumb and forefinger.

I pull on a clean pair of shorts, turn off the overhead light, and get in bed, but I'm still awake when Tommy comes home a couple hours later, sliding the back door shut behind him. He makes his way up the staircase without bothering to turn on a light.

"Nathan?"

I don't answer.

"I'm sorry, Nathan. I'm really, really sorry."

It's dark but I can still make out his body at the top of the stairs. "Go to bed, Tommy. You need to get up early to head back to New York."

Silence. "What about Kyle and Camille?"

"They're your friends, not mine."

He tries to laugh. "I think Kyle likes you better than me, now."

He walks across the room and sits on the end of my bed. "I fucked up."

"Get out of here, Tommy. I mean it."

"Jeez." His voice is sad and gentle. "You'd think I'd pissed you off or something."

I stay silent. He's facing me, but I can't see his features. He smells like beer but he sounds sober; he's always had a high tolerance for alcohol. A minute passes, then another. He finally gets to his feet and steps gingerly toward the stairwell, but he stops again on the top step and turns around. "Can I at least stay until late morning? If I leave too early I'll get stuck in rush hour back in the city."

"Be gone before noon."

"Thanks." He takes another step down. "Is Simon okay?"

"He's fine."

He sighs. "Good. He's a sweet kid. I know you think I'm an asshole for getting involved with him, but . . ."

I sit up. "Shut up, Tommy. Shut up right now, before I come over there and break every goddamn bone in your body."

His laugh is bitter. "Did I use your camera without asking?"

"What are you talking about?"

"Remember? That's exactly what Dad said after you used his camera to get a picture of Andy and Joe. He didn't know what you'd used it for, of course, but he still threatened to 'break every goddamn bone in your body' if you did it again. Your voice even had the same inflection just now when you said it. It's kind of funny if you think about it."

I lie down and roll over so my back is to him. "Get the fuck out of my room."

A few seconds later he leaves. I hear the springs on the futon mattress in the living room protest when he lays down, and I'm still awake ten minutes later when he starts snoring.

CHAPTER 8

I wake up at five thirty. The sky is overcast, and it's almost twenty degrees cooler than it's been for weeks. I try to go back to sleep but it's useless; my mind is babbling like an imbecile, worrying about Tommy and Simon and Ted Baker and the cornfield. I sit up and pull the sheet over my shoulders to stay warm, and I stare around my room, watching as the dull gray light from the east window makes its way down from the ceiling and picks an object at a time to linger over.

Everything is still where Dad had it. The desk is in the same place, and the bed, and the chest of drawers, and the nightstand. There's a pile of framed pictures leaning against the wall that hasn't been touched in years, and a shelf of books over the west window with an upside-down copy of *Robinson Crusoe* stuck in the middle—God only knows how long that's been like that.

Why haven't I changed things around? Why haven't I tossed out everything I don't need or want, and rearranged the furniture, and put up some artwork on the bare walls? And why is this the first time I've thought to ask myself those questions?

A psychiatrist would have a field day with me: *"So, Nathan. The reason you haven't made any changes to your home since your father died is obviously not connected to sentimental feelings. Why do you suppose you've been reluctant to make the cottage your own? Are you uncomfortable with change? Or are you perhaps attempting to establish a connection, however tenuous, with your father (a distant, difficult man, by all accounts) by main-*

*taining the same physical environment you became accustomed
to as a child?"*

I don't know. I like the large things where they are, and the clut-
ter around them doesn't bother me any more than it bothered
Dad. My problems with him had nothing to do with the objects he
collected or how he decorated his home, and to purge the cottage
of all evidence of the man himself would be a pointless symbolic
gesture. I'd have to raze the whole place to the ground to get rid of
him; he's in the ceiling, and in the floor, and in the cinder blocks
lining the wine cellar.

I'm a coward. I'm distracting myself with this shit because I
don't want to get out of bed and face this day. Throwing Tommy out
is one thing—he deserves it, and I want him gone—but I'm also
cutting Kyle's and Camille's vacation short. I could invite them to
stay without Tommy here, I suppose, but given the weirdness between Kyle and me that's a terrible idea. Even so, I don't want to
deal with the hurt looks on their faces when Tommy tells them they
have to go.

Then there's Ted Baker. God only knows what he's told
Madeline, and what action they'll take against me for my "improper" behavior with Simon. I may not have a job by the end of
the day, and if I get fired, I'll be out of money by early August. I'm
not very good with money. I own the cottage free and clear, but the
property taxes are crippling, and day-to-day life in a resort town like
Walcott is twice as expensive as most places. The small savings I had
after Dad died is gone—it got me through another rough patch last
year—and opportunities for employment in the area are extremely
limited. I suppose I'll find something, but who's going to hire me if
Baker starts gossiping with one of his drinking buddies, or a mom
from the local PTA? *("Now I'm not saying that Bishop went so far
as to actually molest that boy, but it sure looked suspicious to me . . .")*
Madeline is decent enough that even if she lets me go she'll stay
silent, but after Baker's done shooting off his mouth I'll be lucky to
find work flipping burgers at McDonald's.

But what I'm dreading most today is seeing Simon. How can I
face him after last night? I treated him so badly, and I'm embarrassed and ashamed that I didn't do more to keep him away from

Tommy in the first place. If I'd been more vigilant this never would have happened. Yeah, I know they went behind my back, but I should have sent Tommy packing the instant after I saw them messing around on the couch. Simon's just a kid and Tommy is, well, Tommy. It was up to me to be the adult around here and keep things in control.

I guess I should just be glad that it's all over.

I push the sheet off and get to my feet. It's almost chilly in here. I put on a pair of shorts and a shirt and head downstairs. Tommy is buried in the blankets on the futon, and all I can see is his nose and one knee.

I get my shower and have some breakfast, then I dawdle around upstairs until it's time to go to school. Everybody's still asleep when I come back downstairs on my way out.

I shake Tommy's shoulder. "I'm taking off."

He pulls the sheet off his head and blinks at me. "What time is it?"

"Eight thirty."

"Are Kyle and Camille awake?" He's got morning breath.

"No. But you'll have to get them up soon so they'll have time to pack."

He grimaces. "I know, Nathan. You don't have to keep telling me."

I straighten. "I'll be back in time to say good-bye."

"How sweet."

I ignore the sourness in his voice and go out the front door. Jane Hampstead pulls into the clearing—Bill's in her backseat and Sally's sitting shotgun—just as I'm getting into my car. I don't feel like talking but she rolls down her window so I'm forced to be polite and roll mine down, too.

"Good morning, Nathan."

"Hi, Dr. Hampstead."

Sally leans closer and also says good morning. Hampstead frowns at the intrusion into her personal space but Sally ignores her. She's wearing lipstick today, and a tight red blouse. I say hello to her and she blushes and gives me a huge smile.

Oh, for Christ's sake.

I look quickly back at Hampstead. "I think I saw the ghost of Ramses running around your cornfield this morning."

She raises a thin white eyebrow. "If he's torn up my grids, I'm going to kick his ass."

I smile in spite of myself. "So what's on the agenda today? More arts and crafts with twine?"

"Nope, that's mostly done. We're going to start digging a trial trench today."

"Sounds like fun. What then?"

"Depends on what we find." Her face darkens. "Or if we're even digging in the right place."

"Well, if you turn up any gold doubloons, they're mine."

She grins and waves. "Finders, keepers."

Class started twenty minutes ago and Simon still isn't here. I'm relieved not to see him, but I'm worried he may be at the cottage with Tommy—though surely he wouldn't be *that* retarded. I go through the motions of teaching, but I'm watching the clock the whole time. I can get away with leaving a little early, but if I dismiss class too soon and Baker finds out it will just give him more ammunition against me.

I'm pacing around the front of the room and trying to engage the kids in a discussion about adjectives. Most of them are at least trying to look interested, but Vernette is blowing bubbles and staring at the ceiling. All of a sudden I'm unreasonably irritated with her.

I grab the wastebasket and hold it next to her desk. "Spit the gum out, Vernette."

She rolls her eyes. "How come?"

"Because I said so."

"You've never made me spit it out before."

"That's because I was waiting to ruin your life until today. Spit."

She takes the glob of pink goo out of her mouth with her fingers—it's the same color as her lipstick—and drops it in the trash. "This isn't fair, Mr. Bishop. Peter's got gum, too."

"Yeah, but Peter's not blowing bubbles and chewing so loudly I can't hear myself think."

She crosses her arms across her breasts. "Why are you always picking on me?"

I set the wastebasket back on the floor by the desk. "Because I've been put on this earth to make your life difficult."

"That's not funny. I think you should . . ."

I'm not in the mood for this shit today and my temper flares. "It's just a piece of bubble gum, Vernette. Stop acting like it's a fucking family heirloom."

There's a collective intake of breath from the rest of the class. I close my eyes briefly, cursing myself. Tommy and Simon have me so rattled I can't even function properly.

I sigh. "I'm sorry, Vernette. I shouldn't have sworn at you. I'm just in a bad mood today, so how about giving me a break?"

I expect a big scene, now, but she studies me for a minute and the pissed look on her face slowly dissolves. "Okay." She smiles at me. "But just this once."

She has large, crooked teeth, but it's a surprisingly good-natured smile.

If I live to be a thousand I'll never understand high school kids. It's not just Vernette, either; for some reason everybody in the room now seems more cheerful and relaxed. Maybe I should make it a point from here on to say "fuck" at least once in every class.

There's a knock at the door and Cleo Norton sticks her head in. She must have just gotten a permanent because her hair is fluffier than usual. "Can I see you in the hall for a minute, Nathan?"

I tell the kids I'll be right back and step out of the room, closing the door behind me. "Hey, Cleo. Your head got big."

She doesn't smile and she leans in close to whisper. Her breath smells like chocolate. "Something's going on, Nathan. Something bad. Ted got a call a few minutes ago from Simon Hart's father. I don't know what it was about, but Ted said your name, and something about the police. When he hung up he went to find Madeline. He looked pretty upset."

"Jesus." The floor lurches under my feet.

She puts a plump hand on my arm to steady me. "What's happening, Nathan? What did you do?"

My heart is pounding and I feel dizzy. Simon must have told his dad about Tommy. But why in the name of God would he have done that? It doesn't make sense.

I force myself to think. "I didn't do anything, Cleo. What exactly did Ted say about the police?"

"I couldn't hear much. I think he was asking Mr. Hart if they'd been notified." She squeezes my elbow. "Please don't tell Ted I told you. I could lose my job for this."

I study her. "So why tell me?"

She shrugs. "I don't know. I just thought I should warn you." She drops her hand. "I know you, Nathan. You're no angel, but you wouldn't do anything too terrible, and whatever is going on must be some kind of mistake. I didn't want you to get blindsided, that's all."

"Thanks." I give her a quick kiss on the cheek. My mind is racing. "I've got to go."

The first hint of distrust crosses her face. "Where are you going?"

"I'll tell you later, I promise." Panic is welling up in me and I start moving down the hall toward the parking lot, talking over my shoulder. "And don't worry, Cleo. You're right. I haven't done anything wrong. It's just a huge misunderstanding."

She's trailing behind me, trying to catch up. "What about your class?"

I don't answer. My feet are going faster and faster, and by the time I hit the door I'm running.

I've got to get to Tommy before the police do.

I drive like a drunken teenager to the cottage, squealing tires around corners and completely disregarding stop signs. I'm vaguely aware of people staring at me as I fly by them, but I don't pay any attention to who they are. The sky is getting darker and by the time I turn off the road onto our lane it's starting to sprinkle.

I floor the car through the woods, ignoring the potholes even when I hit one of them so hard it nearly rips the steering wheel from my hands, and I don't slow down until I get to the clearing. I skid to a halt on the grass next to Cheri Tipton's Subaru and jump out, leaving the keys in the ignition.

Kyle is standing at the kitchen sink with a mug of coffee in his hands. He starts as the screen door bangs shut behind me. "Hey, Nathan. You're home early, aren't you?"

He's relaxed and chipper, and it's obvious that Tommy hasn't told him about our conversation last night.

"Where's Tommy?" I demand.

He frowns. "In the shower. Is something wrong?"

I step over to the bathroom and open the door and a wave of steam engulfs me.

"Who's that?" Tommy calls out cheerfully.

I sweep aside the shower curtain and get splashed by hot water. He's got his head tilted back, rinsing shampoo from his hair, and he yelps in surprise.

I bend down and turn off the faucet. "Get dressed, Tommy. Now. The police are on their way."

He stares at me. "What?"

I grab a towel off the rack and stuff it in his hands. "Hurry up."

He stands there, motionless and dripping. "You called the police?"

"Don't be an idiot." I search the room for his clothes, but there's only a wadded pair of boxers on the floor beside the washer and dryer. "Ted Baker's secretary overheard Baker on the phone with Simon's dad."

He's still just standing there. I put my arms around him and yank him roughly from the tub. His knees bang against the porcelain and he cries out, but I ignore him. "Come on, Tommy, goddammit, move!"

He finally starts to towel off but it seems like slow motion. I snatch the towel from his hands and shove him toward the door. "Forget drying off. Just get your suitcase. You can dress in the car."

He stumbles naked into the kitchen in front of me. Kyle and Camille are both standing by the table, looking anxious. Camille steps toward us. "What's going on?"

Tommy slows to talk to her and I give him another shove in the direction of the living room. He disappears through the doorway and I stare after him. "Tommy's in trouble." I toss the towel over a chair. "I've got to get him out of here right now."

She bites her lip. "Simon?"

I nod. "I think so."

Kyle's face goes white and Camille's eyes fill. "Oh, Jesus. What are you going to do?"

I fight to keep my voice calm. "I don't know. Take him someplace safe."

She bites her lower lip. "Are you sure that's wise? Maybe we should just hire a good lawyer and . . ."

I shake my head. "Clarence Darrow couldn't get him out of this one."

I step into the living room and almost collide with Tommy on his way back to the kitchen. He's got on a pair of shorts and a shirt and he's carrying his suitcase. His clothes are stuck to his skin. "I think Camille's right," he says.

"And I think you're a moron," I snap. "Simon's dad is a district attorney, Tommy. You'll be lucky to be out of jail before it's time to move into the nursing home. Stop arguing and come on."

I take the suitcase from him and lead him to the front door, but he stops to hug Kyle and Camille. Kyle's crying.

I open the screen door. "We've got to go, Tommy. Now."

He pulls away from Camille and lurches toward me. His face looks blurred. "I need my sandals," he mutters. He bends down and starts hunting around in the pile of shoes by the door.

I grab his shirt collar with my free hand and pull on it hard. It rips and he almost falls into me. "Forget your fucking sandals, Tommy! Let's go."

He finally gives up and follows me outside. The rain has stopped again and the temperature is rising. We hurry across the lawn to the car.

I'm opening the door and tossing the suitcase in the backseat and he's going around to get in the other side when we hear a car coming down the lane. We both freeze and stare at each other over the hood of my Chevette. There's a small patch of shampoo in his hair above his right ear, and his face has the same expression it had—terrified, uncomprehending—as when we watched Mom die.

"Oh, Jesus, Nathan," he says.

A police car pulls into the clearing.

*   *   *

The Walcott Police Station is a one-story brick building that used to be a junior high school when Dad was a kid. It still smells like a school, all dust and ammonia and dried sweat and mimeograph machines. I've never been in here before, even though I've passed it on the way to the grocery store two or three times a week for years. There's a flimsy wooden barricade with bulletproof glass protecting the dispatcher/receptionist at the front door, and once she checks you out and decides you're not dangerous, she lets you in to a small waiting area with wood floors and benches and a heavy iron door in the back that leads to jail cells and offices and God knows what else.

Kyle and Camille and I are waiting for Tommy's attorney to come back from talking to Tommy. The pudgy-faced officer at the desk next to the iron door (drinking Diet Coke and eating corn nuts) just told us the set amount for bail for statutory rape in Connecticut is thirteen thousand five hundred dollars.

The cop who arrested Tommy was Paul Joublowsky. Tommy and I both know him because he used to be a lifeguard with us back in high school. We were even friends, sort of, occasionally getting drunk in the dunes after the main gates to the beach were closed for the night. I don't see him very often anymore, but whenever we pass each other on the street we always wave, and sometimes we'll bump into each other at Manchester's and have a beer together.

But he acted like a stranger when he arrested Tommy.

I've never seen my brother so subdued and beaten as when Paul was putting the cuffs on him and reading him his rights. Kyle and Camille stood a few feet away, holding each other, and Cheri Tipton came around front to see what was going on and planted herself next to them, whispering questions.

I tried to act shocked and indignant, but Paul just stared at me as if he knew exactly what I was doing. I demanded to know what was going on and he sighed.

"Don't make this harder than it already is, Nathan," he said. "I just told you Tom's been accused of having sex with a minor. Don't insult us both by pretending you didn't see this coming."

I kept my eyes locked on his. "I don't know what you're talking about."

"Bullshit." He spat a wad of tobacco on the ground. "You're lucky you're not being arrested, too."

Tommy's head jerked up. "What? Nathan didn't do anything."

Paul snorted. "Right. He's as innocent as the Virgin Mary. That's why he didn't report what he saw in the woods last night." He nods at the expression on Tommy's face. "Yeah, I know all about that." He smiled grimly when Tommy looked away. "And what about that suitcase in the back of your car, Nathan? You weren't by any chance headed someplace where I'd have had a harder time finding you guys, were you? Because if you were . . ."

I tried to interrupt. "We were on our way downtown . . ."

"Because if you were," he continued, "that would open you up to charges of giving aid to a suspected criminal."

I rolled my eyes and attempted to sound exasperated. "We were just going to the train station, Paul. He's on his way back to New York this morning."

He looked pointedly at Tommy's bare feet. "So I guess they're not wearing shoes in the city these days?" He flicked the glob of lather out of Tommy's wet hair. "You missed a spot there, buddy. Looks like you were in a hurry." He heaved a sigh and glared at me. "Look, Nathan. I don't like this any better than you do. But your brother's in deep shit, and if I were you I'd keep my mouth shut and call a lawyer."

He put Tommy in the backseat of his squad car and said I could follow them down to the station to arrange bail. I watched them pull out of sight into the lane, and Tommy turned his head so I could see his face through the rear window. His lips moved; I think he said my name.

I'm trying to listen to the cop at the desk. (The silver tag on his shoulder says "Sergeant Darling," and I overheard Paul call him "Rex" a minute ago. He must be new in town because I've never seen him before.) He's telling me about a bail bondsman but nothing he's saying makes sense. Tommy's in jail and I haven't got a clue how to help him. My heart feels as if somebody is kneading it between their fingers like dough.

Camille has her hand on my elbow and Kyle is on my other side, darting looks at my face.

The sergeant is still talking. "The bondsman's fee is usually ten percent of whatever the bail amount is, which is, of course, nonrefundable."

Camille whispers in my ear. "That's over thirteen hundred dollars you'd never get back. Can you borrow money against the cottage instead?"

I stare blankly at her. "The cottage?"

"You can probably get a home equity loan or something, I imagine."

I'm shaking my head before she finishes. "I'd have to go to the bank and that would take too much time. I have to get Tommy out of here right now."

The door behind Darling opens and Martin Melville steps out. Martin moved to Walcott in the late seventies and opened a law practice down the street from Dad's newspaper office. He's a sour-faced, leather-skinned crank who was older than God even back then, but he's still the best attorney in town, and the only one I'd trust to handle something like this. When I called him from the cottage and asked him if he could meet me at the police station to represent Tommy, he said yes before I told him why we needed him, and after I told him all he said was, "I hope your brother keeps his goddamn mouth shut until I get there."

He comes up to me now, wheezing a little and eyeing Kyle and Camille with suspicion. "I need to talk to you in private, Nathan."

I pull my arm away from Camille and follow him out the front door. It's getting hot again and the air feels heavy and wet. Once I catch up to him he doesn't say anything for a few steps and I get impatient. "So what's the deal, Marvin? What do we have to do?"

He stops walking and sets his briefcase by his feet. He's wearing dirty white sneakers that match the bristling hairs of his goatee. "The deal is that your brother is going to prison, and there is no way in hell I can prevent it."

I feel the blood drain from my face. "What are you talking about?"

He shakes his head. "I spoke with Harold Hart on the phone.

He's not going to try the case himself, but he's appointed some hotshot lawyer from his office who's already had Hart's kid tested for samples of Tom's DNA, and from what Tom just told me, that alone will probably do the trick." He meets my eyes. "I trust I'm not violating client confidentiality, here. He told me what happened with you in the woods last night." He picks a crumb out of his beard and waits for me to nod. "I didn't ask if he was guilty, by the way. He just volunteered the information."

I slump against the wall. "Surely there's something you can do. It's not as if Simon was an unwilling participant."

He grimaces. "It doesn't matter, Nathan. The bottom line is that the kid is only fifteen. He could have knocked your brother down on the ground and torn his pants off with his teeth and Tom would still be held liable for everything." He sighs. "If it was just the scientific evidence, I could poke a few holes in Hart's case, but he says he's prepared to make sure his son testifies in court, too, if necessary. That could get pretty ugly. Especially because Tom seems predisposed to tell all there is to tell."

My throat feels thick and I can barely talk. "If you lose, how many years are we talking about?"

"Ten. And the DA will probably manage to attach a fine of ten thousand dollars to that, too."

Ten years. Christ. "Can't you do a plea bargain or something?"

He chews on his mustache. "I'm afraid not. We've got nothing to bargain with, and even if we did, Hart's going to insist on the maximum sentence, no matter what."

"Jesus," I whisper.

A couple of people I don't know walk by and say hi. Melville nods at them and waits for them to get out of earshot. "You're also likely to have trouble getting a bondsman to post bail for you, because the only one in town is a good friend to the Hart family. Do you have access to that kind of cash?"

I nod. "I think so. I'll get a loan or something."

"Well, get over to the bank first or whatever you need to do, I guess, and then get him out of here. We'll talk some more before he goes up in front of the judge on Monday." He studies my face and frowns. "But I don't want to give you any false hope. Hart's out for blood, and unless we get very lucky, your brother's screwed."

"So you're going to tell him to plead guilty?"

He shrugs. "We can go to trial if he wants, but I think the end result is going to be the same no matter what we do. A trial would just prolong the inevitable."

I fight back tears. "I can't believe Simon told his dad about this. It doesn't make any sense."

He purses his lips. "It may not have been Simon. I don't know who told Hart, but we should probably find out. It might help us. Who else knew? Can you think of anybody who might have had a reason to turn Tommy in?"

I close my eyes. Of course.

Philip. That vindictive son of a bitch, Philip.

Tommy's sitting on the cot in his cell with his head on his knees and his back against the wall. He doesn't even look up when I sit next to him.

I take one of his hands and hold it in my lap. His fingers are ice-cold.

I try to sound cheerful. "Hey."

No answer.

"You're not going to believe this, but every goddamn person at the bank who can authorize a loan is out of town today at some stupid wedding. I can't get you out of here until tomorrow morning."

He turns his head and opens his eyes. As usual, I'm struck by how blue they are. He gives me the ghost of a smile. "Did you make a scene?"

I smile, too, in spite of myself. "What do you think?" My smile fades. "I lost control. When one of the tellers . . ."

"Which one? Sharon?"

"No, Bonnie Norton. Remember her? She's even uglier than she used to be. Her warts must breed, or something." I scoot back on the cot until my spine touches the wall, too. "Anyway, when she told me no one could help me today, I pulled a Dad and threw a bunch of deposit slips at her and started screaming like Jamie Lee Curtis in a Halloween movie. If Kyle and Camille hadn't been there to calm me down I'd have probably ended up in here with you." I squeeze his hand. "I'll get you out of here first thing tomorrow."

He shrugs. "It's okay. I guess I might as well get used to this."

His face is still sideways, and when a tear rolls out of his eye it runs across the bridge of his nose. I wipe it away with my free hand. "This is Philip's fault."

He blinks. "How do you figure?"

"He must have told Hart about you and Simon. I can't believe Simon would have said anything."

He shrugs again. "It doesn't really matter. It's nobody's fault but mine." He lifts his head and lets it fall back with a soft thump on the concrete. "I'm so stupid, Nathan. You were right all the way along and I just kept ignoring you and thinking you were overreacting. I am so fucking stupid."

I keep my voice light. "No argument." I close my eyes and rest my forehead on his shoulder. "Jesus, Tommy." The words are out of my mouth before I can stop them. "You can have practically anybody you want. Why did you have to go after a kid?"

He drops his head on mine. "I don't know. It's not like I made a conscious decision or anything. It just happened." He swallows. "I know this sounds retarded, but I couldn't help myself. My body just took over and I didn't have any choice but to go along for the ride."

A flicker of anger runs through me, even though I know that at this point there's nothing to be gained by chewing him out. "That's great, buddy. Be sure to tell the judge that. I'm sure he'll understand."

He starts to cry and my anger is instantly snuffed out. I wrap my arms around him and cradle him against my chest. "We'll get you out of here, Tommy. I promise. I don't care what Melville says. We'll find a way to make this all go away."

He lets me hold him and listens to my lies until the cop guarding us comes to tell me it's time to leave.

When I step back into the waiting area of the police station, Kyle and Camille rise from a bench in the corner and walk over to me.

"How is he?" Kyle asks.

I try to answer but nothing comes out.

Camille puts her arms around me. "I'm so sorry, Nathan. What can we do to help?"

"Nathan Bishop?"

I turn around. A middle-aged man with thinning blond hair who was talking to Darling when I came into the room is now standing a few feet away, glaring at me. "Are you Nathan Bishop?" he asks again.

I nod and he charges me without warning. I let go of Camille just as he hits me in the face with his fist. I stagger back into her and she falls to her knees as I struggle to stay on my feet. Sergeant Darling and another cop grab the guy from behind before he can hit me again.

I wipe the back of my hand across my lips and it comes away with blood on it. "What the fuck . . ."

"You piece of shit!" His face is distorted by rage. "You caught your brother raping my son and you didn't even bother to report it!"

Harold Hart.

Now that I know who he is, I can see the resemblance to Simon. I hope Simon ages better than this, though; Harold's got pasty skin and bad teeth and a pear-shaped ass.

I bend down and help Camille stand up, then turn to face him. "Nice right jab, Harold. You must be used to hitting people." I know I should shut up and get out of here, but my jaw hurts and my head is throbbing and all of a sudden I hate this man more than I can remember hating anybody in my life. "Say, how did Simon get that bruise on his ribs last week, by the way?"

He flinches a little, then struggles to get away from the cops without any success. Darling whispers something in his ear, but Hart ignores him.

"You make me sick," he spits. "The only reason you aren't in here with your brother is because my son swore last night that you never touched him and he begged me not to have you arrested, too. But I'm going to do everything in my power to make sure you never teach anywhere again. Perverts like you have no business being around kids."

I run my tongue across my lower lip and taste the blood. There seems to be quite a bit of it. I can feel myself getting dangerously angry, and Darling and the other cop are both watching me with wary faces.

Darling clears his throat. "Get on out of here, Mr. Bishop. Go home before this gets out of hand."

Fuck that. I take a step toward Hart. "And you're a model citizen? What kind of white trash loser hits his own son?" Camille takes my arm and tries to lead me toward the door but I jerk away from her. "Why don't you tell these nice officers what you did to Simon after you found his pot stash?"

He flushes. "I don't know what the hell you're talking about."

An ugly certainty grips me. "And how about last night, when you 'talked' to him about Tommy? Did you have to use brass knuckles, or were your bare fists enough?"

He drops his eyes briefly and a wave of fury washes through me. "You motherfucker," I whisper. "What did you do to him?"

I put my face next to his, in spite of another warning from Darling, and I make my voice pleasant and conversational. "Tell me something, Harold. Did you get an erection while you were beating up your son? Come on, you can admit it. You popped a little wood, didn't you?"

He tears an arm free from Darling and stumbles toward me, pulling both cops with him. The veins in his neck are trying to crawl through his skin. "You fucking faggot!" he screams. "I'm going to put your brother away for the rest of his fucking life!"

"Get out of here now, Bishop!" Darling bellows at me. "Get out before I kick your ass myself!" He puts an arm around Hart's neck and squeezes. "Goddammit, Harold! Calm down or I swear to God I'll have you arrested, too!"

Kyle and Camille are both tugging on me, and I finally let them drag me toward the door.

"I'm going to bring you up on charges for hitting me, Harold!" I call over my shoulder. "What the fuck kind of queer-ass name is 'Harold,' anyway? Why don't you just change it to 'Cocksucker' and leave it at that?"

Camille shoves open the door and Kyle pushes me through it.

The sun is back out and the heat is stifling. Somebody slams the door shut behind us.

I storm around on the sidewalk for a few minutes, swearing and kicking at the front wall of the station. Kyle and Camille stand several feet away from me, wisely not saying anything.

My heartbeat starts to slow and my feet eventually grind to a halt. I stand with my head down, staring at my shoes and tasting bile in my throat.

When I look up again, my eyes are full of tears.

Camille drives us home. I sit in the passenger seat and Kyle sits behind me and keeps a hand on my shoulder until we get back to the cottage. As we're pulling into the clearing I see Caleb Farrell sitting on the porch between the rhododendron bushes.

He stands up as Camille turns off the engine, but he waits for me to come to him in the shade at the front of the house before he starts talking.

"What's going on?" he demands. "Cheri came to get me a while ago and said Tommy's been arrested for something."

I tell Kyle and Camille to go on inside. Camille just nods and walks toward the door, but Kyle hangs back, oozing concern. He looks as if he's expecting me to lose control again any second.

The last thing I need right now is to be babied by Kyle. I wave a hand at him, shooing him after Camille. "I'll be fine, Kyle. Really. Let me talk to Caleb alone, okay?"

He hears my irritation and he tries to hide the hurt on his face. "Okay. Sure. But I'll be right inside if you need me."

He turns around and wanders off with his head down. I sigh and call after him. "Thanks for your help today."

He glances over his shoulder and smiles a little. "Sure." His head lifts as he disappears into the house.

I turn back to Caleb. He's staring up at me, waiting for an explanation. I don't want to tell him what's happening, but there's really no point in trying to protect Tommy anymore; the story will be all over town by the end of the weekend.

I fold my arms across my chest. "Tommy's been accused of raping Simon Hart."

His eyes widen and he takes a step backward. "Dear God."

Hampstead's clipped voice drifts around the cottage from the cornfield, chiding Sally for something or other. I watch Caleb in silence and wait for him to say whatever he needs to say.

He starts sputtering. "What damn fool liar concocted that story? Was it the Hart boy?" His voice gets louder with each word. "Jesus Christ, it's like Salem. Some sick fucking kid starts pointing fingers and good people get burned at the stake."

He paces back and forth, raging about idiotic cops who believe every cockamamie story people tell them, no matter how bogus it is. I let him rant, not really listening. A ladybug lands on my knuckles for an instant then takes off again.

He winds down after a minute and comes to a halt in front of me. In the silence I can hear shovels clawing through rocky soil behind the house. Hampstead's peons have apparently begun to dig their trial trench in my backyard.

He reaches up and takes my chin in his fingers like he used to do when I was a kid. "Why are you being so quiet, son? You're acting as if . . ."

He sees something in my eyes and suddenly looks away, dropping his hand. "Jesus."

I rub my temples. "You don't happen to have thirteen thousand dollars under your mattress, do you?"

He stares at me blankly. "What are you talking about?"

"Tommy's bail. I can't get my hands on that kind of money until tomorrow morning."

He shakes his head. "I live month to month on Social Security and a shitty pension from the city. You know that." He hesitates. "I could maybe swing a loan from the bank, though, if you need it."

He's trying not to cry, and I feel a pang of love for this crotchety old man. Even confronted with something like this about Tommy, he's still willing to help.

"Thanks, Caleb," I murmur. "But I've got it covered."

Cheri Tipton suddenly appears from around the corner of the house. "Nathan! I thought I heard voices over here. Thank God you're home. What's happening with Tommy and the police?"

Caleb has a right to know what's going on, but I'll be damned if I tell this witless old gossip anything. "Nothing, Cheri. It's just a misunderstanding."

"I thought I overheard Paul Joublowsky saying something about rape?"

"I said it's a misunderstanding, okay?" My voice is frigid. "Tommy's fine."

She recoils at my tone. "I didn't mean to pry. I was just concerned, that's all."

"I appreciate that. But everything's okay."

She searches my face for a moment and looks as if she wants to say something else, but then she winces a little and excuses herself and heads back to the cornfield, dragging her feet.

I wait until she's out of earshot before venting my anger. "That woman drives me apeshit. Why in God's name does she think she has any right to know the details of our family's problems?"

Caleb looks at me strangely. "Surely you know about Cheri and your mom and dad?"

I roll my eyes. "Yeah, she's told me all about how she and Mom were Siamese twins back in the olden days. What a load of crap."

He searches my face. "No, it's true, Nathan. Cheri and your folks were like the Three Musketeers before you and Tommy came along. Your dad never told you what happened?"

"My dad never told me anything, Caleb."

He sighs. "Yeah, I never knew why he kept you boys at arm's distance. But I figured he must have at least said something about Cheri to you. I guess I understand why he wouldn't want you to know, but still . . ."

I throw up my hands. "Just tell me, okay?"

He grimaces and looks at the ground, scratching his head. "It's kind of complicated. Cheri and your mom were real close, just like she says, but things got out of hand when the three of them started doing things together. Cheri and your dad hit it off a little too well, I guess, and one thing led to another, and, well, anyway, they started sleeping together behind your mom's back. It lasted for several years. Your dad felt terrible about it but he couldn't seem to break it off until your mom died, and then he got bitter and it just fizzled out. Cheri really loved your mom, too, and I think they both felt guilty as hell and couldn't . . ."

He stops talking when he raises his eyes and sees the look on my face.

I sit on the ground abruptly and begin to pluck mindlessly at the grass. "That son of a bitch."

He squats next to me with a groan. "It's ancient history, Nathan. I didn't think it would upset you like this. I'm sorry. I should have kept my mouth shut."

I glare at him. "I'm not upset, Caleb. I'm pissed off. If Dad were still alive I'd toss his fat, self-righteous, lying ass into the ocean."

He frowns. "Well, anyway, that's why Cheri's being kind of intrusive, I imagine. She's always thought the world of you and your brother, and I know she wanted to help out raising you but your dad didn't want anything to do with her by that point and told her to stay away. It's kind of a shame, really. I think she'd have made a good wife and mother."

I explode. "A good wife and mother? Tell me you didn't just say that! She'd have humped the milkman and the plumber and every horny poodle in the neighborhood while Dad was at work. Jesus, Caleb, what the hell are you talking about? The Three Musketeers, my ass. I can't believe you."

The corners of his mouth lift.

"What's so damn funny?" I demand.

"I'm sorry, Nathan. I didn't mean to make you mad, but you're so much like your dad sometimes that I get tickled listening to you."

I feel like screaming. "Do you have a death wish or something, old man?"

His smile grows. "There you go again," he murmurs.

"Goddammit, Caleb!" I toss a handful of dead lawn stuff at him. A rhododendron petal gets caught in his hair and sticks up from the crown of his head like an Indian feather. "Why not just compare me to Stalin, while you're at it?"

He sighs, running a hand over his scalp to clear it of the mess. "Okay, okay. I'll stop, all right? Calm down."

He flops down on his scrawny butt and stretches his legs out in front of him. He's wearing sandals and white cotton pants, and his bare ankles are veined and splotchy and so thin I could probably fit one hand around both of them. He looks frail and old. I rub my neck and stare into space, hating myself for losing my temper at him. No wonder everyone keeps telling me I'm like Dad. Jesus. I am so tired of myself.

In the silence my mind shifts from Cheri and my parents back to Tommy, and the last of my anger vanishes, shoved out of the way by fear and worry. I get a lump in my throat and I want to crawl under the cottage like a sick animal.

Caleb is watching me, and he must be thinking along similar lines, because suddenly his gray eyes fill and his face goes slack.

"So what are we going to do?" he asks. His voice is husky and trembling.

I pull a few strands of grass from the ground and let the wind blow them off my palm. "I don't know."

When I step inside the cottage I can hear Kyle and Camille fighting in the guest room. The door is shut, but Camille's voice is so loud that the bookshelves can't begin to muffle it.

"Nice fucking timing, asshole!" she yells. "Why don't you just admit why you're doing this and stop being such a fucking coward?"

I can't make out Kyle's answer but he sounds defensive, and Camille apparently doesn't like what she's hearing: "Oh, Jesus, Kyle! I'm going to drive to Wal-Mart and buy you a new pair of balls! Then maybe you'll at least have the courage not to lie to me anymore!"

I walk quietly toward the living room, trying not to listen to any more of it, but before I get out of the kitchen, Camille yells, "Bullshit! We both know exactly what this is about, and it's got nothing to do with me!"

I step out of the room before Kyle responds. It's too easy to guess what they're fighting about, and I can't handle any more guilt today.

The futon bed has been folded up into a couch and Tommy's

sheets and the clothes he didn't get in his suitcase are piled next to it on the floor. Camille's work, no doubt. She probably thought it would help to clean up a little around here. Part of me is obscurely moved by her gesture, I guess, but when you think about it, it's pretty absurd: my brother's going to jail for the next ten years and she's trying to make it all better by playing housemaid.

The sliding door in back is open and through the screen I can hear the human moles talking to each other in the cornfield. I wander over and look outside to see what they're doing. Hampstead is standing on this side of the field with her back to me, looking down at Bill and Sally in a hole in the ground. They're about a meter deep—Sally's in the earth up to her nipples, Bill to his navel—and Hampstead is apparently pissed off again for some reason. She's pointing to another patch of ground a few feet away from them and kicking at the soil with her boots, and they're both staring up at her with hangdog expressions on their faces.

Cheri is a few feet away, taking pictures of the field. She sees me standing in the doorway and waves. It's all I can do to not flip her off.

What in God's name was my dad thinking? He had a woman who looked like Mom at home and he chose to get in bed with *that* on the sly. Granted, Cheri was probably not the porky, invasive sow then that she is now, but still. As long as I live I'll never understand that man.

"Nathan?"

I turn around. Camille's standing in the doorway on the other side of the room. She's obviously been crying but she seems to have gotten herself under control.

"How are you?" she asks.

I shrug. "I've been better. How about you?"

"Not good. Kyle and I are having some problems."

I'm too tired to act surprised. "I noticed. I'm sorry, Camille."

She nods and her head dips in and out of a patch of sunlight from the west window. Her hair is so red it's almost orange. "We both want to stay and help Tommy and you, but I don't think we should be in the same house right now, so I'm going back to New York this afternoon."

I feel an unexpected twinge of sadness. "Do you have to?"

She seems taken aback. "I thought you'd be glad to get me out of here."

"I'm not." I try a joke. "Ever since you threw up on my crotch I've had a secret crush on you."

She manages a smile. "That was my plan. Vomit is an aphrodisiac, you know."

I walk over and give her a hug. She rests her head on my chest and starts to cry again. I hold her until her shoulders stop shaking. She finally pulls away and wipes her nose on the back of her hand. "I suppose I'd better get my things packed."

A lock of hair is hanging in her face and I tuck it back behind her ear. "So what's Kyle going to do?"

"I don't know." Her voice is flat. "He's in the bedroom right now staring at the wall. But I think he was hoping he could stay here with you." Her eyes meet mine for an instant then dart away again.

I let out a groan before I can help it. "That's probably not such a good idea," I whisper.

She makes a face and shrugs. "That's Kyle for you."

It's early evening and I'm alone in the cottage for the first time in what seems like years. I have the outside to myself as well, since Hampstead and Company have left for the day (Bulimic Bill and Sallow Sally stopped by to make sure I knew about—and wouldn't accidentally fall into—the crater they've dug in my backyard), so this almost feels like a normal night at home, with just me to deal with.

Almost.

I'm sitting at my desk and staring at the phone, trying to control my breathing. The number on the pad next to it is Philip's, printed in Camille's neat, definite script. She gave it to me right before she and Kyle left for New York in Tommy's car. She asked me why I needed to talk to Philip and I told her I wanted to thank him for being such a delightful houseguest. I expected her to try to talk me out of calling him, but all she did was nod and ask for a pen and paper. She told me to be careful and gave me a brief, dry kiss on the lips before she said good-bye.

Kyle hugged me, but he was still angry at me for not letting him stay here this evening. I told him he could come back in the morning, if he wanted, but I needed some privacy tonight. It was obvious what he'd hoped would happen once we had the cottage to ourselves, but the thought of Camille driving home alone while he tried to live out his randy little fantasy with me turned my stomach.

I pick up the phone and punch in the number. I lean forward and rest my elbows on the desk when it starts to ring.

"Hello?"

"Hi, Philip. It's Nathan."

Silence. I shift my weight and the chair creaks under me. "Aren't you going to ask why I'm calling?"

"No. I don't care." His voice is lifeless and distant.

I wrap the phone cord around my fingers tight enough to cut off the circulation. "So how the hell are you, buddy? Are you having a nice day?"

More silence, then he takes a deep breath. "Why are you calling?"

"I just wanted to tell you how much I enjoyed your visit." I fake a hearty chuckle. "Oh, by the way, Tommy is in jail, and I'm probably going to be fired from my job."

"What?" The bastard actually has the balls to sound shocked. "What are you talking about?"

"Oh, I realize it was a complete accident that you called Simon's dad last night. How did you get the number, by the way? Did you 'accidentally' call information, too?"

"I don't know what you're talking about," he blurts. "What's going on?"

I drop the cheerful act. "Don't you fucking dare lie to me." My voice is shaking. "You said you were going to do this and you went ahead and did it. Tommy dumped you and so you decided to get even in the meanest, trashiest way possible. You must be pretty proud of yourself."

"I swear to God, Nathan, I don't know what . . ."

I start yelling. "I'm going to kill you, you sick little shit! You better move away and leave no fucking forwarding address or I'll hunt you down like . . ."

He breaks in, stuttering, "I don't know what I've done to make you think . . ." He's crying so hard he can't talk. The bewilderment in his voice sounds completely genuine, and I feel the first flicker of doubt.

I listen to him sob for a minute and my voice drops to a whisper. "If you're lying to me, Philip, I'll find out. Are you telling me you didn't call Harold Hart and tell him about Simon and Tommy?"

He slowly gets himself under control. "I didn't call anybody. I haven't talked to anybody except my mom and my boss since you dropped me off at the train station yesterday." His voice breaks again. "Tommy's in jail?"

"Yes." I rest my forehead on my desk and listen to him sniffle for a while, then I sigh. "I'm sorry, Philip. I thought you'd turned him in."

He fights for breath. "How could you think that? I love him, Nathan. Jesus."

I tell him I'm sorry again and I hang up.

About fifteen minutes after my conversation with Philip the phone rings. It's Madeline Huber.

"Hi, Nathan." She sounds tired.

"Hi, Madeline. I thought I'd be hearing from you sooner."

She coughs. "I put it off as long as I could. I didn't want to make this call."

After talking with Philip I'd come downstairs and poured myself a triple-shot of Cuervo Gold. I down it now in one gulp, making my eyes water and my throat burn. "How bad is it?"

"Bad enough. But I think you already know that."

I sink to the floor. "What've you been told?"

She pauses to light a cigarette. "Harold Hart says Tommy raped his son on at least two occasions, and even though you were clearly suspicious that something was going on between them you made no effort to contact the police, not even after you became sure of it." She clears her throat. "He's still trying to decide if he's going to bring you up on charges, too, by the way."

My hands are trembling. She waits for me to answer but when I stay quiet she continues. "He also says that every time Simon was a guest in your home there was alcohol involved and what he calls 'grossly inappropriate conversation.' He's demanding your immediate dismissal."

I close my eyes for a second, then reach up and snag the bottle of tequila off the phone table for a refill. "Nothing's been proven about Tommy." I speak slowly, trying to keep my voice placid. "And if I'd known about anything like what they're accusing him of, I would have turned him in myself."

The half-lie makes me want to gag, but I go on, anxious to get back on solid ground. "Secondly, Simon never had any alcohol at my house or in my presence, and the only drinking going on was when the rest of us had a little wine with our dinner." The booze is kicking in; my temper is starting to flare again. "And just what the hell does Hart mean by 'inappropriate conversation?'"

"He says you encouraged Simon to think of himself as homosexual."

"I did no such thing!" I snap. "Simon asked me point blank if I was gay and I told him I was. And that was our whole conversation. Period." I lean back against a bookshelf. "That's the stupidest thing I've ever heard, incidentally. If a kid isn't gay, no amount of 'encouragement' from me or anyone else is going to convince him he is."

She sighs. "Try and tell that to Hart." If she's surprised or upset to hear about my sexual orientation I can't detect it in her voice. "How many times has Simon been in your house, Nathan?"

"I don't know. A handful. He ate dinner with us two or three times."

"And how many times were you at the beach with him?"

The sun has gone down and the lights in the cottage are attracting bugs. A moth the size of my palm beats at the screen door for a minute, then disappears.

"Again, two or three times."

A long silence.

"Madeline, what's going on?"

She drags at her cigarette again and exhales slowly. "Hart called every single school board member, and all of them contacted me individually to insist that I fire you." She snorts. "It's the first time in history they've ever agreed on anything."

"Ted Baker must be dancing in the streets," I mutter.

She doesn't respond. I wait a few seconds and then prod her along. "So what are you going to do?"

I want this over with.

She coughs again. "I'm going to suspend you for now until we see how all this plays out. If Tommy is proven innocent I might be able to make the board come around. But frankly, Nathan, I don't see that happening, do you?" She hesitates. "At the very least, you've displayed remarkably bad judgment by getting this personally involved with a student. Surely you can see that."

Her voice is mild but it still rankles.

"I haven't done anything wrong, Madeline," I growl. "Since when did it become a crime to be nice to a kid?" I know it's useless to keep talking but I can't seem to stop. "Harold Hart is a lying piece of shit who hits his own son. Did he happen to mention that to the school board?"

"What are you talking about?"

"Hart hits Simon whenever he gets pissed off. What kind of a father . . ."

She interrupts. "If that's true, why didn't you say something about it before now? You know better than that. You're a mandatory reporter. A teacher staying silent about domestic abuse is grounds for dismissal, all by itself."

"Oh, Jesus," I flare. "Just fire me and get it over with."

More silence. Her air conditioner shuts off in the background and when she starts talking again her voice is softer. "I'll have Social Services investigate Hart."

Memories of the fiasco with Andy and Joe come pouring into my head. Christ. I've done it again. I wonder how many more families I can destroy before I die. "I'm making it all up," I mumble. "Just let it go, okay?"

"I wish I could." She sighs again. "I'm sorry, Nathan," she says. "I've always liked you, and I wish there were something else I could do about all of this. But my hands are tied."

I take another drink and dribble tequila on my shorts. "So I guess I'm officially suspended."

"I'm afraid so." She sounds genuinely unhappy, and all of a sudden it occurs to me how many times she's intervened on my behalf in the past. I'm ashamed for making her job harder; none of this is her fault.

I swallow my anger. "I've always liked you, too, Madeline. Why have you been so nice to me all these years?"

"Beats me." She laughs a little. "I used to have the biggest crush on your dad when we were in high school. You've always reminded me of how he used to be before your mom died." She sounds embarrassed. "We even dated once or twice, not long after she passed away. Did you know that?"

"No, I didn't." Christ. Dad was probably humping her, too, on the sly. "So he wasn't always the biggest asshole in Walcott?"

"God, no. He was a sweetheart. He had a short fuse, but most of the time he was good as gold, even for the first few months after your mom's funeral. I should tell you about him sometime."

A book is digging into my neck and I shift to get away from it. "Great. I love fairy stories."

"I'm serious."

"I know you are. It's just hard to believe, that's all."

"I understand. You boys always got the worst of him, for some reason. You boys, and the rest of us who made the mistake of trying to love him after he decided he didn't want to be loved anymore."

I wince at the open pain in her voice. "I thought Tommy and I were the only lucky ones. So he treated you like shit, too?"

"He sure did."

We listen to each other breathe for a minute, then she says she'll be in touch in a day or two about my final paycheck, and she reminds me that while I'm under suspension I'm eligible for unemployment benefits.

And then there's nothing else to say but good night.

I'm having a nightmare when I feel somebody crawl into my bed.

I was dreaming about Tommy being surrounded by an angry

mob and stoned to death, Bible-fashion. One rock after another kept hitting him, drawing blood and shattering bone. Through it all he cried my name, time after time, but I stood behind the crowd, too afraid to help him. They didn't stop until he was nothing but a raw, faceless mound of meat on the ground, and when the people finally dispersed and I approached him, he rolled away from me, screaming.

And that's when I feel a hand on my shoulder.

I wake up yelling and fly off the mattress, dragging the top sheet with me and falling to my knees on the floor.

"Nathan, it's me!"

"Goddammit, Kyle!" I fling the sheet off and hurl myself at him, swinging my fists. One misses, but the other connects with the side of his head and he reels back against the headboard, wailing.

"Stop, Nathan, please!"

He's got his arms over his face so I punch him in the stomach instead. He curls up into a ball, gasping for air and whimpering. I stand over him for a second with my heart pounding against my ribs, finally alert enough to realize what I'm doing.

I flop on the bed. "God, Kyle, I'm sorry." I touch his back. "I was having a terrible dream and you scared the shit out of me. Are you all right?"

He's crying softly but he uncurls a little and turns toward me. "It's my fault," he sniffles. "I shouldn't have startled you like that."

He's completely naked. Christ.

I sigh and run my fingers up his arm. "You idiot. What are you doing?"

He wipes his nose with his wrist. "I decided to drive back tonight. I know you told me you didn't want me here until the morning, but I couldn't stand the thought of you being all alone."

I snort. "That's very sweet. And I'm sure getting laid never crossed your mind."

He starts to protest but gives up when he realizes I'm teasing him. "Well, yeah, okay, that was part of it." He smiles and his teeth glint a little in the moonlight. "But if I'd known the foreplay was going to be like this, I might have listened to you and stayed away."

He wets his lips and shifts toward me. His knee touches my

thigh, and my penis stirs in my shorts. He reaches out and lightly rubs my collarbone, then slides his hand down my chest, stopping to play with each nipple before moving on. He sticks the tip of his index finger in my navel.

I swallow in a dry throat. "I don't want to do this," I lie.

"So stop me." He worms his hand through the fly of my boxers and takes hold of me.

I shouldn't let this go any further. I get the feeling he needs a lot more than sex from me, and if I give in tonight he'll just be more hurt tomorrow when I tell him it was a one-time deal. But I'm sick of trying to do the right thing. I'm horny and I'm tired, and I'm half-crazed with worry about Tommy. Kyle's an adult, and he's old enough to know how this is likely to turn out. It's not my fault if things don't go the way he wants them to.

He frees my dick from my shorts and runs his thumb over the tip of it. I close my eyes and lie flat on my back as his tongue flicks at the base of my throat then travels down my sternum.

I want to forget my name. I want to forget my family and friends; I want to forget my job and my house and my past and my future. I want to use this man to blot out my life for a few hours, and I want to fuck him until neither of us can move or talk, or do anything but sleep like corpses.

Dead people don't dream, or so I'm told.

He tugs at my boxers and I lift my hips so he can pull them off. I open my eyes to find him looking up at me. He's breathing so fast he sounds like he's practicing for a Lamaze class.

I tug lightly at his ear. "Housebreaking is a serious offense, you know."

"Yeah?" He bumps his chin against my erection. "You should maybe start locking your door, then, I guess."

I don't have the heart to tell him that after tonight I probably will.

CHAPTER 9

Tommy follows Rex Darling out of the back of the police station into the reception area, dressed in the same clothes he was arrested in yesterday. The second he sees me he stumbles over and wraps himself around me, completely ignoring Darling and the two other officers in the room.

I squeeze him back for a second, then push him away. "Let's go home."

He nods. He looks like he hasn't slept in a week, and he needs a shower and a shave, but other than that he seems okay. I hand him his sandals and he thanks me under his breath and slides them on his feet.

Darling motions us over to the same desk where I just forked over the bail money, and Tommy trails behind me like a stray cat. He has to sign for his wallet and keys but he picks up the pen and scrawls his name without looking in the wallet.

Darling leans toward me. "You accused Mr. Hart of hitting his kid yesterday. Were you serious?"

"Yes. It happened a few days ago. Simon had a big bruise on his ribs."

He frowns. "Can you prove it?"

I shrug. "Tommy saw it, too."

The other cops—Steve Macy and John Ferris—have wandered over to listen, and Ferris smirks. "I'll bet he did."

My head snaps up. "Fuck you, Ferris. Are you still doing the Peeping Tom thing you used to do when we were in high school?"

Tommy grabs my wrist. "Don't, Nathan."

Ferris's eyes narrow and he takes a step toward me, but Darling holds up a hand and stops him. "Stay put, John." He turns back to me. "Cool down, Mr. Bishop. We don't need another scene in here like yesterday's."

"Then tell this dick to get away from me."

"Go get a cup of coffee, John. You, too, Steve."

Ferris glowers at me, but Macy takes his arm and leads him out of the room.

Darling chews on his lower lip. "If you're willing to file a report, I can have a social worker check it out."

"Will it do any good?"

He grimaces. "I'm afraid your credibility isn't worth much, these days. You seem to be developing a history of seeing crimes and not reporting them."

I glare at him. Tommy pulls me away from the desk. "Come on, Nathan. I want out of here."

Darling calls after us. "If you change your mind, come talk to me."

Outside, the sky is getting darker. Tommy doesn't say anything until we're in the car.

He slumps in his seat and closes his eyes. "So where are Kyle and Camille?"

I turn on the engine and roll down the window. "Back in New York. Kyle's got your car, for now."

"Why did they go home?"

I leave the transmission in neutral and put my forehead on the steering wheel. "Well, let's see. After we got back to the cottage yesterday, Kyle told Camille he wanted a divorce. Camille said okay, and I made Kyle drive her home. He was supposed to return this morning, but he decided to come back last night instead and get in bed with me. I beat him up a little first, then we fucked like bunnies on Ecstasy, and then I tossed his skinny butt out right after breakfast." I glance over at him. "That about sums it all up, I guess."

He's opened his eyes and he's watching me. "Why did he take my car?"

"That's your only question?"

One side of his mouth curls up.

I shift into reverse and back up. "I told him to. I knew you wouldn't be needing it for a few days."

He looks away. "That's a fact," he murmurs.

Neither of us says anything on the way home.

Kyle didn't understand when I told him he had to leave. He cried and pouted and yelled, and then he cried some more. He thinks he loves me.

Maybe he does. But I don't feel the same toward him, and I never will.

I was thinking after he left about my conversation with Madeline yesterday, and I'm beginning to believe I may have been wrong about Dad all these years. I've blamed him for withdrawing his love from Tommy and me after Mom died, and I've assumed he did it on purpose, as a way to make us pay for what he saw as our part in her death. But now it seems as if his bitterness wasn't personal as much as universal.

I know what most religions preach: "The more love you give away, the more you have." But as usual, religion is full of shit. That Hallmark theory might work well for a few scattered saints and fools, but for the rest of us, love is a finite commodity.

I think it's likely Dad might not have wanted to be the way he was. It doesn't mean I have to forgive him or anything, but it helps me to understand him a little, because I'm pretty much built the same way.

I've never had love to spare, either. I gave it all to Tommy.

Hampstead's and Cheri's cars are in the driveway when we get home.

I turn off the engine and groan. "It's the weekend, for God's sake. Don't these people have a life?"

Tommy doesn't answer. He opens his door but doesn't make any move to get out.

"What's the matter?" I ask.

He takes a long, slow breath and lets it out again. "I'm pretty tired."

Something in his voice hurts to listen to. I put my hand on his shoulder. "Come on inside. You can sleep all day if you want."

He drops his head on my hand. "I need a bath first."

"Okay."

A tear runs over my fingers. I take a shaky breath and look away.

The sky is filling with black clouds and I can hear thunder in the distance. My eyes fall on Cheri's car and I clear my throat. "Caleb told me yesterday that Cheri and Dad were having an affair behind Mom's back."

He stirs. "You're kidding." He doesn't sound particularly interested.

"Nope. Apparently they were pretty hot and heavy for a while. And Madeline Huber told me last night that she and Dad 'dated' too, after Mom died. Did you remember that?"

"Uh-uh." Two lifeless syllables.

I squeeze his shoulder. "Let's go inside, Tommy. I think it's going to rain."

He nods but doesn't lift his head. "Did I get you fired?"

I hesitate. "No. Just suspended, for now. Firing comes later, I guess."

He sighs. "Well, good. Everything turned out perfect, then." His voice breaks. "God, what a mess. I am so sorry, Nathan."

I lean over and kiss his hair. It's oily and limp. "I didn't like that job, anyway," I whisper. "Come on. Let's get you inside."

Once we're in the cottage he immediately strips off his clothes and gets in the shower. I change the sheets on the bed in the guest room while he's doing that, and after he finishes drying off, he puts on a pair of shorts and brushes his teeth, then crawls into bed like an old man.

I turn off the light and start to leave, but he stops me before I close the door. "Stay with me for a while, okay?"

I lie down next to him and he curls up against me and falls asleep almost instantly. I hold him, and listen to him breathe, and I stare around the walls of our old room. The Yoda clock we had as kids (Yoda's green arms have always kept erratic track of time, losing a few minutes every month) is still hanging near the foot of the bed, ticking out the seconds, one after another. The wind is picking up outside and pushing the curtains around, and I can feel the temperature dropping. A storm is on its way.

When I step onto the back porch about half an hour later, Hampstead and her three little helpers are scrambling around in the cornfield, racing to get a bright blue tarp up over the trench before the rain hits. There's lightning in the sky and the thunder is getting closer and louder. I wander over to see if they need help.

"Hi, Nathan!" Cheri chirps, trying to hold down a corner of the tarp that's flapping in the wind long enough for Sally to tie it to a wooden stake. "How's Tommy?"

There's a stillness to Hampstead and the others that tells me Cheri's been shooting off her mouth. Bill stares at his feet and Sally gives me an awkward smile that's probably intended to convey sympathy.

"He's fine," I lie. "Are you guys calling it quits?"

Hampstead finishes tying down her corner and stands up. "I'm afraid so. It's supposed to rain for the rest of the day."

I kneel down and peek under the tarp. There's nothing to see but a big hole in the ground, but it looks like an open grave and it creeps me out.

I drop the tarp quickly and stand up again. "So how's it going? Did you find anything yet?"

"Nothing interesting." Her lips are tight. "I think we're on a wild-goose chase."

Sally finally ties down Cheri's corner and Cheri gets up, frowning. "I'm sure something's here. We just need to keep searching."

Hampstead scowls at her. "We've poked around enough that we should have come across some kind of evidence by now. A trench this size should have turned up something, assuming we're anywhere near where someone lived."

Dust blows into Cheri's face and she sneezes. "I'm sure if we go a little deeper we'll find what we're looking for. Or maybe we should just dig another trench on the other side of the field."

Hampstead shakes her head. "We'll keep looking for a few more days, of course, but you should realize that this isn't a very promising beginning." She nibbles at a hangnail and keeps her voice casual. "Perhaps if we examined the surveyor's records together, we might come across something that would help our search."

Cheri narrows her eyes. "That won't be necessary, Jane. We'll just continue right here."

Hampstead's back stiffens. "This is insufferable." The frown lines at the corners of her mouth make her jaw look hinged, like a wooden puppet's. "Why have me here at all if you won't listen to what I say?"

Cheri starts to respond but a gust of wind makes her short black hair flutter around her head like a startled bat and a few strands fly into her mouth and shut her up. Hampstead uses the opportunity to press her case.

"People are basically pigs, you see." She gestures at the field. "If a community of any size had lived here for any length of time, they'd have left all manner of things behind. Mostly trash, of course, but other things, too." She eyes the approaching storm and turns to Bill and Sally. "We need to finish cleaning up before the storm hits. Bill, start gathering the tools and the table, and Sally, go get my SUV and drive it around here so that we can load everything up at the same time." She glances at me. "That is, if it's okay for us to drive on your lawn."

I wave a hand and Bill and Sally scurry off to follow her orders. Hampstead faces us again and resumes her lecture. "What I'm saying is that it's human nature to litter. For instance, when we started digging we almost immediately turned up an old oil can and a scrap of cloth, and soon after that we found this little treasure." She pulls a plastic toy soldier with one leg missing out of her pocket and hands it to me. "But the farther down in the soil we go the less we turn up, and that doesn't bode well for our search."

I recognize the soldier; Tommy and I used to have hundreds of the things until Dad got tired of stepping on them and made us throw them away. This one is gray, with a melted face—no doubt another victim of Tommy's sick boyhood fascination with cigarette lighters. (One time he even erected a miniature hospital tent over several dozen of these grisly figures, all lying on homemade match-stick cots. He called it "The Burn Ward.") I hand it back to her and she slides it in her pocket again.

Cheri's picking at the mole on her forehead. "There's no need to be so negative, Jane. We've just begun looking."

Hampstead's face hardens under the bill of her Smithsonian cap. "I'm not being negative, Cheri. I'm being realistic. People *always* leave a record of themselves, whether or not they intend to." She jabs a thumb at the trench. "And as deep as we've gone here, something else should have come to light by now. I see no reason for your optimism."

Cheri rolls her eyes and Hampstead's temper flares. "You can be as childish as you want, but sooner or later you'll have to face the facts." Beads of sweat pop out along her mustache and her odd voice goes up and down like a roller coaster. "This dig is going nowhere, and if nothing turns up soon, we might as well throw in the towel and go home."

Cheri sniffs and looks away, sulking. Hampstead frowns at the back of her head and grinds her teeth.

"Gee," I murmur in the silence. "That's too bad."

Cheri wheels on me, bridling. "You don't have to be smug about this, Nathan. It's far too early to give up our search, no matter what Jane says."

I can't resist needling her. "I told you so."

She glares at me. "What is it with you Bishop men and your incessant need to get under other people's skins?"

I force a smile. "And what is it with you Tipton women and your incessant need to screw other people's husbands?"

Her mouth drops open and she takes a step backward. Hampstead looks from one to the other of us, then abruptly excuses herself.

Cheri watches her go, then turns back to me, running a nervous hand through her hair. She has trouble meeting my eyes for a few seconds, but she finally manages. Her face is pale and grave. "How did you find out?"

"Caleb."

"I see." She drops her hand. "So how much did he tell you?"

A drop of cold rain hits my arm. "Oh, nothing much. Just an interesting little anecdote about you and Dad I hadn't heard before." I scratch my neck. "Incidentally, you might want to revise all those stories you told me about how good a friend you were to my mom."

More raindrops splatter around us. I can smell the dust settling; it's one of my favorite smells. Bill drops a shovel and a rake at our feet and Cheri tries to lead me away from the trench for privacy, but I hold my ground until she gets this pathetic look on her face and starts wringing her hands. "Please?"

I follow her over closer to the cottage and wait impatiently to hear what she has to say. She's fighting back tears, and she has to swallow several times before she can talk. "I loved your mom dearly, Nathan." Her words are hard to make out. "You have no idea how badly I felt about what your dad and I did."

The roots of her hair are white, and under a thick shellac of makeup I can see hundreds of wrinkles embedded in her fat old face. Her lips are trembling and she looks miserable and guilty and I'm suddenly too tired and sad to keep riding her.

I sigh. "It doesn't really matter, Cheri. All I can say is that you and Mom sure had strange taste in men. Madeline Huber, too, I gather."

Hampstead passes by with a handful of tools for the pile, studiously avoiding looking in our direction, and a flicker of humor runs through me. I point at her retreating back. "So did Jane sleep with Dad, too?"

She makes a face. "Don't be ridiculous." She pauses. "And as for Madeline, I have no idea. We've never spoken about it." She looks into my eyes with a wistful expression. "I should have told you about it a long time ago, I suppose, but I didn't see any point. I was afraid you'd be angry."

The SUV rolls around the cottage with Sally at the wheel. She turns away from the field, then pops it in reverse and backs toward Bill and Hampstead by the trench. Bill has retrieved the metal table and folded it up, and now he's leaning on it with one hand while he watches Hampstead wave her arms at the rear of the vehicle. Sally is watching her in the side mirror and alternately stepping on the gas and the brakes, making the SUV buck like an epileptic mustang.

Lightning flashes directly over our heads and is followed almost immediately by a crack of thunder. We all jump. Sally is watching me from the open window of the SUV, and she calls out, "Scary, huh?"

I shrug and she nods and smiles, as if I just said something really witty. Hampstead yells for her to stop and Sally stomps on the brakes and sticks her bleached-yellow head out the window. "What?"

Hampstead comes around to the side so Sally can hear her. "Turn the wheel more to the right, Sally. The tools are by Bill. Can't you see them?"

She turns away and Sally glances at me and giggles, embarrassed, then sticks her tongue out at the back of Hampstead's head. She lets up on the brake and turns the wheel to the right, and she steps on the gas, still watching me.

"I think someone has a crush," Cheri whispers.

I grunt. "Perfect. That's all I need."

She starts to say something else about Dad when without warning the SUV lurches backwards and Sally cries out, "Oh, shit!"

Bill bellows as the SUV swerves around Hampstead and heads straight at him. When he realizes it's not going to stop, his mouth makes an O and he drops the table and tries to run, but he stumbles before he can get out of the way and the fender bangs into his broomstick legs with a loud thunk and sends him sprawling on top of the blue tarp covering the trench. The tarp collapses and Bill tumbles into the hole with it, his long arms clutching at the earth and then disappearing. Hampstead starts screaming and the SUV screeches to a halt, one rear wheel on the mangled table, and the other less than an inch from the edge of the pit.

Sally gazes out her window at Cheri and me, her face blank. Her eyes are as big as egg yolks. "My foot slipped," she says, stunned. "I'm too short to drive this thing."

Cheri and I stare back at her, shocked into silence.

"Oh, Jesus," Bill wails from the trench.

Hampstead charges over to the driver's door. "What in God's name are you doing?" She pounds her fists on the roof above Sally's head. "Have you lost your mind?"

Sally rears back from the window as far as she can and covers her mouth with both hands. Hampstead kicks the door once in speechless fury, then runs over to the trench. "Bill? Are you all right?"

"I don't know." His head and skinny torso emerge from the earth like a zombie stick figure. His hair and face are clotted with dirt and mud, and there's blood on his temple. "I don't think anything's broken, but my right knee hurts like hell." He squints around Hampstead's legs as Sally crawls out of the SUV. "What the fuck, Sally?" he yells. "Are you trying to kill me, you stupid bitch?"

"I'm so sorry, Bill, oh, God, I'm so sorry," she babbles. "My foot slipped and I just couldn't stop in time." She gallops up to the trench, boobs flopping, and bends down to help him climb out. "Are you hurt?"

He pushes her offered hand aside and claws his way out of the hole, dragging a corner of the tarp with him. He's breathing hard and his clothes are filthy. He ignores Sally's repeated apologies and begins to tie the tarp up again, hobbling around the trench like Long John Silver.

Hampstead watches him for a minute, then opens the rear door of the SUV and starts loading the tools without a word, hurling them in one after another with no regard for either the tools or her SUV's interior. Sally tries to help her but Hampstead won't let her. "Just stay out of the way," she growls.

Sally looks over at Cheri and me with a forlorn expression, and we gawk back at her. I don't know what look to put on my face. Bill and Hampstead finish what they're doing and get in the SUV, without once looking at Sally. Thunder rolls over our heads again, considerably louder than before.

Sally steps over to the driver's window on timid feet. "What about the table?"

Hampstead's head spins around like Linda Blair's in *The Exorcist.* "Just get in the goddamn car, Sally!" she snaps, spittle flying.

Sally reels back and flings herself into the rear seat with a little whimper. It takes her two tries to shut the door, then she sits with her head down as they drive off. Hampstead steps on the accelerator too hard and chunks of grass and mud splatter the table and the tarp. None of them look at us as they pull out of sight.

Cheri and I stare after them for a minute, then Cheri finally looks up at me with strained eyes. She shakes her head. "I'm sorry, Nathan. I seem to have lost my train of thought. What was I saying?"

Big raindrops are hitting the dirt hard enough to send up puffs of dust. I shrug. "I haven't got a clue."

There's a short pause as we study each other, and then her face twitches and she bursts out laughing. Her belly shakes like an agitated tub of yogurt and a string of snot spurts from her nose, and all of a sudden I lose it, too. In spite of Tommy, in spite of her and Dad, in spite of everything, all I can do is laugh. I laugh until my stomach aches and my throat feels raw. I laugh until I'm doubled over and my breath is coming in spasms. It lasts forever, and even though I hear a faint hint of hysteria creep into my voice, I don't try to stop.

It may be my last chance to feel good for a long time.

When I finally straighten again I'm still wheezing. "What a bunch of clowns," I gasp.

Cheri nods but doesn't try to talk. She's leaning against the cottage to keep from falling down, and tears are dribbling from her chin.

A visible wall of rain is coming straight for us, but neither of us moves, and within seconds we're both drenched. At first the cold water feels great, and I put my head back and close my eyes and let it wash over me. I shake my soaked head around like a dog, spraying water everywhere, and I laugh a little more and try to keep pretending that everything will be okay. But as my breathing slows and the absurdity of the last few minutes recedes, the raindrops begin to sting my skin, and the nightmare with Tommy comes flooding back full force.

I lower my head and open my eyes, utterly sober and chilled to the bone. Cheri, too, has returned to earth; she's looking up at me with a sad smile.

I raise my voice so she can hear me. "Now's not the time, but I'd like to hear about you and Dad eventually, Cheri. I'm trying to figure him out these days and maybe it would help to talk to you."

She's shivering but doesn't seem to notice or care. "Anytime. It's not all that interesting a story, but I'll be glad to answer anything you want to ask me." She looks down at her clothes. Her blouse is stuck to her skin in unflattering mounds and folds, and her bra is visible under the fabric. "Tell me something, Nathan."

I have to strain to hear her above the rain and wind. "What?"

She fixes her eyes on me again. "Did your father ever . . ." She trails off. "Never mind."

I try to make my voice kind. "He never said anything about you, Cheri."

She looks away and nods. "I guess I'm not surprised." She stares at the back of the cottage for a minute, but then her shoulders lift a little. "Well, I suppose I should get going. We've got an early start tomorrow."

I manage a grin. "You may be digging by yourself. Bill and Sally will probably be in the hospital by then, and Hampstead sounds like she's about ready to quit on you."

She shakes her head. "Jane's wrong. Something's here. I know it. I don't care what anybody says."

I take her arm. "Come on. I'll walk you to your car."

When we get to the front of the cottage the yard is already saturated with water and mud. I help her pick her way through it and she leans heavily on my arm. The only vehicles left in the driveway are Cheri's and mine. She hasn't fixed her side mirror yet; if anything, it's hanging farther down than before. She stops before opening her door and gives me a quick, awkward hug, and a kiss on the cheek. We say good-bye and I watch her back up, making sure she doesn't get stuck in the new mud ruts Hampstead and the Mongoloid twins made in the lane on their way out.

It's still raining heavily when I wake up around dinnertime. Tommy is sleeping next to me on his side, with his mouth open and a little puddle of drool on his pillowcase. He's always drooled when he sleeps and I've always teased him about it.

After I came back inside this morning I took a long, hot shower, then I got back in bed with Tommy and fell asleep. He didn't even stir when I snuggled up next to him, but now when I put my arm around him he shifts onto his back to get more comfortable. I watch his face as his breathing gets lighter and his eyelids start to flutter.

He smells like Tommy: clean sweat, and Ivory soap, and a faint, pleasant odor I've never been able to identify. It kind of reminds me of a cross between almonds and peanut butter, but when I told him that once he laughed his butt off and told me I was crazy.

His eyes open. He blinks slowly, focusing on the big wooden ceiling beams that run the length of the room. I left the door to the kitchen open and I can hear rainwater gushing off the roof and splashing down on the steps of the front porch.

He turns his head and sees me watching him.

"Hey," he whispers.

"Hey, yourself. Feel better?"

He nods. "Some." He puts his hand on my arm. His fingers are warm. "Wow. Listen to the rain."

"Yeah. It's been pouring all afternoon." I yawn. "It hasn't rained like this in years. The wine cellar might flood again."

He rolls over so we're face-to-face and our knees are touching. It's cool enough that we have a sheet and a light blanket over us, but our bodies are generating too much heat and he pushes the covers down to our waists. "It's been a long time since we slept in a bed together," he murmurs. "What's it been? Thirteen years?"

"Something like that." I kiss his shoulder. "You missed all the action this morning. Sally did some minor knee surgery on Bill with the fender of an SUV."

He touches the cleft at the base of my throat and runs his index finger down the center of my chest. "Yeah? Was he hurt?"

"Not really." I play with the lobe of his ear for a minute as he tickles the hair around my navel. "He'll live."

Our eyes meet. His are brimming with tears.

"Want to?" he asks.

I reach down and take his hand, and guide it under the sheets. "Yes."

The rain starts to slow down while we're washing the dishes after supper, and the sky begins to lighten even though it must be getting close to sundown. The cottage smells like grilled onions and garlic, and steak.

Tommy's drying and I'm washing. He waits for me to finish scrubbing the broiling pan and then hands it back to me, pointing at a spot I missed. I drop it in the hot water again without comment.

I keep my eyes on the pan. "We should probably talk about what we're going to do."

"I don't want to." He wipes some soapsuds off the counter.

"I know you don't, but Melville said we need to call him tomorrow."

"Then we'll talk about it tomorrow, okay? I don't want to think about it tonight."

I raise my eyes and look at his reflection in the window. He's dressed in a white T-shirt and black sweatpants, and he's staring at the floor. "Tommy . . ."

Anger edges into his voice. "I don't want to talk about it, Nathan." He moderates his tone. "Please."

I rinse off the pan and hand it to him again. "Melville said we should try to figure out what plea you're going to enter."

"Goddammit!" he snaps. "I said not tonight. Is that too much to ask?"

"This isn't going to go away just because you ignore it."

His eyes burn into mine. "No shit, asshole! Do you think I don't know that?" He slams the pan down on the counter and all the dishes in the drying rack jump. "Do you think for a minute I don't know what's going to happen at the end of all this? Do you think I don't know that I'm going to prison no matter what? Christ, Nathan."

His voice drops to a whisper. "And even after I get out I'll be labeled as a pedophile for the rest of my life, and forced to register as a sex offender in whatever town I end up living in. Do you think I don't know that, too?" His shoulders start to shake and he drops the dish towel on the floor and glares at me. "It doesn't matter a goddamn bit what plea I enter, and you know that as well as I do. So how about giving me a fucking break tonight and let me pretend for a few more hours that the best part of my life isn't already over?"

I turn back to the sink, trying not to cry. He's right and we both know it.

A movement outside catches my eye. I lean forward to try to see better but it's too dark to make anything out, so I reach over to the switch by the door to turn on the outside light. The instant I flick it on, the window over the sink explodes and something the size of a fist flies past my head. Dozens of shards of glass pepper Tommy and me and he cries out as one of them leaves a gash across his cheek. I reel away from the sink and feel a stabbing pain in the sole of my right foot. Neither of us has shoes on.

There's wild laughter outside, and a young male voice screams out, "Fucking faggots!"

I lunge for the door but before I get there I slip on the floor because of the blood on the bottom of my foot, and I fall down hard. My teeth slam together and catch my tongue, and I taste copper in my mouth. I bang my arm against the cabinet while I'm trying to sit up and it leaves a smear of red across the white paint; my left elbow and forearm are torn up, too. Tommy bends down to help me.

"Fuck!" I howl. "I'm going to kill you little sons of bitches!"

More laughter, but moving away from the cottage fast. There are three or four different voices but I don't recognize any of them. Tommy rips the door open and charges out and I follow as best as I can, hobbling in his wake. One of the boys is still in sight when we get outside—I glimpse a white T-shirt and white sneakers, and the ghost of a face—but he disappears down the lane the instant we see him. Tommy grabs a rock out of the driveway and tears after him, screaming.

I run a few steps too, but my foot hurts like hell so I'm forced to stop. I stand in the darkness and listen, trying to figure out if everybody ran down the lane or if any of them went the other way, toward the beach. I stay still and wait, hoping one or two of the bastards will be stupid enough to try to double back. My heart is pounding in my chest and my foot feels sticky in the wet grass.

I hear Tommy yelling, "Come back here you little fuckers!" then there's nothing else to hear but water dripping from the trees and from the gutters on the house. I give up after another minute and pick my way back to the kitchen. Just as I'm stepping inside Tommy reappears out of the darkness.

"Be careful, Nathan. There's glass everywhere." He makes his way around me and gets his shoes by the door, then he puts them on and brings me my sandals.

"I can't put those on yet," I mutter. "I cut my foot."

"I know. Put on the other one, though, and hop to the bathroom. We need to see how bad it is. You may need stitches."

"I don't need stitches. I need an assault rifle and a couple of basset hounds."

I put on the sandal then I drape an arm over his shoulder and we lurch across the floor to the bathroom, glass crunching underneath us with each step. He makes me sit on the edge of the tub and he turns on the faucet and holds my injured foot under the water for a minute. He's got blood on his shirt but I don't know if it's his or mine.

"Did you catch any of them?" I ask.

He shakes his head. "No. It was too dark and they had too much of a head start. Fucking little pricks."

After he turns off the water he probes around the cut gently. "I can't see any more glass, but that doesn't mean there's none there. It's still bleeding a lot but it doesn't look too deep."

I pull it away from him. "It's fine. Just get me a bandage, will you?"

Once I'm back on my feet I check out the wound on his face and get it disinfected and patched up, then both of us tend to the various smaller injuries on our hands and arms. I keep up a steady stream of swearing, but Tommy doesn't say anything else until we're finished and I tell him I'm going to go call the police.

He catches my arm before I leave the room. "No! I can't deal with the cops tonight. They wouldn't be able to do anything, anyway."

I stop still. "I am not going to let those little fuckers get away with this, Tommy. What if we'd gotten some glass in our eyes, or had an artery sliced open?"

He doesn't let go of my elbow. "Please, Nathan. Let's just clean up the mess tonight and forget about it. You can call the police in the morning if you want." His voice is desperate.

I give in. We go back in the kitchen and pick up as best we can, then he gets the broom and dustpan and I get the vacuum. The window was shattered; nothing is left in the frame except a few jagged edges I knock outward with a hammer onto the lawn. The rain has stopped but a cold wind is blowing directly into the house.

Glass is everywhere, but most of it fell between the table and the sink in a kind of inverted pyramid shape. After we're done sweeping up, I get a beach towel and tack it up over the window, standing on the counter to reach the top of the pane, and he stands behind me on the floor to make sure I don't fall. It takes a couple of minutes but neither of us says anything while I'm working. The towel billows in the wind now and then like a parachute, making it hard to handle.

Something about cleaning up the wreckage has calmed me down. I almost feel peaceful when I finish pinning the towel in place.

I look down at him. "I've always wanted a tapestry. Not bad, huh?"

He nods and holds a hand up to help me back to the floor. I land next to him, wincing at the impact on my sore foot.

He notices. "Are you okay?"

"I'm fine." I take off my sandal and inspect the bottom of my foot. "I just need a fresh bandage, that's all." I straighten up and notice a tiny sliver of glass in his hair and I tell him to hold still until I get it out. "We should take a shower. We're probably covered with stuff like this."

He bends over and picks up the rock that shattered the window. It's rough granite, and flat on one side like a paperweight. He holds it in his palm and studies it without expression. "Previews of coming attractions, I guess." His voice is toneless.

I take it away from him and set it on the table, but he keeps staring at it. I put my hands on his shoulders and turn him toward me, but even though his eyes meet mine it's as if I'm not in the room with him.

I make my voice brisk. "Okay, that sure was fun. What should we do for an encore?"

He blinks a couple of times and eventually manages to focus on my face. He reaches up and touches my cheek, and he tries to smile. "Let's go to the beach."

The clouds are dissipating and the moon is out, but the ocean is still worked up from the storm. Angry five-foot waves are coming in at an angle and beating on the shore, and the surface is boiling with foam, and the beach is littered with seaweed and shells and fishing nets and beer cans.

We have the place to ourselves tonight. It's cold enough that we're both wearing long pants and sweatshirts, and every time the wind hits my face I shiver. The walk from the cottage took longer than usual because I'm limping, but Tommy didn't seem to mind going at a slower pace. He stayed next to me the whole way, occasionally taking my arm to help me slog through patches of sand and gravel, and when we reached the lighthouse and the rocky path to the beach, he made me get on his back and he carried me like a child past Caleb's house. The lights were off at Caleb's; he goes to bed early.

Tommy leans close now so I can hear him. "Remember when we came down here after Hurricane Gladys?"

I shudder. "Don't remind me." We found a small hammerhead shark that day, dead on the beach. It was crawling with maggots, and the seagulls had been breakfasting on it for several hours by the time we saw it. "I threw up on the spot."

"Yeah. And on your pants, too." He covers a nostril and blows snot out the other one. "I had nightmares about that fucking shark for a week."

We pick our way down to the smoother sand by the ocean and start walking south. We take off our shoes and let the waves wash over our feet; the water is cold but not unbearable.

"You'll open up that cut again," he says.

I shrug. "The saltwater will be good for it."

About a mile ahead of us the lights are on at the Newbury mansion. The Newbury House was built about a hundred years ago on a hill overlooking an old fishing village at the mouth of the Walcott River. The Newburys died off a long time ago (Henry Newbury— the patriarch of the clan—committed suicide during the Depression), so now it's a state historical site, which probably pisses off Cheri Tipton no end, since she seems to believe anything of interest in Walcott should fall under her jurisdiction. Tommy and I went on the mansion tour once, but the only thing I remember about it is that there used to be a full-sized bowling alley in the basement.

I point at it. "Looks lonely, doesn't it?"

He shakes his head and says something I don't catch. I ask him to repeat it.

"I said, I think it looks kind of peaceful."

We walk for a while without saying anything, and my foot starts to ache. He notices my limp getting more pronounced, and he asks if I want to sit down for a minute. I nod and we make our way over to the dunes, out of the wind. We flop down on the sand and sit side by side, staring out at the water. It's almost warm here.

He drops his head on my shoulder. "So what will you do if you can't teach anymore?"

I put a broken moon shell on my knee and flick it away with my middle finger. "I don't know. I haven't thought about it much." I sigh. "I hear Kmart is hiring."

"Don't joke. It's not funny."

"I know. I just don't know what else to do." I put the soles of my feet together; the bandage on the right one is coming loose. "We may have to sell the cottage so I can move someplace else."

His head jerks up and he stares at me. "You can't. You love this place." The way he says it sounds like an accusation.

"So do you." I rest my chin on my knees and listen to the surf. The waves are gradually getting smaller. "But my employment options in Walcott are somewhat limited. And besides . . ." I trail off.

He prods. "Go on."

I turn my head to look at him and I try to pick my words carefully. "I'm not sure I want to live here anymore."

He winces. "You're only saying that because of what I've done. I've turned you into a pariah."

I shrug. "It just might be simpler if I moved someplace where I don't know anyone. Then when you're ready . . ."

"When I get out of prison, you mean." His voice is matter-of-fact, but there's an undertone of fear.

I pause. "When you're free again, you can come live with me, if you want. By then I'll probably have a decent house and a good job, and you'll be able to get a fresh start, too."

"And then what?" His sudden bitterness takes me by surprise. "Your neighbors will find out about me and start posting fliers with my picture on it, and soon after that your nice new house will have rocks thrown through its windows, too, and then we can move someplace else and do it all again. Sounds great, doesn't it? I bet we can keep doing that routine for years."

I don't know what to say. I pull my arms out of my sleeves and hug myself under my sweatshirt. My hands are ice cold against my ribs.

He stares out at the water again for a long time. I watch his face in the moonlight; there are shadows under his eyes and the muscles in his jaw are clenched. He doesn't look like he's breathing. I wait for him to move, and I listen to the ocean, and I try not to cry.

It's the only thing I can do for him now.

I have no comfort to offer, and no hope. Whatever I say is useless, and whatever I do won't change what's happened, or shield him from what's coming. But the last thing he needs from me right now is tears. I will keep control of myself, and I will speak calmly, and I will not give him cause to worry about me, no matter what. He needs strength tonight, not hysterics.

For his sake, I will not fall apart.

He finally shifts and looks back at me. "I don't think I can do it, Nathan."

"Do what?" My tongue feels heavy in my mouth.

"Prison," he murmurs. "I'll die in there."

The long grass in the dunes behind us rustles in the wind. I force my lips to move. "It hasn't come to that yet."

"No, but it's going to. And when it does, I won't survive it."

Something about his certainty terrifies me. "What are you saying?"

"I'm saying I need to get out of here. I need to go someplace they'll never find me. If I don't . . ." He swallows hard. "I won't die in a cage."

I want to tell him he's being melodramatic, but I can't. I want to tell him he'll be okay, but we both know better.

I breathe in and out a few times and fight back panic. "Where will you go?" I blurt.

He doesn't answer for a long time. "I don't know. Someplace safe." The sadness in his voice tears at my heart.

Far out at sea there's a flash of lightning. It burns through the sky and reflects in the water for a split second before it disappears, swallowed up whole by the darkness. I wait for another outburst but nothing comes.

What are we doing here on this beach talking about the things we're talking about? How did we get here? When did our lives become completely unraveled, like so much yarn? Just last week Tommy was home in New York, out of harm's way, and Simon was only a kid in my English class at school.

Now look.

I can handle losing my job and my home, but I can't bear to lose Tommy for ten years, not when I know how much those years are going to hurt him. All my life I have loved him and looked out for him, and seeing him like this is killing me. I would do anything to make things right for him again. Anything.

But how can I possibly fix this? Even if I murdered Harold Hart and every single cop in Walcott, it wouldn't change things for Tommy. His only choices are to run away or to stay put, but no matter what he does, he's screwed, and I can't help him. This fucked-up mess will follow him everywhere he goes, marring everything he touches. All he might have done with his life—and all he might have been— is gone.

And I don't know how I can live with that.

I wipe my nose on my shoulder and try to sound cheerful. "I'll come with you, then. I hear Canada is nice this time of year."

He shakes his head. "No. You need to be safe, too, and if I'm around, you never will be." He doesn't let me argue. "You know I'm right."

He scoops up some sand with his hands and lets it run out between his fingers. It's wet so it falls in small clumps, and it sticks to his skin. He shifts to look at me. "Do you ever wonder what our lives would have been like if we'd never crossed the line?"

I don't want to talk about this. "What line?"

"You know what I mean."

I meet his eyes. "It's a little late for us to be having this conversation, isn't it?"

"I suppose. But I was just thinking that one of the reasons I never worried about getting involved with Simon was because in my mind I'd already done something much worse hundreds of times."

His voice is mild and has no blame in it, but pain stabs through me anyway. My throat closes and I can't seem to breathe. "You mean what we did."

What we're still doing.

He glances down at his hands and brushes them off on his pants. "Yeah." He looks back up after a while and his face is suddenly old. "We never really had much of a chance for a normal existence, did we? Not after something like that." He pauses and his eyes fill. "Though I guess if you think about it, it's a fucking miracle nothing else bad has happened before now, considering the odds."

All this time. All this time, and I never knew what he thought. I never let myself know, never admitted to myself what was right in front of my face all along.

Dear God. What have we done to each other?

I close my eyes and try to stop the tears. "I'm so sorry, Tommy. I should never . . ." I break down.

"Don't, Nathan." He puts his arm around my shoulders and holds me tight against his side. "I'm not sorry at all, and you shouldn't be either. You've always been the best thing in my life, no matter what. Nothing else even comes close."

He holds me for a long time. When I finally open my eyes again, there's a blinking light far out at sea, probably on an oil tanker, and closer to shore I can hear a bell ringing on one of those safety floats the Coast Guard puts up to mark the channel into the harbor. I focus on the sound and try to find the float, but the wind and the ocean are distorting the sound and making it impossible to tell where it's coming from.

Tommy's pulling off his sweatshirt.

"What are you doing?" I ask.

He tugs off his T-shirt, too. "I'm going for a quick swim."

"Are you nuts? It's freezing."

He starts to stand up and I stuff my arms back in my sleeves and reach up to grab him. "It's too dangerous out there, Tommy. The waves are still really strong, and there's going to be an undertow, too."

He pushes his pants and boxers down to his ankles and steps out of them, then he leans over me, naked. There's enough moonlight for me to see the gooseflesh on his arms and shoulders.

"You worry too much," he says, smiling. "I'll be okay." The smile fades as he meets my eyes. "Promise me you will be, too."

"What are you talking about?"

"Just promise. It's been kind of a rough week and you don't do so well with depression sometimes, remember?"

I look away. "That was a long time ago."

"I know." He takes my chin and makes me look at him. His hand is surprisingly warm. "Promise me anyway."

I roll my eyes. "You're being stupid." I sigh at the look on his face. "Okay, I promise. Now will you shut the hell up?"

He grins again and the bandage on his cheek crinkles. "I love you, Nathan."

I don't remember the last time he said that. I'm not sure he ever has.

He kisses me on the lips, then he straightens up again and takes off for the water at a sprint. He hits the first wave at full speed and yells out at the cold right before he dives from sight.

"Don't do this, Tommy," I say aloud.

I can't handle his stupid little underwater trick this evening. I want him to get out of the ocean, and come dry off and get dressed so we can go home and figure out how to smuggle him out of town and wherever else he needs to go. But of course he has to fuck around first, as if he has all the time in the world.

Half a minute passes. The water is churning like a potful of soup on a stove. I wait for him to give up and surface, since there's no way even he can make any headway against this kind of current. Forty-five seconds go by, then a minute.

I get slowly to my feet. I think I see him for an instant, but the dark blob on the water gets a little closer and it turns out to be the lid to a Styrofoam cooler. By the time I get that figured out, Tommy's been under at least a minute and a half.

God damn him. Here we go again. He knows how much I hate this. I start running. My foot throbs with each step and my breathing is loud in my ears. I reach the ocean and scream his name.

I can't hear anything but the wind and the waves. It has to have been at least two minutes by now. I plunge in and gasp when the water hits my crotch, and I immediately feel the drag of the undercurrent. I force myself to stop while my feet are still touching the bottom.

"Tommy!" I scream again. My eyes sweep frantically over the surface. The waves break over me every few seconds, one by one, pushing me back toward the shore.

I glance at the lighthouse, hoping that Caleb has woken up for some reason and has seen us down here and called for help, but there's still no other light coming from the tower and the house except for the revolving beacon at the top. I take a step toward it and stop immediately.

Three minutes. I stumble over a rock or something and fall on my ass in shallow water, and when I try to stand up I get knocked down again, twice, before regaining my feet. I come up thrashing and swearing.

He'll resurface now. This is the longest he's ever gone, but he's done this a million times and he'll pop up like an ice cube in a punch bowl, and he'll be laughing at the look on my face. No one swims like Tommy. Even when he was a little kid he swam like a seal. He's got a third lung or something.

Four minutes.

"Tommy!" My throat feels as if its ripping down the middle. I throw myself at the ocean and start flailing my arms and legs as fast as they'll go. I keep my head up, but all I can see is the next wave, and the next. The cold is wearing me out fast; my limbs are already numb. I glance back at the shore and scream in rage. I've barely moved forward.

I drop my feet down again and touch sand. The water is only up to my armpits. He couldn't have gotten too far out in this. I plow back to the shore and run up and down the beach, howling his name again and again.

Nothing answers but the ocean, repeating itself like an idiot. I fall to my knees and start to pray, eyes still fixed on the water. I don't even recognize my own voice. "Please God please, oh God please, not this. Anything but this. Whatever you want, whatever you ask, anything. Just not this. Not this, God, please not this . . ." The words stream from my mouth until I don't even know what I'm saying and my lips finally stop moving.

Ten minutes go by, then twenty. I drop my head and stare at the sand; my hands and feet are aching from the cold. Part of me knows I can't stay out here much longer, but I can't make myself care enough to move.

The look in his eyes should have warned me. I should have known.

Maybe I did.

"Oh, Jesus, Tommy," I whisper. A single sob bursts from my lips, but I stifle it instantly. I wrap my arms around myself and rock back and forth on the beach. Something inside of me is disintegrating, crumbling into powder like old parchment.

This is not happening. This cannot be happening. He was just here with me, holding me. We were just talking. He was here beside me, on the beach, just the same as when we were kids. We were talking. He had sand on his feet. He smiled at me, and he kissed me on the lips. He's never done that before.

He was holding me.

When I look up again I see him. He's fifty feet to my right and facedown on the sand. The ocean is nudging his naked body as if it's trying to wake him.

I make a low noise in my throat.

He's fucking with me. He's just pretending. He's waiting for me to come running, and when I get two feet away he'll jump up and scare the shit out of me and he'll laugh his ass off. I'll kill him for this, the stupid asshole. He's fine. He's only pretending.

He's naked in the surf. His body looks fake, like a blow-up doll, like one of those Resuscitation Andy things they use in CPR courses. He must be freezing. It'll serve the little son of a bitch right if he gets frostbite and has to have his dick amputated.

He had goose bumps on his arms and shoulders, and a bandage on his cheek. There was sand on his feet. The bandage moved when he smiled, and then he kissed me. He's never done that.

He must be freezing.

He was just here beside me. He was holding me.

He's naked in the surf, on his stomach. One arm is under his body, the other is above his head, on the sand.

I can't feel my hands. I can't feel anything.

He was just here. My little brother.

Tommy.

He was just

CHAPTER 10

Caleb's back. I hear the key turn in the lock and a few moments later he sticks his head in the living room doorway and says hello. He's got a bag of groceries in his arms and he asks if I'm hungry. I tell him no.

He frowns. "You need to eat something, son. You're wasting away." He wrinkles his nose. "And you need a shower, too, by the way. Not taking care of yourself isn't going to help anything."

It was Caleb I went to first. He opened his door at three-fifteen in the morning with a fuzzy, pissed-off look on his face, which quickly turned to horror when he saw what I was carrying in my arms. I don't remember anything else about that night aside from sitting on the beach with Tommy's corpse for five or six hours, but Caleb says after he helped me lower the body to the floor I passed out, apparently from loss of blood and shock. I also had hypothermia. I woke the next morning in the hospital, but after the doctors poked and prodded me and the cops finished questioning me, they let me come home. That was a week ago.

There was no memorial service in Walcott, even though Caleb and Cheri both thought I should have one. They kept using the word "closure," but I told them there was no point. Most of the town was (and still is) thinking "good riddance," and I couldn't stand the idea of sitting around listening to the eulogies and prayers of hypocrites, and worse, enduring their clumsy sympathy.

I called Camille to tell her the news, but after I asked her to pass it along to Kyle and Philip and anyone else who needed to know, she began to sob, and I hung up. I'm sorry for her pain, but I can't do anything about it. I know other people loved Tommy, too, but I don't want anything to do with how they handle losing him.

Does that sound harsh? I don't mean it that way. But I'll be damned if someone else will orchestrate how and when I grieve for him, or try to "share" what I'm feeling. My grief is not a fucking spectator sport.

"Nathan?" Caleb is standing over me. "Did you hear me?"

His eyes are red. He's been crying all week and it's getting old. "What?"

"I asked when was the last time you ate anything."

I shrug. "I'm fine, Caleb. Don't mother me."

He purses his lips together and glares. I suppose I should be kinder to him, but I'm not in the mood. I just want to be left alone, and he keeps showing up two or three times a day, letting himself in with the key Dad gave him years ago. Several other people have come by, too, but I haven't answered when they've knocked, and they've eventually gone away. If Caleb doesn't back off soon I'm going to ask him to return the key so I can get some peace and quiet.

He sighs and his knees pop as he sits beside me on the couch. "We should talk, Nathan."

I stare at him. "I don't feel like talking right now." My voice is cold. "I appreciate your concern, but it's misplaced."

He nods. "Yeah, anyone can see you're doing real well." He snorts. "You're a mess, boy."

I start to get up. "I'm going to go take a nap. Thanks for stopping by."

He catches my wrist. His fingers are fragile and I could easily break his hold, but I let him pull me down again.

He clears his throat. "You know what you're doing, don't you? You're acting exactly like your dad did after Vicki died."

I get up immediately and this time when he tries to grab me I step away. "This conversation is over, Caleb. I don't need a lecture."

He looks up at me, lips quivering. His left eyelid droops in a way I've never noticed before.

"I'm not lecturing you, you stupid little son of a bitch," he snaps.

"I'm trying to tell you something important, and you can damn well do me the courtesy of shutting up and listening."

I glower back at him and stuff my hands in my pockets, waiting.

He points at the seat next to him and rolls his eyes when I stay standing. "Fine. Don't sit, then." He rubs his temples. Everything about him looks tired, from the set of his shoulders to the slight tremor in his hands.

Against my will I sit down again. I force myself to sound patient. "What do you want to tell me?"

He studies my face and takes a deep breath. "Remember when you stuck that pencil in my eye?"

What the hell does that have to do with anything?

I nod and grimace. "If I'd known what a pain in the ass you were going to be I would have used the pointed end."

He grunts. "You might as well have, for as much as it hurt." He takes my hand and holds it in his lap. His skin is cold and dry. "Do you remember when it happened?"

"Not really. I was too little. But Tommy and I were staying at your house for a few days for some reason, weren't we?"

"That's right. Your mom had just died a couple of weeks before that and your dad was in the hospital."

"I'd forgotten that. He had appendicitis, right?"

"No, that's just what he told me to tell you boys." He squeezes my fingers. "But what really happened . . ."

I pull away from him. "Great. More lies from Dad. That's exactly what I need to hear today. Thanks, Caleb, you always know just the right thing to say to make me feel better."

He reclaims my hand. ". . . but what really happened is he tried to kill himself."

I fall silent and gawk at him. "What are you talking about?"

He licks his lips. "Know that bayonet of your grandpa's that your dad used to keep upstairs?"

"It's still there." I slump back against the couch. "Jesus."

He spreads my fingers flat against his, palm to palm, comparing our hands like an adult does with a baby—except in this case my hand dwarfs his; the tops of his fingers only extend to the top knuckle on each of mine.

He sighs again. "Anyway, he went for a walk in the woods one day while you boys were in school, and he stuck that thing in his gut up to the hilt. When I found him the blade was sticking out his back about five inches, and he'd lost an enormous amount of blood."

"Christ." I glare at him. "I can't believe you never told me this before."

He looks away. "He made me promise not to."

I drop my head on the back of the couch and stare at the ceiling. A spider is building a web around one of the wooden beams. "I also can't believe no one else said anything. Lots of people must have known."

He nods. "A few did, but your dad begged them not to tell anyone because he didn't want you boys finding out. He somehow even managed to convince the doctors and the cops not to say anything to Social Services, for fear someone would try to take you and Tommy away from him." He chuckles a little but it sounds forced. "I still can't believe he pulled that off. If it had been anyplace else but Walcott, he'd never have gotten away with it."

"What did he do? Bribe them?"

"Of course not. You forget how much people liked Vernon Bishop in this town. He just told them you'd already gone through enough, and the last thing you needed was to get ripped out of your home and sent off to live with strangers. After that, no one had the heart to do what they were supposed to do."

I turn my head to face him. "What a load of crap. Since when did he give a shit about what we'd gone through?"

"He cared, Nathan. He just didn't know what to do with himself without your mom, and he had no idea how to raise you and Tommy." He sees my expression and frowns. "I know you won't believe this, but the only reason he stayed alive at all was because of you and your brother."

I laugh. "Yeah, right. He was a devoted father."

He squeezes my fingers. "No, he wasn't. But he didn't treat you bad on purpose. He just had nothing left in him after Vicki died, and he did the best he could."

I work my hand free from his. "Well, let me tell you a little secret, Caleb. His best sucked."

He nods again. "I know it did. But you should forgive him if you can. He was in a lot of pain his whole life. All that stuff with Cheri, and then how your mom died . . ." He pauses. "And you should also know that he tried to kill himself again."

"What?" I jerk my head up. "When?"

"A couple of years later. Pills, this time. He did it one night after you and Tommy were asleep, but then he stumbled over to my place in time for me to get an ambulance." He pats my leg. "I guess gutting yourself in the woods is a lot different than swallowing some pills at home and then realizing your little boys are going to be the ones who find you in the morning."

I pause. "So why didn't he try the bayonet again?"

He pulls at his ear and laughs a little. "He said it hurt too much."

I bite my lip and turn away. "It always does." I watch a wasp climb up the screen on the back door.

We're silent for a minute, and when I face him again, his eyes are keen with understanding. "I figured you'd know something about that." He worries at a cold sore with his tongue. "I think your dad thought about killing himself all the time, Nathan. I don't know if he ever tried again, but he'd go through these black periods when I was sure he was about ready to."

"So what stopped him?"

"You and Tommy, of course. He was in a bad way after your mom died, but after a few years I think his grief got a little easier to handle, and he knew what his death would do to you boys and he couldn't go through with it anymore."

I make a triangle with my thumbs and forefingers and stare through it at the floor. "Dad told you that?"

"Well, no, not in so many words, but I know he didn't want to leave you boys by yourselves." He frowns at my expression. "You can believe what you want, but that's the truth."

I bring my knees up and drop my face on them. My head is pounding. "Why are you telling me all this, now, Caleb?"

He hesitates. "Because you're acting just like he did before he hurt himself. I never told you before because he didn't want you to know, but you've been scaring me lately and I figured maybe if you knew you'd think twice before doing something that stupid. Especially after Tommy . . . " His voice breaks. "I asked your dad before he died if he was glad he hadn't killed himself. He told me he was, Nathan." He bites his lip. "I know it's not much, but even though he hated a lot of things about his life, he was glad in the end that he stuck around."

He chokes up again. "What I'm trying to say is that I don't want to outlive you, too. I don't think I can stand to put another Bishop in the ground."

I take a deep breath and wait a long time before letting it out. My voice comes out gentler. "What were you going to tell me about the day I hurt your eye?"

He clears his throat. "Yeah, I forgot." He pulls out a hanky and blows his nose. "I was typing and you were sitting beside me in my den. You and Tommy had only been with me an hour or two." He shifts and his ankle pops. "Anyway, do you remember what happened after you poked me?"

I shake my head and look up at him. "Not in any detail. I remember you were pretty mad, is all."

He grins. "Damn right. I wanted to toss you through a window." The grin fades. "But when I asked you why you'd hurt me, you just stared at me like I was talking in a foreign language."

I get impatient again. "This is really fascinating, Caleb, but why do I need to hear it?"

He rubs his jaw and his voice gets rough. "Because of what Tommy said when he heard me asking. Remember?"

"No. I don't even remember him being in the room."

"He was." He tries to talk and he can't until he swallows a couple of times. "He said 'Nathan and Daddy hurt other people when they're sad. It's the only thing that stops them from hurting themselves.'"

I drop my feet to the floor. "That's a lie." My voice is shaking.

"It's true. I swear to God."

"Bullshit." All of a sudden I'm infuriated. "Tommy would have been three years old at the time. You're trying to tell me a three-year-old said something like that?"

"What can I say? Tommy was a pretty special little kid."

I drop my head on the back of the couch again and close my eyes. "Go away, Caleb."

I don't open my eyes until I hear the front door shut behind him.

Hampstead abandoned the cornfield four days ago, after Cheri Tipton showed up late and asked me to come outside for a minute to speak with them. When I joined her and Hampstead, Cheri, red-faced and stammering, said, "I'm terribly embarrassed. It seems I've made a teeny little miscalculation after all."

Until then, I'd had next to no contact with the dirt people since Tommy's death. Cheri had inflicted herself on me several times, of course, and Bill and Sally came to the back door and forced a bouquet of flowers into my hands, but for the most part they'd respected my privacy. I could hear their conversations through the windows, though, and I knew that the dig was not going well at all, because Hampstead's voice kept getting more strident with each passing day, and Cheri's was more defensive and stubborn. When I finally came outside they all called "hello" to me, but Cheri was subdued, Hampstead barely civil, and Bill and Sally—looking beaten down after digging yet another useless trench in a different part of the field—listless and bored.

Hampstead and I listened wordlessly as Cheri explained that she'd reexamined the old surveyor's records once again and discovered that Minister Shepard's old farm had actually been in the woods on the other side of the cottage, near the site of the foundation where I'd caught Tommy and Simon fucking.

"I got looking at the old maps last night, and I discovered one simple little error in my calculations, but it threw absolutely everything off." She shifted her weight from foot to foot and clasped her hands in front of her crotch, anxiously searching our faces as she babbled. "I am so, so *sorry* about this. I don't know how I could have made such a stupid mistake. I'm just mortified, you have no idea."

Hampstead's initial outraged expression slowly turned to stone. Her eyes were bugging out, and her mouth was wide open with her tongue in plain sight; she looked like a gargoyle. I couldn't help but guffaw.

Cheri ignored me and focused on Hampstead. "I don't blame you at all for being furious with me, Jane. You were right all along, and I was wrong. I should have listened to you, but now I'm openly admitting my mistake and I'll do anything you want, no questions asked, and no more arguments. That's a promise."

Bill and Sally stood a few feet away, side by side, apparently friends again. Bill was leaning on a shovel (with an Ace bandage wrapped around his right knee) and Sally had her hands crossed in front of her stomach; the two of them looked like that dour old couple in Grant Wood's painting. Bill kept shaking his head and muttering, "Unbelievable. Un-fucking-believable," and Sally nodded every time he said it, her head bobbing up and down like one of those kitschy toy dogs you see in the rear windows of cars.

When Cheri finally wound down, Hampstead turned to me and raised her eyebrows. I shook my head and she grimaced and nodded and said she didn't blame me, then she ordered Bill and Sally to start packing up. I turned to go back inside.

Cheri didn't know which of us to chase after. She had tears in her eyes as she cornered me. "I don't understand, Nathan. Why won't you let us keep searching?"

I looked over her head into space. "Because I don't care if something's there or not, Cheri, and I want to be left alone."

She tried to sound reasonable. "I know this is a difficult time for you, but surely you can see the value in continuing this dig. What harm is there in allowing me another few weeks to try again? Now that we're on the right track, it will be easy."

I made myself look at her. "Why do you care so much, Cheri? Say you eventually find your lost village. What do you get out of it?"

She bit her lip and hesitated. "Peace of mind, I suppose."

"I don't understand."

"I don't either." She hugged herself. "I think if the village were anyplace else besides on your property I wouldn't care half as much." She gripped her flabby triceps for a minute and then let go. "This won't make any sense, but ever since we've been digging around out here I can't stop thinking about your mom."

She waited for me to say something but when I stayed silent, she went on. "I've felt so awful for years about what your dad and I did to her, and being here again is bringing everything back to the surface." She tried to smile. "Your mom would have loved the idea of finding an Indian community, you know. She'd have grabbed a shovel and charged into the woods ahead of all of us if she thought something was there. She was always so curious about everything, and she loved history."

Her double chins trembled and her voice dropped. "I know how stupid this sounds, but I keep thinking how excited she'd be, and it makes me feel like I have to do this for her. I keep thinking if I find something, it will somehow make up for . . . ."

She grimaced at my expression. "I know what you're thinking. You're thinking, 'Why should I help this fat old slut feel better about herself?'"

I barked out a laugh. "Pretty much."

She took hold of my wrist. "Please, Nathan. I know I have no right to ask, but I need to know what's causing this feeling in my gut. I think it might be something your mom would have wanted. Let me do this. It won't take long."

I stared into her eyes. "No." She started to argue but I cut her off. "I'm sorry, Cheri. I truly am. Believe it or not, I'd like nothing better than to help you ease your conscience, but I think we both have enough experience with guilt by now to know that no amount of excavation is going to get rid of it." I pull away from her gently. "For people like us there's no getting around that."

She looked at me curiously, her eyes forming a question. I didn't let her ask it. "Go home, Cheri. Please. I've got enough dead people in my life without going out of my way to dig up more."

She eventually gave up. I watched her trudge away, defeated, and after she drove down the lane and Hampstead led Bill and Sally away like a couple of pack mules (they took all the tools and their new metal table, and they cleared away all the stakes and twine, but they left the Porta Potty for tomorrow), I went inside and stood by the screen door for a while, thinking.

Save for the Porta Potty, the cornfield looked like the surface of the moon, pocked with craters and scars, and barren of any living thing. The longer I stared at it, the more my heart ached. I eventually went upstairs and got the urn with Tommy's ashes in it, and I went outside and dumped it in Hampstead's first trial trench. After I filled the hole in, I didn't mark the ground in any way.

He belongs there, where no one but me will ever know what happened to his remains.

Archaeology is a useless vocation, because the only stuff worth owning never gets left behind. Love and hate and guilt and lust are so much more real than first edition books and antique furniture and Hummel figurines and bright scraps of cloth—but then again the only thing that nonmaterial objects leave to mark their passing—at least in the case of people like Tommy and me—is ruined lives, and distorted echoes, and crippled footprints on the earth, so I guess there's nothing wrong with digging around in the dirt for baubles and gewgaws to line your shelves and mantels with. I suppose it passes the time.

But Cheri's lost village needs to stay lost. Let the vines and shrubs covering it stay there, let the trees continue to block out the sunlight above it, let the dead rest in peace.

God knows the living never will.

I want Dale to plant his corn again. I want Tommy's ashes to fertilize the soil, and disappear utterly in the silent darkness beneath the surface. I want to look out the back of my cottage and see green things growing, and I want to forget what I buried here this summer.

Tommy and I meant no harm all those years ago. We coasted through the last decade and a half, thinking we'd never have to pay a price for loving each other the way we did. And the funny thing is, we actually thought we'd gotten away with it.

God, we were such fools.

About fifteen minutes after Caleb leaves someone knocks on the front door. I ignore it. They knock again, and then I hear the door opening.

Goddammit. Caleb must not have locked it on his way out.

"Who's there?" I yell.

No answer for a second, then a subdued voice calls out, "It's me."

Simon. I get slowly to my feet. "Come on in."

He steps into the living room. He's wearing green shorts and a red tank top, and his face is puffy and bruised. He looks scared.

We study each other. I'm suddenly aware that I haven't shaved or showered in days, and I'm wearing the same clothes I had on yesterday, a white T-shirt and surgical pants. His face is working.

"Hi, Simon." My voice is quiet. "You look like a damaged Christmas ornament."

He tries to smile. "Hi, Nathan."

An awkward silence. I clear my throat. "Does your dad know you're here?"

He shakes his head. "No. But it's okay. Mom drove me over here."

I raise my eyebrows and he shrugs. "She made Dad move out last week after . . ." he swallows. "After the shit hit the fan. She's divorcing him because of what he did."

"I don't understand."

He bites his lip. "That night . . . you know, after you found Tommy and me in the woods and walked me home?"

He waits for me to nod before going on. "Dad was still awake when I walked in the house. I was crying pretty hard because, well, you know, and he asked me what was wrong and I wouldn't tell him and he just kind of lost it, then. I guess he'd been drinking a lot."

He pushes his hair off his forehead nervously. "He tossed me into a wall and started beating the shit out of me, and when Mom tried to make him stop he hit her, too, and then he locked her out of the room so he could be alone with me." He drops his eyes. "She was outside the door the whole time, screaming to be let in. But he didn't stop until I told him everything."

He looks back up at me. His eyes are streaming tears. "I am so sorry, Nathan. He was going to kill me. I swear to God he would have. He kept hitting me and screaming and pushing and every time I tried to leave something out or lie he'd . . ."

I take a deep breath. "It's not your fault," I whisper. "I figured out what happened."

He nods slowly and pulls himself together. "Mom made him leave that night. She and I are getting ready to move away someplace where I can get a fresh start." He makes a face. "Some lady from Social Services came by the other day asking questions, but Dad was long gone. Did you call them?"

"No." I hesitate. "But I might as well have."

He nods again and shrugs. "It doesn't matter. I just wondered." He pauses, his lips trembling. "Anyway, I had to come see you before we go because I couldn't leave without telling you how much . . ."

His voice breaks. "I wish I'd let my dad kill me. Then Tommy would still be here, and . . . Oh, God, Nathan, I am so sorry."

My throat is swollen shut. We stare at each other for a second longer, then he runs across the room and throws his arms around me. We rock back and forth and something inside of me shatters and I start to cry for the first time since Tommy died. The sobs wrack my body and I want to die because it hurts so much. Simon is crying, too, but I can barely hear him above my own noise. His thin arms are wrapped tightly around my ribs and his wet face is against my throat and I'm holding him in a death grip. It goes on forever. I cry until there's nothing left in me but dust and ashes and empty rooms. I cry for Tommy and Simon and my dad and mom, but mostly I cry for me.

It's sunset on the beach. I'm standing with my feet in the water and the sun on my back, and there's a warm wind coming from the south. I've seen several people I know since I got here, but no one has spoken to me or made eye contact.

Simon left the cottage about an hour ago. He said he'd write when he gets wherever he and his mom are going, and I told him I'd like that and I kissed him on the head and said good-bye. He may write or he may not; I hope he doesn't. I don't need reminders of this summer showing up in the mail.

But I suppose it doesn't matter. I won't be in Walcott much longer anyway. I'll sell the cottage and the land and I'll move someplace I've never heard of, and I'll try to find a reason to get out of bed in the morning. It's not much of a plan, but it's the best I can do for now.

Is this despair? I don't know. All I know is I want it to stop.

The ocean is friendly again, all smiles and soft words. It accepted Tommy's sacrifice and seems to be sated for the moment. Yet I feel the pull, and I know what it wants. It's already sniffing at my shins and wetting its lips. If you listen closely you can hear it chuckling to itself.

Two boys run by behind me, and an Irish setter chases along behind them with a stick in its mouth. It sees me and pelts into the water to say hello, but when I bend to pet it, it leaps back out of reach, then charges after the kids again. One of the boys waits for the dog to catch up, then wrestles the stick out of its mouth and tosses it ahead. The dog tears off immediately, but the boy grins at me and waves before running after it. I watch them until they're too far away to see clearly.

I drop my head and feel tears run down my face.

After Simon left, I dug out Dad's old copy of Emerson again. I thumbed through the pages, reading what somebody else—probably Dad, I suppose—underlined years ago. I guess I hoped I'd find something that would give me a reason, yet again, to go on living. Something to help mitigate all this pain and guilt. I found nothing but senseless words.

Emerson was an innocent man, and hope is for the innocent.

I started to put the book back, but then I dropped it on the floor, facedown. When I picked it up again, I read one final phrase: "My life is not an apology, but a life." For some reason, it was the only sentence in the book underscored in ink instead of pencil. It went through me like a knife.

Maybe Dad was trying to tell me something. He must have known I'd read that book again someday; maybe those words helped him get through his life, and maybe he thought they'd help me eventually, too.

I don't have any real reason to believe that, but at this point I'll take what I can get.

The sun is almost down now. I stretch my arms above my head and breathe in salt air. Each breath hurts, but I keep breathing, because what else can I do? I made a promise, and this time I wasn't smart enough to cross my fingers.

Tommy's way out is not for me, not anymore. Nor is my father's.

I will not end with despair, or bitterness. I've had enough of both.

I squat down and put my hands in the ocean. It runs a smooth tongue over my palms.

"Go on and have a taste, you son of a bitch," I whisper. "I will not be your next meal."